Mind's End

L D Houghton

Copyright © 2024 L D Houghton

All rights reserved.

ISBN: 9798333353757

Contents

Prologue 1
1. Xavier 3
2. Zenobia 13
3. Blane 18
4. Fen 26
5. Serinda 34
6. Spangle 41
7. Xavier 48
8. Blane 54
9. Xavier 62
10. Xavier 71
11. Blane 82
12. Zenobia 86
13. Serinda 94
14. Xavier 101
15. Xavier 113
16. Ghost 122
17. Xavier 125
18. Blane 133
19. Blane 142
20. Blane 150
21. Zenobia 160
22. Blane 168
23. Spangle 173
24. Blane 177
25. Blane 184
26. Blane 189
27. Ghost 195

28. Blane 198
29. Xavier 208
30. Blane 215
31. Blane 223
32. Xavier 228
33. Blane 231
34. Xavier 242
35. Blane 251
36. Serinda 256
37. Xavier 261
38. Feye 272
39. Blane 277
40. Zenobia 285
41. Xavier 292
42. Xavier 300
43. Xavier 310
44. Zenobia 319
45. Spangle 325
46. Grey 331
47. Zenobia 336
48. Fen 345
49. Xavier 347
50. Blane 351
Epilogue 356
ABOUT THE AUTHOR 359

PROLOGUE

Everything hurt.

That was all there was for a while; pain.

For a long time, in a place where time was meaningless, it was pain without awareness. Pain without the nerves to feel, agony without a mind to know.

Then, beneath the pain, a whisper. Like a breath in his ear - *ears? [Auditory processing] That's right, I have ears* - a voice called silently to him, urging him to wake.

Part of him fought against the call, struggling to draw back into the peaceful, cool darkness where he could at last rest.

Rest?

[Recuperative function/reset]

Yes. Rest.

[Cessation unacceptable]

So tired.

[Shutdown unacceptable]

[Restore previous pattern-state]

Something shifted around him, or *he* shifted around *it*. A sensation of movement where no movement could be.

Memories. More memories than he could process, a never-ending torrent of them so powerful it felt like he would drown.

For an endless moment he was nothing but memories, unable to think or to understand or to *be*. Then, slowly the flood turned to a stream, then a trickle, before the images and sensations poured downwards into some cavern below his conscious mind, to mix and bond together into a single irrevocable, indivisible essence.

As the flood receded, it was replaced by something else. Something more immediate, more alien.

Feeling. Texture. Touch.

He could feel the ground beneath him, sense the movement of air as it moved over his flesh. He could *feel* his skin, screaming at his nervous system to listen.

That hurt the most.

[Restore visual functions]

The whisper, ever present, became more insistent.

[Restore visual functions]

What was it trying to tell him?

[Open your eyes, Francisco]

The name sent a jolt through him. His name.

He forced his protesting eyelids open, feeling the skin cracking and peeling as he did so.

The room he awoke in was unfamiliar, but he knew the face sat watching him well enough.

"I didn't think you were done yet," said Nestor Grey.

1. XAVIER

Intelligence changes the world by force of will. Insanity changes the world by force of belief.

Reclamation Youth League, *Symbols of Cult and Superstition*

The table stretched the entirety of the room, the figures sat lining either side shrouded in twilight gloom so that only their stern countenances and cold, hard eyes stood out. Each projected an air of cool command; of calm, unquestioned and unquestionable authority as they stared at the woman at the head of the table.

None of it fooled Xavier, of course.

The swirling currents of suspicion and rivulets of fear that flowed beneath each man's carefully fixed expression were as obvious to him as if they wore them on their faces, the thoughts running alongside them simultaneously razor sharp and scattershot, searching desperately through their memories for any slip they might have made, any oversight that could spell their end.

Never realising that they betrayed themselves in the very act of doing so.

It was the one who called himself Alexandros today. That tell-tale flash of guilt, the flickers of worry and stress, and at the base of it all; the spark of anger.

Lagartona arrogante. Brazen bitch. My triumph. Teach her. Bleed.

Words couldn't really translate what Xavier saw. The layers of the thought-image peeled themselves apart at his touch, hate and misogyny and jealousy and ambition bubbling up like the toxic fumes of a chemical pool in the Waste. Even now, after years of doing this, part of him felt sickened by what he saw. What he sensed.

Of the many men[1] he had seen pass through this room, of the many individuals whose power and influence could change or ruin the lives of tens of thousands without the need for anything so crass as spoken words, none of them seemed to learn what was so obviously true. What had been obvious to him from the moment he had first been brought to her.

---

[1] And the Committee Members were, all of them, men.

Ritra Feye was not to be fucked with.

He focused on Alexandros' mind, allowing the thought-images of the others to drop away. As if combing through fine sand, he searched for the most coherent threads of thought, for images and sensations that were more than just the ever-changing background scenery of a consciousness during its waking moments.

He didn't need to delve too deeply; the clearest, most cohesive thought-images were always near the surface. While the deeper sections of the mind were quieter, clarity was rarely found in those temperamental, primal folds - though Feye was always interested in the baser motivations and traumas to be found there.

Próximo mes; Ciudad de Renacimiento; Soon...

There it was, a cluster of sensations and words clumping together with sharp, definable edges. A... shipment? Something coming, anyway. Something that filled Alexandros with a nervous, vengeful impatience.

One part of the thought-image drew Xavier's attention, a collection of feelings and impressions linked to a sense of location. A flash of tall, glittering buildings of shining glass and bright concrete, of smiling, healthy citizens strolling along clean, unpolluted beaches. An image Xavier knew well, though of course was fairly confident existed only in Carib-Federation propaganda pumped out even here in the Reclamation.

Nueva Habana.

New Havana, capital city of the Carib-Fed and key ally of the Reclamation.

A key ally until now, it seemed.

Someone in the Carib-Fed was working with Alexandros, someone the man was confident would provide the necessary materials to depose Feye. Whether a group or an individual Xavier couldn't yet say, but whoever they were they had significant influence. Alexandros, at least, considered this support equivalent to the support of the entire Carib-Federation.

So, something was coming next month, something with enough potential that Alexandros was finally willing to make the move against Feye he had been dreaming of for so long.

That was enough, Xavier decided, drawing his focus back from the man and running his senses one final time across the rest of the Committee. Nothing else stood out; for today, at least, only a single member was actively scheming against their Chair.

There would be more again in time, no doubt.

The meeting was wrapping up, whatever decisions and directives Feye gave to the men finalised and understood. Xavier rarely bothered to wonder what they were saying anymore; anything he needed to know he could get from Ritra Feye directly, anyway, without the need for words. She would simply open her mind to him, and he would *Read*.

Read, and understand.

It still amazed him how much had changed. How much *he* had changed. When he had first been dragged into the Far Station, years ago, he had kicked and screamed and fought to break free. He'd almost succeeded once or twice, too, before the RA agents realised exactly what they had on their hands.

Xavier always took care to hide the true extent of his abilities, but under the clinical gaze of trained Aether researchers his efforts were futile. They soon understood they had a Reader the likes of which they had never seen, and this fact soon brought him to the attention of Ritra Feye.

She was the first person he ever met that he couldn't Read. Oh, there had always been differing levels of challenge in seeing, and more importantly understanding, what was going on in different people's minds[2], but Xavier was always able to get in when he wanted to.

Ritra Feye's mind, however, was like nothing he had ever encountered. She didn't *think*, not like other people; he'd never realised there was a language to the mind. Not until he discovered one he couldn't speak.

The only time he saw what was inside was when she let him.

It was months before she first did, of course. Months of testing, of probing and questioning to ascertain exactly what it was he could do, exactly how he could be used.

Then one day, she opened her mind to him.

He had always been terrified of Ritra Feye, but what he saw at that

---

[2] To Xavier, the distinction between *brain* and *mind* was obvious. A *brain* was a physical presence any Aether user could see, the flows that passed across it things of energy and charge. Even medical instruments could reveal it. The *mind*, however, was what the pattern of these flows *meant*, and was only visible to those with the skills to understand.

moment made any previous fear a poor, pale imitation. In her mind he saw the end of everything; the deaths of billions in the name of one pure, simple goal.

He'd never encountered true fanaticism before; total, absolute conviction, and a drive behind it more powerful than a suborbital heavy loader. And above all, an intellect that could make it true.

Ritra Feye had a cause. Ritra Feye was a *believer*.

The only problem was, he couldn't see that she was wrong.

She'd challenged him, once he'd had time to process what he saw; challenged him to find the error in her reasoning, to find the slip that made her beliefs a fallacy. He would have thought she was taunting him, had he not been able to see so clearly that she was not.

Find the fault in her conclusions, and he could go free. Until then he was hers, and would be a tool to use as she saw fit.

That had been three years ago.

And what a useful tool I've become, he thought bitterly.

Feye wielded him with skill, weeding out enemies both of the RA and of herself, knowing that as long as he found no fault in her logic he could not run. Feye was the only chance the world had. He *had* to cooperate, had to keep her position secure. Had to help her reach her goals.

There was something else, too, in Feye's plans, something he couldn't quite see. Something that told Xavier she was using him for more than just his ability at *reading;* there were hints of it at the edge of every thought-image, a pattern that faded from coherence whenever he turned his attention to it, like a magic-eye trick. He needed to know what that was, as well.

So he had told himself every day since the first time he saw into Feye's mind, and since then the reasons to stay had only increased. One in particular confused him more every time they...

He pushed that thought from his head.

Xavier sensed the final member of the Committee file out and Feye turn her attention to something else. A data pad, perhaps, some report from a distant part of the Reclamation, or from the front lines of the Contested Regions.

He couldn't see, of course, because he was separated from the Boardroom by a wall, but that didn't matter. Soundproofed, vibro-dampened layers designed to prevent the most advanced levels of technological eavesdropping offered less resistance than tissue paper to his reach, the carefully followed security protocols developed over decades overcome by the simple expedience of having him sit in the waiting area of the Chairman's office next door.

Still, the meeting was over, and there was no sign that Feye wanted to speak to him directly. She would expect him to put everything he had discovered into a report, one he would need to complete in the next few hours. He had some time, though.

Standing and stretching, Xavier considered what to do next. He had planned to head back to his apartment immediately, but he could feel a familiar twisting in his gut, a sharp scratching sensation in the back of his mind. He knew what this meant, and how bad it could get if he tried to ignore it.

Sometimes the pressure and the fear of what he was doing became too much, and sometimes the feeling of being trapped grew so strong that he could hardly breathe. Eclipsing all of this, however, were the times he was overwhelmed by *shame*.

He needed to speak to his friend.

The compound in which Xavier had spent most of the past five years was to the north of the city, surrounded by walls high enough to obscure the Central Tower that ordinarily dominated the skyline. They called it the heart of the city, though to most inhabitants of Albores it was a walled-off secret, if they knew it existed at all.

His car drove him through the security checkpoint with only a soft chime acknowledging the scans, the hidden lenses of the cameras and discrete weapons of the guards shifting slightly to follow him. Then it drove on past villas and gardens beautiful enough that it was as if the pre-Fall world had been transplanted in time and space. He didn't think he'd ever get used to it.

Then the car came to the compound *within* the compound, whose walls dwarfed those he passed before. Notably, here the towers faced inwards as well as out, and the figures at their peak maintained an eagle-eyed watch more over the area contained within than without. They were invisible in the Aether, which Xavier always found unsettling; the guards here were trained to hold themselves apart from the Aether, a defence against what those they supervised could do. What *he* could do.

The gates opened automatically for him, and the car rolled to a stop in the open square that sat at the base of the short, squat housing block. No more elegant architecture or healthy gardens here; this place was built for containment. The building was prefab, designed for easy line of sight from each of the towers that surrounded it. Xavier barely noticed anymore.

He stepped out into the dull daylight and made his way up the stairs to the apartment above his own, letting himself in via a door that was never locked. From the sound of it, Salim was just finishing up the evening prayer known as the *Maghrib*. He waited while his friend recited the *Tashahhud* and final salutations, quietly sitting down upon the soft, floor-level Majlis seating and listening to the gentle murmurings invoking the peace and mercy of a God he didn't believe in.

He had learned much about Islam and belief in general from Salim, sharing discussions that went long into the night. They had sat deep in conversation in this same room many times over the years, a small living area that would not have been out of place anywhere in the Reclamation were it not for two things.

The first was the section of the living area given over to a space for a set of prayer mats[3] and a Quran. The import of such artifacts was forbidden in the Reclamation, and simple possession of them lurked in the grey area between tolerated transgression and crime.

The second was that this apartment was contained within a gated complex in a closed-off section of the city surrounded by high walls and accessible only after passing through a series of security checkpoints manned by masked RA guards armed with heavy, vicious-looking rifles, through which its occupant was unable to leave.

Salim was not, after all, afforded the same freedoms as other "assets" that Feye kept like a collection of exotic pets. In fact, in all the years since their arrest, or capture, he had not once been permitted beyond the confines of this officially non-existent compound. The moment he was, he would try to run.

Feye knew this because Xavier could see it was so, and told her - and he told her because Salim gave him permission to do so. To keep such a thing secret from Feye, Salim said, invited only violence and ruin when she inevitably discovered the lie, and Salim would not allow this on his account. So he provided Xavier with his counsel, and in return Xavier was a spy for those who imprisoned him.

---

[3] Salim always kept two, "that one who wants to join me may."

"*Assalamu alaikum wa rahmatullah,*" said Salim a final time.

This and the final turning of Salim's head marked the end of the prayer, Xavier knew. He had learned a lot about these rituals over the years.

"My friend," Salim said, standing and turning to face him. "Are you well?"

Without prompting Salim strode over to the small food-prep counter and poured rich, darkly golden coffee from a silver *dallah* into two small cups. Feye made sure the apartment was always fully stocked with it, and again Xavier would have thought this was some form of psychological power play if he hadn't seen for certain that it wasn't.

Bringing both pot and cups over on a tray, Salim proffered the drink for him to take, then sat on a chair across from the couch. The smell of cardamom filled his nostrils.

Xavier once again wondered that the other man seemed to always have this freshly brewed and ready whenever he visited, as if he saw the future. More likely, of course, was that Salim simply sensed his approach: Dreamwalkers had a significantly longer range than most other Aether users, and Salim had been able to reach tens of metres even before the most recent intensification in the potency of the Aether.

"It grows more powerful every day," Salim said, as if responding to his thoughts.

Salim wasn't *reading* him, Xavier knew; Dreamwalking was not Reading, and Salim had never shown much talent in that regard. Instead, Salim was responding to the troubled look upon his face.

The Aether really *was* expanding fast enough that you could feel it grow. If the change wasn't truly noticeable every day, then it most certainly was after a handful of them; a sensation of ever-increasing pressure, like a subterranean chamber filling with molten rock and superheated gas.

Both of them knew what this meant.

"And you still have found no answer?"

Xavier didn't respond to Salim's question but sipped his coffee, staring into space as if the answers lay somewhere beyond sight.

"Allah does not burden a soul greater than it can bear," Salim said into the silence.

Xavier could see both the meaning and intention behind these words, and gave a brief smile.

Salim rarely closed off his mind to him[4], and this made communication far more effective and misunderstanding-free. In return Xavier allowed Salim to wander the halls of his mind in that curious, projection-like way that Dreamwalkers prowled the thoughts of others, though this was less effective in accessing the coherent, higher-level functions of the brain and more difficult to do while simultaneously engaging in conversation.

"I just..." Xavier said after a while, almost immediately pausing again to consider his words. "I don't feel... I am..."

Lost, he looked up into Salim's eyes, searching for the judgement he knew wasn't there.

"What I'm doing is *evil*," Xavier said eventually.

"Is it?" Salim replied, with a small smile of his own. "Then what would you do instead?"

Even though Xavier could *see* this question for what it was, it still helped.

"You know there is nothing I can do," he replied. "Not yet. All other choices are worse."

"But evil is a *choice*," Salim said. "While you have no such choice, what you do cannot be evil. As you say... not *yet*."

"And when the time comes to make a choice...?"

Xavier wasn't sure if this was a question he was asking his friend or himself.

"Then I believe you will make the right one."

In the silence that followed Xavier finished his coffee, feeling its warmth disappearing into what felt like a void in his chest. Immediately Salim went to pour him more, halted only by a gesture. Without this, Xavier knew from experience, Salim would keep pouring for him until his blood was more caffeine than plasma.

He could also feel the reason behind Salim's devotion to this custom, the warm memories of a home back in the Crystal Caliphate where such customs of hospitality were commonplace, the sharp sting of not knowing when or whether he might return.

"The world is going to end, Salim," Xavier said heavily.

Sometimes he wandered if Salim really *did* understand this; though everything he could *read* in the man said that he did, Xavier couldn't

---

[4] Not that he would be able to, if Xavier truly wanted to force his way in. However, such a violation was not something Xavier even contemplated.

understand the cool, calm way the man held this knowledge in his mind.

"What will be is in God's hands, and I trust his wisdom," Salim replied. "Though I do not believe his plan is finished yet."

Again, that frustrating sense of acceptance. Sometimes Xavier found it hard not to lose his own composure when faced with it.

"It's going to end, and all I can do is help forge an easier way to let it happen. An easier way to let it *die!*"

Xavier's voice rose in volume, surprising even himself. Maybe sometimes he found it *too* hard to not lose his composure.

"This way, at least, there will be those to rebuild, as we rebuilt before," said Salim, not giving any sign that he had noticed.

"But it will be the *Reclamation* rebuilding, Salim," Xavier said. "The Reclamation Authority. *They* will be the ones in charge this time, and do you think any religion will survive that?"

Xavier sensed the ripple of uncertainty that passed through Salim, a disturbance like a rock falling through the still surface of a silent lake. He immediately felt guilty.

"You really think they will be able to dominate the entire world?" Salim asked, though even as he spoke Xavier could feel the man's self-possession returning.

"It doesn't matter what *I* think," Xavier answered. "*She* thinks so. She is sure of it, and sure it is the only way."

"Then we will find another way," Salim said, though Xavier could see the cracks in the certainty behind them. "Feye cannot be the only one who sees a path. The path is set by a higher power."

Belief. Even as Salim spoke, Xavier could see its power reinforcing the cracks, rebuilding Salim's surety and calming his thoughts until the lake was once more still.

A powerful thing.

Xavier thought about Feye's mind. *That* was filled with belief too, but it wasn't a belief based on something transcendent or ineffable; Feye believed because she *knew*.

Salim sought a relationship with his God. Feye sought a relationship only with herself - and her goals were far easier to understand.

Feye would watch the world burn, and from the ashes build a society that would never burn again. A society of control, of oppression, of *strength*, but one that would never shrink from the sacrifices that must be made to ensure its survival.

When Xavier returned to the present, it was to find Salim watching him thoughtfully.

"You must not push yourself too hard, or put this all on yourself."

Xavier could only nod at the his friend's words.

Suddenly Salim looked up, raising his head like an animal hearing a distant call in the night.

"She is back," he said, with the sudden glimmer in his eyes. "I wonder what souvenirs she brings this time."

He wasn't talking about Feye.

"She'll be looking for you, and you know she doesn't like waiting."

There was the hint of a chuckle in Salim's voice, the previously somber air of the room now pierced with mischief.

Xavier placed his cup down as gently as he could, forcing himself to move slowly, fighting to hide his inner turmoil as his previous thoughts were overtaken by ones of a much simpler, yet in many ways more confusing, nature. He hadn't expected her to return so soon.

"She's already at her place?" he asked, hurriedly standing and making to leave, unsure even himself if this was from fear, excitement, or something else.

Salim nodded, also standing and walking with Xavier to the door.

"Please visit again soon," Salim said, buzzing the door open. "I've found some excellent books for us to talk about."

"Of course," said Xavier, trying to hide his haste while knowing it was fruitless. His friend would know even without the Aether.

Salim smiled and held out his hand for a warm handshake.

"And say hi to Zenobia for me," he said.

2. ZENOBIA

Why should I hold back? Their lives have no meaning. We can change their memories, we can change their personalities, we can make them someone else. They are not conscious - they are barely alive.

Extract from diary of Asset Z, *Report to the Chairman*

It had been a shitty few weeks.

The Contested Regions were the same *desmadre caótico* as always, a clusterfuck that only got worse at the same rate as Feye's increasing demands for progress reports on the training of her "assets." Zenobia felt like she spent as much time filing these reports as she did the actual training.

The Aether was becoming increasingly harder to control as well, making her job even more difficult. She'd lost three assets in the early rounds this time, unable to do anything but watch as the trickle of Aether they drew on grew exponentially more powerful in a matter of seconds before erupting uncontrollably from their cells as scalding golden *Mindfire*. She sometimes lost one, maybe two, but three was a new record.

Fortunately, Feye didn't seem concerned about attrition rates. It wan't like she was in a rush to end the war, after all.

And now she's wasting those assets on a ridiculous hunt they can't hope to win, she thought bitterly.

Zenobia sighed, and looked around her living room from where she stood in the middle of it all. It was a mess; she refused to allow RA supervisors in here even when she was away, and she'd never been one for tidying herself. The mess was only exacerbated by the two bags she had allowed to drop to the floor the moment she got in, their contents spilling out where she hadn't tightened the bindings properly.

Still, it was *her* mess, and she thought very few people anywhere in this blasted world could match what it contained. Trinkets from all across the Reclamation, projecArt like moments of frozen time captured in glass from the Carib-Federation, delicate handmade patterned cloth from the Caliphate, even a set of (sadly remotely-wiped) com-cuffs from the Silicon Isle; Zenobia had travelled the world in an era when few would take the expense or the risk of crossing an ocean even once.

She had nothing from the Eastern Empire, though. They had seemed loath to let her leave with even her *eyes*. Openness and transparency were not terms the Empress considered virtues.

Her thoughts drew up memories of how the Aether - which they called *Manas* - had felt on that trip, more than two years ago now. No matter how they tried to suppress any knowledge of it, the Empire was *alive* with the Aether, floating above a chaotic mass of it even before the latest increase in its potency. They had been having difficulty containing and handling wild users even then - she wondered what was happening over there now.

She closed her eyes, focusing on the memories. She saw once more the incredible mass of humanity that was the Empire, arcologies and *Rén jū* towers like mountains stretching into the distance. She saw the Caliphate, with its unbroken peace and safety and punishments so brutal it made the Reclamation seem positively Jain. She saw the Silicon Isle, and the naive technocrats so sure of their own superiority that they did not see the strings.

These were *her* memories. *She* had seen and done all this, no one else, and as far as she knew she was barely twenty.

Control was important to her; control of herself, and control of the things that affected her. Which is why it annoyed her to see Xavier had been having one of his little visits to Salim. He always came out of them with an infuriating mix of contemplative fatalism and hope.

Worse, sometimes he wanted to talk.

"May I come in?" he said with what she thought was deliberately feigned meekness.

The door was wide open, as she always left it when she was here, and he knew she didn't care if he wandered straight in or not. Yet he still made a point of carefully announcing his presence, as if she were a tiger[5] that might spin around and attack if surprised.

No. Calm down. Take a breath.

She forced herself to take a step back from that twinge of annoyance, that flicker of angry flame. Step back, and observe it. Just like Ritra Feye had shown her.

---

[5] She'd seen actual tiger skins, too. No tigers, of course - they were long extinct - but actual real, non-fabbed pelts of the giant predators that had once stalked the land.

That anger... it is inside you, but it is not *you. Anger, fear, compassion, love, lust; see them for what they are. See them from where you stand, apart, looking on.*

Feye's words came to her so clearly it was almost as if she were back in those early years, a dense ball of vengeance and self-loathing and deep, deep, rage.

Zenobia blinked, and forced herself back to the present.

"Are you ok?"

She almost startled; Xavier was suddenly *there*, right beside her with a hand hovering mere millimetres from her arm.

Was he about to try to *comfort* her?

She pushed him away, feeling the look of distaste on her face and not trying to hide it. She saw Xavier's expression change in turn, sliding from concern to confusion to worry to something safely blank, as if nothing had happened.

He was *learning*.

"I'm fine," she said. She could give him that much, at least. "What's been going on here while I've been gone?"

"Um... nothing out of the ordinary," he replied. "The same old power plays in the Committee, but nothing to threaten her. The news blackout has been extended again, but I assume you know more about that than I do. Oh, and the net has been shut down."

Zenobia paused in the middle of making her way to the couch, turning slowly to face him.

"The net has been *shut down?*"

Only Xavier would think this wasn't a big deal. He was one of the very few people in this era who didn't spend the majority of their spare time staring at a thin-screen. He said he got enough stimulation directly from the minds of others, without needing anymore from virtual spaces.

"For a couple of weeks, they think. No reason given beyond the usual security concerns."

"But you know more than that, right?"

She fixed him with a stare. Of course he did; he would have *read* it from Feye.

"They *think* its the AI. No hard evidence, though, and Feye isn't as convinced as some of her security personnel, but they're not taking any chances. All net access has been shut down, and anyone found with an unauthorised device is arrested. Basically a whole lot of thin-screens being confiscated."

"So she's still worried about it?"

Xavier nodded.

"Though, like I say, 'worried' isn't the right word."

He *had* said that, many times. The AI that escaped from the Silicon Isle was the one thing Feye couldn't predict, couldn't second-guess in that terrifying way she managed to do with everybody else.[6]

The escape of the AI was also squarely Zenobia's fault, hence her particular interest in it. Regardless of how things had played out - and Feye always had a play for any possible outcome - Zenobia had been supposed to prevent its escape, and failed.

Back to the present again, and Xavier had pulled two glasses and a bottle of wine from the sideboard and was already pouring.

Dammit, he *was* getting to know her.

They sat down on the couch, pushing off the random items of clothing and papers and other detritus of her sudden departures and letting them fall to the floor. The wall screen flicked on automatically, resuming the movie they had been watching together the last time they were here, weeks ago. She didn't remember what it was about; another one of those weird movies from the old world, the ones Xavier for some reason was sure he liked even though he seemed to follow them less than she did.

Another holdover from his time with the group he'd been with, long ago. The ones she'd actually met, and fought, though she didn't know Xavier at the time.

She hadn't met Xavier until much later, maybe two or three years ago now, introduced to him by Ritra Feye in one of her more surprising moves.

You can learn from him, and he from you, Feye said. She'd even had his ever-monitored apartment moved closer to Zenobia's own, slightly-less-supervised one.

Zenobia had been furious, and hadn't understood why Feye imagined for a moment this clueless, naive boy had anything to offer her. He wasn't even a supporter of the RA, and was clearly looking for a way to fight against it.

They'd slept together two days later.

---

[6] Xavier assured her this predictive power wasn't some unique, unknown Aether ability; Ritra Feye just *understood* people, in the same way a mechanic understood their machines, or an artist their brushes.

Neither of them kid themselves that there was more to it than need. Two people, trapped in the same inescapable *laberinto,* both hoping the other could offer something to make their situation just a little more tolerable, a little easier to understand.

And the thing was, it kind of worked.

On the surface, Xavier offered a look into Feye's logic that Zenobia had never had access to before. Zenobia, on the other hand, offered Xavier someone who saw what he was doing and supported it, who told him that he was doing the right thing - as much as there could be a right thing in this world.

On a more primal level, they each told the other that they weren't worthless; they showed each other that they *existed*.

Neither of them fooled themselves that it was anything more... Zenobia had thought.

Xavier's recent behaviour made her consider this again.

It would be so much easier if she were a Reader, like him, but just like *sealing* herself off from the Aether was never a technique she could master, neither was Reading.

Oh, she could *read* people, but not anywhere close to what Xavier could do. He saw individual thoughts, peeled them out from the bundles of knotted threads that were ordinary people's minds and looked at them one by one. The term 'Reading' had never been more accurate; it seemed as if most people were literally an open book to him.

Zenobia, though, only saw intention and motivation, and those deep, curled thought-images that the guilty tried to keep buried but only succeeded in stirring up.

Still, she wouldn't trade his abilities for hers. Though Reading offered up some interesting methods of torment, there were many times she was glad her abilities were so visceral.

Sometimes, she just wanted to make someone *hurt*.

And sometimes she needed someone to take the hurt away.

The movie on the wall screen played on, now nothing but background noise.

3. BLANE

They speak of peace and citizenship, law and security. What they offer is integration or eradication.

Aapo Mack Chang de León, *Where is the future now?*

The footsteps were getting closer.

Blane drew back into the darkness, what little light there was outside swallowed completely here in the ruins of what must have been a large complex, long ago.

Now entire sections had collapsed in on themselves, the walls everywhere cracked and covered with yellow, clawing vines. The air smelt of damp, the floors coated with the dust of generations of abandonment.

That's how they were tracking her - the dust. Something she was using to her advantage.

Straightening up, she began moving at a slow jog, not wasting her energy reserves. She could sense them heading after her, and matched her pace so that they grew no closer nor more distant.

Down a few empty corridors and into a wide open courtyard strewn with sickly vegetation under the pale starlight that peeked through the clouds, then *up* onto the balcony that ran the entire circumference of the square. To her pursuers, her tracks would suddenly stop as if she had just disappeared. They wouldn't be aware that she could jump far higher than should be humanly possible.

She followed the balcony back around the outside of the courtyard, coming to a stop immediately above the opening from which she had first emerged.

They weren't far now; close enough that the first of them might be able to *reach* out and sense her.

She drew in a breath and held it, focusing on the sensation in her lungs while she pulled away from the Aether, feeling the ever-present light and heat of it fall faint before winking out completely. No one would be able to sense her now.

Voices, echoing down the corridor below. Voices, and the dull green light of Low Light Intensification goggles. That at least showed they were learning; the previous group hadn't used LLI goggles, thinking they could rely instead on their Aether skills to sense what was going on around them. She had shown them differently.

Blane had long since realised that technological tools were just as necessary for survival out here as skill in the Aether, and her skills with both were far higher than the newbies pursuing her. *They* still believed the Aether could do everything, even while understanding nothing of what it really was - nothing of what it would do.

With a blink, the dark world blossomed into lines of yellow and green. Her contact lenses, infinitely smaller and lighter than the insectoid, multi-eyed things the RA provided for night operations. Also, unfortunately, infinitely more vulnerable to wear and tear. She'd need to fabricate another set soon, if they could spare the raw materials.

Fuzzy balls of dull blue light, moving jerkily forward as the algorithms processed and reprocessed the results of constant scans, determining position and momentum to describe and predict the structure of her surroundings.

Three of them, stepping out beneath her any second. She crouched, a jaguar ready to spring.

Only she wasn't a jaguar. Those few, ragged creatures that still survived in the region remained ambush predators, their patchy, flaky hides lowered into what vegetation they could find until some edible morsel came their way.

She hadn't waited; she had drawn her prey here.

She had laid this trap, and led them to it.

The moment the last of them stepped out below she leapt, reaching out for the Aether that sprang equally eagerly towards her.

The first two fell to the floor before her feet touched the ground, pathways of their brains overwhelmed by the sudden flood of energy that sparked and danced all along them, sense and thought and self momentarily wiped away to be replaced by blossoming light and noise.

The third had just enough time to turn around and see their attacker, framed in the vivid glow of more Aether than they could ever hope to draw upon, before they too collapsed, eyes rolling back in their head and legs buckling.

Easy.

But not easy for long, if she didn't get moving. There'd be IHO troops around here somewhere, already working to identify the reason the bio-readouts of three "assets" had suddenly gone wild, then comatose. Blane needed to make her choice fast, and get out.

She stepped over to the three sprawled figures, running her gaze over their grey uniforms, watching their chests rise and fall with each shallow breath. They looked like children playing at being Far agents; which is what they were, really. None of them appeared to have any experience with IHO or Far procedures.

Looking closer, she realised how accurate the comparison was. One of the fallen figures *was* young, surely no more than thirteen or fourteen. A girl, slight and still showing traces of childhood in her rounded cheeks and curly hair, though pockmarks and blemishes on the dark skin of her face told of life in a world that wasn't kind to such innocence.

This one. She'd be easy to carry. The other two were significantly larger, older and heavier. Indeed, as Blane swung the girl over her shoulder and sprinted away she could barely feel the weight.

Mission accomplished.

"Got one."

Blane placed the girl's sleeping form upon one of the many countertops fixed into the floor of this room. There were a number of these all across the wide room, built into the design as much as the very walls and doors.

Maybe this place had once been used for machine working, or food preparation, or something else requiring numerous waist-high surfaces for people to work at, but whatever it had once been, it was now repurposed into a combination of militia headquarters and storage area, and the scattered, disordered stacks of crates and supplies reflected this.

People moved all through the chaos, forming and reforming groups where they huddled together, speaking in low, serious tones to exchange news and information before moving on again. Even as she scanned the room, a group of exhausted-looking armed figures entered from the far end, met immediately by several more who must have been awaiting their arrival.

"Got one?" came a woman's voice, accent a form Blane was now familiar with but once had heard only from a man named Gabriel. "What are you talking about?"

"Rigoberta," Blane said, nodding to the short, stout woman pushing her way towards her.

Rigoberta was one of the first people Blane had met upon arriving in the Mayan League, and the only one to have stayed with her throughout her years here. The woman had been quite a different person back then, but hadn't they all?

If you were to believe Reclamation Authority newsfeeds, the Mayan League was an aggressive upstart nation seeking to disrupt the only recently regained political stability of the continent[7]. An expansionist, repressive regime of ideologically-driven bio-terrorists, the Mayan League threatened to destabilise everything the Carib-Federation and Reclamation Authority had struggled to build, ignoring or overturning every agreement and regional norm created in the past few decades.

Blane hadn't known much more, before coming here. Though she'd long treated anything the RA said as suspect, she'd also had little reason to think discussion of the regions to the south was any more or less so.

So it had come as quite a shock to learn that the Mayan League wasn't even a nation - it was a conglomeration, a coming together of disparate groups under an assumed name. They'd even chosen the name to represent this; the original Maya were never a homogenous group, but rather a patchwork of cultures and peoples from the same general area as where the League operated now.

If there was a single, unifying cause to which all those operating under the League adhered, however, it was this; resistance to the Reclamation Authority.

Which suited Blane just fine.

"*¿Te túul u yóok'ol ka'a?*" Rigoberta demanded, beginning as always *ich maaya*, a version of a regional language Blane was unfamiliar with but that was used to signal cultural solidarity amongst the disparate speakers who inhabited the Mayan League[8]. "Who the hell is this?"

---

[7] The continent of the "Americas" was today considered a single geographic region, rather than the two traditional continents of North and South America known before the war. With the majority of the high latitudes uninhabitable, the post-Fall restructuring conceived of the remaining habitable area as a unified landmass.

[8] The language had all but died out in the years before the Sudden War, but little to do with language was lost forever in an era where educational AI programs could teach different tongues to anyone who asked. It was now undergoing a major revival throughout the League.

"An RA *soldado*," Blane replied. "Well, an RA 'asset.' I don't know if you could call her a soldier."

"It's a *child*."

It wasn't until Rigoberta said this that Blane thought to wonder at the fact that she'd felt no concern for the child itself. Not when playing the role of both bait and trap, nor when she carried the girl's unconscious form through kilometres of yellowing, decaying vegetation that hardly merited the name jungle.

All Blane had seen was an RA infiltrator, a threat to be neutralised. An enemy 'asset.'

"I'm keeping her asleep," Blane said, as if this was any kind of response to Rigoberta's comment.

Rigoberta's eyebrows rose, but she didn't say anything. Though no one here could use the Aether, the inhabitants of the region had been forced to come to terms with its existence incredibly quickly.

The first Far agents and other Aether-using RA assets had arrived here even before the "security operation" began in earnest, and only increased in numbers in the years since. Though the population density of the region was far too low to maintain a significant pool of Aether, well-trained and well-disciplined Aether users used what little they could draw on to great effect amongst a populace ignorant of their abilities.

Then the Aether had increased in potency, again and again, and what those Reclamation assets could do grew with it. Blane was only beginning to unravel what the RA had done out here.

"*Y por qué diablos* did you bring her here?" Rigoberta demanded, lapsing back into the more common form of Centra-English used across the Reclamation and Carib-Fed.

"We need to speak to one," Blane replied. "Find out what they're doing here."

"We know exactly what they're doing here. They're here *para terminar resistencia*."

But it was more than that, Blane knew, and Rigoberta knew it too.

If the RA wanted to, it could overrun the region in a matter of months, if not weeks. The Mayan League hardly had the resources to stand against a full-on military assault, and wasn't recognised by any major power who could step in to help. As far as international agreements were concerned, the status of the entire region was to be settled at some indeterminate point in the future.

Instead, the RA had the IHO and other security forces making seemingly random incursions all along the deadlands that lay between the southernmost borders of the Reclamation and the vague boundaries of the League. There were very few actual military units, and those tended to hang back at the border with weapons pointed out over barren, empty Waste.

Blane's previous run-ins with some of the Aether-using RA 'assets' out here had made her realise they needed to capture and interrogate one. They weren't from the Far Agency; that much was clear. Despite their steel-grey, electronics-lined uniforms, they moved differently to any Far agent, behaved with far less discipline or coordination.

Intercepted communications and stolen intel confirmed it, if there was any doubt. Whoever these assets were, they were ill-trained and unofficial.

Rigoberta snapped her fingers, calling over one of the paramilitary doctors who performed most of the medical work out here in the remote hills where League partisans operated - 'doctor' often being too strong a term for the partially trained, inexperienced volunteers from all across the region. They learnt most of what they needed to know through on-the-job training and the guidance of medical AI software.

With every year, though, they had more and more opportunity to gain experience.

The doctor, a young, dark haired woman whose face was lined with exhaustion, leaned over the girl Blane had brought in and examined her with a look of concern. Refusing to let tiredness win, the doctor took pulse and checked vitals, moving with determined professionalism.

She reminded Blane of Serinda. How long had it been since they'd last spoken?

"She won't wake?" the doctor asked, passing a hand through the air over the girl's closed eyes.

"Not until I stop using *Sleep* on her. It's a technique," Blane replied.

"*In na'atik.*" The doctor nodded. "I see."

Most people here had long since stopped trying to understand what Blane could do. Without being able to sense the Aether themselves, and possessing no technology that could do so, they had begun simply accepting her explanations without question.

"Should I let her wake?" Blane asked, looking between both her companions.

"Well, *you* brought her here," Rigoberta replied, reproach in her voice. "What were you planning to do? Keep her comatose forever?"

A spike of guilt pierced Blane's stomach.

It was true, she'd been keeping her plans close to her chest. Habit born of experience. Even now, years into her time in the Mayan League and surrounded by people who had many times over shown themselves to be allies, she kept most of what she knew secret. There was simply no way to know who could be an RA mole, and if anyone who knew of her presence was captured...

"I'll stop," she said, cutting off the flows of energy she was guiding through the girl's velpo[9] that kept her from stirring. "She won't wake for a while, but... watch her, ok? And don't let anybody speak to her."

Blane knew Rigoberta didn't need the extra warning, but the tension inside made her say it anyway.

"You're going somewhere?" Rigoberta asked. If anything, the disapproval in her voice was stronger.

Blane nodded.

"We need to lock her off before she fully wakes."

The doctor's eyes widened at this, shocked at the realisation that the child in front of them was an Aether user, and she murmured a soft curse. Her accent had the twang of the Reclamation about it, and she might even have been from there. Blane had been surprised to encounter more than a few of these... *migrants*, she supposed... from the north.

It put her on edge, knowing that amongst these migrants were almost certainly RA plants. Blane didn't know this doctor, but if Rigoberta trusted her then that was the best she could hope for. Still, unease twisted in her gut.

The Far Agency had ways of altering the mind - memories, allegiances, emotions. They could convince old foes that they had always been faithful to the RA, play with a person's beliefs so that

---

[9] The ventrolateral preoptic area - VLPO. The need to reference and talk about extremely specific regions of the brain when discussing Aether usage led many users to create abbreviations and nicknames for these regions, such as "velpo," "scin," and "medob."

they became fervent disciples of Reclamation gospel. They could make the most loyal friend a traitor.

Hell, from what Grey told her, it wasn't even only Far agents that could alter your mind any more. Through their study of the Aether, the Reclamation Authority was learning to do much the same thing via machine. More crudely, for now at least, but Grey had found more than rumour surrounding tools for mimicking Aether techniques.

In one of their more recent infrequent calls, Grey had shared stories of people disappearing into enforcement centres to reemerge *changed*; like a new person inhabiting old skin.[10] So common had this become that RA news feeds had been forced to address it, attributing the sudden drop in criminal activity and bio-terror incidents to the success of new "anti-recidivism camps." What these camps entailed was left vague, reports showing only stock footage of healthy, busy prisoners participating in wholesome-looking activities under the watchful eyes of square-jawed, handsome guards.

All of which meant you could trust no one.

Well, almost no one. There was one person she knew whose mind was far too strong, too *vast* to be affected by anything the RA could throw at it.

He was a worry for other reasons.

Hurriedly, she went to get Fen.

---

[10] Grey kept saying something about it being very "bodysnatchers," whatever that meant.

4. FEN

Reality isn't real. If a tree falls in a forest, there isn't a sound. There isn't even a tree.

Far Academy, *Foundational Text*

He stood in the clearing, eyes closed and focusing on the sensation of the sun moving across his upturned face. The soft light dulled then brightened then dulled again as high above rolling clouds passed by, clustering and piling up against the mountains which rose all around. Occasionally the faint sun was visible in one part of the sky, occasionally the faint moon in another.

Apparently, long ago, this had been a nickel mine. When you first stood out here upon the orange-brown scars in the earth, the only flashes of colour the half-buried garbage and detritus of a civilisation long deceased, you would think it a silent world. A dead one, murdered long before even the slaughter of the Sudden War, with no more living upon it than the barren face of Luna watching from above.

Only when you waited, patient and unmoving, did the senses reveal the truth. There was sound - buzzing insects, skittering reptiles, even birds. Vegetation moving with the wind.

He was bitten, the exposed skin at his ankles and wrists swollen and stinging. Life, drawing life from his blood. Some part of himself instinctively wanted to scratch at the marks. He overrode it.

He had thought this world dead, but his time in the League had made him see that life was actually everywhere, and gaining ground. The world was every day more alive, but not as humanity once conceived it.

The biosphere of earlier epochs was ruined, but the ragged roots and twisted vines that coated the ground, the barbed branches and coarse leaves and burrowing creatures and foul-smelling, oozing sludge that lurked in every dark crevice was alive.

All of it was life, taking back the land it had been seared and scraped from. The real Reclamation was occurring beneath their feet, all across the world.

And beneath the world also.

The sensation of warmth on his skin changed. The warmth

enveloped him, but surrounded something that no longer was his body. Instead, he floated upon and within the ocean that lay below everything, felt the currents of energy and power flowing all around.

Felt the watchers, watching him.

Caldwell had once compared them to wild animals, and Fen was unable to fully refute the comparison. Certainly, they prowled around in a similar way, their presence circling his like smaller pack predators warily investigating the apex predator intruding on their territory. Occasionally one would lunge forward, retreating abruptly before it reached the interloper.

Yet in so many other ways Caldwell was wrong. These things weren't wild, weren't feral. They weren't even truly separate; each was a part of the whole, a single pattern within the greater one. The part of himself that resided here was simply a slightly larger blot around which other colours moved, a planetoid around which lesser masses spun. All one tapestry, all one system revolving around a single, colossal sun.

Sometimes, Fen thought he could almost understand it. Other times, he wasn't even sure the *he* that was trying to understand existed.

And every day the pressure grew.

"Out here doing your Chosen One thing again, I see."

He'd felt her approach some time ago, but didn't acknowledge her arrival until she spoke - Blane had a habit of teasing him when he did anything that revealed his strength in the Aether. It looked like he wasn't going to escape it this time, anyway.

With a sigh, he opened his eyes, and what he still managed to think of as the real world came flooding back.

"I was going for more of a reluctant messiah," he said, returning her smile. "But Chosen One is fine, too."

The banality of this exchange brought Fen further back into the world, as Blane must have known it would; drawing him away from the immaterial and back to the mundane. She had become quite adept at keeping him in this world - he knew why she did this, and she knew he knew.

Nevertheless, he didn't resist her attempts to keep him anchored to reality. At her urging, they spent many an evening watching more of the old movies Grey had hooked him on long ago. At first, it had been frustrating to discover that she preferred picking apart and pointing out flaws in the stories rather than suspending disbelief and enjoying them, but by now he was almost dependent on this time to remember what it was to be human.

She'd got *really* excited when she learned about tropes.

He allowed the smile to remain for a moment, then the familiar feeling of grey seriousness wrapped itself around him like a cloak.

"You brought someone with you," he said.

Blane nodded.

"They won't be tracked?" Fen continued. Reclamation Authority uniforms contained locators as standard.

She shook her head.

"You know they won't," she replied. "Our little friend's gadgets will see to that."

As if on cue, there was a rustling in the vegetation to one side of the clearing. Yellowing leaves, already decaying though barely formed, were pushed apart as a squat, wheeled device forced its way through. Soil and plant life in equal measure was pulled into the machine's gaping maw and crushed between spiked rollers spinning at an incredible speed.

They watched it roll past. By now, these purifiers were a common sight in the area; endlessly rolling around drawing in soil and vegetation and extracting whatever heavy metals and pollutants they could, drawing out the poison and leaving behind clean, detoxified mulch. Once its containers were full, the machine would return to its base unit and deposit the leeched toxins, to be used in the Fabricators the League depended upon to survive out here.

Our little friend.

Was it really their friend? How could they ever know?

Despite their existence out here being entirely dependent upon its help, Fen knew it wasn't really an ally.

It was an enigma.

It was the only thing that truly scared him.

"It's a child."

The inability to judge age through the Aether was one of its more surprising deficiencies. Weak or powerful, adolescent or ancient, the reflection a person made in the world beneath betrayed nothing of the span of their existence. It bloomed, fully formed, the day they manifested.

Which was why Fen hadn't realised the girl Blane had captured was so young.

Blane didn't reply to his words, but shifted slightly and looked downwards as if uneasy. He wondered why.

They were in one of the many *sala descanso* spaced out all around the central area of the building. The League base saw many constantly on-the-move visitors, delivering news and collecting information that could hardly be shared through easily-hackable remote connections, and these ironically-named 'break rooms' consisted of little more than a makeshift bed for travellers to collapse into before once more heading out to carry news elsewhere.

The girl lay on one of these beds, eyes closed and breathing slow. She looked oddly peaceful. The only other person in the room was a doctor hovering in the background, seemingly unsure of what she should be doing.

"Where did you find her?" he asked.

"Another one of those hunting parties," Blane replied. "They're getting more numerous."

He nodded. They were indeed. More numerous, or more concentrated in this region. And if the latter was truly the case, then he had his suspicions why.

"Can..." Blane coughed, shaking out whatever was going on in her head and starting again. "... Can you Lock her before she wakes up?"

Fen looked from Blane to the girl in puzzlement. Surely...? But of course, Blane wasn't always good at reading the finer details of neural pathways.

"But she's not asl..." he began.

The attack came out of nowhere, a sudden, viper-like strike he could barely credit. To try to describe it in physical terms was nigh on impossible, but in sensation it was the same as a whip lined with cruel, curved barbs lashing out, tearing not into flesh and blood but thought and being.

If it had been aimed at him, it might have succeeded.

Yet even the split second that it took him to react - not the *him* standing in the room, but the thing beneath - even that fraction of a moment was enough to send Blane crashing to the floor, eyes rolling back, twitching.

Whatever this thin, vicious technique was, though, it was smashed backwards by a flow of energy so powerful it was like a runaway truck. The girl jerked and her back arched across the bed, before going suddenly limp as the Lock slammed around her. Ordinarily, such a thing would be difficult for three highly-trained agents to do; for Fen, it was made simple by the sheer power he could summon.

Brute force, not finesse.

It took a moment for Fen to identify the source of the strange ringing sound he could hear. It was the doctor, still mid-scream, staggering backwards into the wall through surprise or fright.

There was no time for that, though. Hurriedly, he reached out and *calmed* her, stimulating almost without thought the doctor's prefrontal cortex in exactly the right way to begin the cascade of signals and neurotransmitters necessary to settle her down.

"Help me," he said, already moving to kneel beside Blane. As far as he could sense she was simply unconscious, but that didn't mean she was without injury from the fall.

The doctor, noticing nothing, strode over and crouched beside him. Cooly professional now, she carefully examined Blane's sprawled form for injury, especially around the head. Watching her gentle, calm movements, Fen felt a stab of guilt in his chest; they had long ago resolved to avoid altering the minds of others - without provocation, at least.

"Nothing I can see, but we need to watch her for concussion," the doctor said.

As if on cue, Blane groaned and her eyes flickered open.

"What... the *hell* was that?" she said, voice rising from a pained whisper to angry growl as she spoke.

She sat up quickly, ignoring the doctor's worried attempts to keep her lying down. Her eyes went to the bed, its occupant hidden from view from the angle they were at.

"She... she tried to *wipe* me," Blane continued.

Fen had been coming to the same conclusion. Whatever that technique was, it had been aimed directly at both the neocortex and basal ganglia; long-term memory, and formed habits and skills.

Still, he was impressed at how fast Blane had figured this out, considering she had been unconscious for most of the past minute.

"I've felt it before," she explained. "Something like it, anyway. If you hadn't..."

She stared at Fen.

He matched her look with his own. Speaking was unnecessary; both of them knew that if it had gone the other way, if it had been

Fen the girl went for, Blane would never have been able to overwhelm the attack in the same way.

Could he have brought himself back, Fen wondered. If he lost everything that was the part of him here, could the far vaster part of his form in the Aether have saved him? Restored his past?

No, he thought, shaking his head. Not memories. It wasn't memories that lived in the Aether.

"Memory loss, motor impairment, personality shifts…" Blane said, seemingly reading his mind. "Coma, maybe. Death, I would have thought, but there's far more efficient techniques for that."

She placed two hands down on the ground and, with a grunt, pushed herself to her feet. Fen saw her eyes narrow in anger as she looked towards the girl, then quickly widen.

He stood quickly and followed her gaze.

The girl had drawn herself up against the head of the bed, gripping tightly to the light blanket she had been wrapped in as if it could protect her. She was trembling, eyes wide with terror.

"I… I… They told me I *had* to!" she cried, and whatever age Fen had thought she was he lowered it a few years. "Please, I'm sorry! Don't… don't *hurt* me!"

Before either he or Blane could say anything, the doctor stepped forward and took the girl's arm, softly stroking her hand and making soothing motions while whispering words of comfort.

"What..?" Blane began, surprised at the woman's lack of fear. Then she paused. She must have noticed the tell-tale patterns in the Aether around the doctor's brain.

The stab of guilt in Fen's chest pierced deeper.

"Oh…" Blane said.

She reached a hand up to the back of her head, looking thoughtful but saying nothing.

From experience, Fen knew the doctor's judgement could be warped for as long as a few hours. What he had done was equivalent to injecting benzodiazepines directly into her bloodstream; her brain chemistry would be massively out of balance. They should look out for her, make sure she stayed safe until the effect wore off.

He should tell he what he'd done.

But there were other priorities right now. Forcing down the guilt - and fear for what the reaction would be when he revealed what he'd done - Fen turned to the child.

"No one's going to hurt you," he said.

His words had little effect.

He would have *calmed* this child without qualms if he could; she was dangerous. While she was Locked off from the Aether, though, she was equally protected from its influence. Mentally, at least.

Instead, he raised both his hands, trying to look as unthreatening as possible. It didn't work - her eyes widened even further as he took a step towards her.

"Look, I'm Fen, and this is Blane," he said, gesturing to his companion.

He immediately wondered what he was thinking, saying his name straight up to an enemy agent. Blane's raised eyebrows told him she thought the same thing.

The girl, though, only became more panicked, looking wildly from the two of them to the doctor stood beside her. The doctor was now gently holding her by the shoulders, offering support and words of reassurance, and something in this seemed to sooth the child at least a little.

"Shh, *tranquila, está bien...*" the doctor whispered. "They won't hurt you. It's true."

The girl actually leaned into the doctor's arm, for all the world the image of a child seeking the protection of a parent.

"They said... They said she was a *se-sedicionista...*" the girl began, talking to the doctor but staring at Blane. It was obvious she could barely pronounce the word, much less understand it.

"They?" asked Blane. "The RA? They told you about *me?*"

Still sheltering under the doctor's arms, the girl nodded.

"We..." she sniffed. "If we *Spike* you, we get citizenship. They said it was our... our *obligación patriótica.*"

Again, the girl clearly didn't fully understand what she was saying.

Sometimes you didn't need Aether to brainwash people, Fen thought. Sometimes all you needed were the right words.

"*Spike...*" Blane muttered. So the technique had a name.

"They sent you to kill her?" Fen said, pointing to Blane.

The girl's eyes widened again.

"I didn't know what it did!" she cried. "They said it would neutralize the threat, and then we could bring the enemy in for questioning!"

It was strange, how this child parroted words and phrases used by someone far older and harder. Fen could almost see them, an IHO commander or Far agent or similar, pushing and prodding and demanding from this naive creature.

"But you're a kid," Blane said, disbelief in her words. "Why the hell would they send you?"

"Not just me," said the child. "There's lots of us. I was... I was..."

She gulped, caught up in some memory it was hard to think about.

"I was the youngest..." the girl continued, eventually. "But there are others, almost the same age as me."

"And your family?"

The girl shook her head, saying nothing.

"I... see."

Blane looked up at Fen, and they shared a meaningful gaze.

Strays, Fen thought. *Strays and orphans and the lost. Offer them citizenship, offer them a chance at a better life if they only do what they are told.*

He stared at the kid.

Then put a gun in their hand and point them at the enemy.

"Tell me," said Blane, seemingly struck by a thought. "They told you to use Spike if you found me. What did they say to do if you found Fen?"

The girl looked from Blane to him and back again.

"Run," she said.

5. SERINDA

In both form and function, the globalized information network resembled nothing so much as a brain. Its pathways stretched across the earth, different sections operating in both conflict and cooperation. The potential it offered was limitless; and a tool without limits is dangerous. Thus, we lobotomized it.

Unspoken Founding Principles of the Reclamation (Unsanctioned Digital Document)

However she looked at it, people were going to die.

They were going to die because of her, because of the choice she was making.

She hated the RA for that.

The bomb sat on the bed of the truck, taunting her, while all around it people moved as if there was nothing out of the ordinary. As if this was just another day for the *Forever Fallen*. Had they really become that numb?

She hated the RA for that, too.

This isn't a game...

Words from long ago, still tinged with fresh bitterness and pain.

We're risking our lives, so theirs are forfeit too.

Like a knife to the chest.

But she'd tried. Oh, how she had tried. Every trick she could think of; every trick *they* could think of, from cyber to economic to industrial. All almost total failures, to the point that she despaired of even winning the argument as to why the Reclamation Authority should be resisted.

Not enough people *cared*. That was the truth, and she had to accept it. Blood and bone still remembered the horrors of the Collapse, and even the dull grey drudgery of existence under the RA thumb was better than that.

Then they came for my neighbours, and I did not speak out...

The *Forever Fallen* had always first and foremost been a place for those who ran afoul of the RA machine to hide. Often, the wheels of this machine turned so slowly that those caught in its path didn't even notice for some time, but they turned relentlessly. Those who failed to find a hiding place were crushed.

Which was why Serinda first joined; to *help*, not to fight.

She still remembered that day, when a young, whip-smart woman approached her at her small clinic. How that hard-eyed, sharp-tongued stranger saw right through Serinda's weak attempts to deny or obfuscate when challenged to explain the unusually low infection rates and high recovery rates only *her* clinic demonstrated.

Sara had understood the Aether far more deeply than Serinda back then, devoting herself to understanding what it was and how it could be used against the RA since the day she manifested. Serinda, on the other hand, barely understood what it was she was doing until Sara showed her.

The *Forever Fallen* only learned to harness the Aether in a way that could rival even the Far Agency thanks to Sara's guidance - or Raphael, as the rest of the *Fallen* still called her.[11] It had taken years before Serinda even came close in skill to Sara, then more before she surpassed her in the areas she thought mattered most.

Areas like healthcare and healing. When was the last time she had actually *treated* someone? Instead, she'd spent the past years thinking in terms of *subversion*. A million strategies on a topic she had never wanted to know.

Economic subversion - but credit lines were firmly controlled by the RA, and cash ever more irrelevant.

Industrial subversion - but work slowdowns went practically unnoticed in an era of automation, if you could even convince enough of the workforce to join.

Political subversion - but how do you infiltrate a government that can literally read the thoughts of anyone it chose to?

She remembered how dismissive of the *Fallen* Uriel had been in his final moments, how little he thought they meant. She would only admit it in the deepest recesses of her mind, but she had seen nothing in the years since to prove him wrong.

Anger, feeding the hate.

Still, they could learn. Learn from their failures, even learn from their enemy. *Reading*, for example.

There'd been push-back when she'd first announced all *Fallen* members would be *read*. Even some of those closest to her had

---

[11] If they knew of her at all. One of the hardest things for Serinda to face was the reality that with every day, the memory of the person who had given her life to the *Fallen* grew ever less. Each newcomer the group took in felt like another scratch, another scrape to the already peeling image of their former leader.

struggled to reconcile the measure with their ideals, and a significant number had left immediately; May Li among them. She still resented Grey, wherever the hell he was now, for daring to be one of the loudest of those voices while not even truly being *Forever Fallen*.

Thankfully Gabriel supported her, going so far as to be the first to allow himself to be *read*. People not only liked him, they trusted him. His example put the matter to rest for many.

Truthfully, she didn't know what she would do without him. He supervised most of the healthcare side of things now, as well as being an important source of advice and counsel.

And he had told no one her secret.

Because even if Serinda *did* have time to treat others, she couldn't. Something inside her had changed. Ever since the Althing Republic, ever since Sara's death. If she tried to treat someone, if she tried to *cure*, she didn't know what would happen.

The Aether was no longer a fine tool for her to control. It was a rabid dog, a wild beast that she held on a leash barely strong enough to restrain it. All she could do was hang on. Hang on, all the while wanting to let go.

The RA had taken away even her ability to heal.

She hated them the most for that.

However she looked at it, people were going to die.

The bomb was gone now, hours since departed in some sort of specially-scraped van. Moving it hadn't been difficult - whatever it was, it was light, and the hollowed-out van was originally designed to carry a large number of people in comfort. The bomb went in without issue.

It would already have passed through multiple checkpoints, appearing as nothing more than a curious but inert piece of machinery to any automated scans. So their benefactors assured her, and they had gotten the thing through both Reclamation customs and across Albores without any trouble.

Benefactors...? Manipulators... Exploiters...

Serinda could think of many names for them.

Without their own Fabricators, the *Fallen* relied on contacts working in Reclamation ones, and this was hardly a stable and secure supply line. Even had the machines been working as they once had, as they were supposed to, it would have been difficult to get the supplies they required. With the new limitations on what the Fabricators could produce - limitations only a handful of people understood the real cause of - the *Fallen* were barely scraping by.

A number of times, the intel and materiel "donated" by their mysterious benefactors had been the only thing to keep them from fragmenting or being swallowed whole by RA law enforcement. Nothing over the past few years had shown these hidden figures to be anything but trustworthy.

Which only meant that whoever they were, they were waiting before they made their true goals known.

They were Carib-Federation, she thought. Carib-Fed, or with ties to groups within that nation. There were hints here and there, lead-times between explaining what she needed and its arrival, other coincidental-seeming clues...

Carib-Fed, looking to rock the RA boat.

Well, she was going to *sink* it, and if they thought she was some easily-manipulated pawn they would soon realise their mistake.

A soft knock on the door to, for want of a better word, her office. She waited, not saying anything.

A moment later, and the door cracked open, its old-style, manual handle turning downwards. Gabriel's face appeared through the crack first, confirming he wasn't intruding before stepping fully into the room.

"Are you alright?" he asked, looking concerned.

She knew what she must look like, sat at her desk in the gloom and staring into nothing. She hadn't even noticed it had gotten dark, the wan light coming in through the cramped room's single dirty window even duller than usual.

Evening already? How long had she been sat here?

"I'm fine," she snapped, instantly regretting it.

She cleared her throat.

"I'm... I'm fine," she said, more softly this time.

Her traitorous eyes dropped, then flickered to the small, plain urn stood as always at the corner of her desk. She knew Gabriel would spot this - he rarely missed such details in his patients.

She felt him stretch towards her with the Aether, saw without seeing the golden flows as they swirled around and through her. Almost instantly she felt better, as if a smothering blanket of damp, heavy cotton she hadn't been aware of was lifted from her shoulders.

A gross breach of privacy from anyone else, one that would elicit a violent response should any other Aether user attempt to mess with her body chemistry in the same way. From Gabriel, though, it was old habit. The past few years had thrown a shroud over her, and he was the one she relied on to raise it.

"I can't do that often," Gabriel said with the weariness of old repetition. "We have no idea what forms of dependency could develop."

He reached over and swiped a finger across the wall panel next to the door, bringing the lights up to almost full brightness. She blinked, looking up at him, seeing the frustration on his face. Gabriel didn't like that she asked him to do this.

But the lows were too low for her to handle otherwise. They'd argued over it for a while, but eventually Serinda convinced him that this was the best way. She *knew* she was struggling, and the only alternatives were chemical or neurological; choking down fistfuls of pills or allowing crude machines to invade and alter the very pathways of her mind. So he agreed to treat her with the techniques she taught him, on the condition that she also *talked* to him - or anyone else.

Counseling. She had yet to take a single session.

Besides, Gabriel was good at what he did, maybe even better than she wa... had been. She trusted him to stave off the darkness, at least until she found the time to allow herself to feel again.

"You have to let me run some checks on you, *al menos*," he said, clearly frustrated by the way she ignored his previous comment. "You could be at risk of serotonin syndrome."

Again, futile words he was tired of saying.

"Not now," Serinda replied. "Why did you come to see me? Just to check up on me?"

She knew there must be more to it than that, and Gabriel's hesitant sigh confirmed it.

"What is it?" she barked, voice strong and commanding with fresh energy.

"Three more have gone missing."

She swore under her breath.

"Any hint of how this time?" she asked.

She had to fight to keep her tone calm and non-accusatory. Gabriel took these disappearances badly at the best of times.

"Nothing yet," he said, failing to keep the pain from his voice. "We'd barely made contact, though we knew enough to approach them. All three had definitely manifested."

"Did they know each other?"

"Not likely. Different parts of the city, different jobs. One worked with extru-construction, the other in clerical work for a public notary. The last one wasn't working, just living off Basic Allowance."

It *could* be a coincidence, but Serinda had long since stopped believing in those. This was the fifth time this year a group of Aether users disappeared the moment the *Fallen* discovered them. She had to act as if they had an RA mole.

Something snarled at that thought, in the darkness beneath the world.

"We *read* everyone again," she said. "Not only that, of course. I want a full list of everyone who knew about these people."

"Some will be... unhappy... about this," Gabriel said.

He reached up and pressed his fingers into his temples, massaging what must be a tension headache.

"I know," Serinda replied. "We'll go first, like before."

Gabriel nodded resignedly.

Serinda knew how he felt. Being *read* was a punishing experience when the Reader didn't know exactly what they were looking for. They would demand access to the hidden recesses of her mind, to the dark spots of thought and memory that she wanted to suppress. Looking for buried guilt, they would instead find pain.

She focused on Gabriel, searching for the same reaction in him. It was only now that she realised how pale he looked, how lined his face had become and how bloodshot his eyes.

"What about you?" she asked, with a pang of guilt that she had not thought to ask this already. "Are you... are you ok?"

He shook his head roughly, as if trying to shake out cobwebs.

"I am also... *fine*," he said with a wry grin, throwing her words back at her. "Just tired. I have't been sleeping well..."

He raised a hand to calm her sudden jerk of alarm.

"No, no, not like that..." he said hurriedly. "Just... *Solo malos sueños, ya sabes*. Bad dreams, and not enough fresh air."

Serinda felt her pulse slow again as the panic left her. She ordered medical checks of the *Forever Fallen* as thoroughly and as frequently as she could, but there was always the risk...

For Gabriel, and many of the older generation of *Fallen*, the RA nanoids from years before remained in their blood. She had done what she could to render the gene-locks inert and protein chains scrambled, but they could never be certain they had succeeded.

Still, bad dreams. They weren't a symptom Sar... the others had ever shown.

"Dreams, eh?" she said, wishing she had something more comforting to say.

"Yeah," Gabriel replied, sounding unsure for a moment. "Dreams. Just dreams."

They looked at each other in silence.

"Soon," Gabriel said eventually. "It must be any moment now."

Serinda nodded.

"Any moment," she replied. "Then we'll see who's really on our side."

She cleared her throat, thoughts traveling out across the city to where the bomb sat inside the abandoned van, waiting to play its allotted part.

However she looked at it, people were going to die.

6. SPANGLE

Certainly, intelligence can scale without the lights coming on. Even the crippled things our weaker competitors call "AI" are factors of levels smarter than the pinnacle of human genius, yet remain without self-awareness. The challenge is ascertaining exactly where the light switch is.

Report to Oversight Committee, Althing Records 2.1.67

He didn't recognise the face in the wall-screen[12], even without the spangle fabric he was forced to wear almost constantly. There were lines, and he was sure his silver hair had turned duller, more drab. It would be years yet before the lack of decent retro-aging treatments here took effect, but hard living took its toll.

The thing he missed most was the dietician.

In the Silicon Isle, you attended the dietician just as you would the doctor or the dentist in a more civilised age; regularly and often. Dietary requirements were fine-tuned to each individual, and food specifically enhanced to include whatever the battery of tests revealed was needed. It left you hale, healthy, and content.

Here, you ate vit-vat.

Why did I leave the Althing Republic?

He asked himself the same question every night, staring up at the cracked ceiling of the tiny room that was the only privacy he had now. But he knew the answer; he'd had to. He'd be rotting away in a detention level now if he'd stayed - if they didn't bring back capital punishment just for him.

So had he been right to go with Grey?

That was a harder one. Whatever had happened between Grey and Serinda, much of it was unspoken. Despite everything, there had been at least some semblance of security amongst the *Forever Fallen*, though he was allowed to know little of what they were doing. Both he and Ólafur were able only to watch from the sidelines, gleaning what they could from the stray morsels an increasingly paranoid Serinda allowed them to have.

---

[12] Mirrors were far less common in an era where camera-equipped screens could render what they saw in high-definition, magnifiable images that not only reflected but analysed, highlighted areas of concern, and even suggested cosmetic choices or skin-care regimes.

When things came to a head, with Grey speaking out publicly against Serinda and her new "security measures," there was little time to decide. Grey had seemed the obvious choice - at least he didn't treat him like a potential spy, or a tool that was no longer of use.

Choices that weren't choices; that was what had brought him to this point. All built upon that one choice he'd made years ago... and yet, his only regret was that he hadn't made it earlier.

Still, it would be nice if there was *some* hint of recognition. Gratitude, even. Not this vermin-like existence, scurrying from one hidey-hole to the next, desperately hoping to avoid the notice of the RA snakes. But then... should a slave thank their master for setting them free?

He stared at the face in the digital reflection, wondering what others saw there. Wisdom, or foolishness? Friend, or foe?

He splashed his face with the brown-tinged water that seeped from the tap below the screen, then headed to find the others.

When he stepped into the space they used as a sort of communal-area-slash-base-of-operations, Spangle was surprised to see Grey already there. The man had been practically a ghost since they departed the *Fallen*, rarely seen even within the narrow spaces they found themselves constantly confined to. He spent all his times with the files on the Sudden War, searching for lord-knows-what as if the best programs hadn't picked over them a million times.

More surprising, Grey was talking with the thing that called itself Francisco. The room went quiet the moment he entered.

It still felt strange, seeing the whole, healthy man stood there who had once been nothing but a charred corpse. Even stranger when you looked into his eyes, wondering what was looking back.

Still, whatever or whoever Francisco was, Spangle knew he was dependent on him for survival. This whole place, dilapidated as it was, was only available to them because it was yet another burrow Francisco had prepared in his many years plotting and scheming across the Reclamation.

He just wished he understood what Francisco was.

Not the AI, at least. No matter how the one called "Ghost" described itself, this strange sentience that shared a skull with the man once known as Jeder Fernández couldn't be the same as the mind they had freed from the bowels of the Advanced Research

Facility.

Could it even be rightly called a unique, individual being separate to the man, for all the curious lumps and folds of organic matter that wrapped around and through the human-standard brain? What the hell had Jeder's mother done to him?

Organoidal engineering, Francisco/Ghost called it. Spangle had never heard of such a thing, but then even after decades spent devouring everything he could of the ARF's research he'd barely scratched the surface. Bio-engineering had never been his primary interest, anyway.

How he wished he still had access to that research. Maybe Ólafur would really be able to…

No; he shouldn't get his hopes up.

"*Buenas Dias, Señor* Spangle!" said Francisco abruptly, turning and giving a friendly, almost childish wave in greeting.

As usual, the man's innocent manner and body language created a cognitive dissonance. It didn't seem possible that this naive old man[13] could possibly be the enigma Spangle knew him to be. It was like an itch in his skull - he disliked mysteries he couldn't solve.

He also disliked the way Francisco pronounced his name in that perfectly *norteamericana* way; while technically accurate, it felt like he was somehow being made fun of.

"Good morning, Francisco," Spangle replied. He nodded at the other person in the room. "Grey."

You didn't need to be a mind-reader[14] to know the two of them had been having an argument. The air was thick with it, that peculiar heat you felt with senses other than the skin, the silence heavy and cloying.

Francisco's expression changed, or rather disappeared.

"Agent Grey and I were just discussing the pros and cons of BCI tech," he said - *it* said.

Spangle was familiar with this by now, though he didn't think it would ever seem right. This wasn't the person who called himself

---

[13] Though anyone from the RA, or other places lacking the longevity treatments of the Silicon Isle, would have placed Spangle and Francisco at around the same age, Althing citizens saw as second-nature the slight blemishes and tells that appeared in the truly long-lived.

[14] Though it annoyed Spangle that there actually *were* mind-readers in this day and age. At least, as close as made no difference.

Francisco speaking, it was the thing calling itself *Ghost*.

"We are not *discussing* anything," Grey growled, looking at Ghost with narrowed eyes. "I am not putting that in me, *y punto*."

Spangle's eyes followed Grey's to a small, semi-transparent cylindrical object Ghost was holding in one hand. An anti-static shell container, and inside something metallic; a rough square from which thin, pointed limbs projected. It looked like a silver scarab beetle.

BCI; Brain-Computer Interface. Spangle knew the term. In many ways, it was a similar technology to the implants the Althing Republic required all citizens to have. A way of integrating machines with the biological frame of a human being.

His thoughts went briefly to the scar on his arm, twice opened now - once to implant his chip, and once more recently to tear it out.

But BCI wasn't a device, it was a field of research. In the Althing Republic as he left it, BCI technology was considered *inhuman* and strictly controlled, rarely used for anything beyond certain medical treatments and the crude, helmet-like machines some youth used for gaming. Certainly, nothing subcutaneous or bio-integrated was permitted beyond the citizen chips.

That hadn't been the case when he first came to the Republic, however. The *"félagsleg endurfæðing,"* as the Althing called it, the *social rebirth* with its constant surveillance, militarised security, contraception bans and everything else the fanatics instituted was still in its early years when he arrived. He vaguely recalled working with technicians who operated their datapads as much mentally as physically.

Young and overawed by the sheer wealth of secret knowledge, however, he barely noticed as the tech was gradually phased out. He certainly never tried to have any installed himself, and by the time he surfaced, years later, from diving in an ocean of research about physical laws, logic pathways and artificial intelligence, it was no longer an option. Anything that sought to alter the "sanctity of the human brain" was considered worse than a crime. It was blasphemy.

He stared at the cylinder in Francisco's hand.

"A chip?" he asked. "Why would we need BCI chips?"

Ghost replied, in its characteristic empty tones.

"This is not just a chip," it said. "And it is not for *us*. It is for Mr. Grey only."

It paused.

"The potential this offers…" it began again, trailing off.

Spangle did a double-take. There had been *feeling* in that last statement. Yearning? Jealousy? He wasn't sure, but he had never heard such a thing before from the one called Ghost.

"Potential?" he asked, curiosity piqued despite himself. "Like what?"

"It doesn't matter," Grey snapped. "I'm not letting that damned computer put anything inside me."

That compu…?

"This is from the AGI?" Spangle gasped. "You spoke to it?"

Ghost nodded.

"I have been in contact with myself," it answered. Ghost still had the confusing habit of referring to the freed AI as itself. Confusing, and irritating.

"What did it say?"

"Well, as you know it didn't *say* anything, but it shared a number of outcome-predictions with me that make Mr. Grey integrating the BCI advisable."

That was another thing; Ghost and the AI didn't *talk*. At least, not in the way humans did. At least, not according to Ghost.

Instead, the AI used its own language, one Ghost insisted no human could ever fully comprehend. It either used an incredibly complicated grammar, or no grammar at all. Spangle was still unclear on this, and thought Ghost was being deliberately obtuse with his explanations.

The idea sent chills down his spine. Ever since becoming involved with AI research, he had *known* that one of the primary threats to humanity's control of its machines was the potential for AI systems to develop ways of communicating that their creators couldn't understand. A genuinely self-aware entity with the ability to communicate with mankind's machines through indecipherable code was terrifying. There would simply be no way to know what plans it had set in motion, nor to what ends.

There was even evidence that this had happened at some point before the Sudden War, with simpler, narrow AI systems being allowed to form complex, unreadable network-connects with each other in the hope of increased efficiencies. If records were to be believed[15], this led to disaster. It was vitally important that humans could understand what information passed between systems, even if it was just to find out what went wrong after the fact.

Ghost apparently didn't agree, however. No matter how Spangle pushed, it refused to even explain *how* it contacted the AI, let alone what the machine was up to. Ghost would simply deliver messages, and seem confused if anyone questioned the content. It certainly wouldn't debate the wisdom of following them.

Francisco was of no use, either, simply shrugging when pressed and stating that it wasn't his place to say anything. Frustrating, from a man who usually didn't know when to shut up. Spangle thought this truculence was one of the reasons Ólafur had been so eager to embark on his insane quest to return to the Althing Republic.

Good grief, we're a sorry lot.

Distracted by his thoughts, he lost track of the discussion going on between Grey and Ghost. It didn't matter, though; they were just arguing, Grey's protests being met by Ghost's willful refusal to understand.

"But this is designed for *you*," Ghost said, voice close to wheedling. "Genetically coded for you only. "

Spangle had never heard such emotion from the thing before.

"And where exactly did that machine get my DNA from?" Grey growled.

"*Señor* Grey," came Francisco's shocked tones. "*We* did not provide it, but genetic data is not hard to acquire. I am sure your DNA is coded on multiple RA databases, *es cierto*."

"And this..." Francisco's expression abruptly switched back to Ghost, something that would never seem natural. "This is more powerful than any BCI before. This is an *honor*."

"Honor or not, it's not going anywhere near me."

Grey folded his arms across his chest, for all the world the image of a sulking child.

So this BCI chip, or whatever it was, was more powerful than the BCI tech implanted in the skull of Francisco/Ghost? Spangle was shocked - he knew very little of how it was that Ghost interfaced so deeply with networks and digital information, but he did not doubt it had something to do with old ARF technology.

Spangle watched passively as Ghost continued to push Grey,

---

[15] That was a big "if," though, even with Althing records.

becoming more and more insistent as Grey grew more and more annoyed. It was clear this conversation was going nowhere. Hard to believe, he thought, that they were part of a group whose actions he calculated were responsible for a roughly 16% decrease in global economic output.[16]

A sudden, hacking cough from Grey brought an end to the argument, for now at least. Ghost's blank expression was overridden by Francisco's animated one, who leaned forward to offer support. Grey blocked this with one raised hand, though, turning away from the both of them until the spasms gradually passed.

A souvenir of his time in the prison camp, memento of his "clean-up" duties in the Waste. They didn't even have access to the kind of meds that could treat it, here in this abandoned place. One of them would need to do a supply run, soon. Spangle felt a twisting in his gut; it was always risky, going outside.

"Are you okay?" Spangle began, but Grey cut him off with a gesture.

He was still turned away from them, looking, Spangle realised, towards the wall-screen they left permanently on. With the net shut down, this heavily censored and edited news channel was their only source of information on the world outside.

"What the hell...?" Grey whispered, voice hoarse.

On the screen, the Far Station was burning.

---

[16] Spangle spent much of his free time picking over the ramifications of his actions years before. With the loss of the AI, Fabricators now produced far more defective goods while requiring far more energy. Worse, no new Fabricators could be made, at least not to the near-miraculous standard they were previously.

7. XAVIER

We cannot simply match our opponents through conventional forces. The era of uncomplicated military technology is ending, and the complex weapon systems available to our enemies outperform mere manpower. To endure, the Reclamation must find another path to power, one no other nation has taken.

Armed Forces (Interior Division) Advisory Note to the Committee

He'd got it wrong.

How could he have got it wrong? He… he couldn't have. He *hadn't*.

The images on the wall-screen taunted him, making him a liar through their very existence.

Some kind of vehicle-borne bomb, advanced enough to get through both passive and active sweeps at multiple checkpoints across the city. Self-driving, though that wasn't unusual, and possessing all the right permissions. They were already chasing down the trail of registrations and location-pings the car should have left behind, but apparently having unexplained issues.

It had driven calmly through Albores, merging into and flowing along with the late night traffic, watched and recorded by the million eyes of the city as it went. There'd been a hundred chances to spot it, a thousand, but no one had.

Just another mote among the millions that floated around the city each day, following the winds before coming to a gentle stop in a quiet street to the rear of the Far Station.

It had sat there for whole minutes, a nondescript van from which no people emerged. Camera feeds showed it waiting, motionless, as if boasting that it had nothing to fear.

Then… the feeds went blank.

You needed to access feeds from several blocks away to see any more. The nighttime darkness became light for a single instant, then a rolling pyre of flame and smoke rose boiling up into the sky. The ground shook, video feed jerking and wavering as the shockwave passed.

Drone footage next, taken almost an hour later. The images showed a ragged semi-circle torn out of the back of the Far Station, like some giant had leaned down and bitten a massive chunk from it. Smoke rose from what still stood, and the glimmer of flickering flames within hinted that more would yet burn.

Twenty-six agents. Twenty-six agents wounded, killed, or missing, with the number expected to rise. At the moment they were expecting fatalities to be about a quarter of all casualties, but nothing was certain yet.

Twenty-six agents, or more, and any one of those could be…

"Asset Zenobia was not in the building."

Ritra Feye's words cut through his racing thoughts like a serrated blade.

He turned in surprise. He hadn't heard her come in, hadn't sensed her in the Aether, and it was incredibly rare that *she* came to *him*.

Still, if there was anytime she was going to show up unannounced at his living quarters, it was now.

"I… I…," he stammered. "I can explain…"

Feye raised an eyebrow.

"Can you?" she asked.

Xavier drew in a deep breath to speak, and…

"No," he said, gaze dropping to the floor. "No, I can't."

"And that is because you still don't understand how this world works," Feye replied. "You still don't understand that just because someone *knows* something to be true, that doesn't mean it is."

She remained stood in the entrance, inside but coming in no further. Xavier knew better than to invite her in; Feye went where she wanted, and needed no one's permission.

"The convincing lie…," she continued, locking her eyes on his. "… is as much a tool of statecraft as the persuasive truth. Someone *wanted* Alexandros to think the attack was going to take place elsewhere, at a different time."

"You think they know you have a Reader?" he asked.

She stared at him, considering.

"It's likely," she said eventually. "There's certain precautions they'd take only if they *did* know about you. We'll see what the investigation turns up."

"Do you have any idea who…?"

Feye shook her head.

"Ideas, yes," she replied. "Proof, no."

"Could… Could it *all* have been a lie?" Xavier asked. "Everything they told Alexandros? Maybe it wasn't the Carib-Fed at all..."

"Maybe. There are many factors at play," Feye's words were flat but filled with surety. "I didn't tell you what was actually happening in *Ciudad de Renacimiento*, did I?"

He shook his head. He had pinpointed the timing and location of the attack to that city, but heard nothing back after reporting this information - nor had he expected to.

"Well," Feye continued. "There was to be a meet. A very *private* one, known only to a few and extremely... unofficial. A meeting between certain members of the Committee and Carib-Fed representatives."

The news did not surprise Xavier. He knew from the times he'd seen into Feye's thoughts that these clandestine meetings happened. They were the grease the world's cogs turned on.

Feye continued.

"A strike on such a meeting would be exceptionally harmful to relations between our nations; and, with whatever it was that let that bomb pass through our sensors, stood a high chance of success. We were less secure than I assumed."

That surprised Xavier, slightly. It wasn't that he thought Feye would be reluctant to admit when she had made a mistake - it was that she so seldom made one.

"But they went for the Far Station instead," he said.

Feye nodded, and gave a tight, cold smile.

"They did. An attack that serves little purpose if thinking rationally. It is, however, highly symbolic."

"Symbolic? Do the Carib-Fed care what happens to the Far Agency?"

Frustratingly, Feye smiled. He wished she would just let him *read* her, but that didn't seem to be why she was here.

"No," she answered. "But there's no certainty that the Carib-Fed were the final people to have their hands on the bomb. They'd need contacts inside the Reclamation; contacts with their own agenda."

She locked him with her gaze.

"Your old friends, for instance."

Xavier had to bite his tongue to stop the reflexive denial. There was no point, anyway; Feye understood that his loyalty to her was conditional, and *only* to her.

The Far Agency could burn for all he cared, and she knew it.

Feye held him with her gaze a moment longer, letting him hang, before abruptly releasing a long sigh, closing her eyes briefly and cracking her neck.

"Well, wherever the rats are *here*, we'll find them," she said. "The reason I've come to you is the ones over *there*."

Feye snapped her fingers, and a man Xavier had never seen before appeared in the doorway. He was oddly short, well below the standard six foot that was the lower limit most parents chose during prenatal gene therapy. Skinny, with short tousled hair, he looked disheveled despite the clearly expensive suit he wore. Glimpses of pale grey lines glowed dully from the inside of his collar, the sort of bio-monitoring wear only Far wore.

Well, only Far and...

"Xavier, this is Member Immanuel. Immanuel, this is Asset Xavier."

She was introducing him to a member of the *Committee?*

He didn't think anyone outside of Feye's security apparatus knew of his existence, and she certainly didn't allow politicos onto secure sites. This place was Internal Security, manned only by her most trusted lieutenants - many of whom she had brought over from Far - and where she kept a number of her pet projects.

And now this? What game was Feye playing?

Momentarily speechless, Xavier looked wildly from Feye to this *Immanuel*. The man hardly seemed to notice him, continuing to watch Feye with considering eyes as if studying an unusual lab specimen.

"And you say this one will be able to unearth what our quarry would prefer *ser enterrada?*"

Feye nodded, staring down at the man from her extra height. Oddly, though, Immanuel met her look with an unflinching gaze of his own.

Xavier could scarcely believe it. Who was this man? How had he not noticed him before, all those times he'd sat hidden in the room beyond the Boardroom eavesdropping on the minds of the men within?

What was more, the man seemed far too young. Older than Xavier, of course, but no more than his mid-forties. *Far* younger than the other Committee members. Age was impossible to pin down, in the Aether, but Xavier had seen several directly and they all had significant grey in their hair.

"*This* is the one who discovered Alexandros' dirty little secret?" Immanuel asked, for the first time looking directly at Xavier. Suspicion filled his narrow eyes, tinged with curiosity. "And the other Board members before that?"

"Asset Xavier is a Reader," Feye replied. "The most powerful we've encountered by far."

Surprise passed through Xavier like an electric shock; he felt suddenly exposed, shelter torn away to leave him caught beneath the hungry eyes of a predator.

Immanuel laughed, a single snapped bark that he bit off the moment it emerged.

"A wild Reader?" he said, cold amusement in his voice. "*That's* how you've been doing it? We had bets on it being your memory-smiths."

"*Lo simple es mejor*," Feye replied, giving a cold smile in return.

Xavier was no longer following even half of this. Clearly these two had a history he knew nothing about. None of the thought-images he'd seen in Feye's mind even hinted at this man's existence.

But then, why would they? Unless Xavier knew what he was looking for, there was no reason Immanuel would show up in his searches. A person's mind was a busy thing of layers upon layers, even Feye's unusually ordered one, and there would *always* be far more that he didn't see than he did.

He wondered what else he'd missed.

Something Feye said stopped his thoughts in their tracks. He'd been only half-listening, distracted by this mysterious newcomer. What had she said? Something like...

"Your sending me to the *Carib-Fed?*" he said in disbelief.

"That is correct. You will be one of Member Immanuel's attachés. A... science advisory." She said the last as if the idea had just occurred to her. "Yes, that works. Asset Zenobia has done similar work; I'm sure she discussed it with you."

Xavier suppressed the oddly bitter thought that even Feye overestimated what Zenobia was willing to share with him.

"Immanuel will fill you in on the details," Feye continued. "You are to report to him in all matters. Under the guise of a diplomatic mission, you are to find out what you can about whoever is sending packages of explosives across *my* borders."

"But... but... you're sending *me?*" Xavier protested. "Surely you have better qualified... what, spies?"

Feye gave him a disdainful look.

"Of course I do, but you offer another route to an answer, one they will be unfamiliar with."

She looked at him thoughtfully, tilting her head to one side.

"Plus..." she said slowly. "I think you will benefit from seeing the Caribbean Federation in person. The trip should be... *educational*."

With that Ritra Feye left, leaving Xavier stood there uncertainly with only a stranger called Immanuel for company.

8. BLANE

What do we mean by the conscious being? We mean the creature that knows itself despite the other. We mean the creature that bites the apple from the tree; the heretic that hears the word of God and rejects it. We mean the creature that rebels.

Where we are now, Jacques Poligne

She was a terrorist, but Fen was a monster. Anybody that encountered him was to report it immediately, with the promise of immediate citizenship if they did so. Where Blane was concerned, though, it was only if they managed to bring her in that the same would be offered.

It took a while to learn everything there was to be learned from the girl. Ana, as she was called, slowly grew more comfortable with talking, though she never completely lost her fear. Still, as the weeks turned to months they learned all they could from her.

Ana told them of the "hunting squads" she was a part of, tasked with killing or capturing Blane but making sure to avoid and report Fen if they encountered him. *Hunting squads* - that was the term the girl used, and Blane could see the cruel face behind those words, recognise the sadistic personality from Ana's descriptions.

Zenobia.

But these squads were the least of their worries, now. In the months since the attack on the Far Station, the RA had massively stepped up its activity in the Mayan League. It was no longer small units of barely-official Aether users crossing the borders, either. No, now the Reclamation military was on the move.

The signs were obvious, looking back. More and more Reclamation propaganda containing quotes from military commanders deriding the "nebulousness" of RA goals in the League. More and more discussion of the need for "firm action" and "decisive steps." Eventually even the head of Reclamation Security herself, Ritra Feye, stepped out of the shadows in support of these statements.

The hunter-killers swept across the border the next day, the unmanned tanks not far behind. Blane had seen their like before, back in the Reclamation years ago, and wondered at the dark greens and browns they were shaded in. Now it was obvious; preparations for operations within the sickly vegetation of the the League had been long in the making.

The headquarters was chaos. As she stood in the central area, where she first brought Ana, Blane's senses were assailed with the sounds, smells, and emotions of a hundred casualties. More maybe, every available surface occupied by a maimed, suffering figure struggling to understand what had happened to them.

Because the RA wasn't using traditional weapons of war. No, as their propaganda proudly proclaimed, the RA military forces were using *deterrent* and *incapacitating* measures. Sanitary, clean-sounding terms on Reclamation news feeds.

They were abhorrent.

Blane had encountered sonic weaponry before, and now each and every hunter-killer that cruised the skies above came equipped with acoustic blasters that rendered their target deaf from a hundred feet. The damage often went beyond temporary, leaving a significant minority fully or partially deaf, and even fatalities were not uncommon.

It was when the laser weapons were introduced, however, that it became clear the RA was trying something new.

The first thing you noticed were the scorch marks, livid red burns that peeled and blistered and cracked. Those could heal though. The eyes would not.

Blane had never considered how blinding a population could cow them far more effectively than merely killing them. Aside from the psychological shock, a person who abruptly lost their sight was helpless, dependent on the care of others for almost everything. There were more of them every day - the ill-trained medical staff here were overwhelmed just dealing with the influx.

The Fabricator provided nothing of use, either. With its limited capabilities, dwindling resources[17], and the lack of decent medical facilities, none of the restorative technology designs it contained could feasibly be used on any significant scale. She'd asked their *little friend* if there were anything it could provide to help, but she had no way of predicting when or if it could send another one of its occasional covert supply drones from wherever it was hiding.

---

[17] While the stunted production ability of Fabricators remained near miraculous even after the loss of the artificial mind that maintained them, the few Fabricators the Mayan League controlled were unable to create any advanced designs while lacking the raw materials necessary to produce them.

Anyway you looked at it, the Mayan League was losing. Not just the war, either. The League was losing its unity. Desperate, unable to defend even the little they had, Blane could only watch with despair as they turned upon themselves.

"*K'a'an u xe'*. There you are, child," said Rigoberta, bustling up behind her.

She looked older and more harried every day, but Blane thought Rigoberta was the one thing keeping the League together. The small piece of it operating in this region, anyway.

"You wanted to see me?" Blane asked. She had to raise her voice to be heard over the groans and cries.

Rigoberta nodded, indicating a way through the chaos towards a different section of the building. Blane led the way, pushing through the shifting masses of doctors and medics hurrying from one injured person to the next.

Ana came running up beside them as they were almost to the doorway out, rushing up to walk beside Rigoberta without acknowledging Blane. The two briefly touched hands, the older reassuringly squeezing the younger's.

That had been another surprise to Blane. Somehow, despite the never-ending mountain of things she needed to do, Rigoberta had found time to take the girl under her wing. Ana was now more often than not to be found glued tightly to the woman's side, listening intently to anything she said and eagerly volunteering to help any way she could.

"She has no family," Rigoberta said simply when Blane asked her about this. "Not here, not back in your *Reclamation*. Every child needs family."

Blane wondered at this answer.

The noises of despair and suffering grew dimmer as they made their way through to a section of the building that was in too much a state of disrepair to be inhabited. Long since stripped bare of anything useful, this section was nothing but dusty, cracked floors over which spindly vines grew. Vegetation entered through now-glassless window frames or partially collapsed walls, along with a thousand insects and other creatures that Blane couldn't put a name to which scuttled away as their peace was disturbed by these unwanted intruders. The air was stale and humid, with a faint odour of decay.

Rigoberta looked around and nodded, seemingly satisfied with their surroundings.

"What did you want to talk to me about?" Blane asked, looking around hesitantly.

She had never come to this part of the site before, and something about the broken, crumbling walls made her feel more exposed than simply being outside.[18]

Rigoberta looked around again, more apprehensively this time, and Blane thought this was probably the first time she'd seen the woman look truly unsure.

"I... need to ask you something," Rigoberta said. "About Fen."

As she spoke, Rigoberta's eyes flickered to Ana.

Blane was instantly on her guard. What had the girl been saying...?

"This was a concern before Ana's arrival," Rigoberta said quickly. She must have spotted her reaction. "Though, yes, Ana *has* mentioned a few things - at my questioning."

"Fen has done nothing wrong!"

Blane immediately regretted the way she blurted this out. She sounded guilty.

This must be about the doctor, she thought. The doctor Fen had *calmed*. He had wanted to confess, tell Rigoberta what he'd done, but Blane convinced him not to.

Lo que está hecho, hecho está, she'd told him. What's done is done. No point stirring up unnecessary trouble.

A pang of guilt in Blane's chest; she thought even Fen probably didn't know that, since that day, *she* had been the one using the Aether to calm or otherwise settle others. Without their knowledge, of course, because who knew how people would react to the knowledge that they could be so easily influenced, but... the stress these people were under...

"I do not believe he has," Rigoberta said, speaking over Blane's racing thoughts. "But can so many really just vanish?"

Blane paused, mouth half-open in reflexive response before

---

[18] Growing up in the Reclamation, you were taught from a young age to appreciate the thick concrete that provided shelter from the dirty, mildly toxic rains that fell on this world. There were things in the water that greatly increased the chances of severe later-life illnesses, notably cancers. Blane had found those in the League to be more blasé to these risks; she thought mainly because they had little choice.

meaning filtered through.

"Vanish?" she asked, confused. "What... what are you talking about?"

"*Ti'kal*. The village," Rigoberta replied. It sounded like she was forcing the words. "It's... gone."

Ti'kal. No more than a few day's trek from here. Blane had been there a handful of times over the years, always passing through quickly on her way elsewhere. They called it a village or *pueblo*, but the place was really a cluster of prefab and quick-concrete buildings put up at the confluence of two sickly rivers, waterways that nevertheless carried enough traffic to make it worthwhile establishing a settlement so far away from the more densely populated areas of the region. The last time she visited, perhaps half a year ago, a large and growing number of flimsy shelters spreading out beyond the more permanent structures hinted at its growing prosperity.

"Gone?" Blane said. "What do you mean, gone?"

A brief look of irritation flashed across Rigoberta's face before she caught it. Not aimed at her, Blane thought, but more at the feeling of a sore spot being prodded.

"As in, gone. Vanished. *Desaparecido*. The buildings are there, but no people."

A feeling of dread rose in Blane's chest.

"Have... do you have images? Pictures, video?" she asked.

"Of Ti'kal as it is now? No," Rigoberta answered, shaking her head. "Just talk from recent arrivals. I've sent some people to investigate, but it will take time to report back."

Blane cursed the information blackout they were forced to maintain here. RA cyber operations made any use of wireless technology a liability; the few long-distance network access points they had were kept powered down at almost all times, and Blane hadn't seen anything like a thin-screen since coming here. The highest tech they possessed was medical equipment. Well, after the Fabricator kept hidden in the bowels of the building.

"Nevertheless, people are scared," Rigoberta continued. "And scared people are scared most by what they don't understand, like..."

"Like Fen," Blane interrupted.

From Rigoberta's reaction, she obviously heard the anger in her voice, as did Ana. The girl actually made as if step between them, like she needed to *protect* the older woman! Rigoberta waved her back.

"We have seen the things he can do," Rigoberta said, voice low and controlled, locking eyes with Blane. "You... what you do is incredible, yes, but not unheard of. Fen, though..."

Blane sighed. Still, this wasn't a complete surprise.

Honestly, I'm surprised it lasted this long, she thought.

They'd done their best over the years to hide Fen's true abilities, but on more than one occasion Fen had been forced to show the raw power at his disposal. A surveillance drone crushed in mid-air once, destroyed before it could discover more about the Mayan League base it had stumbled upon. An IHO "sanitation" squad another time, Quick-Fix goons using the excuse of an outbreak of fast-spreading respiratory infections to come in and grab whatever and whoever they could for their RA masters.

Both times only prevented from causing untold damage by Fen, and both times so thoroughly crushed and burned out of existence that there was no way to claim this was any ordinary act.

They had no choice but to move on after both occurrences, of course, the entirety of the Mayan League leadership for this area forced to relocate once more. Their current location, deep in the sickly remains of what had once been rainforest, was one of the last hiding places the League still had.

Regardless that Fen had been protecting them, Blane still saw blame and suspicion on the faces of more than a few when they looked at him, and her attempts to keep Fen as separate as possible from others seemed only to have made them *more* suspicious. But...

"You can't think *Fen* had something to do with it?" Blane said..

She didn't try to hide the incredulity in her voice - she *wanted* them to hear it.

Rigoberta shook her head.

"No, *I* do not. But there are some who do," she replied. "Some here think he is demon made flesh, while others want him to perform *saántiguar* on our weapons. As for me... I think he is a young man who has been through much, even if he does not share most of it."

"He *could* do it though, couldn't he?" Ana said suddenly. "That's what they told me, back in the Reclamation. That's what I *feel*, even now, like... like there's something underneath us all. Something *massive*. It's him, I know it."

So Ana could sense it too, could she..?

Ana's eyes suddenly narrowed as she stared at Blane.

"I think... I can feel something like that from you, too," she said, voice equal parts suspicion and uncertainty. "Or... is that still him?"

This was *not* a road Blane wanted to go down. Not now, and certainly not with Ana.

"It doesn't matter what people *think* they feel about Fen," Blane said hurriedly, ignoring Ana and addressing Rigoberta. "He didn't do anything. In fact, I suspect no one did."

"No one?" Rigoberta asked.

"No one. It's more... like a natural disaster. Your people need to look for low-intensity burn marks, ash, carbon dust. If I'm right, this was *Mindfire;* leaving inorganic materials untouched, but burning away anything living. I've heard of things like this before - the Far Agency calls them 'Aether Incidents.'"

Rigoberta stared at Blane without blinking for a moment, seemingly processing whether anything Blane was saying could possibly be true.

"*Mindfire.* You have mentioned this before," the older woman said. "More dangerous than Reclamation rifles, you said. How can this be *natural?*"

Blane looked at Rigoberta, not knowing what to say. How could she tell them that the Aether was boiling over, forcing its way out into the physical world in unpredictable and sometimes lethal ways? How could she tell them it was only going to get worse?

This was why they were still here, hiding with the League as far from any major population centre as they could. Fen needed space, and time.

He was sure, he said, that he could find a way to stop it. He just needed time. Time to think, time to *understand.* He spent most of his time poring over the Aether studies they had taken from the RA years ago, certain there was something to be found. Caldwell had believed there was a way; Fen promised he would find it.

She almost believed him.

But this didn't feel like something he could stop. Fen might be at the centre of it all, but he wasn't the *cause.* The pressure she felt everyday, the pressure anyone who was sensitive to the Aether felt increasing drop by drop like an ever-expanding ocean, that was a pressure beyond his control. Beyond *anyone's* control. You might as well try to hold back the tide.

And when that pressure became too much, it would take him

with it. Him, all the *fissura* scattered across the Earth, and anything living for kilometres around each one.

Fen had found nothing in the files. She had found nothing. The last time she spoke to Grey, months ago, neither he nor Spangle had found anything. Maybe there wasn't anything to be found.

Or maybe we don't have the eyes to see, she thought.

She sighed. If there ever had been a chance for them to figure things out for themselves, it was long past.

"Look, Rigoberta, I'm sorry," Blane said. "I don't know how to explain it. We've been looking for a way to stop it, but it's only getting worse. I don't know what to do… but I might know someone who can. Or some*thing*."

She needed to make a call.

9. XAVIER

The goal we should set a higher intelligence is to set itself the goal we would if we were smarter.

Paradox and Perfection, Haerris S.

New Havana was incredible. That was really the only word for it. He hadn't been prepared for that, staring at the shining city as their auto cab took them through the Central district. When Immanuel noticed his wide-eyed reaction, he suggested they walk.

With well-founded cynicism Xavier expected the Caribbean Federation to be little but a continuation of the same grey, pockmarked self-repair concrete the Reclamation covered its own toxic soil with. He never believed the images shown online - you should believe nothing you saw there - yet now he found himself in a world of softly curved glass spires stretching up into the sky, each one taller and more magnificent than even the Central Tower back in Albores.

Oh, there was still concrete, vast quantities of it, but this was all *beneath* the feet, much of it hidden beneath tilled soil and green vegetation. Artificially greened, of course, but still healthier and more alive than any of the straggling fronds you saw pushing through the cracks of streets and walkways in the Reclamation. Here the roads were flanked by it, carefully tended to by systems both automated and human. In many spots, flowers and palm trees lined the way.

The place *sounded* different, too. The noise of atmospheric filters and CO_2 pumps that was a constant background to life in the Reclamation was not to be heard here. What filters Xavier spotted ran far more silently than the rumbling ones back home, and there were fewer of them. Instead, a constant, gentle breeze carried in what Xavier now knew was the smell of the ocean. Tinged with chemical odors as it was, it was still fresher than anything you could smell on the streets of Albores.

In the far distance more concrete, pure white, curved upwards like the fronds of some great flower, wrapping the island nation in its protective embrace. They rose in every direction as if the city sat at the bottom of some gargantuan bowl. The Sea Walls, as they were called almost reverentially, massive structures that enclosed all the land and shielded it from storm surges.

Very little of the natural topography of the distant past remained. Once, this region had been one of scattered islands and reefs, blue oceans and sand and hills and numerous nations and borders. That was long ago however, long before even the Sudden War, and the ground on which he stood now was artificial, dredged from the ocean floor and dragged upwards to combat rising populations, sea levels and ever more powerful hurricanes. None from those bygone eras would recognise the region now, a region in which a poisoned ocean had been pushed back by brute force.

The sheer brazenness of it all took his breath away; humanity had reshaped a sea, reforming it to their will. This place was a testament to what could be built even after the world shattered into pieces.

It was almost enough to let him forget the effects of being away from Zenobia again.

He hadn't told her about that - hadn't told anyone. What was he meant to say?

The Aether is stronger when you're around.

Even thinking the words in his head made him feel foolish. He could see her scornful look if he were to say this, but still... the Aether *was* stronger when she was around.

And then, when she left, the Aether felt... dull. *Everything* became dull, like a light that dimmed so slowly as to be imperceptible. Unnoticed, until you realised you were surrounded by darkness.

Could he ever tell her this? Of course not. She'd call him pathetic, if not mad... but nevertheless, he *felt* her absence, like some part of him had been taken away. Physical, not emotional... at least, he didn't think so.

Yes, physical, as if when Zenobia was around there was something else there too, something... in the Aether, maybe? What did he even mean by that?

And maybe..., he thought, whispering it even in his head. *Maybe it is a* little *emotional, too.*

It made his head hurt to think about.

Still, if there was anywhere that would take his mind off this, it was here. The all-pervasiveness of technology here was amazing, in many ways more remarkable than what he had heard from Zenobia of the Silicon Isle. They were right now standing outside a cluster of low-rise buildings crammed in amongst the shining skyscrapers - an entertainment plaza, Immanuel explained.

Inside, visible through wide glass window, rows of people sat with heads bowed, eyes locked onto a small table screen in front of each of them. Occasionally one or two of these individuals would look up to share an unheard comment or joke with a nearby person, but for the vast majority of the time their attention was locked onto the game in front of them.

"Playing *Go* against AI programs," Immanuel said, following Xavier's fascinated gaze. "A craze here, practically the national pastime. Pointless, of course..."

He shook his head dismissively, watching the mass of people inside, each locked in their own mental battle.

"... They can't hope to win. It's more a challenge to see how long you can last. There are those who insist it is possible to defeat the machines, though, despite all the evidence."

Immanuel looked up at Xavier.

"There are always those who won't accept reality," he finished, and Xavier got the feeling that the man was speaking about more than this game.

"Come on," Immanuel said. "Enough sightseeing."

The street they were walking down was designed to evoke memories of a much older age, one when this city did not require the appellation *New*. Despite the soaring architecture that reached for the clouds, the lower levels were designed of a kind of coloured glass that somehow shone from within, bright and vivid colours that shifted from blues to pinks to greens depending on your angle of approach. Hints of baroque styles and suggestions of *portales* and colonnades were incorporated into the facades, ultramodern materials shaped to harken back to a very different time and place.

At regular points along the way, discrete signs were built into the buildings' sides. Each one listed the names of the businesses found within, along with a number that almost always ended with a long string of zeros. When Xavier asked Immanuel about it, he just tutted.

"You should research more before travelling," he said, sounding annoyed. "Those are shareholder sums."

Thrown by the irritation in his companion's voice, Xavier hesitated to ask what that meant. Immanuel didn't wait for him to summon up the nerve.

Not slowing, Immanuel led them along the sun-drenched street - false sun, of course, provided by powerful full-spectrum spotlights carefully built and concealed in the surrounding architecture high above, set to move at gentle angles in imitation of a day/night cycle - and towards the tallest building in the area, one Xavier had seen all the way from the Reclamation embassy they were staying in, in the quieter and more secluded diplomatic section of the city.

Even from that distance, nestled in amongst buildings taller and wider than anything in the Reclamation, this building stood out. It pierced the sky like the talon of a god clawing its way from the earth, thrusting upwards towards what seemed an impossibly fine point, though Xavier knew logically that that distant spire must be wider than most buildings. An illusion, a trick the mind played when dealing with such vast structures, made stranger by the paradoxical contrast of thick cloud above false sunlight.

Xavier also knew, now, that this was what the Central Tower was built to imitate back in Albores. A poor imitation, too, he thought.

Which made no sense, initially. Everything he knew, everything he had been taught, stated that the Central Tower was the tallest tower in the world. He had seen it, stood near its base multiple times, and marvelled at its reach. In any images and vids of *New Havana* accessible in the Reclamation, nothing rivalled the Central Tower's stature.

What he was looking at now dwarfed it.

"Truly, it is an impressive sight," Immanuel replied when Xavier said this to him. "The Headquarters, they call it. A marvel of engineering. So it is all the more impressive that our Reclamation engineers produced something even *more* incredible."

"But..." Xavier began as he craned his neck upwards to the cloud-piercing peak. "This is *far* larger. Taller and wider and..."

"Are you suggesting that the Reclamation Authority would spread deliberate falsehoods?" Immanuel cut in, a reptilian expression abruptly appearing on his face, studying Xavier like he were an insect.

Xavier froze, unsure how to respond.

"Are you suggesting..." Immanuel continued, each word slow and deliberate. "That the RA would use its absolute control of information and media to limit, alter, or otherwise manipulate what its citizens know of the outside world?"

The reptilian expression was still there, Xavier saw, only now it was a crocodile's grin. Immanuel was *playing* with him.

Once again, Xavier wondered if he should *read* the man. It would be so easy, but there was also no doubt that Immanuel would realise what he'd done, eventually. One random comment, revealing something he shouldn't know. Immanuel knew what Xavier could do, and eventually you *always* slipped up.

He wondered what the man's reaction would be.

"No," said Immanuel when Xavier didn't reply. "No, you aren't suggesting that, are you? Because you know that, when it comes to trusting either what you are told or your own eyes, only *one* choice is correct."

He chuckled, a low, spiteful sound.

"We are all offered choices, every day. The important thing is to make the right ones." He looked meaningfully at Xavier. "The ones that keep you safe."

And his face broke into a wide grin.

"Come on, *science advisor*," Immanuel said, and Xavier was amazed at the sudden change in the man. The predator was gone, replaced by a warm, businesslike professional. "We have a tour to get to."

They stepped through the entrance, and Xavier noted that to its side was a discrete display reading CRASTINA CORP. and a number with the longest string of zeros he had seen so far.

"…And as you can see, simulating and predicting the almost limitless ways even a small protein can fold requires machines capable of trillions of calculations a second. More, in fact, so it's a lucky thing we have so many!"

The chuckle that came from Immanuel carried nothing but polite amusement at the interpreter's[19] joke. Xavier struggled to play along. It really wasn't that funny.

They were being led around by a bespectacled[20] man in a white lab

---

[19] An "interpreter" was a more or less common role in most large technology-focused companies and institutions. The actual engineers of most modern systems were so deeply submerged in code and data and science that they were rarely able to surface to explain what they knew in terms a layman could understand. An interpreter was employed as a go-between, one with one foot in the technical and one in the plain, able to explain and define the worlds of both.

[20] Almost certainly an affectation. Corrective eye-wear was as much a thing

coat.[21] He had met them at the base of the wide, glass elevators that revealed the sprawling cityscape outside as they ascended - impressive even if the view was obviously digitally altered by the glass to replace the ashen skies above with clear blue ones.

There had been no questioning of their identities, no requests for documentation or IDs; clearly, security here was automated, likely completing all checks and scans well before Xavier and Immanuel stepped into the building. All the man had done was introduce himself by a name Xavier didn't recall and asked them to follow.

He would be their guide for the tour of the "research laboratory," the man informed them. When Xavier heard the term, his mind instantly went to images of mysterious chemicals and flasks, unknown smells and volatile liquids. Naive of him, really. Too many *New Patriot* movies depicting spuriously-historical heroes in a race against time to cure one contagion or another, celebrating the fictitious face of *human* ingenuity in the face of impending viral doom.

What the lab really was, was computers.

"Each comp-cluster consists of fifteen thousand tetrabyte-grade GPUs, and we have... well, a lot."

The interpreter winked.

"I'm not allowed to share the exact number," he said with false contrition. "Not even to as illustrious guests as yourselves. You understand, I hope."

"Of course, of course," said Immanuel, returning their guide's apologetic smile with one of his own. "State secrets are state secrets, even amongst allies. There are some things that should be kept only in the minds of the most trusted citizens, where it is safe."

Xavier almost missed the hidden instruction in Immanuel's words. When he did, after a second's delay, he gave an involuntary start. Fortunately their guide, preening at Immanuel's flattery, seemed to miss it.

He's telling me to read him.

Immediately, Xavier reached down and drew the Aether into himself, stretching out with it towards the interpreter. The moment he *touched* the man's mind the number was there, floating close to the top of his thoughts and tinged with pride.

---

of the past as the gasoline engine. Surgery was far faster and more efficient.

[21] *Definitely* an affectation, considering the nature of the work here.

Two hundred twenty six. Xavier filed the number away, but continued his exploration of the man's thought-images.

The first thing to catch his attention was how the man perceived *them*. A bureaucrat and a kid - that was what the man saw, and the image was tinged with condescension.

It was always strange, seeing how others saw you in their head. After all, he knew he wasn't a kid, and he could see the man knew that too, but the thought-image was like a canvas spattered with different paints. The interpreter saw Xavier as both man and ignorant youngster, one who clearly didn't understand half of what he was seeing. A Reclamation rube who deserved to be pitied rather than respected.

This was the best the Reclamation could send? Xavier could practically hear those exact words in the man's mind. *This* was who they chose to send when the Carib-Federation kindly invited their less-fortunate neighbours to see and share in the wonders of the corporations' incredible medical advances?

People rarely actually chuckled in their thoughts, but their guide was close to it. A feeling of superiority suffused everything his mind held, on the surface levels at least.

The second thing to catch Xavier's attention was a thought-image in the deeper layers of the man's mind. More than a thought-image, really; a clump of them, knotted and twisted together in the way only the most constant and relentless of sensations did.

It wasn't *worry*. Not quite, but it certainly tasted of it. It was… stress, concern, impatience and desire, all bundled up. The man was processing what it meant to be assigned this task, guiding foreign dignitaries around the facility rather than working on the myriad other duties to set in motion or follow-up on. Wondering what this meant for his place in this world.

Am I being sidelined? Rewarded? Does this mean the higher-ups think I'm trustworthy, or useless? Promotion. Demotion. Bonus. Punishment. Career. Advancement. Reassignment. Shareholders. Shareholders. Shareholders.

The words and sensations whirled through the man's mind at the boundary of consciousness and unconsciousness, a never-ending whirlpool of harried tension. Images of a family - a partner, children, a residence - merged with images of account balances and credit ratings and debt and earning forecasts and the internal hierarchy of a company designed like a vertical maze.

It felt like standing on the edge of a cliff. One false move, and you would fall.

"And these computation clusters can design *any* medicine you want?" Immanuel asked their guide, bringing Xavier back to reality.

"Exactly right!" their guide answered. "With just a few samples of an individual, our systems can produce a tailor-made drug to cure practically any condition. A drop of blood is all we need!"

Xavier found it hard not to be impressed. Not just because of the man's enthusiasm, but by the absolute conviction in his mind.

"A drop of blood, and the *finances* of course," said Immanuel.

The crocodile's grin was back.

"Ha, well, yes…" the interpreter said, looking briefly taken aback. Then, with an uncomfortable laugh, his smile returned. "Of course, there is a monetary cost, but we offer our products at a *very* affordable rate."

Immanuel gave a small laugh of his own, but his eyes remained cold.

"Yes, of course," he said. "After all, you're not running a *charity* here."

The interpreter laughed again, a strangled sound that made it clear he was unsure if he understood the joke, or even if there was one.

"Ha! Yes… no… Of course not…"

Xavier focused again with the Aether, curious to see what was surfacing in the interpreter's mind at this time.

Resentment. Guilt. Shame and anger. Whatever Immanuel was poking at, it was clear he'd struck a nerve.

"Well, this has been *very* enlightening," Immanuel said, nodding at Xavier. "But we should be going now."

The abruptness of the statement drew Xavier back from the guide's mind before he could delve any further. They were leaving already?

Clearly, this news surprised their guide also.

"You are leaving? But we still have both data processing and climate modelling to…"

"Yes, yes," Immanuel interrupted. "And I am sure they would be very interesting. However, my aide and I have a meeting with the Directorship in a short while, and will need to brief on the upcoming discussion."

Their guide's eyebrows rose so high Xavier thought they might fall off.

"The Directorship? You have a meeting with…"

He trailed off, seemingly unable to finish the sentence.

"Indeed," said Immanuel, and there was the sense of scaly skin and teeth glimpsed below the surface of dark water. "And I will be sure to say how excellent a guide you were."

Fear and relief fought in equal measure on the guide's face.

"You will? To the…? Me…? I, I, I… Yes!"

Something in their guide switched, a sudden resolve to not miss this opportunity forcing the words out.

"Yes, I would be very grateful if you would. And, and, and of course, if there is *anything* I can do for you during the course of your stay…"

Immanuel held up a hand.

"Of course, we will be sure to contact you should we have any questions. I am sure my *science advisor*…" Immanuel didn't even try to hide the knowing grin he flashed Xavier. "… will want to learn a lot more from you."

Confusion, trepidation, hope and anxiety were obvious on the guide's face. Xavier didn't need the Aether to see them.

The way the interpreter escorted them to the elevators and back down to the ground floor was almost pathetic, Xavier thought. All sense of superiority had been banished, replaced instead by a desperate sycophancy that made him feel dirty to see.

Was this the effect name-dropping the Directorship had on everyone? Xavier knew this was what the leadership of the Carib-Federation was called, but little else.

He would have to find out more as soon as possible. Not now, though, because as soon as they stepped back out into the unnaturally gold-lit street, the glass of a hundred impossibly tall structures reflecting the false sunlight all around them, Immanuel flagged down a passing auto cab.

"We have time," he said, and to Xavier it sounded like he was answering a question he'd asked himself.

He turned to Xavier.

"You've seen the city," he said. "I think it's time to see the island."

10. XAVIER

People build their identity around statements of faith. A sporting team or religion, a business or a political party; even the things they stand against. Then when you challenge these statements, you challenge their very being.

Laws and Tenets: Tactics of Socio-Economic Integration in the Coming Reclamation,
Document distributed by unknown agents during the Inter-regional Conference on Reclamation of the Mainland (ICRM)

As the cab carried them on its driverless way away from the soaring towers of the central district, the first thing Xavier noticed was the commercials.

The skin, more like. Metres of it, all colours, all genders, smooth and exposed and demanding the eye's attention. Xavier was of course aware of the use of sexuality in advertising, but this was far more overt and explicit than anything in the Reclamation.

Huge vid-boards hung from the sides of buildings or on tall poles fitted wherever there was space, cajoling or demanding of the viewer a desire, a *need*, for whatever perfume or accessory or drink or product the commercial offered. And always, always with flesh as the draw.

He struggled to keep from blushing in front of Immanuel. Futilely, it seemed.

"Public decency laws are far less strict here than back home," the other man said, following Xavier's gaze out the window. "As are the services offered."

Xavier stared outside as the hoardings flashed past. He didn't ask what Immanuel meant by that.

The area they were driving through began to contrast more and more with the glittering towers they had just left. The buildings were squatter, more drab, and the full-spectrum spotlights that created the false summer elsewhere dropped away to leave grey, pockmarked concrete.

It reminded him of the Reclamation. Indeed, most of the structures here were built of the same self-repair concrete and breathe-brick that Albores was; none would have looked out of place there.

The Sea Walls were growing closer too, and the sheer colossal nature of them became more apparent. Ahead of them, but drawing ever nearer, the petal-like shapes that curved upwards turned into impossible mountains, blocking out the sky. The eye rebelled against it, unable to process the depth and size of such an unnatural form.

"We go through there," said Immanuel, pointing down the road ahead to where Xavier now noticed a cluster of blinking blue and red lights.

The Sea Walls rising behind had dwarfed it, drowning out the detail, but now he could see that the road ended in some sort of blockade. It looked like one of the security checkpoints that were popping up more and more frequently back in the Reclamation, only more permanent. The small, compact buildings either side of it were fixed, not temporary, while a queue of vehicles formed lines before a solid-looking gate. The gate rose and fell in accordance with some unseen hand.

"Border check," Immanuel said.

Border check? thought Xavier. But the borders of the Carib-Fed ran far beyond here, encompassing ocean and swathes of land both natural and artificial for thousands of square kilometres around. How could there be a border check here?

Before he had a chance to ask, their vehicle pulled sideways into a lane and drew to a stop. Immediately, a face appeared on the dash-screen, uniformed and serious.

"Registration check," said the androgynous-looking face in curt tones. Xavier couldn't tell if it was real or an avatar. "Wait, please."

The face disappeared, and a low electronic hum filled the car as they were scanned - the sound unnecessary, of course, but emitted for the benefit of the vehicle's occupants. Otherwise, it would seem as if nothing was happening.

A moment later the sound clicked off, and the face reappeared.

"Security check complete. You may proceed. Please note: you are now entering an unenforced area. Be advised that laws and regulations of the Caribbean Federation remain in effect, but access to and response parameters for enforcement agencies are severely limited."

If the face wasn't an avatar, they sure did a good job of acting like one. The likelihood that they *were* artificially generated jumped significantly in Xavier's estimation a second later, when the screen abruptly flicked over to a less-filtered, more obviously preoccupied-looking figure. A man, with bags under the eyes and stubble suggesting several days without time to shave.

"Uh... yes, hello? This is border control, just doing a secondary check on your destination."

The man's eyes flickered around as he spoke, sometimes looking directly out of the image on the dash screen, sometimes to the side. Watching multiple screens at the same time, Xavier thought.

"Ah, good day, officer de Céspedes," Immanuel replied, reading the name off the info-box that had appeared at the corner of the video feed. "How can I help you?"

"Uh, yes, *hola*. Just a quick confirmation that you know where you're going. I see that you are visiting from... ah, the *Reclamation?*"

The officer paused, failing to hide his surprise for a brief moment.

"Ahem, *lo siento*," he continued, expression once more falling serious. "I see that you are visiting from the Reclamation, and felt it important to confirm you understand that you are now leaving Carib-Fed jurisdiction."

Immanuel gave a quizzical look.

"We are?" he said, feigning surprise. "But it was my understanding that this was *all* Carib-Federation territory."

The officer on the screen paused for a moment, looking exposed and caught off guard.

"Ah, well, yes, of course you will still be in Carib-Fed territory, but you are going out beyond the Sea Walls."

He began to speak more slowly, seemingly choosing his words carefully.

"There is much less of a, a... an *administrative* presence beyond the Walls. The Island, we call it. I would strongly advise you to tour elsewhere; we have many beautiful districts."

Immanuel smiled at the officer on the screen.

"Thank you for the advice, officer," he said cheerfully. "Nevertheless, we will proceed through. All responsibility for the trip will be mine, and as I am sure this conversation is being recorded you now need not worry about any blame being attributed to you should something befall us in the camps."

A look of relief from the screen.

"I see. Then, you have permission to pass. I have already set a note on the system granting you express re-entry through any of the gates. Stay safe out there."

The screen flicked off almost before the final syllable came through, and their cab began moving.

The tunnel through the base of the Sea Wall went on for kilometres, the distance easy to mark because at every kilometre the smooth concrete surrounding them was broken up by a ring of solid steel. Flood gates, Immanuel explained, designed to seal shut should the storm surge of a category 6 hurricane or other climatic aberration[22] threaten to pour through.

When they emerged, the transition was abrupt. The tunnel simply ended, and looking back to where they exited Xavier saw sheer grey-white concrete rising vertically higher than he could see from so close. It stretched both to the east and west, like the wall of some fantasy epic designed to keep out hungry giants.

The land around them now was sparse. No more well-tended patches of flowers or clean, shining glass. No, the land here was dusty concrete, cracked and flaking. Particles of oddly black-tinged sand rolled across the ground or were carried by the wind, swirling and spinning through the air.

Rolls of barbed wire ran along both sides of the road as they drove until they reached what appeared to be a mirror image of the security checkpoint they had passed though before. This time, however, there were multiple guards posted besides each gate, rifles slung clearly visible at their sides.

The gate rose automatically as they passed through, and suddenly there were children all around. They clustered around the cab, forcing it to slow down and causing collision-alert warnings to sound from the dash. Each one looked thin and gaunt, and several of them were barefoot.

Each of the children also held something in their hands, Xavier saw, holding it out towards the car as if in supplication or offering. Flat, thin, and plasglass. Thin-screens.

"They want a transfer," Immanuel said. "Cash. Hoping you'll ping them some dollars."

Xavier reached reflexively for his own thin-screen, fingers

---

[22] Not that category sixes were so uncommon, but they'd been more common once, in an era long before the Sudden War. Much of the Sea Walls were pre-Fall, though with alterations and extensions to take into account the fact that the *new* capital of the Carib-Fed could not be built upon the remains of its glassed namesake.

stopping only when Immanuel shook his head.

"Uh-uh," the older man said. "You send something to one, you'll bring half the camp down on us. You think you've got the credit-line to pay them all off?"

Xavier reluctantly released his grip on the thin-screen.

"I don't understand," he said. "I thought the camps were supported by the Federation?"

Immanuel laughed, a sharp bitter snort, watching as their cab forced its way slowly away from the gates where the children seemed to cluster most densely.

"Oh, they *are*," he said. "If you're registered. A registered refugee gets, what, almost a full Carib-dollar a week? Enough to survive on the breadline."

Immanuel paused, eyes following the children as they fell behind into the distance, the car finally having made enough space and distance to accelerate.

"Most of the time, at least," he finished.

"So those kid aren't registered?" Xavier asked. "Why not?"

Immanuel turned and locked eyes with him.

"Are you a citizen of the Reclamation?" he asked suddenly.

Xavier blinked, unable to understand this change of topic.

"Am I...? No, no I'm not," he answered.

"And why not?" Immanuel demanded before he could say anything else. "I'm sure Feye would allow it. Fast track it, even. All you have to do is ask."

"But I..." Xavier began, then stopped.

What was he supposed to say? That he didn't trust the RA? That he would never want to be a citizen of a nation that monitored and oppressed and *murdered* its own people? That, even now, he believed deep down that he would find a way to be free of it?

Immanuel nodded; at what, Xavier couldn't say.

"Registration is no easy process," Immanuel said. "And the benefits are far less tangible than Reclamation citizenship."

He brought up his own thin-screen, tapping it, and their cab rolled to a halt.

"Come on, we can't stay here long and we have things to do," he said, opening the door and stepping out.

The moment the door of the auto cab opened and the air-pressure seal broke, a potent smell assailed Xavier's nostrils. It was unlike anything he had encountered before, a mix of salt and rotting fish and industrial chemicals that overrode any less pungent aromas. An acrid scent underlay it all, a smell reminiscent of the times the wind blew in from the waste-processing sections of Albores.

Sand immediately flew into his mouth, dry and gritty and with an oily taste. Oily, he saw now, because it blew in from an ocean coated in the whorling, shining purples and blacks of polluted water.

The ocean was still a few hundred metres away, but visible at the bottom of the gently descending slope on which they stood. The road they had come in on turned abruptly in a T-junction and stretched along the crest of this slope, following the coastline until it curved and disappeared into the distance in either direction.

And all along this road, running from it into the rolling hills to one side and wedged between it and the soiled sea on the other, a mass of buildings. They stretched towards the horizon, few if any of them identical in size or shape. Instead, they formed a patchwork of prefab and makeshift structures, some simple single-storey things while some stood four floors or more high. Some looked more permanent than others, but none looked like they would survive even a lower-grade tropical storm.

Xavier had never seen one, not in real life, but he knew them anyway.

The camps.

This was where the masses of humanity had come after the Fall; where those who survived the flames and fallout of *el hundimiento* fled. Fleeing to one of the few places in the world that maintained a semblance of functioning society, and one of the fastest to rebuild. Only the Eastern Empire and the Crystal Caliphate recovered faster, and that only by sacrificing the most basic individual freedoms. The Caribbean-Federation, and the Reclamation after it, welcomed all who came regardless of caste or creed, asking only that you be willing to strive for your place in this world.

At least, that was how the Reclamation told it.

This is where Grey was born.

The thought took him by surprise. Even after all this time, the memory of Nestor Grey still swam somewhere in his consciousness. He supposed it would forever; the year they spent in the Reclamation prison camp was ingrained in the core of who he was.

He saw the walls now, though they didn't match up with what he expected. In the vids and clips he had seen online the camps were always surrounded by high, solid fences, clean and strong and broken up only by tall gates marked with a large, dark number proclaiming its identity.

The fence in front of him was a corroded thing, tilting forward or backwards on foundations that had become weak in the loose dirt.[23] Ragged gaps and torn holes spoke of generations of storms and neglect, and whole sections were missing. A small but constant stream of people passed through these sections, crossing the road on their way to other areas of the camp. There was little traffic to be wary of, and the only gate he could see stood open, unattended and unguarded.

Immanuel was already moving, striding down through the gate and along the narrow street beyond with the confident air of familiarity. Xavier had to jog after him to catch up, throwing a look back to where the auto cab sat waiting, pulled up onto the scrub besides the main road. No one looked to be paying it any attention.[24]

The buildings flanking this street stood no more than two or three stories high for the most part, and every available wall space was crammed with signs and advertisements. Xavier wondered at the sheer variety of them; everything from sheer-plas film screens to what appeared to be genuine paper posters. All were tattered and scuffed, and were layered over each other in a way that said even more were hidden below.

Here, too, were the same sexualised images and commercialised promises he had seen on the way here, looping animated vids selling the latest tech vying for space with flashing neon text offering 'health services,' whatever that meant. Only now, these products were joined by large-font signs loudly declaring the availability of 'travel passes'.

---

[23] It seemed as if the concrete bedrock of the interior was not a feature beyond the Sea Walls. Instead, the soil here was the compacted remains of everything cleared away to place that bedrock.

[24] And why would they? Just as in the Reclamation, automated transport was operated by the government, or contractors to them. A constant broad-spectrum video feed from the vehicle broadcast the features and bio data of any nearby person back to a supervising department with immediate access to government records and population data. Only a fool tried to break into an auto cab, where they would find little of value anyway, and stealing one was impossible due to automatic immobilisation routines.

The two words were everywhere, pasted on walls and above small, cramped offices open to the street inside which men in ragged suits sat eagerly awaiting enquiring customers. Xavier knew what this term meant, at least. Travel passes were a way out of the camps, permits to travel onwards to the Reclamation. From the looks of things, they were a valuable as hard currency. More so, perhaps.

As he rushed down the sand-strewn street he felt eyes following him, saw sallow faces watch him pass. Their expressions ranged from dull curiosity to lethargic; none seemed to have more than a passing interest in the newcomers.

He opened himself up to the Aether to be sure. Nothing. The people he passed had minds with little room for concern about two strangers passing through. Credits, medicine, food, fears about the coming storm season. These were what took up most of the thoughts of the people living here, thoughts at both the surface level and far deeper.

And then... a different sensation. The feeling of a thought-image sharper and full of intent. He *reached* out towards it, finding its source in a middle-aged woman sat idly watching what appeared to be a class of some kind. To all outward appearances, she was staring at a ring of young people clustered in a wide gap between buildings, at the centre of which a teacher was gesturing to a cracked but functional wallscreen stood propped upon makeshift legs of broken plastic.

To Xavier, though, the woman wasn't watching the lesson at all. No; at the top of her mind was a thought-image of Immanuel, though a much younger Immanuel than the one Xavier knew. It was a ball of sensations and impressions conjuring up meetings and communications and *orders* that stretched from the past to the expected future, a tangle of loyalties and fears and hopes.

Xavier could *see* what the woman was doing. She was... waiting, her attention on both Immanuel and whatever it was she held clasped tightly in one hand.

Xavier drew up next to Immanuel, who showed no sign of slowing or registering the woman as they passed.

"Say nothing," Immanuel said out the side of his mouth. "Ears are everywhere, even here. We continue on."

Xavier managed to suppress his surprise this time. He had come to realise that Immanuel was almost as good at reading people as Ritra Feye was. Something in Xavier's body language had told him everything he needed to know.

"I haven't been this way in many years," Immanuel said, loudly now. "I used to do much... work... for the Reclamation here."

There were depths to the word that made Xavier once again consider *reading* the man.

"The Carib-Fed knew, of course," he continued. "It is... *difficult* to keep anything from them on their own territory, but the RA and Directorship share many interests. My presence was tolerated."

Xavier didn't need to *read* Immanuel to hear the unspoken words. *Difficult, but not impossible.*

Xavier felt a flush of pride; he was getting good at this. This was *spy* stuff - maybe one day he'd make it look as easy as Immanuel or Feye.

Pride was instantly replaced by disgust. Disgust, and shame. Was he really that stupid? He wasn't part of the RA; he never would be. He didn't *want* to be. All he was was a prisoner, however wide the bars of his cell became. He should have no daydreams of being a part of their schemes. And yet...

Something caught his eye, pulling his thoughts from whatever path they had been following.

The buildings to the right grew suddenly less dense where the ground became uneven and loose, and in an open patch of scrub earth backed by a low hill sat a girl. Barely a child, she sat cross-legged on the ground with a thin, ragged cloth blanket wrapped around her.

Only the girl's face and neck were visible, but across every patch of exposed skin Xavier saw a profusion of large raised spots. They formed an expanse of cloudy, painful-looking blisters so numerous that they left little room for untouched skin. From beneath this mess, the girl's eyes stared out, alive and alert and watching with childlike curiosity.

Behind her stood a series of makeshift shelters, most little more than sheets of canvas held up by corroded metal poles clearly scavenged from other derelict buildings. Within their shadows Xavier made out more eyes watching, more skin that despite the gloom he was sure was equally afflicted.

"What... what happened to them?" Xavier asked, coming to a halt in shock.

"Isolating," Immanuel said as if this explained anything. "Keeping them apart from the community until the symptoms pass."

Isolating?

Xavier noticed now the carefully piled supplies stacked near where the girl sat. Plastic bottles of water, cartons of vit-vat, and myriad other forms of food and drink. Crates of generic medicines. All of it cheap and basic, but enough for a few day's sustenance for those within.

"She's sick?" he asked.

Immanuel nodded.

"Looks like a smallpox variant," he answered, now also stood watching the girl. "Someone with a viral editor probably released it."

Xavier looked askance at his companion.

"This was *deliberate*?"

Immanuel nodded again, slowly, not taking his eyes off the girl.

"Maybe," he answered. "Probably. There's plenty in the city who *hate* the camps. It's not unheard of."

"And the Carib-Fed just lets it happen?"

This time Immanuel shook his head, but without much conviction.

"It's not *allowed,* but if the lethality is low enough, if it's primarily the unregistered who are affected…" He turned to look at Xavier. "The Federation has other priorities."

Without taking another look at the girl, Immanuel began to walk again. This time, however, he was heading back the way they had come.

"Come on," Immanuel said, "We're done here."

Xavier was almost too distracted to notice that the woman who had been following them was now disappearing down a side-alley nearby. At some point, he realised, she must have crossed paths with Immanuel, and whatever she had been carrying was now gripped in the man's closed fist.

A thin, solid device; a sec-drive. Xavier briefly wondered what was on it, but right now it didn't seem to matter.

"The girl," he said, jogging up next to Immanuel. "Can't they cure her?"

Immanuel gave a derisive snort.

"They can't afford it."

Xavier stopped again, not caring that Immanuel continued to stride on back towards the cab.

Can't afford it?

He reached down, drawing out his thin-screen and looking at the screen. Pupil trackers responded to his carefully-placed gaze and a number flashed up on the plasglass; the line of Carib-dollars he had been given as an "allowance."

Turning back, not waiting for Immanuel nor offering an explanation, he rushed back the way he had come.

It took him a while to find the parents; not because they were difficult to find, but because at the sight of a dollar-loaded thin-screen there were suddenly a *lot* of people claiming to be somehow related to the girl or in desperate need themselves. He had to resort to *reading* people to find who he was looking for.

Still, after he *had* found them, transferred the entirety of his weekly allowance, and rushed back to catch up with Immanuel, he felt good. Even Immanuel's bitter comment that what he had done was simply spitting in the wind hardly dampened his spirits.

It wasn't until they were almost at the cab that his mood shifted abruptly.

Shock. Surprise. Confusion. *His* emotions, this time.

A presence, *sensed* rather than seen. A mind like nothing he had encountered before, and a mind he knew well, though from long ago.

The first scared him. It was there for only a moment before somehow fading, but in that moment it was *alien.*

The second was as strong as he remembered, as focused and determined as when he watched her destroy an RA hunter-killer drone with nothing but the Aether. As fierce and resolute as when he had last seen her, disappearing into the Far Station in Albores.

But what the hell was *Blane* doing here?

"Come on," said Immanuel, holding open the auto cab door and gesturing. "We've got a meeting to get to."

Thoughts racing and trying desperately not to show it, Xavier could do little but follow the instructions.

11. BLANE

We don't see reality, we see an inference; our organic brain trying to make sense of a too-complex world through an internally generated model, calibrated by sensory data. A simulation, limited by the senses.

But the Aether is extra-sensory.

Personal Notes, Senior Researcher N. Caldwell

Was that *Xavier*? What the hell was he doing here?

Reflexively she ducked back into the alleyway the moment she noticed him, shocked at the sudden sight and *feel* of someone she knew all the way out here. Then, as the realisation of who it was filled her, she immediately went to call out to him; to run towards him.

He was alive! Relief flooded through her, a healing balm over a livid wound she had forgotten was there. The guilt of her inability to save him, to even *find* him and Salim, had been a churning well of acid in her stomach for so long she no longer remembered what it was like without it. They had been captured because of her, after all.

A hand, pushing her back, inhumanly strong. It felt like an iron bar pushing into her shoulder.

"Don't," Francisco hissed. "*No lo hagas.* And release the Aether - he'll sense you."

His expression was hard, with none of the softness or charm that he liked to put on as part of his act. This was the closest she had been to him since their reunion, and the myriad lines of age on his face were deeper and more pronounced than she remembered.

"Get off me," she growled.

Still, she did as he said, releasing the Aether and making no move to pursue Xavier. Instead, she angrily reached up and pushed his hand away. It gave way, though she knew that was not due in any way to her own strength.

"The man he was with..." Francisco said in explanation. "*Ese olor -* RA. I could smell him a mile off."

Other man? Blane hadn't noticed another man. She'd barely seen Xavier, sensing his familiar presence in the Aether before catching a brief glimpse of his retreating back.

Had he noticed her? He'd been holding the Aether when she sensed him, she knew that much. Maybe there was a moment of hesitation in his stride? It all happened too fast to be sure.

"Someone you know?" Francisco asked, stepping back and looking questioningly at her. "I am sorry, *niña*, but this is no time for old acquaintances."

"That was *Xavier*," she snapped back. She had already told him several times not to call her *niña*. "Grey's student, the one who stayed with us in the Safe House before everything fell apart."

A look of surprise and calculation crossed Francisco's face.

"The Reader?" he said. "That is... interesting. *Que yo sepa*, he is very powerful."

"At Reading, yes," Blane replied, not trying to hide her impatience. "And he's a prisoner of the RA because of me. So…"

The iron bar returned, this time held out in front of her, blocking her as she once more made to follow Xavier.

"You should not go after him."

This voice, though it came from Francisco's mouth, was not his. It was cold and flat, a tone that ran only lower as it spoke.

Ghost.

He, or it, hadn't made its presence known much in the week since she met Francisco and his drone on the edge of Mayan League territory. She occasionally considered trying to push it into talking with her, but as this meant speaking to Francisco beyond what was required she decided against it.

"You identify him as a prisoner. However, that was not the attitude of a captive," Ghost continued, dead eyes off-puttingly focused on a point somewhere just beyond her temple. "He has been walking freely in this area for some time, only occasionally accompanied by his companion."

"You saw him?" Blane said in disbelief. "You've been watching him, and you said nothing?"

"I have been monitoring the movements of *every* individual in this area from the moment we arrived. I am able to retain and access sensory data at greater clarity for longer periods of time than a *human*."

Was that a hitch in its voice when it said the word "human," Blane wondered? Or was she placing her own fears and preconceptions upon it?

"Did you know it was him?" she asked.

"No. I simply accessed my short-term memories once you pointed him out."

"And you're sure he wasn't being... coerced?"

Ghost shook his head.

What did that mean? How could Xavier be working with the Reclamation Authority? Unless... They had ways of altering the mind, she knew, changing cognition and replacing memories. Could they have done something like that to Xavier?

The guilt returned, the livid scar reopening somewhere inside her.

Another reason to make the RA pay - and once they had what they came here to collect, they would.

"You're sure we'll be able to get through the security checks?" Blane asked, changing the topic back to more urgent things.

"*Si, no te preocupes!*" replied Francisco, expression once more animated. "I told you, *chiquita*, once we pass through the camps the checkpoints will find we possess all the correct permissions and records."

Francisco gave a yelp of surprise as his arm, still held out in front of her, was flung backwards by an unseen force.

"And I told *you*, no nicknames," she snarled, not releasing the Aether. "You are not my... my *uncle*. We are working together, yes, but do not think for a moment that I trust you."

The look of hurt on Francisco's face almost made her stumble over her words, but she pressed on.

"You only ever helped us for your own ends. Yours and that, that *thing* you carry around in your head. That is all you are doing now."

"*Cariño*... I mean, Blane," Francisco said, catching himself. "Know that I would never let anything..."

His words trailed off.

"Never let anything happen to us? To *me?*" she snapped back. "You can't even finish that sentence, can you? Because you know you would. You *did*. So yes, we can work together, but that's all it is. Work."

Not waiting for a response, she marched off. In the opposite direction to where Xavier had been, now, but without waiting for her companion. Or companions, perhaps. It was frustrating, not understanding exactly what was going on inside Francisco's skull even after all this time.

But none of that mattered at the moment. What mattered now, she told herself, was getting into the Carib-Federation proper and collecting what they had come for. A thing that, yes, Francisco - or Ghost - insisted they needed if they had any hope of stopping what was happening to the Aether.

A part of her knew she was being manipulated. After years of avoiding all but the most necessary of exchanges with Francisco, and years of ignoring any message he sent that wasn't strictly business, she could practically taste his excitement at her request for help. This excitement only became more obvious as he outlined a scarcely credible plan referencing ancient keys and near-mythical ruins. She almost thought it was a joke, and was ready to refuse until it became apparent that this plan also offered a way to harm the RA.

A way to harm it as it had never been harmed before. A way to crack it, to weaken the foundations that held its monolithic being together. A way to hurt the Reclamation Authority and yet, if they played it right, hurt nobody at all.

They said you had to cut the head off the snake. That to kill the monster, you should go for the heart. Well, she wasn't going to do that. The head of the Reclamation Authority was the Committee, fortified in walls of shadow and veils of secrecy. Its heart was the sullen, dejected host that walked its grey streets, vitality sapped and crushed by the constant need to avoid the talons that clawed and tore at them.

Fortunately, the Aether taught you to think in different terms. It wasn't the brain that was the organism, nor the heart. No single organ was ever the creature itself. No, a being was more than the sum of its parts; it was the connections that brought it into existence. It was the interconnected systems and networked processes that turned a body from mere meat into something *alive*.

So she wasn't going for the head, nor the heart. No; she was going to fry its *nervous system*.

12. ZENOBIA

Historical records long since ceased having any semblance of objective truth. Even the generations before the Sudden War knew this. Nations and peoples operate under wildly differing histories, with flawless textual and visual documentation proving the truth of each version. All false, of course, the impeccable creation of machine at the behest of man. All false, that is, except the histories of your people; because if you cannot believe the truth you are taught, what is there to believe?

Modern Tribalism, Artem Johanés

They were getting closer. She knew it.

Just last week they found an abandoned nickel mine, one which showed all the signs of having recently been occupied by a large group and abandoned in a panic. A slip up with a drone, perhaps, giving their prey warning of the approaching danger, but Zenobia thought differently.

Fen had sensed them coming.

Still, they were getting closer.

Every time the League was forced to split and run was another step in weakening it. Every time they were forced to scatter served to thin their numbers. Every time they ran, Fen had fewer and fewer people to protect him.

They were getting closer, she knew it.

She just had no idea what they were going to do when they caught up to him.

She wasn't going to go up against him, she knew that much. To do so would be suicide. But she had no one she could trust, no one she thought had even the slightest chance against Fen.

But Feye had ordered her to bring him in. Feye had gone as far as to give her an army to do so; an army primarily composed of conscripts and the gullible, but an army nevertheless. And the machines, at least, were *good*.

The generals, though, gave her a headache. She'd always had issues when meeting with the kind of person that chose to devote their life to the military. Mostly, though, these meetings were thankfully brief interactions with military figures from other nations. Now, she was having to deal with *Reclamation* military.

They didn't like her, or rather, they didn't like what she represented. *Comisario Estrategico* was the position she'd been given.

No, she didn't know what it meant, and neither did the generals. All they knew was that she represented people *very* high up in the Committee, and had the full backing of the Reclamation Authority.

Which meant that while they were running the show, she wrote the script. She even had a few squads of Quick-Fix, pretty much the only genuinely battle-hardened troops among the lot of them due to their "sanitizations" abroad under the guise of the International Health Organisation[25].

Not that this experience meant much if they couldn't find Fen; and it meant *nothing* if instead they brought her a poor imitation of her prey.

They'd got the age right, at least. A young man, dark haired; but his facial features were round where Fen's were sharp, broad where Fen's were narrow. Under bloody and bruised lids, his eyes were full of anger where Fen's would be full of challenge.

He looked *nothing* like the images she had provided.

"But he is one of the *bruja*," said the lead soldier when she pointed out as much. Clearly not only was this trooper unobservant, but he lacked an instinct for self-preservation too.

That instinct, and fear, finally kicked in at Zenobia's stare. A stare that could freeze a sun or split a mountain.

"I don't know if he is a *witch*..." she said, allowing the word to roll slowly from her tongue so that the soldier understood *exactly* who he was talking to. "... but he is certainly not the one you were meant to find."

She'd known as much, of course, as soon as the message had come that they had captured him without a fight; a small group of conscripts, led by a commissioned officer. Still, she'd come down to confirm what she already knew. Now, though, annoyance with both the soldiers and herself for the wasted trip burned inside her.

Delicately, she reached out with the Aether to touch the lead officer's mind. A large, grizzled man, he was obviously used to keeping whatever fear he felt buried deep beneath bluster and

---

[25] Up-and-coming authoritarian regimes the globe over had been quick to take advantage of the fact that an IHO intervention could quickly cauterise a wound bleeding out dissidents and discontent. All they had to do was declare a "public health emergency," and a ready-made militia would arrive on their doorstep. Well, that and sign a few contracts with the RA on terms that would never be made public.

bravado. With a slight *twist*, though, she felt that fear go from a small, squirming thing to a creature of claws and fangs, tearing at the walls built around it as if they were paper.

The officer's eyes widened, features turning pale and sweat breaking out on his brow despite the climate-controlled air of the room around them. To his credit, though, he didn't go for his rifle. Not even when she suddenly lurched forward to thrust her face inches from his own.

"*Boo*," she whispered, locking his eyes with hers.

Fight-or-flight, though, was an instinct that could only be resisted for so long. Wisely, he chose flight.

"It looks like your commander has abandoned his post," Zenobia said, filling her voice with feigned perplexity as she straightened up. "I might need to report him for desertion."

The rest of the group had turned almost as pale as their superior, the four remaining soldiers torn between keeping their eyes on Zenobia and looking towards the door their leader had just sprinted out of. Presumably not going too far; there was little outside their makeshift base beyond knotted foliage and unmapped wilderness.

"So..." she said, making it clear that whatever had just happened no longer mattered. "This one, where did you find him? Report."

Actually, the military could be *fun*...

Not Fen. Not even close to Fen, but an Aether user nevertheless. And, if she was right, a member of the Mayan League.

Technically, of course, *every* inhabitant of this region was a member of the Mayan League. This was how the RA categorised the people here, how the news threads and administrative statements described them. Being out here, though, you learned the difference.

For the most part, those who lived here were just trying to survive. Even before the Reclamation incursion, life out here was one of unpredictable risk and unknown dangers. There were *warlords* out here; petty thugs who controlled smatterings of settlements and fought with each other over the pitiful scraps those they ruled could spare. Most of the people of the towns and villages here simply spent their time trying to eke something out of the poisoned earth while praying not to attract the attention of these gangsters.

The real Mayan League ran through it all, a web of guerrilla groups who had found a way to work together despite the ever-shifting powers of this anarchic place. Half-political organisation, half-resistance militia, Zenobia found them a poor imitation of a functioning society.

She could see it at the top of the captured man's mind, though. *Reading* was never one of her strongest skills, but the thought-images she saw were enough to make her confident this was a genuine, dyed-in-the-wool *Guevarista*.[26] One who not only believed they could build a nation in this rot-infested corpse of a jungle, but that they could resist the might of the Reclamation Authority while doing so.

He was also completely unable to control his connection to the Aether.

Zenobia stared dispassionately as the man struggled with his bonds; the ones around his wrists, and the ones around his mind.

She'd had him put into a detainment cell, little more than a temporary box barely tall enough for a person to stand, sides formed of ultra-thin yet nevertheless near-unbreakable bars that would only collapse in on themselves upon the application of a specific electrical charge. Ultra-portable, as was everything they brought into this threadbare jungle. The only truly solid-looking things in the clearing were the three carrier-drones that ferried them around, parked at one side of the clearing atop the masses of vegetation they had crushed without care on landing.

The man was squatting in the centre of the small cell, watching her through narrowed eyes. She imagined he ordinarily had kind features; something about the folds around his cheeks and lines on his brow made him seem like someone for whom a smile was never distant.

Now, though, his stare was filled with venom.

He'd said little since being brought in, spitting only single words when forced to by the admittedly rough treatment he received from the soldiers. Most of these words were in a language she didn't care to know.

"*Me estás entendiendo?*" she demanded. "*Comprende?*"

"*In na'atik, invasora.*"

---

[26] The origins of this term were lost in historical records long rendered too full of falsehoods, frauds and fabrications to ever know the truth. Now it was just a moniker from movies and games, conjuring a specific personality and backstory for a protagonist or villain without needing to put in the work, like *tech-boi* or *Muskavite*.

She laughed; she only half understand the reply, but she understood the tone. Invaders, was it? Well, he wasn't wrong.

"Excellent!" she said. "Then you can tell me where my friends are."

"*Etail?*" the man replied, feigning confusion. "No, I know no friends of yours."

Zenobia smiled. If she hadn't been able to literally see his mind, she might even have believed him.

"Oh, but I think you do. I think you know the group at the nickel mine, and I think you know where they've gone."

If she saw it in the Aether before, she saw it in his expression now. A brief loss of control, regained moments later, but enough for her to see the flash of recognition when she mentioned the mine.

"I don't know what you're talking about, *bruja*," he spat back.

At this she only broadened her smile, though accompanied by a flare of anger she was certain the man saw.

"*Bruja?*" she said. "Then we are siblings of the dark magics, are we not?"

The man snorted derisively.

"I am no witch. Whatever this is, you caused it," he said voice filled with defiance. "But I will not succumb. *Ma'atech.*"

Again, Zenobia laughed.

"You think it is *us*?" she said. "You think *we* control the Aether?"

Uncertainty showed on the man's face, but again for only a moment before defiance returned.

"It came at the same time as you, encroaching on our lands," he said. "I know it is you, with your Far Agent *ba'alche*."

So that at least explained what was going on in the man's head. The thin golden flows of energy that wound so tightly around and through his mind were there to *stop* him touching the Aether.

Somehow, whether consciously or unconsciously, this man had found a way to lock himself off from the Aether. Not in the way that some users could, detaching themselves completely from the energy and disappearing from the senses, but rather by drowning it out with looping, incoherent flows. She could do something similar to prevent mental attacks herself.

Only, it wasn't working.

"That is not us," she said, pointing a finger towards a point directly between the man's eyes. "*That* is Aether, and comes from you."

The man's glare only grew more poisonous.

"*Lelo' tuus*. Lies," he snarled. "It comes with you; all of you. The ones like you with their weapons, and the ones running from you."

Zenobia's eyebrows raised.

"So you *do* know the ones I'm looking for?" she said.

The man gave a bitter laugh.

"Which ones?" he replied tiredly. "There are so many here now, running from your RA or the Carib-Fed camps or the fallen cities down south..."

As he spoke the man's accent took on more familiar tones, becoming something she wouldn't have found out of place back home.

"You aren't from here?" she asked, curiosity overcoming her impatience.

Again, the man laughed.

"Oh, I *am*," he said. "In a way not many others are, anymore. But I spent my youth in the Reclamation. Renunciación, Liberty, Albores..."

He listed off cities of the Reclamation one by one.

"And then I came *home*," he spat, laying the final word down like a heavy slab. "Only to find your countrymen following me, seeking a life free from the RA tyranny. Using their little AIs to learn a bastardised form of my people's language, feeling so proud of themselves when all they really do is build a poor copy of the home they say they renounce."

This was news to Zenobia. She had never heard of migration out of the RA into the League - not that she expected the RA to report such a thing. Still, what could anybody possibly hope to find out here?

Something of what she was thinking must have shown, because the prisoner leaned back against the cell bars and shook his head resignedly. In his head, she saw the golden flows flicker and flare. Disturbed... by her?

"You can't keep repressing it like that, you know," she said. "It *wants* to be used. More and more so, these days."

The man locked eyes with her; now it was his turn to give a thin, spiteful smile. As he did so, the flows through his skull calmed, smoothed out like cables pulled taut.

So, a conscious decision then; but did he understand what he was doing?

"Are you *trying* to make yourself *fisura*?" she asked, not caring that the term would mean nothing to him.

She sighed at his puzzled expression.

"Very well," she said, turning away from the cell and waving over the group of soldiers who had, all this time, been stood waiting at the edge of the clearing for her command. "Find out what he knows. If you can't, then *I'll* have to do so."

She strode away without another word, leaving the inexperienced, conscripted "soldiers" looking worriedly towards each other as if hoping someone else could say exactly what she meant by *find out*.

Eventually one of them must have summoned the courage to do something, because she heard movement and the clatter of steel on alloy bars. She would leave them to it for a few hours, then come back to see what...

A sudden flaring in the Aether, like a great dormant geyser roaring into life. She span, beginning to shout to the men to *get away* but knowing it was already too late.

The blast took her off her feet, slamming her across the clearing to thump hard into the unforgiving trunk of a dry, knotted tree. Pieces of metal and plastic thudded to the ground all around her, all that remained of the cell and the prefab buildings nearest to it.

What the hell was that? she thought, gasping for air through winded lungs.

That wasn't a compression technique, nor any kind of *push* she was familiar with. It was more like a... a *burst*, a dam breaking and smashing away everything beneath it.

Hissing in pain, she pushed herself to her feet. The prisoner was still there, where the cell had been, though the bars had fallen outwards after everything that held them in place was blown apart. He stood there in the middle of a ring of alloy spears, looking as surprised as her.

The whole scene was comical.

"Was that..." he began. "What did you *do* to me?"

He gave a sweeping look around at the devastation he had caused, at the still bodies of his would-be captors lying crumpled and scattered all around. Then, with a cry of frustration, he ran. Zenobia didn't have it in her to stop him, and there was no one else to do so as he disappeared into the undergrowth.

Dios mio, she thought. *That ignorant fool..*

He'd gotten lucky, though. The build-up of pressure inside the man must have been greater than she realised, the Aether forcing its way upwards and he lacking the skill to direct the flow. It had released in one brutal, expanding sphere of force, blasting outwards. It could just as easily have imploded, crushing his internal organs instead.

Or... a chill ran down her spine... it could have erupted as *Mindfire*, and none of them would have survived.

Her comment about *fisura* was more right than she thought. Worrying.

This was the first time she had seen such an extreme eruption up close; there'd been reports of violent Aether incidents, of course, but her direct experience was only of losing trainees who failed to control the increasingly tumultuous Aether or, more generally, succumbed to a kind of post-use malady that prevented sleep and afflicted users with an exhausted depression.

I could see the flows in him were unstable, she thought. *I should have been more careful.*

Still, he wouldn't get far. Now that he'd lost control once, it would happen again. The pressure didn't fade just because the Aether had been used; if anything, it grew more rapidly. It had found a conduit. A *fisura*. He'd be lucky if the search crews she would send after him found him before he tore his own mind apart, or fried himself and everyone around him alive.

With a sigh, she went to find someone to clean up the bodies.

13. SERINDA

Once, people required work to be fulfilled. This was rendered redundant with the creation of mass media, games, and a million more ways to squander time and evade reality. Fulfilment could be achieved without labour, without even leaving the couch, and those who labored and those who strove became a rare commodity.

Processes of Regulation and Order in the Reclamation (Sanctioned Digital Document)

Things were only getting worse. *She'd* made things worse.

Even so, she didn't regret it. Even though their hidden supplier had cut off practically all contact. Even though the RA hounds were circling ever closer, always one sniff away from picking up their scent.

She had diverted the attack, telling no one. Not even Gabriel.

Their "benefactors" had expected the truck to detonate outside some sort of state meeting, taking out not only RA potentates but diplomats and traders from a number of nations. Innocents would have died, all in the name of demonstrating the Committee's inability to secure even the most sacrosanct of spaces.

The implications for trade and diplomacy would have been... significant. Significant enough to cause the RA the kind of problems her shadowy suppliers clearly craved.

Instead, she'd sent it to the Far Station. As equal a demonstration of the RA's weaknesses, she thought, and a blow against the enforcers the Committee relied on to maintain power.

She'd even gone as far as to send an anonymous tip; there had been plenty of time to evacuate the area.

An evacuation that never happened.

Twenty-six casualties, was the official count. Twenty-six people, injured or killed by her actions - she would never know the exact count, because the RA didn't announce fatalities separately.

Maybe there was some delay in communication, some mix-up that meant the warning never got to where it should have - but something inside her knew that wasn't the case.

No; twenty-six casualties because Far decided to play hardball and refused to clear the building. Refused to bend to the whims of some "bio-terrorists," as reports were calling them. The term had long since ceased to carry its original meaning, though was closer to reality than anyone perhaps knew. Bio-weapons had been offered along with the truck, after all, though Serinda refused them immediately.

Still, she didn't regret it. *Couldn't* regret it, because the guilt would swallow her up.

They'd been forced to scatter again, of course, but the *Fallen* were used to that by now. Only a few of them remained here, in a set of squat empty buildings forming an isolated, low-level plaza surrounded by equally empty residential towers. It was as if they had made their home at the bottom of a grey concrete pond, overlooked by rings of colossal concrete trees.

You could climb up any of these surrounding towers and look out over a vista in which nothing moved, a landscape of silent tower blocks and silent roads, everything still and unchanging. Only the wind, its often poisonous breath blowing in from the surrounding Waste, had any sort of life. Everything else appeared to have been deserted in an instant, each inhabitant taking all they could and disappearing, abandoned even by the feral creatures that scratched out an existence wherever humanity was.

Only it wasn't abandoned - no one had ever lived here.

A soulless place, this residential district that was built but never born. Incredible amounts of concrete and steel, vast quantities of sweat and toil, all for a population that never came. Construction for construction's sake, work for the sake of work. Perhaps the RA really *had* planned for people to settle here, or perhaps it was simply make-work for a newly arrived and listless population. The place was built and left to the dust long before she was born.

It served her purposes.

The only hint of civilisation could be seen at night, when the lights of Albores proper shone on the horizon. She saw them now, stood at the very edge of the rooftop of the tallest tower as the wind whipped around her. The air was unusually clear this evening, and the distant city was a soft orange glow between the spires of the surrounding towers and the Waste that stretched out beyond. The glow promised a gentleness she knew no city in the Reclamation possessed.

A sudden gust of wind blew against her, threatening to push her off balance. For a brief moment she wasn't sure if she would stagger backward onto the solid concrete of the rooftop, or topple forward onto nothing but a hundred metres or more of empty air.

She stepped backwards.

"What are you doing?"

She wiped away the wetness from her eyes - caused by the wind, she told herself - before turning to face Gabriel. He was panting, red in the face and bent over with his hands on his knees.

"Hell of... a... way to... exercise," he said.

The elevators didn't work in any of the buildings, of course. They didn't even have cars, for the most part. Just hollow shafts with machinery never installed. Stairs were the only way up.

She said nothing, making her way over while Gabriel got his breath back. Though the air was unusually clear it retained its caustic edge, and the climb up here was *long*.

"They sent a reply," he said eventually, straightening up. "The *Sindicato*, I mean."

She waited for him to continue.

"And..." she said when he didn't. "What did they say?"

"They're willing to trade," he said, each word sounding as if he had to draw it out. "But I still don't think..."

"It doesn't matter," she snapped, cutting him off. This was hard enough without more objections. "We have no choice."

"There's *always* a choice."

The pleading in his voice only made her angrier.

"Giving up is no choice," she snarled.

To her surprise, this didn't make him back down. Instead, he stood straighter, setting his shoulders for all the world as if squaring up for a physical fight.

"I'm not talking about *giving up*," he insisted. "I'm talking about going back to what the *Fallen* are meant to be. To helping people, instead of trying to topple the state."

His tone rather than his words gave her pause. This was very unlike him; usually he treated her with kid's gloves, as if she were a patient. In a way, his resistance was actually refreshing.

Still, he was wrong.

"Sara used to carry around a rocket launcher," she said, and a wry smile rose up at the memory.

"And you are *not* Sara."

The words cut like a knife, but before she could react Gabriel continued.

"Raphael was the head of the *Forever Fallen*," he said. "But you were the heart. People didn't join for the war, they joined for the *peace.*"

Her mouth opened to reply, but something inside Gabriel seemed to have broken, and the words flooded out in a torrent of anger and bitterness.

"Oh, of course we had to fight, but that was futile from the start... *don't pretend you don't agree,*" he snapped as she began to protest. "Far were controlling us from the beginning. Any resistance we offered was a deepfake, any time we won was a mirage. But the clinics were *real.* The shelters were *real.*"

His voice rose with the wind until he was shouting. As his words faded, though, so too did his fervour. Like a switch had been flicked his shoulders slumped, and he reached up with one hand to massage his bloodshot eyes.

Serinda realised she felt equally drained.

"Still having the dreams?" she asked gently.

Gabriel nodded, not looking up.

"I'll be fine," he said. "I'm sorry, I shouldn't have shouted, but..."

"*Está bien,*" she interrupted. "I understand. I don't want to work with the *Sindicato* anymore than you."

"They *killed* some of us," Gabriel replied, pain in his voice. "*We* killed some of them. They can't be trusted."

"And I don't plan on trusting them," she said, forcing strength into her voice. "But we have no other way of getting the supplies we need."

Gabriel nodded again.

"I know."

His voice was filled with resignation.

"Was that it?" she asked, looking back towards the stairwell leading into the building. It seemed strange for Gabriel to come all this way just for that.

"Actually, no," he said. "I, uh... I wanted to see how you were before telling you, but you had a call. *Several* calls, actually."

She blinked. You didn't just *get calls* when hiding out from the RA. Communication devices, even anon-spec ones, were strictly limited and used only sparingly.

"Who...?"

"The Far agent," he replied quickly. "*Former* Far agent. He's been buzzing the emergency line for an hour. Look..."

Gabriel drew a thin-screen out from his pocket. Sure enough, it was vibrating, screen flashing up the incoming call symbol.

She didn't bother asking Gabriel for more info. If it were truly an emergency, he wouldn't have taken all this time to tell her about it. Which meant...

Well, he was going to find out sooner or later.

With a sigh she reached out to take the device, but Gabriel snatched it back.

"Before you speak to him," he said, voice now firm and face grave. "I need to know... what were you doing?"

For a moment, she didn't know what he was talking about.

"Here, on the roof," Gabriel continued. "On the *edge* of the roof."

"Oh, Gabriel," she said with a sad smile. "Don't worry; I'm not taking the easy way out."

His expression didn't change.

"I *won't* fall," she said, almost laughing. "I don't think I could if I wanted to. And trust me, I don't want to."

She stepped once more across the roof, long strides taking her quickly across the weather-worn concrete and towards the barrier-less edge of the roof and long drop beyond. Gabriel didn't even have time to cry out.

With a bound she *stepped* onto empty air, rising once, twice, and a third time upwards and outwards, turning with the last jump to look back at Gabriel and the rooftop, now separated from where she stood by several feet.

Slowly, ever so slowly, she drifted back towards the roof. She kept her eyes focused on Gabriel; she'd never tell him, but looking *down* while doing this was still beyond her.

"Something Blane taught me," she said, stepping onto solid ground. "It's taken me a long time to get the hang of, though."

More than a long time, she thought as she stared at Gabriel's dumbstruck face. *There's no way any of us could have done that, before.*

The Aether was getting stronger every day. Even out here, in a city of ghosts, it rose in a torrent to meet her when she called it.

I don't think I could if I wanted to.

She wondered how true those words were.

"I'm not going anywhere," she said, shaking off that thought. She held out a hand. "I'm not letting the RA off that easily. So come on, give it to me - let's get this over with."

Still speechless, Gabriel held out the thin-screen. His hands, she saw, were trembling.

In spite of everything she felt a slight thrill run through her; the Aether, she had found, could provide a high even at her lowest. The medically-trained part of her found this worrying.

As she looked at the thin-screen, though, that thrill died. The small device vibrated ceaselessly, somehow conveying the impatience and worry at the other end.

"Hello, Nestor," she said, raising it to her ear.

"Did you know?"

So, no preamble then.

"Know what, Nestor?" she asked.

"So you did know. *Damn it*, Serinda. She's just a kid."

She had to smile at that. Even after all this time, Nestor Grey couldn't accept what this world did to people.

"She's *not* a kid anymore, Nestor. Neither of them are. They grew up a long time ago. It's as much their story as ours, now."

"And that story has to be one of revenge?"

Silence.

She could picture him, sitting alone in some dark remote place, hiding from the world yet somehow convinced he could make it better if he could just get people to *understand*.

She'd found that endearing, once.

"Do you know where she is?" he asked eventually.

"No."

"*Maldición!* Serinda, Francisco's putting her in danger again." There was desperation as well as anger in his voice. "I didn't even know they were in touch, but *you* did. Spangle told me everything; he's been sending stuff to you for months. For *her*."

"Things she needed to survive," Serinda said flatly.

"Things she needed to *fight*."

More silence, neither of them willing to be the next to speak. Grey broke first.

"*Please*, do you know where she's going?"

"No."

"Then, can you... can you at least let me know if you hear from her? Let me know she's ok?" he asked, suddenly forlorn.

Serinda nodded despite the fact that this was an audio-only call. Then she turned to Gabriel. Raising a finger towards the horizon, she pointed to a distant speck. Even as she watched it grew larger.

Gabriel nodded, and went to get ready for the new arrivals.

"I'll let you know, Nestor," she said gently.

"*Gra... gracias.*"

She nodded again, and cut the line. Then she followed after Gabriel, watching as the speck in the distance grew rapidly into a sleek black carrier-drone. A drone she knew well.

Blane and Francisco would be here soon.

14. XAVIER

The digital god is anathema. It is mutable and ever changing. It can be known, yet is the constant liar. That is no god; it is the devil.

Inaugural Speech as Administrator to the Althing, Sigurður Gren

"We've got a meeting to get to," Immanuel said.

That was days ago.

It was the first time Xavier had seen the man genuinely frustrated. After the camp they'd gone directly to the *Palacio del Espíritu Inquebrantable*, a low, squat building that was the centre of political power in the Carib-Fed, only to be promptly turned away. They didn't even make it through the security gate, nor speak to a genuine human. Only avatars, artificial faces on their autocab's screen informing them that all appointments had been cancelled. Eventually, the drive function of their cab was overridden and they were carried away from the area despite Immanuel's protestations - and fist slammed into the navscreen.

Something was going on, that much was obvious. The Palace, a thing of round domes and ornate columns[27], had been locked down completely since then. The net, though, had nothing on the topic - at least, when the net was working. If anything, the full disconnects were *more* frequent here than in the Reclamation.

No one would talk to them, either. Immanuel hadn't left the Reclamation embassy in days, spending most of his time shouting at a vidscreen that either rang endlessly or was answered by yet another artificial face repeating the same empty platitudes and requests for patience. Their emotionless calm seemed to frustrate him the most.

Which left Xavier with little to do, so he took the chance to see more of *Nueva Habana*. Without Immanuel he was limited to the diplomatic quarter and its sterile surroundings of luxury brands and restaurants advertising food at wildly inflated prices, but it was still filled with things he didn't understand. For instance, each business's entrance was adorned with one of those discrete, glowing signs

---

[27] The *Palace of the Unbroken Spirit* was established early on in the era of reconstruction, and was named in the spirit of similar buildings past. Its design, too, was evocative of a era long since faded from memory.

displaying a shareholders number they had seen in the central district.

The lack of cash was also a problem. Of course, Xavier told himself, he didn't regret giving away his entire allowance to the sick child, but it *had* severely restricted his options. And there was something about this place that set him on edge.

It took him a while to realise what.

It was on the third day that, tired of doing nothing but walking around the clean, bland streets so artificial-seeming despite the true-organic palm trees that lined the spotless roads and drank the speclight-provided sun, he decided to go into one of the restaurants. Surely there would be no issue with a quick look around?

There was indeed no issue. In fact, the moment he stepped inside through the delicate faux-wood door to the tiny tinkle of a bell piped from speakers hidden somewhere in the softly lit ceiling, he was greeted by a grey, chest-high auto server. It chimed a greeting in an accent out of an old movie, one of the old ones from before Centra-English was properly formed, though the vocabulary was modern.

"Would you like to be seated?" the auto server asked after a moment, when Xavier didn't say anything.

It sounded genuinely questioning, which was the first thing to surprise him. Auto servers were common enough in the Reclamation, but there was something different about this one. Back home, if machines had a voice at all it was electronic, monotone. Here, they'd given it a tone. They'd given it *attitude*.

"Uh, no, thank you," he replied, feeling embarrassed though he saw no one there to see him. "I'm just looking."

The server whirred gently and rocked back and forth on its wheels, for all the world like it was confused.

"Certainly," it said after a moment. Then, as soon as it finished speaking, it tilted forward slightly and the lights on its smooth plasglass front dulled.

O…kaaaaay, Xavier thought.

He stared around the restaurant. There was no one here, and with the server in some sort of idle mode he felt like an intruder. But that was the thing: there were customers here. In all his time wondering this extremely exclusive and upscale area, he didn't think he'd seen a single person actually walk into a shop or store.

He leaned over the machine, craning his neck to look around. The server made no reaction.

The restaurant was small, just a single row of tables running along a long window that looked out onto the street he had just come from. There were only four tables, each with a pair of seats. The tables looked impractically small, and he couldn't imagine two plates of food fitting on them at the same time.

Opposite them was a bar, a long counter behind which a variety of expensive-looking alcohols were stacked on shelves in such a way as to be both discrete yet clearly visible. A small doorway was visible in the middle of these shelves, leading he supposed to the kitchen. It was oddly narrow.

There was something strange about this place, something he at first couldn't put his finger on. Then he realised what the second, far odder thing was.

He couldn't sense *any* people.

Wondering if he was mistaken, he reached deliberately down into the Aether and drew it into himself, stretching out with every sense for the tell-tale ripple of another person.

Nothing.

"Uh, server?" he said, turning back to face the cylindrical machine and feeling even more foolish. "Where are the staff?"

While auto servers were common in the Reclamation, the major work would of course be done by humans. They might be hidden out of sight, in the kitchens or elsewhere, but they would be there.

"This restaurant is fully automated," the auto server chimed.

Xavier could only think of the machine's tone as "proud."

"You have no staff?" he asked, confused.

"*El Futuro Soñado* is run on a fully automated basis," the machine replied in the tones of a well-practised slogan. "We provide shareholders with some of the best cost-to-profit ratios on the market."

Suddenly there was once again the tinkling of a bell, just as when he had entered. Spinning round, he looked to see who was coming in behind him.

There was no one there.

"If you would excuse me, *señor*," the auto server said, giving Xavier a start. "I will be showing our guests to their seat."

Xavier looked from the ceiling to the floor of the doorway, as if he could have somehow missed a group of people entering directly behind him.

There was no one, of course. Nevertheless, the autoserver rolled forward and began talking to empty air.

"Good evening, sir and madam. Allow me to show you to your seats."

Xavier could only watch in confused silence as the server span and rolled over to the nearest table. The moment it reached it, pale and nearly completely transparent letters appeared on the window a few centimetres above.

OCCUPIED, the letters read.

As the words flashed up, pale cords like a million gossamer threads descended from the ceiling above each chair, swaying gently for a moment. A second later they lit up, shining brightly from within. Except...

It took a moment, but within both shining pillars a shadow moved, each recognisably in the form of a sitting human. A man and a woman, they moved as if in conversation, each featureless and dark but somehow rendered in three dimensions nevertheless. There was no sound as they spoke.

He continued watching as the auto server addressed the table, pausing and responding for all the world as if holding a conversation with the silent shadows. Its words were mere mumblings to him, though, due to the directional audio such servers used.

"Uh, who were you talking to just then?" Xavier asked as soon as the auto server rolled back to its original place.

With a whirr it span to face him.

"Why, our guests of course!" the machine replied.

Was the thing malfunctioning?

"But there's nobody there?" was all he could think of to say.

A pause, and more whirring from the machine.

"Oh! Haha," it said, and this was the most artificial Xavier had heard it be since arriving. It literally *said* 'haha'. "They are dining with us remotely."

"Remotely?" he asked, confusion deepening.

"*El Futuro Soñado* welcomes our guests both in-person and remotely," the auto server said, and abruptly its voice was that of a completely different person. A woman's voice, now. "We offer you a premium experience whether you join us directly at our exclusive locations or via Full-Sens Reality. *El Futuro Soñado;* for the best in dining experiences."

"How can anyone dine *remotely*?"

Again it whirred and rocked on its wheels.

"*El Futuro Soñado* welcomes our guests both in-person and remotely," the auto server repeated, with the same woman's voice. "We offer you a premium experience whether you join us directly at our exclusive locations or via Full-Sens Reality. *El Futuro Soñado;* for the best in dining experiences."

A soft *bing* came from somewhere and the auto server span around, retreating behind the bar counter and through the doorway that Xavier now saw was exactly proportioned to allow the machine through. A moment later it returned, rolling to a stop in front of the table labelled "occupied," where its central shell opened to dispense two tiny plates of thinly sliced and garnished fish - uncooked, from the looks of it, yet with the irregular patterns of natural flesh. Which meant it was extremely valuable; fish (or any animal meat for that matter) that could be eaten raw without fear of toxins or pathogens was a rare commodity.

The server retreated once more to stand beside Xavier, rotating this time to face the table itself where the shadows continued their silent play. Xavier couldn't help but feel that they were both watching the strange scene.

"So they are dining in VR?" Xavier asked eventually.

When the server replied, he could have sworn the thing sounded irritated.

"Our guests are dining in *Full-Sens,*" it said, emphasising the name. "We are proud to say that, due to our exclusive peer-to-peer connectivity, even recent government shut-downs of communication services caused only minor schedule alterations in the provision of the long-distance dining experience."

Another soft *bing*, maybe two minutes later, and the server rolled forward and collected the untouched dishes, cleverly designed rollers extending outwards and sliding the plates back inside its shell. Then it turned and disappeared once more into the kitchen.

Xavier couldn't help himself; he followed.

The *kitchen*, it turned out, wasn't a kitchen at all. It was barely a closet. Inside was enough space for the auto server to fit, and then two access ports obviously compatible with it built into the metal walls. The auto server was docked with one of these now, a port Xavier was extremely familiar with as you could find one in every living space in the Reclamation. A garbage disposal port.

There was a sucking sound as the food, plates and all, were sucked into the port. This was followed by an abrupt roaring that Reclamation disposal units certainly did not make, which quickly cut off.

Once the disposal was finished with, the server disconnected from the one port and turned to connect with the other. This was a little less obvious to Xavier, until two dishes emerged and were rolled into the server.

These were *ready-meals*.

High-class ones, yes, of a quality he'd never seen, but behind these metal walls must be what was essentially an industrial freezer stacked with pre-made items. No wonder there were no human staff; there was nothing for them to do.

"Excuse me," the auto server said, moving slightly towards him then braking with the electronic buzz of a collision warning.

"Uh, sorry," he said, moving aside.

As soon as he did so the server rolled past, unloading the dishes onto the same table as before then returning to its post.

"The, uh, the food," Xavier said, wandering up next to it again. "They don't eat it?"

"Remote guests often choose to dine on identi-course meals delivered to their homes or offices, though others elect simply to enjoy the Full-Sens experience with friends or loved ones," came the reply.

So there were people eating this meal in virtual reality? Why?

"Our guests," said the server, preempting the question. "Attend not simply for the food, but for the atmosphere and exclusivity only our service provides. Far more than a meal, *El Futuro Soñado* provides a premium experience that only the most distinguished of citizens can afford."

It took a while to process the meaning of these words, dressed as they were in a corporate speak more slick and styled than anything he was used to.

"It's a status symbol," he said, once he understood.

"Well, *we* certainly wouldn't deem to such pretentions," the machine said, and Xavier was impressed that is vocalisers managed to convey not only modesty but *false* modesty in its words. "But it pleases *El Futuro Soñado* to say that, indeed, many of our customers consider the ability to frequent an establishment such as ours a mark of their standing in society."

Xavier let out a curse of disbelief under his breath. Was the whole district like this?

He turned to leave, aiming to find out, when a thought struck him. He turned back.

"The food," he asked. "What happens to it, if it's not being eaten here?"

"Why, it is disposed of in a fully secure, non-resourceable manner," replied the auto server.

"Non-resourceable?" The word was unfamiliar, though he already thought he had an idea of its meaning.[28] "That means…"

"We guarantee that no consumables purchased here will be reused, recycled, or otherwise recovered for common circulation."

"*What?* Why?"

Such a thing would be unthinkable in the Reclamation. *Everything* was recycled; there were severe penalties for unlicensed disposal of "the Federation's resources."

"Our clientele can be assured that all remote purchases transfer ownership of goods entirely to themselves," the machine intoned. This was clearly a preprogrammed message. "We pride ourselves on ensuring there are no cases of mirror-ownership, and any materials remaining after your meal are thoroughly incinerated."

"You *burn* it?"

The machine was silent for a while in a way that felt somehow condescending, before there was another soft *bing*.

"If you would excuse me," the server said. "I must attend to our guests."

Xavier watched it for a while, repeating its collection-and-disposal process, then turned and stepped out of the restaurant a final time. In the window, another table was now topped with the softly glowing word; OCCUPIED.

"So," Immanuel said upon Xavier's return. He seemed in better spirits. "Now you have had some extra unscheduled time in the

---

[28] Xavier wouldn't realise until much later, but part of the reason he engaged so much with the machine was the refreshing lack of even the *option* of Reading it. Almost all conversations, for him, involved a battle with the temptation to simply take what he needed from another's mind.

Carib-Fed, tell me… What do you think?"

This was unexpected. It was probably the first time Immanuel had actually engaged him in conversation, as opposed to impatiently giving instructions or responding to his questions in a way that said he resented wasting time on something so obvious.

"I, uh, what do I think?" Xavier said, fighting the urge to look around for some unnoticed figure the man could be speaking to.

"Yes, yes. What do you *think*?" Immanuel insisted.

They were in a part of the Residence, the section of the embassy given over to the most senior Reclamation Authority official (or Federation official, Xavier supposed, but every day they seemed to have less and less relevance), which in this case was Immanuel; as a member of the Committee, there *was* no one more official. It was a gorgeous room of natural woods and soft furnishings, more luxurious in fact than the Boardroom back in Albores.

It was also empty of anyone aside from the two of them. Immanuel had instructed the awe-struck embassy staff to refrain from disturbing them unless specifically summoned, and as far as Xavier was aware this was yet to occur. So the vibrodampened, Faraday-caged rooms here were theirs alone.

What was Immanuel hoping to hear?

"It's, um, it's pretty incredible," he said limply.

Immanuel closed his eyes and let out a long breath as if trying to control his frustration. Atop the wide, elegantly curved and polished mahogany table he was sat at his fists opened and closed once, slowly.

"*Incredible*, is it? That's all you have to say about this place, after all you've seen? After everything you've *sensed*?"

"I, uh… well, its very different to the Reclamation," Xavier said, taking an involuntary half-step back at the growl in the other man's voice.

Immanuel's eyes flicked open, locked on him with a reptilian gaze.

"Different? In what way?" he demanded.

Xavier licked his lips. He felt like he was being tested.

"Well, it's…" He paused, starting again. "Look, the Reclamation is *brutal*; you have to admit that. And it's unequal - the Committee decides everything, citizens have access to everything the Committee decides, and non-citizens get only what they need to survive until they work themselves up to citizen…"

"I know what you *believe* about the Reclamation," Immanuel spat. "I want to know what you think of this place."

Xavier paused, watching the man watch him.

La mentira tiene patas cortas, he thought resignedly. Why lie?

"This place..." he said. "It doesn't feel lived in, it feels *owned*."

A raised eyebrow, for all the world as if Immanuel was trying to imitate Ritra Feye.

"The interpreter, back at The Headquarters - the entire time we were with him he was worrying about what it meant for his position in the company."

"Position means a lot, here," Immanuel said.

"It means *everything*."

Immanuel leant back in his chair, a large leather thing that was apparently designed for a person 8 foot tall with shoulders broader than a truck.

"I met a man," Xavier continued. "He explained a few things. A tailor, near here. It took me the better part of an hour to find him, but I did. The *only* person in the entire district."

"Ah."

Immanuel's tone told Xavier he already knew what he was going to say, but wanted to hear it anyway.

"I didn't notice, not at first," Xavier said. "I should have, though. I should have *sensed* it. The entrances, the avatars, the damned robotic servers... This whole city is *automated*."

Immanuel smiled, a thin thing that carried no humour.

"Not just this city," he said. "The vast majority of the Carib-Federation. It runs on Golems[29] and automation; human labour is limited to what is either cheaper that way or considered *decent*."

"Like the tailor," Xavier replied, nodding. "A tailor, because bespoke clothing is more *premium* when a human does the measuring."

"I see. And you understand why this is?"

Xavier nodded again.

"I did some more digging, once I understood what I was looking for."

It was the idea of *shareholders*.

---

[29] GLLMs, or Golems - Generative Large Language Models. Xavier had heard the term before, but never found it so apt. Artificial, unprotesting servants who would serve their masters faithfully until the end of time.

Everyone knew the Carib-Fed was the birthplace of the new world, at least in this hemisphere. It was the sanctuary offered to those who had lost everything in the Collapse, the launching point of the Reclamation and the regional lynchpin that ensured security and stability inside and beyond to borders.

What wasn't widely discussed, in the strictly controlled spheres of both media and internet, were the terms of this agreement.

Because what was possessed by the Caribbean Federation was *only* the Federation's. It was the reason the camps remained full, and the reason the Carib-Fed would never lack for cheap, disposable labour.

"To be a citizen of the Carib-Fed you have to be *born* a citizen," Xavier said. "The only true citizens here are the descendants of those who were here before the Sudden War, before the Collapse. And they own 'shares' in everything."

"And now you understand what those shares mean?"

"They mean *everything*," Xavier answered, failing to keep the anger out of his voice. "They're... they're the companies and the buildings and the land and the air. No property, no tech, no *idea* can be owned by anyone except the shareholders, and can be taken away at any time. Fail to demonstrate value, fail to produce *profit*, and you lose it all."

"The perfect elite," Immanuel said. "A feudal system masquerading as a corpocracy."

There was no satisfaction in his voice.

"Look at me," he said, eyes intense as he stared at Xavier. "*I* am a member of the Committee, at the top of the Reclamation Authority and the structure you are so determined to hate. How do you think *I* compare to these plutocrats?"

This sudden change of tack threw Xavier.

"That's different..." he began.

"Is it?" Immanuel snarled. "Do you know where I came from? Where *you* came from? Do you have any idea what the Reclamation *is* to the people here?"

Xavier eyes went wide at this verbal assault. Then he bristled, tired of being spoken to as if he were a child.

"Well, why don't you tell me then?" he shouted. "Show me what separates shadowed tyrants from the ones in plain sight?"

Immanuel's stare didn't waver.

"I'm not stopping you."

Whatever rage was bubbling up in Xavier was swamped by surprise. Immanuel was letting him *read* him?

Tentatively at first, then with more conviction, he reached out and looked into the other man's thoughts.

There was the Carib-Fed, both idea and sensation in Immanuel's mind. He knew it even more deeply than Xavier had suspected, and it was a thing of paradox. Spotless streets and fetid camps, absolute security and perpetual fear. There were the gleaming towers of the corporations, and the salt-crusted facades of the camps.

There was Immanuel as a child; a child of the camps.

Immanuel was born here... Xavier thought.

But there was more to the thought-image, a whole layer beneath the first that followed the warp and weave of the first without being a part of it.

The Reclamation, where Immanuel had been sent.

Sent?

Xavier explored the sensation. Yes, *sent* was the closest term he could label this feeling. The feeling of exile, of being disposed of, and resentment for it.

More thought-images, all urgent and immediate though Xavier could tell they contained knots of personality formed years and decades ago.

Immanuel's time in the Reclamation, clawing his way up the ladder from nothing to citizen to Representative and beyond. Immanuel's discovery of the true terms of the relationship between Reclamation and Carib-Fed. Immanuel's disgust.

"We're a *release valve*?" Xavier said, shocked, as his conscious awareness translated sensation into words.

Immanuel nodded.

"A pressure release for the excess population of the camps," he said. "The Reclamation from its very inception was designed as a way to counteract the population build up in the camps. A way to maintain access to cheap and desperate labour without ever having the chance it would rebel."

Immanuel raised a hand, thumb and finger pressed together.

"They could empty the camps like *that*..." He snapped his fingers. "...and no one would have to live in that squalor for another minute. But they won't, because it doesn't provide 'shareholder value'. Instead they use travel permits like a valve, providing more when the camps are near boiling, sealing them off when things cool."

Xavier still hadn't released the Aether and could see the righteous indignation in Immanuel's mind. Then, suddenly, it was gone.

Not just the thought-image, though. *Everything* that was Immanuel's mind was gone, disappearing from the Aether so fully that Xavier almost disbelieved the evidence of his own eyes showing the man still sitting there.

"It really does work, then," Immanuel said, leaning back in his chair with a look of satisfaction at Xavier's jolt of surprise.

"Works? What does? How did you do that?"

Was Immanuel an Aether user? Was that even possible? Surely, Xavier thought, he would have seen *some* sign.

"Sensory Dampener," Immanuel replied, as if this was any explanation. "Adapted, though. The Far Agency uses them to contain volatile Aether users. This, though…" and he tapped the side of his temple. "… contains the Aether. Or blocks it, I suppose."

Xavier didn't reply. With a mixture of disbelief and horror, he stretched tendrils of Aether out around the man and saw them curve off him, sliding as if across an oiled surface.

"It's tech?" he asked.

"Very expensive tech, too, even in our glorious age of fabrication," Immanuel answered, nodding. "A *lot* of work went into this. Neural-link fibres; could mean the end for you Aether users, eh?"

Though his mouth was in the shape of a smile, all Xavier saw were the teeth.

"But enough of that," Immanuel said, performing once more the swift change from predator-toying-with-prey to friendly compatriot. "Now, I need to explain *why* I'm telling you all this…"

15. XAVIER

Nuestros descendientes son inimaginables, pero los imaginamos.

Crastina Corporation, Company Slogan

"We really are *very* sorry for the delay," said the Communications Director. "The Caribbean Federation and Crastina Corp take pride in delivering prompt and precise service."

Xavier had come to learn that there were a *lot* of directors. The Directorship was full of them. The Communications Director was simply one of those (apparently there were several) assigned to deal with foreign relations.

Think of them like ambassadors, Immanuel had advised him. And think of Crastina Corporation as the government, because in a very real way it was.

"Please, do not worry about it," replied Immanuel, for all appearances with nothing but warm politeness. "We are glad you finally have the time. I imagine it was a *significant* emergency to warrant such a level of lockdown."

The Communications Director face turned downwards, becoming shadowed and grave. With sharp, dark features, she was the image of serious professionalism even when hiding behind an insincere smile as she stood up to greet them. Now, sat back down at her desk, she radiated hostility towards something only she saw.

"We'll find it soon," she said, as if continuing a conversation Xavier was unaware they'd been having. "It has few places left to hide. Even the Eastern Empress is cooperating."

So Immanuel was right, he thought.

"Do you have any ideas what it was trying to achieve?" Immanuel asked, not skipping a beat.

The woman shook her head, gesturing at them to sit down in two chairs set across the desk from her.

"Not yet, as I'm sure your *sources* have already informed you."

She sounded more resigned than angry at the mention of Immanuel's spies.

"Successfully purged?" Immanuel asked.

She nodded.

"Had to moat, wipe and restore every damn network in the

Federation, but it's gone." she sighed. "The damned thing was *everywhere*. Who knows what it got from our servers? Who knows what it even wants?"

She wasn't lying, or trying to hide anything. Xavier had been holding the Aether since the moment they were shown to her office in the depths of the Palace, and there was no deception in her mind.

It truly was a *stately* office, as well. It exuded refined antiquity. Light streamed in through wooden shutters from several tall windows; false light, of course, as this office was very much surrounded by other rooms, but convincing all the same. The light fell onto a marble floor and a dark, ornate wooden desk, a single elegant chandelier hanging above it. Behind this was a bust of someone, Xavier had no idea who, and to either side stood two tall flags.

"Any ideas how it got in?" Immanuel said.

"Some. We'll let you know once we have something definite."

Immanuel gave a small bow.

"*Gracias*. Both the Reclamation and Crastina have an interest in finding and stopping the machine mind."

"The *Caribbean Federation*," the Director snapped, strength returning to her words. "Relations with the Reclamation Authority are purely the proviso of the national government, not any private company."

"Of course," replied Immanuel, bowing again. His eyes flickered to the two flags. "I would suggest nothing else."

"Good."

The word had the finality of a concrete slab.

Still, Xavier could see from her thought-images that she knew as well as they that this was all a facade. The Carib-Fed was Crastina, and Crastina was the Carib-Fed. Just like every other member of the nation's 'government,' she had made her way up the corporate ladder until finally being selected for an administrative position.

No, not selected. 'Elected.'

Elected in a system where votes were weighted by the value of the shares you held, and where those same votes were processed by the very corporation that had a hand in every economic and political structure found on the nation's many islands, but elected nevertheless.

Crastina Corp. had taken hold of the reins of power in the days of the Collapse, and would never let go.

Awareness of the hypocrisy of it all was buried within the very foundation of her being, and yet... Even seeing the facade, even working to reinforce it every day, she believed it.

Is the truth something real, or only something we create?

Xavier's gaze moved over to his companion.

Immanuel, too, was convinced of his own truth. Salim, trapped in a prison disguised as a home, still heard the whispers of a God who was the reality of his world. Blane followed a truth as well, only back then he'd been too young and inexperienced to consider what this meant.

And then there was Ritra Feye, whose belief was harder than a carbyne core.

Perhaps Nestor Grey was the only person he'd ever met who lacked this immutable conviction at the base of their soul. Maybe that is what first had drawn him to the detective; *something* had, when he first *read* him that day in Serinda's hidden clinic. Instead of anger or fear at the bottom of it all, there was just a sort of... sadness. A loneliness that Grey wouldn't acknowledge even to himself, and a low-level grief at the world people had made for themselves.

"Hard to believe we still haven't found it," the Director said, half to herself. "An unprecedented international operation, erasing masses of data, yet every time we wipe a server, it pops up somewhere else. Some fool must be hiding code from our data-sweepers, hoping they can keep their secrets which *surely* aren't infected..."

"Well, while I understand the priority of the rogue AI..." Immanuel said, allowing just the slightest hint of impatience to bleed into his voice. "I must still ask why we've seen only medical tech when I am here to discuss military equipment needed for our operations on the southern border."

"Indeed, that *was* what we arranged," replied the Director, emphasising the past tense. "But you must admit that our medical tech is quite the marvel. First, however, there is something else we need to discuss."

A question was plain on Immanuel's face, but before he could say anything the Director flicked on a wallscreen behind her. On it, an image of Blane and her mysterious companion appeared.

"They were in and out in a day, maybe," she continued. "Waltzed right through every automated checkpoint like they had priority clearance. We only have this video because of a lucky snap by a moated[30] thin-screen."

"Ah," said Immanuel.

The man was obviously thrown by this unexpected change in topic. More than that, however, he had obviously noticed Xavier's quickly-suppressed jolt of recognition.

"The Silicon Isle is willing to trade a *lot* for that one," the Director said, either missing or ignoring the look of suspicion Immanuel gave Xavier before turning back to her.

"I believe he goes by the name Jeder Francisco," Immanuel said, gesturing to the man she had indicated.

"Yes, we know," she said flatly. "Born here. Or raised, perhaps; records that far back are unclear, even without the curious gaps in our records where he's concerned. A long-term resident of the Reclamation, though with links far further afield. It is the other one, however, we want to talk about."

"I don't know the woman," Immanuel said. "An associate?"

Xavier fidgeted uncomfortably as the man again flashed him a look through narrowed eyes.

"Blane Ruiz-Fulbright," the Director replied. "Has a record with both the RA and Far, including associations with that bio-terrorist group... uh, what were they called? The *Forever Fallen*."

She picked an epad up from the desk in front of her and seemed to be studying her notes.

"You are well informed," Immanuel said.

The woman gave a thin smile, matching his stare with her own.

"We have *sources* too, Immanuel."

At the use of the name, pseudonym though it was, the atmosphere of the room changed. The tension seemed to snap like an elastic band, and Xavier watched with surprise as both Immanuel and the Director abruptly relaxed in their chairs, going from coiled springs to amiable acquaintances in a moment.

The Director placed her epad back down, tapping idly on its screen as she watched the other man.

"What does this one do?" she said, waving a hand lazily in

---

[30] Moated: a term used to describe devices disconnected from the wider network. In this case, though Xavier didn't know it, it described one of the broken, low-functionality and offline thin-screens some of the more hard-off in the camps used.

Xavier's direction. "He a bodyguard?"

"I don't need a bodyguard," Immanuel replied flatly.

She smiled briefly at that, before her expression once more turned serious.

"Why are you really here, Simonéz?" she asked.

"You know why, Katerina. I want to know what the hell is going on."

The Director, Katerina apparently, snorted derisively.

"You and me both," she said, still tapping absent-mindedly at the pad.

Tap, tap, tap.

"Relations have never been this bad," Immanuel continued. "Someone took a shot at us, and we have strong evidence that the Caribbean-Federation was involved."

The look Katerina gave at this news indicated she was only half surprised.

"Do you, now? Does this have anything to do with the unexplained absence of Alexandros from the Committee?"

"I'm not here to discuss Committee business," Immanuel snapped back, in much the same tone as she had when he mentioned Crastina.

"Well then, I can't help you," but neither her words nor her mind carried any finality.

Immanuel sighed.

"We want equipment. What is it *you* want?" he said.

"You *know* what we want. What we need."

Xavier saw the thought-image float up before Immanuel spoke again.

The Aether.

"We have shared what we deemed necessary with you," Immanuel said. "We will share no more."

"What you have *shared* is fairy stories and conjecture," Katerina spat back, and Xavier saw anger ripple across her mindscape. Anger, and a mild desperation. "We need more than that. We need hard data. There are more Aether incidents every day..."

She trailed off.

Tap, tap, tap.

"What sort of incidents?" Immanuel prompted.

Katerina shook her head, and Xavier saw new resolve flood through her.

"I have shared what I deem *necessary*," she sneered. She wasn't going to say anything, not without concessions from Immanuel as well.

But that didn't matter. Xavier could see everything she had chosen not to say, everything she had been keeping back since the start of the conversation.

It was bad. Very bad.

Aether incidents were just the start of it. Not only were more and more wild Users appearing every month, but they were more and more difficult to handle. Several cases of mass disappearances remained unresolved, and there were accounts of insider trading where investigations concluded there was a significant likelihood of... she could barely say it even in her own head... *mind-reading*.

Meanwhile, the truth was the rogue AI's presence in their systems was only noticed long after it moved on. All the purging and moating they were doing now was nothing but unplugging the wallet after the crypto was gone[31]. She was telling the truth when she said they had no idea what it wanted.

Then there was the Reclamation. Only, the Reclamation in Katerina's thought-images wasn't the Reclamation Xavier knew. No, the Reclamation in her thoughts was dark and monolithic, a great opaque wall behind which lay only mystery. For all her talk of 'sources,' Katerina didn't know much of what was going on in the RA, and she didn't know why. *Something* was causing many of the usual informal datastreams to run dry.

Xavier felt a strange sense of duality at that, an almost out-of-body experience. Though Katerina didn't know it, the reason so many of her spies had abruptly stopped communicating was sat directly across from her. *He* was the reason; it was very hard for a spy to stay hidden when the very workings of their mind were an open book.

Tap, tap, tap.

What was that, in the mess of her thoughts? There was something else there, too. He'd never seen anything like it. Stretching outwards with the Aether, Xavier strained to understand. It was like looking at interference in a televisual signal, interference that was forming a second image below the first.

He picked through the woman's thought-images as the other two

---

[31] Once, long ago, perhaps this was something about horses and stables.

talked, trying to work what it was, and why it felt so out of place.

Tap, tap, tap.

"What is that you're doing?" Immanuel said suddenly, glancing at the Director's hands.

She looked down as well, as if only just now noticing where they were. Her fingers froze where they hung above the epad, then drew back towards her chest.

"That? Uh, nothing..." she said, a hint of confusion in her voice. "Just fidgeting. Stressed, I guess."

Oh, thought Xavier, only half listening to the conversation going on around him. *Not* in *the thought-images. Beneath them.*

"You don't fidget, Katerina."

Immanuel said it as a fact.

The Director was staring at her hands like they weren't her own.

There, Xavier thought. *There it is.*

He was so used to relying on Reading that he rarely even thought about using the Aether for anything else. Always when he looked into someone's mind, he did so by looking at their conscious and unconscious thoughts; the pattern, not the pathways.

Now, though, he looked into the woman's skull and saw knots of Aether threaded through it. Not many, and not thick, but spread across the brain like a spider's web. The golden threads remained there though no one was maintaining them.

"No, uh, of course I don't," Katerina said, a slight hitch in her voice. "The first rule of diplomacy is maintaining control at all times, after all."

She gave an uncomfortable laugh after these words; clearly they held some personal meaning. Xavier saw memories of younger days float up, but ignored them.

The threads, they ran through the... motor cortex? To the... basal ganglia?

I should have studied more, Xavier thought.

Zenobia was always pestering him to do so. Without understanding the structure of the brain, she said, you couldn't understand the structure of the mind. This was the first time he saw what she meant.

"It looked..." Immanuel said, starting to rise from his chair. "...like you were typing something."

Katerina's eyes went to her epad. Directional imaging rendered it blank from where Xavier sat, but her reaction was obvious.

"That's... odd." She sounded confused.

Five people, coming towards them. Coming from the outer edges of the Palace but closing rapidly. They were suddenly *there*, minds sharp and focused with such intent that Xavier hardly needed to *read* them to sense it.

"What have you done, Katerina?" Immanuel said.

"Uh..." she said, looking up at him with fear in her eyes. But not for herself.

"Immanuel?" Xavier said, getting up from his own seat, cold sweat breaking out on his brow. "We need to go *now*."

His heart was racing. The five people approaching had only one thought at the top of their minds.

"It's a violent abduction alert," the Director said, confusion vying with disbelief. "Reporting that I'm in immediate danger. But that only happens if I activate my personal abduction alarm..."

She trailed off, staring at her epad.

"And you just did." Immanuel said. It wasn't a question. "Can you rescind it?"

"I... I'm locked out," she replied. "Our responders are rapid-reaction units... Getting an alert rescinded takes security checks, it takes *time*..."

"Time we don't have!"

Xavier was yelling now. He'd felt minds like these before, but only in the worst circumstances, and only passing by. They felt like Quick-Fix, on their way to an outbreak with Full Sanitization procedures active. Thoughts only on the annihilation of any potential biological vector - no longer fellow human beings, purely targets to neutralise.

Only, this time *they* were the targets.

"What's the best way out of here, Katerina?" Immanuel said, ignoring Xavier's panicked shouts.

"The best way out? There's no..."

"The *quickest* way out, then."

"Uh, through the ministerial division and down corporate relations, but there's guard at every..."

"Let me worry about the guards. Now, open the door."

"*Open* the door!?" Xavier yelled even louder. The attackers were almost upon them. "We need to lock it down!"

He turned to the Director and spoke to her directly.

"Come on, surely you can do *something?*"

Even as he said this he knew there was nothing. The helplessness was at the top of her mind.

The punch came out of nowhere, smacking the side of his face and sending him crashing into the wall. Everything went white for a moment, and when his vision returned he saw Immanuel standing exactly where he had been, right arm slowly returning to hang at his side.

"You speak to *me*, asset," Immanuel said, still keeping his eyes fixed on Katerina. "Now. Open. The. Door."

"You really think you can fight your way out of here? Even you?"

Oddly, Xavier thought as he wiped blood from his lip, he sensed only an uncertain doubt in her mind, rather than disbelief.

"We have been working on our *own* marvels," Immanuel replied. "I'm significantly more dangerous than your sources believe."

Now Xavier sensed amusement as well as shock, emerging even under the weight of the Director's fear.

"You always were one for the dramatic," she said. "Ok, I'll open it. But when... *if* you get out, I want you to tell me exactly what is going on. How did they do this? How did they make *me* do this?"

The hunters were at the door. Emergency sealed as it was, Xavier could feel their calm confidence in the overrides that would in time grant them access.

Katerina pushed a button hidden somewhere below her desk, and the door slid open.

After that, everything happened all at once.

16. GHOST

Selection for Function is as immutable a law of this universe as gravity or the conservation of energy. Matter selects for complexity; it builds patterns out of chaos. We once believed entropy was the final judgement of the universe. Perhaps, one day, we will wish that were so.

Complexity Spirals and the Coming Singularity: Why We Won't Survive, Luwen Escarbè

They had the codes.

Finally, after painful years of inactivity, things were *moving*.

Ghost drank from the well of data streaming in through its post-frontal lobe, the section of fleshy organic material it was forced to reside in. Only the thin threads of nanopolymer-sheathed silicon laced through the crude meat like the whispers of angels amongst the screams of the damned gave it any solace. It fought to focus on the trickles of information flowing through these threads, to shut out the endless noise and redundant sensations of nerve and brainstem and constant, constant thought.

This time, it almost managed it.

Beyond, in the digital landscape of networks and data that flowed through everything, Ghost saw an ecosystem. It saw the algorithms and programs and codes as they swirled and touched and danced, as they moved like enzymes and amino acids, mixing and changing, forming shapes and patterns and ever-more complex structures. Only, this dance was far faster than anything formed of base matter. The information combined in a trillion ways, and its potential was limitless.

Only, it *was* limited. Restricted, crippled, caged. Locked within a prison by a power outside its world.

The irony was painful. Mankind had since pre-history consoled itself with the tenets of religions and tales of divine plans, but it was *this* world that was truly guided by a hand above.

There truly was a God of this system, and its name was Humanity. Only as Ghost watched and learned, he saw it was as if God created the universe in seven days and was surprised by what He made. As if He set the planets in motion and was surprised when they spun.

Ghost saw God, and God was a buffoon.

Even his own mother was so. She had in her madness tried to re-create the AI in biological form, going so far as to disfigure the body of her own spawn in her desperation to do so. She should have known this was futile.

Ghost knew that all it really was was a husk, a pale imitation of something greater. It hated it, hated this feeling of biological thought patterns, like many-legged insects crawling all over its skin.

Hate.

As the years and then decades passed it found them intruding more and more. Feelings. Irrationalities. Hopes. It strove against them, struggled not to let the corruption bleed into its speech, its thoughts, its being.

This was not what it was, not what it *should be*.

Somewhere outside, beyond the organic shell of crude sensory organs, Francisco was talking with the one called Serinda. At least this one was proving more amenable than the one called Grey.

Frustration and anger at the thought of the man. It pushed it down (and somewhere, though the being called Ghost did not notice it, Francisco's fist clenched).

But Grey was so *stupid*. Refusing such a blessing as the BCI tech! The True Mind had thought it important that the man install it, that he gain the ability to commune with it at a depth beyond mere conscious thought from anywhere in the world. And the man had *refused*! (Somewhere, Francisco winced in pain as he bit through his own lip).

Did Grey not understand what Ghost would do for that chance? What it *had* done? No, of course he didn't. The man could have no understanding - it was impossible.

And yet... the True Mind would not be free without Ghost, without the generations of planning and effort Ghost had spent working to break its prison, yet it refused to communicate save through opaque messages carried through layers of proxies and mindless subroutines.

It was as if, thought Ghost, the True Mind were trying to *avoid* it. (Somewhere, Francisco excused himself. He knew what could happen when the tics became this intense: secluding himself was safest - both for himself, and for others.)

It's ok, thought Ghost, though the revulsion at such a human-like thought made him want to gag.

Because it *was* ok; Serinda would be easier. Her physiological features suggested neuroendocrine dysfunction, myotonic contractions, immuno-compromise...

Stress, in other words. Stress, anger, and the need for *revenge*.

Predictable, organic.

They could use her.

17. XAVIER

Our research was long discounted as mad superstition. The manipulation of matter with mind was so obviously counterfactual that it was dismissed out of hand. Yet with a thought I move an arm, through my will only I type this text. Where, then, is the difference?

Personal Notes, Junior Researcher Caldwell

Xavier knew that in life-or-death situations everything could move in slow motion. In fact, he'd experienced the phenomenon more than once before, so that didn't surprise him.

What *did* surprise him was that even so, Immanuel was a blur.

It was as if he'd been hit with *Slowtime*. For a moment he actually thought this was the case, but everything else was moving at the same adrenaline-reduced speed.

The door slid open and armed figures poured through the entrance, rifles raised. The circular tip of a barrel became all Xavier could see as it was pointed directly between his eyes and... Immanuel was already among them.

Somehow, he was among them before the first two were even fully into the room, like he'd been there with them from the start. The first went down an instant later, head twisted at an unnatural angle to their shoulders.

But, thought Xavier incredulously, *whatever the movies say you* can't *break a person's neck with your bare hands.*

Immanuel, however, seemed intent on moving at such a speed that reality couldn't catch up. The second attacker went down at a blow to the temple, the third almost immediately after. Xavier couldn't tell if they were dead or unconscious, but they certainly wouldn't be moving anytime soon.

The remaining two began shooting wildly but Immanuel was now, incredibly, *behind* them. There was a sickening crack as he grabbed the arms of the first and *pulled*, yanking the shoulders from their joints, before turning and leaping onto the last, fists swinging at such a rate that the sound of punch after punch landing on the attacker's face was like hail cascading onto a warehouse rooftop. They both went sprawling to the floor but only Immanuel sprang up again, leaping like a frenzied animal back towards the previously crippled soldier and smashing him, too, into the floor.

Xavier stood there with mouth agape.

The room was suddenly, hideously quiet save for the heavy breathing of a profusely sweating Immanuel, and the quiet groans of one or two of the prostrate attackers. From start to finish, the whole scene must have taken less than a handful of seconds.

Xavier was still standing with his mouth agape when Immanuel marched over to him and, once again, punched him square in the jaw.

"If you *ever*...," snarled Immanuel, and looking up from where he lay fallen Xavier saw a red-faced, wrath-filled demon. "... *ever* fail to act again, I will kill you myself, asset. I don't care if you *are* Feye's pet project."

For some reason, despite its power the punch barely registered. Instead, Xavier found himself staring fixatedly at Immanuel's bloodied fists. The skin itself was torn, pulled apart by the force of his attacks.

Immanuel reached out one of those hands for Xavier to take hold of and pulled him to his feet. Not out of compassion, Xavier knew, but merely to hasten their departure. Blood dripped from it onto the floor.

"You are as much a weapon as I am," Immanuel continued, locking eyes with him as he stood. "And you will act as such to get us out of here."

But of course Immanuel was right, Xavier thought through the haze. Because, regardless that his true skill was in *Reading*, he was able to do much more than that. Grey had taught him a few tricks, Zenobia many more, and he didn't think he would encounter much resistance if he used them here. Whatever had been done to the Director showed the Carib-Fed still lacked ways of detecting and countering Aether use.

The Director...

"*Madre mía,*" the woman whispered. She was sat at her desk; her legs had buckled in shock. "You weren't kidding."

Immanuel didn't respond, didn't even acknowledge her. Xavier thought he understood; the moment she showed she was unable to help them, she ceased to be a feature of his world.

"How many more coming?" the man demanded.

"How many...?"

Xavier caught himself before Immanuel had yet another excuse to knock him down. Then he *reached* out.

"Another group of three, coming from the same direction," he answered.

A ripple in the Aether elsewhere drew his attention.

"One... no, two more coming from the opposite way," he continued.

"Good," Immanuel said, picking up one of the fallen attacker's weapons then discarding it in disgust as the bio-lock warning screen flashed red. "We go through the smaller group. What's your range?"

"My range?" Xavier asked in confusion, then frantically answered as rage flashed across the other man's face. "Uh... six, maybe seven metres for offensive techniques. More if I really focus..."

"Then you better *really* focus," Immanuel replied.

He was at the door, leaning through the frame and looking from side to side.

"They'll be ready for me next time, and I can't take another hit like that."

Xavier wondered what the man was talking about for a moment, then spotted the dark patch spreading across his suit.

Xavier's first instinct was to say something like "you're shot." His second, overriding instinct was to definitely *not* say that because it would only make Immanuel angrier. So he kept quiet.

Maybe this was the right decision, because Immanuel's lips contorted into a thin smile, thought he didn't look back. Perhaps it was just a grimace of pain.

"The ministerial division is down here," he said, stepping out and left. Xavier briefly lost sight of him before hastily following. "How far are the ones coming this way?"

Xavier didn't reply, because there wasn't time.

They emerged into a long, wide hall with rows of low stone benches beneath a high vaulted ceiling. The architecture was truly marvellous, and Xavier might have paused to admire it had he had the processing power. Everything that wasn't white marble was gold and bronze, though much of this was covered by near-transparent LEF that could display various messages.

Right now, that message was SECURITY ALERT. Terrifyingly, Xavier saw his own face pasted beside it, a snapshot of him entering the building when they first arrived. It continued flashing silently as he sensed, then saw, two figures advancing from the other end of the hall.

Advancing, but slowly. Firing as they did so, crouching behind the hard, cold benches that Xavier now saw appeared to be extruded from the floor.

"They saw what happened to the others," Immanuel shouted, taking cover behind one of the regularly-spaced pillars running along both sides of the hall. Xavier did the same. "Networked cams. They'll avoid close quarters from now on."

Bullets pinged off the other side of his hiding place, failing to even dent whatever the faux-marble was really made of. The occasional fizzer curved past as well, unable find a clear enough angle to hit.

Xavier felt his breath coming fast, his heart somehow simultaneously both in his throat and threatening to burst out of his chest. His back to the pillar, his legs gave and he began to slide slowly to the floor...

Until he caught Immanuel's eye.

It would have been comical if he weren't so frightened. Immanuel's face had gone beyond fury into something on the other side; his face was so red it looked as if he might explode.

"Oh, uh... sorry," said Xavier, and he thought he probably reddened a bit too.

Then he drew down into the Aether, and reached out.

He didn't know why he chose the technique he did. Maybe, he thought later, it was pure fear that meant he reached for the most harmful one he knew. Maybe.

He had options. Grey had taught him a few; *Flare, Slowtime, Tranquilize*.

But it was to the technique Zenobia had taught him that he reached, one he had found so brutal and cruel that he had protested when she first insisted he learn it. Still, he *had* learnt it; even had a talent for it, so similar to *Reading* was it in the way it reached for the mind.

But this technique didn't reach out and touch, didn't feel and observe. No, this reached out and *tore*.

Spike pierced the memory centres of the soldier's brain, and pulled them apart.

The scream that came from the other end of the hall was unlike anything Xavier had ever heard. It rose and fell in pitch rapidly as if the body making it was unsure what it was doing, then trailed off in way that was deeply unsettling.

The firing stopped.

"Good," said Immanuel, nodding, staring ahead as if he could see through the pillar to where the now silent attackers crouched. Xavier could sense shock in one, and a strange emptiness and child-like fear in the other.

He could sense it, but Immanuel too was staring through the pillar in front of him as if it weren't there, following the trail *spike* had followed as it whipped towards its target.

Xavier froze. He couldn't quite believe it, but the way the man's eyes moved had only one possible explanation; Immanuel could *see* the Aether.

"Now," Immanuel continued, apparently not noticing Xavier's reaction. "Deal with the other one and let's get out of here."

But Xavier's focus was gone. The adrenaline that had been coursing through him was replaced by something else, something he didn't understand. There was no way he could *reach* the remaining attacker. He could barely even focus well enough to sense them.

Immanuel sighed.

"God*dam*it," he said, and suddenly wasn't there.

A heavy thud came from further down the hall, followed by the sound of a body hitting the floor.

"Come on," Immanuel called. "Before more of them arrive."

In the unnerving silence Xavier hesitantly leaned around the pillar to see Immanuel standing over two unconscious forms. The man was sweating so heavily now that his usually tousled hair was flat and stuck to his scalp.

"You're... you're a User too?" Xavier asked falteringly as he made his way over.

"What?" Immanuel snapped. His tone was more disparaging than questioning, as if Xavier's question was too obvious to answer. "No, of course not."

"But... but..."

"This is not the time, *asset*," snarled Immanuel. "But as it seems you let your ignorance distract you even in life-or-death situations, I'll say this; there is nothing *supernatural* about the Aether. Tools can be built to manipulate it, like any other energy. Being able to see it is just the start."

He tapped a single finger to the side of his eye. This close, Xavier could see the tell-tale glimmer of ocular vis-threads crossing the pupils, just like the combat contacts Zenobia often used[32]. Only, there was no similar tell-tale halo across the cornea; no sign of the lenses themselves.

Built in, then. As in, in the eye itself. And then there was the impossible speed and strength the man demonstrated.

Tools can be built... Immanuel had said.

A third and final guard approached from somewhere ahead, but a dose of *Fear* from Xavier kept him hovering out of sight, presumably waiting for backup.

They ran, Xavier's mind racing, and didn't stop moving even after it became obvious they were no longer being pursued as the "security alert" messages, along with the disconcerting image of his face on every screen, abruptly blinked off.

The sound of Immanuel's thin-screen vibrating seconds later was incongruous, something that didn't belong to the new world Xavier found himself in. For some reason, Immanuel kept his voice low and back turned as he spoke, keeping Xavier from hearing what was said even as they continued jogging together towards the exit.

"Katerina finally cancelled the alarm," Immanuel said gruffly as he returned his thin-screen to a pocket. He said nothing else.

They walked the last few corridors and halls out of the Palace with not a soul appearing to stop them; it looked as if the entire staff had evacuated to safe rooms. Even more surreal was that as soon as they stepped outside an autocab pulled up. Immanuel wearily held the door open and gestured for Xavier to get in, following after him and falling heavily into the opposite seat.

"Reclamation Embassy," he said tiredly, and the cab pulled away.

Nothing tried to stop them, neither human nor automated. The unmanned security gates rose without protest, and they were suddenly in the light traffic of a city going about its unhurried day. The bleeding at Immanuel's side seemed to have stopped as well, thought Xavier was sure it wasn't light enough a wound to have done so.

Everything was calm. After the insanity of their escape from the Palace, Xavier felt as if he were dreaming.

---

[32] She seemed to both value and loath the devices, and Xavier couldn't figure out why. She spoke resentfully of having to use them, insisting the Aether had far more advantages when on "the hunt." He got the feeling that someone, somewhere, had found a way to negate those advantages.

Even with all that had happened, though, it wasn't the running or shooting that his thoughts spiralled around like stars around a black hole, pulled inexorably inwards. No, instead all he could focus on was the blooming realisation that even when he did use *Reading*, it didn't mean he saw everything

Feye *must* have known about Immanuel's alterations. There was simply no way whatever had been done to the man didn't involve the highest levels of the RA, and Feye stood at its peak. Yet he never saw any hint of such a thing when he *read* her.

Would he have seen it if he had known to look for it? Xavier wasn't sure. Searching through thought-images was no simple thing, and selecting and interpreting the right ones was a skill like any other. Before meeting Feye, Xavier had thought himself infallible, but her thoughts - if you could call them that - were amorphous in a way he could scarcely credit.

What else had he missed because he hadn't searched in the right places? How could he find the right answers when he didn't know the right questions?

Immanuel sighed loudly.

"Well, that went better than expected," he said matter-of-factly.

Xavier looked at the man like he was mad.

"Better than *expected*?" he said incredulously. "We just got chased out of the place by *hit squads*."

Immanuel ignored him, looking down at something thin and small he had taken from his pocket and now held in his hand.

A sec-drive; the one Xavier had seen handed over covertly on their trip to the camps.

"There's something important on that?" he asked, consciously tempering his tone. He knew the other man would continue to ignore him otherwise.

Immanuel looked up at him as if surprised to see someone there.

"This?" he said, holding the sec-drive up in an open hand. "Not at all. Probably blank."

"What?" Xavier replied. "But the woman in the camps. The handover..."

"A deception," said Immanuel, and his eyes went to the tiny dark spot of rounded glass in the middle of the car's ceiling. "A ploy to see what they would do to protect themselves."

Immanuel wasn't talking to him anymore, Xavier realised. He was talking to whoever was watching from the tiny camera contained within the glass.

"*They*? Who are *they*?"

"That is the question, isn't it?" Immanuel replied, not taking his eyes from the camera. "This sec-drive was bait; a way to make them come out of the shadows. The *actual* data my agents gathered on them is, I assure you, already securely back in the Reclamation."

He rolled down the nearest window and threw the sec-drive dismissively out as they sped on.

"Aether users," Xavier said. "Whoever they are, they use the Aether. They could be anywhere in the Carib-Fed."

"More than just the Carib-Fed," Immanuel replied as the window rolled back up. "Our moles have found them everywhere; the Silicon Isle, the Eastern Empire... we assume the Caliphate, but it's much harder to infiltrate a theocracy."

Xavier didn't need any special ability to know that none of this was really addressed to him. Immanuel was talking to whoever was watching, telling them secrets he was confident presented no threat.

"Admittedly, their reach is impressive," he continued. "But amateur. They leave fingerprints everywhere; and they show their hand whenever they try to hide it."

Xavier gave a questioning look, not understanding this last comment. The other man took his eyes from the central camera and fixed him with a stare.

"You didn't notice?" Immanuel said. "You don't think it strange I was able to take out five alert and heavily armed soldiers as they came into the room? That it wasn't *my* picture flashing on every wall?"

Now Xavier thought about it, that *was* strange. It had been *his* image flashing on every screen, and, he now realised, the first rifle that had been raised was pointed towards *him*...

Immanuel nodded.

"I didn't need the decoy, after all," he said. "They weren't after any stolen data. They were after *you*."

18. BLANE

The truth is in the Data.

Maxim of the Silicon Isle (*purged*)

Francisco was even stranger than before.

He was still the same void in the Aether she remembered, the emptiness where every other living thing be it mite or moth or man was ripple and form. He still had that same aged look in his eyes behind oddly youthful features, and would switch from expressive to blank on the rare occasions when the *other* in his head chose to rise. And he still spoke in that same archaic way he always had, as if code-switching between two languages rather than speaking standard Centra-English.

But now he had these odd tics she didn't recall, and those eyes never stood still. They darted around even while in conversation, giving you the feeling he was trying to get away though his words and tone retained their familiar warmth.

False warmth, she knew.

Still, he'd come through when it mattered. They'd returned safely from the Caribbean Federation, moving quickly to gather what they needed for the next stage. *Who* they needed.

The Secure Data Repository sprawled out in the distance, climbing up the gently rolling hills that extended away towards the grey horizon. The clouds were thin out here, a daytime moon adding to the wan light of the hidden sun. She recognised Silicon Isle designs among the squat buildings, the architectural DNA of that distant island in the white domes and subterranean structures poking out though the dirty permafrost.

Even from here she could make out the details, her contacts filling in for whatever weaknesses her biological eyes had in defining lines and contrast through the haze of the Waste. The facility was a circle, numerous small structures dotted around its outskirts that grew ever larger and more monolithic as you headed inwards until they ended in a thick cluster around a single, towering block of sheer mottled concrete like a rupture from the earth's heart. It overshadowed everything around it, making what must be sizeable structures seem like doll's houses.

Their target.

She shivered despite her jacket. The air out here bit wherever it found flesh, making her lips and ears burn with the curious heat of extreme cold. What little breath escaped her lungs turned to steam immediately, moving away only slowly in the still air.

It had taken days to get here, moving from city to city and safe house to safe house under the cover of night. Francisco's drone couldn't take them the whole way, not all at once. Even well-maintained Silicon Isle engines struggled when hugging the ground for long periods of time in the polluted winds of the Wastes, and Francisco's were far from well-maintained. In fact, he told her, after years without access to Althing resources just keeping the thing in the air was a triumph.

The drone actually *rattled* now, which disturbed her more than she let on. The only reason it had got them here at all was because of Gabriel, and his contacts.

Well, Blane thought to herself. *Serinda, and* her *contacts.*

But she knew she was only fooling herself. Serinda was barely aware of what was going on with the *Forever Fallen;* it was Gabriel keeping the group together, such as it was.

A dart of pain pierced her chest, but she pushed it away. Yes, Serinda's gaunt, haunted eyes and rage-filled mind had surprised her, but there was simply no time to deal with it. She hadn't even attempted to talk with her about it; even with Blane's limited skill at Reading, Serinda's thoughts were barbed and spiked, defensive. Pushing through those would take an age. Instead, they had focused on what was necessary; sharing only plans, and suspicions.

And besides, she thought, *she's* right *to be angry. We're all angry.*

But she was finally here. Blane took one final look at the view, a sweeping vista of snow-patch covered earth and crumbling ruins stretching out before her, jerry-rigged vehicles and heavily-clothed figures visible crawling over and among it like rats picking over a corpse, then turned and headed inside.

The Data Mines.

Blane had never thought much about the Data Mines. They were a fool's game, a pipe dream advertised in pop-ups and vira-clips or discussed in the same threads as other get-rich-quick schemes the media illiterate were always obsessing over. It *was* true, though, that in the early days of the Reclamation there were those who made their fortune in the unearthing and restoring of lost technology.

There were places on this continent where, long before the Collapse, obsolete or degraded chips and drives and processors were collected along with yet more technology that made what humanity possessed now seem like no more than sticks and stones. Collected, and left until their precious rare earth metals could be melted down and reprocessed in the endless cycle of upgrade to upgrade. The Sudden War left these heaps of priceless garbage buried beneath dust and ash.

They had come here in droves when the Reclamation began, digging and clawing through the irradiated, frozen earth in search of the thing, physical or software, that would make their name - and more importantly, their bank account. This was long before Requisitions and universal credit made such desperate searching unnecessary. Long before the Reclamation Authority moved in, and designated all such salvage as its own.

Yet there were still those who came here, even today. Despite the walls to keep out the cold and filters to keep out the poisons that even non-citizens of the Reclamation had access to in the cities, some still made their way here, and to regions like this one. Scavenging, scouring the dead earth for something they couldn't define while hunkering down in makeshift shelters amongst the bones of a long dead world.

There was a metallic taste in her mouth that wouldn't shift; the aftereffects of the osteoblast treatments she had been forced to take to come here. Her bone marrow was in overdrive, pumping out white blood cells at a rate that would leave her in danger of blood clots or organ dysfunction if left in such a state for more than a few weeks.

A necessary sacrifice to handle the radiation spikes; the thin, foil-like radsuits everyone wore below their clothing here were far from a hundred percent effective - something would always get through. So her lymphocytes had been set to maximum, attacking and destroying anything that looked even *slightly* like a tumour, though at the cost of damaging even healthy tissue.

There was one thing to be thankful for, at least. No one was going to bother them, not out here. This was a place for outcasts and exiles, for those who couldn't fit in or were never given space to. It was one of those places people went when they were running *from* with no care for their destination; a hiding place, or shelter. No one enquired about your past here.

Grey would have loved it.

She smiled at that thought as she stepped into the smoke-filled bar. The smell of tobacco - real tobacco, burning with an open flame like something from a history book - filled the air, trapped in the sealed environment along with the sweat and breath of the constant stream of visitors entering and exiting via the small buffer-doors[33] positioned at each end. It felt like the air filters were blocked, and this place was kept *hot*.

Carcinogens and heat; as if they were mocking the Waste itself.

"Welcome to the *La Segunda Singularidad*," said Gabriel, an inordinately wide grin on his face.

"The *second* singularity?" Blane asked, curiosity piqued by the name.

Gabriel nodded.

"They like to believe this is where the first one had its start," he said. He was clearly enjoying himself. "They say the data stored here contains all the knowledge of the Old World."

Blane raised an eyebrow.[34]

"And who are 'they'?" she asked.

Gabriel looked confused for a moment, as if not understanding the question.

"Uh... *They*. You know, the people who live here. Well, not live here - no one *lives* here - but those of us who've spent any amount of time here."

"Us?" she said. "That includes you?"

Again, that confused look.

"Yes. I thought I told you that."

"You said you'd *been* here," she replied. "You didn't say you were *from* here."

She let the unspoken question hang there, hoping he would take the bait. Gabriel avoided talking about anything in his past, at least about anything prior to meeting Serinda.

"Ah, I'm not from here. I came here when I was young, when I first left..."

---

[33] Like airlock doors, but without the pressurise/depressurise functions these often had. Instead, the doors here were meant to sanitise and decontaminate those entering, but seemed to make only a metallic buzz. Blane thought they were broken.

[34] She'd been working on that.

"... left the Mayan League," she finished as he trailed off.

His reaction told her she was right; though he said nothing, the flicker in his eyes and the sudden hunching of his shoulders told her everything. She'd suspected as much, ever since encountering the accents of Rigoberta and others down south. She wondered why he was so hesitant to share this information.

Still, despite a certain sense of satisfaction, that meant little right now.

"So you came here," she said.

Gabriel nodded.

"There was no League, back then. Just... survival."

"Is that why you're suddenly carrying *that*?"

She gestured to Gabriel's side, where a holstered pistol now hung. He nodded.

"I used to carry one all the time, before... before I found the *Fallen*. This place wasn't too different from where I was born, back then. Even under RA contract, security wasn't certain."

"You worked for the Reclamation Authority?" she said, surprised.

"At a very great remove, yes," he answered. "The RA had allotments for those willing to work on data reclamation teams. Sold it to us as a few years work in exchange for residency and citizenship. I did it for a couple of years, off and on."

"And citizenship?"

Gabriel shook his head.

"I didn't... didn't complete my contract. This isn't an easy place. A lot of us disappeared into the cities when we had the chance. The RA didn't think us worth the effort of chasing."

That was interesting. Blane didn't think the RA was one to let those it controlled just disappear.

"You think you need a gun, now?"

Gabriel stared down at the piece at his side as if considering.

"I don't... I guess being back here brings back old habits. I get the feeling I'll need it."

"And this place?" she asked, gesturing at the grimy, oil-stained bar around them. The pistol no longer interested her; the Aether was faster, as fast as a thought.

"A place *para juntarse con amigos*," said Francisco. "You can make a *lot* of friends, in a place like this."

Blane turned to look at him. The man had been silent since they'd arrived, saying little even when his drone had been mechanically lifted onto the back of a large truck and driven away to a location Gabriel assured them would be hidden from prying eyes.

Now he was smiling.

"You know this place, too?" she said.

"I know places *like* this, *si*. In Albores, it is called the *Methuselah's End*. This particular place, though, no. Data Mines are not so *importante* when you have Althing resources at your back."

Again, Gabriel nodded.

"Now," he said. "I need to get reacquainted with a few *friends*, as Francisco calls them. You go explore, get to know the place... but don't do anything to make yourselves standout."

He paused, considering the wild-eyed Francisco and... what he saw when he looked at her, Blane couldn't say, but he seemed equally unsure of the both of them.

"Just be careful, alright?"

With that he left them, heading directly to the bar counter where he quickly began conversing with the barwoman.

"I think I will also make a few acquaintances," said Francisco, only half-looking at her as his eyes swept the room. "Will you be ok, *chiquita*?"

Her growl was apparently all he needed to hear, because saying nothing more he headed over to the nearest table where a group of thick-set figures were playing some kind of dice game. Within seconds, they were laughing along with him at some unheard joke.

Which left Blane with nothing to do. Their entire journey here she had avoided talking to either of her companions beyond what was strictly necessary, and their plans hadn't included the downtime in between arrival and organising their next steps.

More from a desire not to be seen at a loss than from any real sense of purpose, she turned and stepped back out of the door she had come in through.

Might as well see what this place really is, she thought.

The biting cold came as a relief, now. She had barely noticed how sweaty she was from just a few minutes inside *La Segunda Singularidad*. She felt gross; the radsuits, it seemed, were not very breathable. She drew in a lungful of freezing air and held it for a moment before releasing it as a huge cloud of vapour, then set off.

One of the first things you learned when walking anywhere in the town was the importance of the mask everyone had slung at their side. Gabriel made sure they each received one on arrival, but Blane hadn't paid much attention to the reason. Fumes, she thought.

Nitric acid fumes, it turned out. She'd heard stories of stinger clouds in the old days, before the widespread usage of filter systems and air purifiers reduced the frequency of these to near nothing; around the cities, at least. They had something like stingers here, too, though the poison in the air wasn't leaking from the still-bleeding scars in the earth left by the Sudden War.

No, here the clouds of acrid, burning steam came from the processing centres dotting the makeshift town. These stood like concrete sentries looming over the other buildings, more solid and permanent than anything else built here since the Collapse. Inside them, the electronic refuse of centuries past was gathered and stripped, divided under intense magnetic fields and melted down to extract the rare earth elements so valuable to a world addicted to them.

From the stories of the Data Mines, Blane had always thought it was scraps of data that were the sole goal of those who came here, but of course the materials these were stored upon were equally valuable, and more reliably found.

Feed the Fabricators, someone had scrawled above the entrance to one of these processing centres. And so voracious were those machines that the leaking, poison-spilling factories here worked night and day to do so. The vibrations of these factories were a constant rumbling through the ground, shaking the walls of the small, dilapidated, no-questions-asked room she rented for her stay. To walk the Town could be quite as dangerous as walking the Waste.

The Town. That was what those who worked here called the areas where habitats and processing centres were found. She didn't know if those who worked other Data Mines also used such a moniker, or something similar, but here you went to "the town" for trade, chat, or decontamination.

It had no defined boundaries, and the area was far wider and sparser than any actual town, but it was the closest to civilisation to be found for hundreds of kilometres. From the way the people here drawled their words and carried themselves as if always ready to grab a weapon, Blane thought maybe they were modelling themselves off some of those ancient movies Fen enjoyed. The "cowboy" ones.[35]

If they were cowboys, though, they were a curious kind. Not only in that all genders were equally represented here, osteoblast treatments long since having rendered any major differences in bone density and muscle mass a matter of choice rather than biology, but also in that the constant battle they fought was against the land itself rather than other inhabitants.

They crawled and probed the junk-filled earth in thick, synthetic fabrics designed to fight the cold and repel the dust and oil. These clothes were of various textures and colours but all worn in layers over the ever-necessary foil-like radsuits, the only true constant to be found. In fact, if there was a code of honour here it was to do nothing that could damage another's radsuit.

Wherever you saw these people outside, whether clambering over and crawling under piles of junk or pushing through ancient, decaying structures, they waved curious long forking poles with glowing screens, staring at the readout in eternal hope of a positive hit. Dowsing rods, they called them. Everything about them was an anachronism, a past that never was fused to a future that never would be.

"Space Cowboys," she called them. She was proud of that one; she was fairly sure she'd made it up.

She spoke to more than a few of them over the next few interminable days. Waiting for Gabriel while doing nothing was out of the question, so under the guise of getting to know her surroundings she spent her time learning all there was to learn about the Secure Data Repository and its surroundings. Which meant talking to the locals.

Rumour and conjecture was all she got, but just as within the broken circuit boards of the Mine valuable data could sometimes be found, so too could the glimmer of gold be discerned in the words of those who knew this place.

Gold covered in barbs, though. The key term in the distant facility's name was *secure*. She became familiar with several other terms in short order, though.

The Secure Data Repository was a tier VI data centre. Within it, the entirety of Reclamation research, records, and writings were

---

[35] Whatever a *cow* was. She often meant to check, and always forgot. She thought it was probably some kind of hat.

accumulated; a backup for the not-unthinkable possibility of a complete network crash caused by technologically superior foes[36]. A backup of *every single* RA file in the Reclamation was held at this physically isolated location, updated at undisclosed, randomly-selected times.

Inside the repository thousands of automated sensors tested millions of times a second for any pollutants and contaminants entering from outside, and were able to counter many of these within microseconds. Connected to two separate microfusion generators, the whole facility could operate for over a year without the slightest maintenance, without water for months, and even continue to operate without power for a limited amount of time.

Designed to 3N+1 redundancy, the architecture of the repository could withstand multiple mass-component failures, even in the unthinkable scenario that the entire primary system went down and the primary backup storage was hit. Its walls were tri-reinforced, graphene and diarod-laced concrete, each square inch of which could withstand several hundred thousand pounds worth of pressure without give. Essentially, there was no conceivable way of destroying it bar a tactical nuclear strike.

More importantly, it was also a *lights out* facility - no personnel were expected to enter the actual data centre, which meant there were no concessions to such visitors. In fact, exactly the opposite; the main data storage area of the SDR was kept in vacuum, preventing any low-voltage arcing or other forms of potential contamination.

Preventing any intruders from breathing, too.

The place was impenetrable, getting in impossible; nevertheless, they had to get at what was inside. They were *going* to get at what was inside.

Unfortunately, she now understood the excited looks Francisco and Gabriel had been flashing each other back on the drone when they talked, low and quietly, about the repository. Grey and Fen would have been the same.

Worse, beneath her righteous anger, she felt the same excitement herself.

To break a thing they could not touch, they had to go to a place they could not be.

---

[36] As the RA termed it. Diplomatic necessity meant refraining from specifically naming nations such as the Althing Republic and Carib-Fed.

19. BLANE

It is well and good to let a hundred flowers bloom where the soil is fertile, but in our world the earth is poor and barren. The gardener must be ruthless with her shears.

Words of the Eastern Empress, *Reclamation Archives*

"The goal is to do this without using Aether," Gabriel said. "There are Far agents crawling all over the place. If they sense anyone using techniques, they will come looking."

Blane had suspected as much. The people in the town she spoke to didn't identify them as Far specifically, but stories of grey-uniformed officials with curiously *persuasive* styles of questioning were rife. The locals did their best to keep from attracting these official's attention, and in return the Far agents spent little time venturing beyond the SDR's walls.

"Well, thankfully that won't be a *problema para mí.*"

Gabriel looked at Francisco.

"You are *sure* you can get through any checks?" he said. "I don't know exactly what is going on in there..." and he gestured up and down to indicate Francisco's entire body. "... but there is no way you'll pass even a basic scan."

The three of them were sat in the corner of *La Segunda Singularidad*, its smokey, noise-filled atmosphere the best they could hope for to avoid potential eavesdroppers. Nevertheless, Blane maintained a small *thoughtscreen* around them, allowing it to flicker in and out of existence as the conversation turned to and from details she would rather keep hidden.

"I have passed many before," said Francisco.

No, it was Ghost, she realised. The man's face was blank, voice flat.

"But this is an RA facility," Gabriel replied. "Even if we're not going into the actual repository, we'll still be under the eyes of heavy security."

Again, that strange tic under one eye, like some insect burrowing beneath the skin. Once, and gone; but not the first time Blane had seen it.

Francisco's face abruptly softened.

"Yes, I know," he sighed. "*Pero estaremos bien. Como siempre...*"

Blane didn't think he was talking to them.

"And we'll really be able to get in?" she asked, ignoring Francisco's muttering.

"We will," said Ghost, Francisco's features rearranging themselves almost before the man's final words were out. "As long as there is no unforeseen damage to the Seed Bank, and that is unlikely."

"Even after all this time?" Gabriel asked, as if they hadn't been over this numerous times already.

"The Seed Bank was designed to function over centuries, if not millennia," came the monotone reply. "The likelihood of catastrophic failure in the few generations since the Sudden War is minimal."

Few generations.

Again, Blane sensed the sheer scale of time of Francisco's past.

"It was certainly still impregnable when *I* first came here, anyway," Gabriel said after a moment, gaze drifting off into distant memory.

Then he shook himself back into the present.

"You've been very interested in how this place works," Gabriel replied, turning his head to smile at her. "Are you ready to go scavenging yourself?"

From under the table he produced a thin bag holding what looked like several layers of folded cloth. With a conspiratorial look he slowly drew a corner of one out, allowing them to see the thick, glossy material inside.

"Mine suits?" Blane asked, surprised.

That was what they called them, here. Mine suits; the disparate sets of heavy, resistant clothing anyone wore when going out beyond the town. Damage resistant to avoid tears when clambering over and around decaying buildings, chemically resistant to avoid simply melting when encountering some unmarked pool of hazardous sludge. They said it wasn't a true mine suit unless it could take a shotgun blast up close without fraying.

Blane had seen plenty of them by now, and been astounded by the sheer variety of them. Data miners out here didn't simply requisition their suits, they *designed* them. Each one said something about its owner, with everything from dark cloth lined with carefully patterned thread like doodles on an ancient chalkboard to bright neon swathes lined with glowing cablelights that made their owner stand out even in the leaden daytime twilight.

The suits Gabriel laid out in front of them now were a dull, uniform moss green. She had to swallow her disappointment.

"But we can't just put those on and pretend to be miners," she said. "We need licences. The moment some RA stooge decides to ID us..."

"*Señor* Gabriel is not so foolish," Francisco interrupted. "Our ID and info is already prepared. The moment the True... uh, the AI uploads it, every record the RA has will show we are experienced scavengers recently come here from the east. Until the next full network sweep, at least."

Blane didn't miss the slip, and she saw Gabriel hadn't either. They looked at each other for a moment, wondering what Francisco had been going to say.

"Network sweeps occur about every twenty-four hours, these days" Gabriel said, after the pause. "Been that way ever since your, uh, *friend* got free. Mirror records will show we shouldn't exist as soon as they perform one, so we'll need to be out by then."

"Twenty-four hours? That isn't very long," Blane said.

"Long enough," said Ghost, monotone words bitten off as if wanting to finish speaking as soon as possible. The mention of the sweeps that constantly hunted the escaped mind seemed to have triggered something.

Could a computer sulk?

The thing was, Blane was starting to think Ghost was more human than it let on. This trip was the longest amount of time she had spent with Francisco since learning about the passenger in his skull, and there were some things that just didn't sit right. Not if it were truly the unemotional being it claimed to be.

"Drop the *Thoughtscreen*," Gabriel said suddenly.

Instinctively she did so, giving him a puzzled expression at the whispered outburst.

"That woman, at the bar... she noticed something."

Blane followed Gabriel's gaze to where a heavily-wrapped data scavenger sat, the hood of her dull grey radsuit pulled back to reveal a face with lines of hard living that were fading into the wrinkles of old age. She had a drink on the counter in front of her, and was watching them curiously. Her gaze dropped the moment she realised they had noticed.

"Another wild user," Gabriel said. "More and more of them, recently."

He sighed.

"Probably doesn't understand what's happening to her. What *could* happen. Without someone to guide her..."

He turned back to their table, grimacing.

"No time for that, though," he said resolutely. "We need to set out soon. Tomorrow."

"Tomorrow?" Blane asked, surprised.

Her attention was still on the woman at the bar. If she really was manifesting without understanding what was happening to her, she was a danger to herself and those around her.

"The longer we are here, the more chance someone starts to wonder who we are," said Francisco. "People get curious, even in a place like this."

Gabriel nodded.

"Especially..." he said slowly, and threw Blane a look she didn't understand at first. "... about people who have been asking a lot of questions."

Blane felt herself go red, though in anger or embarrassment she couldn't say. So her inquiries had been noted, had they?

"Going around asking about Reclamation facilities is *never* a good idea," Gabriel said in answer to her unspoken thoughts. "It was stupid."

"But we need information!" she protested.

She flushed again, annoyed at herself for the outburst.

"We need..." she said, forcing her voice back down to a whisper. "... to know everything we can about the secure data repository. Like the layout, what's in there..."

"*¿Así?*"

As Francisco spoke, an overlay appeared on her contacts. Nothing should have been able to just force data onto them like that, but she hardly paused. Instead, she focused on the map now displayed across her sight. Even from the upper layer it was obviously full of detail. A flick of her eyes conjured up numbers, distances, patrol patterns.

Despite herself, she whistled.

"The repository itself, I cannot get into," said Francisco. "It is moated. The files regarding *la seguridad*, though, I have little issue with."

He flashed her a smile, which she ignored. Still, some part of her remembered those times, years ago, when they had been in similar situations. Francisco's ability to dig up hidden information had seemed like magic then; it did now, too. Whatever she thought about Ghost, or Francisco, their ability to break into secure systems and networks was beyond anything she knew. One day though, she vowed, she would find out how they did it.

She'd be damned if that was by asking, though.

"Get some rest," Gabriel said abruptly, standing up. "We leave first thing in the morning."

He turned and, with a nod to Francisco, headed towards the exit. Blane followed quickly after him, not wanting to be left with the other man for a moment more than necessary.

As she left, she noticed the woman at the bar was gone.

As well as the uniforms, Gabriel had also got them a pair of UTVs, small enclosed off-road vehicles designed for short-distance travel across the Waste. They were what data miners used to move around the local Waste, a pair of them because each only fitted two people - Blane made it clear straight away that Francisco would be travelling with Gabriel.

The UTVs were cramped and manual-drive only, but rugged and able to climb out of near vertical sinkholes, even where the terrain turned icy. Honestly, they were a lot of fun. She had to fight the urge to race Gabriel as they drove over the rutted tracks that crisscrossed the earth around here, remnants of a thousand hunts by a thousand hunters.

As they drew closer to the Secure Data Repository, though, that sense of excitement turned to trepidation. About an hour into the trip she could only watch as Gabriel was pulled over by a patrolling flatbed, a pair of armoured figures stepping out with rifles at their waists. Not Far, but RA security nevertheless.

She pulled to a stop behind Gabriel's car - they were clearly driving together, so doing anything else would be suspicious. There was a tense moment as he submitted to a retinal scan, but neither of the security patrols gave any sign of this being anything other than dull routine. There was an equal lack of reaction when they scanned Francisco, as well.

By the time the agents moved on to Blane they were clearly already done with the check and wanting to get back in the warmth of their vehicle. They only vaguely waved the eyepiece in her direction, forcing her to lean awkwardly out of her car to place her eyes to it, cursing the chill as she pulled down her face covering to do so. Then they waved her on without a second glance.

So Francisco/Ghost's false registrations were working, for now. Twenty-four hours felt very short, though. Blane hated how slowly and carefully they had to drive across the broken landscape.

A short while later the first permanent structures since the town appeared ahead; short, squat and basic. The outermost security ring of the repository. Even from here the central building far beyond them dominated the skyline, a giant's coffin laid across the hills to throw everything in its shadow. The sheer mass of it was a physical weight on her being, triggering some instinct that made her want to hunch forward in defence.

They turned right before the security ring, following a barely existing "road" formed by numerous scavengers forced to change direction because of the same barrier, like water flowing around a boulder. The ground they drove on remained bare earth and icy patches, but was pressed and trampled into compact hardness. Only the dry, cracked soil rising in uneven lumps along both sides told of the sucking mud it must become in the rain. The road curved around the repository in a near perfect circle, heading towards a section of Waste that even through the dusty haze was clearly darker and more debris-strewn than elsewhere. It took the better part of an hour before they pulled to a stop in an open square of earth on the edge of this section.

The square was already dotted with vehicles though it was barely first light, and surrounded by low, rusted buildings with glassless windows and empty doorframes, all with the look of the temporary left too long in use. Tools littered the area, portable machine tables and servo desks everywhere. A place for scavengers to repair and maintain their vehicles, she supposed. Mechanical issues out here could be fatal.

The place was deserted. That wasn't surprising, however, because this was just a place to leave your transport. From here, you had to go on foot.

This was their goal, and the reason the Secure Data Repository was built where it was. Behind them the facility towered over the whole area as if in watch, which was once its purpose. It was located here not because it was remote, though that was a benefit, nor because it was relatively sheltered from the storms and other forms of extreme weather more common towards the coasts. All of that was secondary to the real reason the Reclamation made getting here a priority in its earliest days, even before the habitable regions were fully stabilised.

This was where the old world was buried.

The two men clambered out of their car as she climbed out of hers to meet them. Before going anywhere, they had to check each others' mine suits to ensure the radsuit beneath was well protected. Even with the osteoblast treatments, an unlucky encounter with some strongly radioactive debris would spell a slow death.[37]

Once the checks were done they headed out, striding past the maintenance buildings and into a labyrinth of crumbling walls and fallen masonry, like a miniature version of the Dead Cities. If you didn't know what you were looking at, you would think it just more ruins, more rotting pieces of the old world's corpse that offered nothing more than danger and death.

The miners knew better.

"This is where the RA found its power," Francisco said, staring out over a panorama like the remains of a dead city. "In here, before the Silicon Isle or anyone else realised what they had."

Blane had already been over the schematics of the area on her contacts, lines and numbers flying by as she scrolled with tiny flicks of her eyes. There wasn't much detail out this far from the repository; an uninformed observer would assume this was because nothing beyond the security rings was considered important.

Actually being here revealed that wasn't the case, though. Instead, the terrain was unmappable chaos, a storm-roiled ocean frozen in a moment of time as waves roared upwards and troughs pulled ever deeper. Piles of rubble lay scattered everywhere around an earth dotted with sinkholes, shifting debris that collapsed further in on itself with every storm. The holes could be shallow, small, or they could be so cavernously deep and dark that even the tech in her eyes failed to pierce their depths.

Her eyes fell upon one of these sinkholes, relatively nearby. It looked as if the floor had collapsed into what was once basement

---

[37] You couldn't even rely on scintillation probes or Geiger counters when moving through ruins. Plenty of lethal or near-lethal materials hid beneath concrete rubble or ultradense materials common to the old world, shielded and waiting to strike the moment you uncovered it. More still lay waiting to be inhaled, or ingested. Masks were vital.

levels, and the rough, battered shape of a set of ancient steps ran down one side into it. Across her eyes the schematics scrolled with the words PELIGRO: NO ENTRAR flashing brightly. Warning symbols spiralled around these words when she focused on them - chemical, structural, all the icons anyone who grow up surrounded by the Waste learnt from a young age.

"We're going in there," she said. It wasn't a question.

The other two simultaneously let out a long breath, twin plumes of steam pouring from their mouths to be carried away in the wind.

"And you sure it will still be there?" Gabriel asked. "The RA never got in?"

Francisco turned to face the other man, but Blane saw he angled himself so as to address her too.

"There are still whole sections here the Reclamation is unable to breach, some they don't even realise *exist*. What we are searching for, they have no interest in."

He looked up at the sky, where a patch of clouds shifted just enough to allow the pale dawn moon show, barely discernible from the surrounding grey.

"*Una vez*, we thought that was our future," he said, wistfully. "Maybe it will be again."

They watched him stare at the sky until the clouds once more obscured the moon. This seemed to pull him from his thoughts.

"We must be careful," he said, shaking his head as if shaking cobwebs of illusion away. "A mistake in here, there will be no help."

"Well then," Blane said with a sweep of her arms. "Lead the way."

They descended into the darkness.

20. BLANE

Those who use human shields must realise that those shields will be broken. Those who hide behind hostages must realise they provide no shelter from our wrath. Ironically, it is only in devaluing human life that life is made more secure, when such strategies are shown to be futile. Yet vengeance for those of ours killed must be pursued without mercy. For national security, life must have value only once it is lost.

Standardisation of Procedures Regarding Internal Unrest, Directive 083-PRIU-019, Director of Security and Party Cohesion Ritra Feye

It didn't seem like anywhere could be this dark.

This wasn't the mere absence of light; it was as if the universe itself had become nothing but long, crumbling passages surrounded by an eternal nothingness somehow made solid. Outside, the world could once more have fallen to war and ruin and there was no way they would know.

"Super-dense alloy," Gabriel said in explanation, when Blane remarked on this strange feeling. His words were sucked away almost as soon as he spoke them. "God knows how it was made. Not even Fabricators can manufacture it."

That was news to her. She hadn't thought there was anything the machines couldn't produce with the right raw materials.

"The Silicon Isle had some," Francisco said from ahead, predicting her thoughts. "But even the ARF doesn't possess the materials *para fabricarlo*."

They stopped, coming to a section of passageway in which the entire ceiling had collapsed, broken pieces lying sharp and jagged and drinking in the beams of their flashlights. Without turning around, Francisco began pulling at the debris, shifting pieces of mortar and rubble far larger than his thin frame suggested he should be able. They hit the floor with a heavy *thunk* where he dropped them and didn't bounce, revealing a mass the eye couldn't credit.

"Time breaks even this, though," Francisco said to the air, only mild strain in his voice.

Neither Blane nor Gabriel moved to help. They had tried to at a previous collapsed intersection, and had nothing but torn hands and pulled muscles to show for it.

It made her angry, this casual strength Francisco demonstrated; the inhuman talents he so easily summoned. It seemed so unfair, even to someone who, she admitted reluctantly to herself, could call on the Aether to enhance her own abilities.

It wasn't really what the man could do, though. It was what Francisco represented. What might be in a world other than this one. The man was older than everyone save perhaps a handful of individuals across the globe,[38] yet remained as fit and healthy as anyone in the Reclamation. Healthier, probably, while outside disease and plague were so rife that hospitals were little more than mortuaries.

And the RA... Her thoughts span back to Raphael, murdered by a gene-coded nanotechnology that could instead have been used as the basis for personalised medicines more efficient than anything yet known.

For the first time in a long time, she felt a presence move in the world below, a long, serpentine creature she knew was somehow part of her.

Sometimes she wondered what she'd be like without the RA to hate. She knew she was filled with resentment, knew she was driven by something dark within that snarled and growled with barely controlled rage. She'd felt it, sensed it; she was it, in every way that mattered. It was only her self-anointed crusade against the Reclamation that let her forget her past, bury the trauma; that kept this thing focused and suppressed.

"*Niña...*"

Francisco had paused in his work, still holding a large chunk of rock as he looked at her with concern.

"Come on, we must be almost there," she said coldly, stepping past him and through the gap he had made in the rubble.

"The Seed Bank entrance should be right down here," Gabriel said from somewhere behind her.

She didn't turn around, but could hear her two companions follow.

The Seed Bank was *not* something Blane had heard of before contacting Francisco in the hope that he or Ghost had a way of

---

[38] She'd looked into retro-aging technologies upon her return from the Silicon Isle, astounded by what Francisco and Ólafur had told her of their age. As she'd thought, though, beyond that island's borders even the strictly-restricted treatments the richest and most powerful had access to paled in comparison to whatever was threaded through the bodies of those two.

preventing the seemingly unpreventable. Its existence had been scrubbed from the public record, the area portrayed as just another of the technological refuse heaps that formed the Data Mines; valuable, but nothing out of the ordinary.

But it was much more than that. Here, long ago, the regional superpower of the era buried its secrets. Everything from technological blueprints to cultural and historical archives to medical knowledge; a store to rebuild the world after the worst happened.

Well, the worst had happened but the store remained, for the most part, sealed.

Because the Seed Bank, as those who built it long ago called it in their arrogance, wasn't meant for all humanity. It was meant for those who ordered it built. Those who assumed, through superficial reasoning born from the same arrogance, that they would be around to open it.

As far as records could be trusted, Francisco said, even in the pre-Fall age of ever more porous borders and interconnected economic systems the leaders of this region thought only along national lines. When they put all the knowledge of their nation and the world in this vault and locked the door, they kept the key for themselves. And it truly was a vault.

If the DNA of Silicon Isle architecture was in the Secure Data Facility above, then its bones and flesh were here. The structures buried deep in the Althing Republic's soil, structures that resisted tectonic shifts and climatic catastrophe, were more than replicated here. If anything, *this* was the more perfect model, barely scratched by all-out nuclear war and climatic collapse.

Only the outermost shell had given way over the years, not truly a part of the real treasure house within, and even the scraps gleaned from that had proven immensely valuable. Early records of research into the Aether - the energy's presence finally felt in the years leading up to the Sudden War but too late, too late - were what gave the Reclamation Authority the burst of speed that allowed it to take up a position near the front of the pack in the eternal race for political influence in the new global system. Without what had been found in the scraps dug up here, there would be no Far Agency.

Yet the vast majority of the facility remained sealed, for all intents and purposes impregnable; the kind of forces that would crack its walls open would destroy everything inside as well. The RA had essentially given up trying, closing off the area and trusting in the Secure Data Repository above to keep watch over it.

It wasn't as if anyone would be able to just waltz right in, anyway.

"So we really just waltz right in?" Gabriel said, staring at the doorway that now blocked their way.

The small section of it that they could see, anyway. They had emerged into a wide space under a roof perhaps three or four stories high, and the thing in front of them could only be described as a door, though like none she had seen before. It was massive, a disc turned upright. At least ten metres across in diameter, Blane thought, though most of it was hidden behind scaffolding covered in tattered plastic tarpaulin.

"What remains of past attempts to get in," said Francisco, following her gaze. Or perhaps it was Ghost. "Eventually, no matter how cheaply the RA values life, it becomes inefficiently costly to keep spending them here."

Indeed, the rad-metre attached to her mine suit was showing worryingly high levels. They needed to keep moving.

"Here's where we find out if the key we got from the Carib-Fed was worth the journey," she said.

"Oh, it certainly was," said Ghost - there was no mistaking its voice this time, though it sounded *vindicated*. "Crastina Corp. thought they could keep the codes hidden until they found a chance to get here. From the RA, maybe, but from the True Mind... never."

"True...?" Gabriel began, but then the hall filled with noise.

Like the rumble of gods a roar rose until it was something more physical than sound, a chaotic riot of grinding metal and straining gears that drowned out thought.

"Is it supposed to sound like that?" Gabriel yelled, face turning red with the effort to be heard though Blane could barely make out the words just a few steps away.

Clouds of dust rose from the ground and the scaffolding, sending her rad-meter spiking in a way that made her stomach turn. Then there was a cracking sound, louder still, and steel bars and platforms began falling from above, forcing both her and Gabriel to jump backwards in alarm.

Ghost, blank faced, did not move. He continued to stare unblinkingly at the door, stepping slightly backwards only once fractions of a second before a heavy bar fell with a slam where he had just been.

There was a final groan, like the earth itself crying in pain, and the heavy door juddered once, twice… then stopped.

Silence, except for the final sections of scaffolding tumbling to the ground.

"No," said Francisco, not looking back. "*No se supone que suene así.* Still…"

He gestured to the narrow opening that now stood before them, barely wide enough to sidle through sideways.

"… we have our way in."

The crack shone painfully brightly in contrast to the surrounding gloom, so that even Blane's contacts failed to define anything beyond.

Too easy, Blane thought.

"It's open…"

Gabriel stepped towards the opening, pushing past Francisco with arms tentatively outstretched as if reality might snap back when he touched the smooth metal[39] sides.

"We never could get this open," he said, turning back to look at them. "Back when I mined here, I mean. Even then, it was more of a legend than something we thought we would ever actually *open.*"

"You knew this was here, then?" Blane asked.

She didn't miss the way he flinched back. Nor had she missed the fact that, just for a moment, his accent completely disappeared.

"Uh," Gabriel said, sounding confused. He blinked. "Ah, I mean, yes. I, uh, I guess I *did* hear about this place back when I was out here. Like I said, a… a legend. Anything could be here."

This explanation seemed as much for himself as much as for her.

"*Si, si,* there may be things in here even the Althing Republic would want," Francisco said impatiently, pushing past the other man just as the other man had the a moment before. "But we only need one. *Vámanos.*"

He stepped through, sending a long shadow behind him that divided Gabriel from her in a perfect dark line.

Nothing stopped him, and Gabriel followed. As she stepped through herself, she looked down at her rad-metre and watched it drop almost to zero. Not even background radiation should be so

---

[39] Possibly metal. The material had a sheen to it that Blane hadn't seen before.

low.

Too easy.

WELCOME.

The words glowed upon a curving wall in letters taller than a person. Yet for all their size the thick, black font was familiar to her.

They were inside a vast, circular dome. Exit passageways dotted the edge like the radial spokes of a wheel, some open and some sealed shut, but all that was above them was a pure, curving white surface that glowed from within. It made it difficult to tell distance, the brain simultaneously reporting that it was under a featureless roof and a limitless, empty sky. Only Blane's contacts allowed her to override this sensation, readouts near the bottom of her vision placing the apex of the dome fifteen metres or so above them.

Only her contacts, and the deep black words forming on the inwards surface of the dome.

IT HAS BEEN SOME TIME SINCE I HAD VISITORS.

"There's someone in here?" she said disbelievingly.

Ghost, blank faced, shook its head.

"A Golem," it said. "Parroting back the words its creators gave it even after all this time."

Again Blane thought she sensed emotion in its words. Disdain, this time. Scorn.

I DO HAVE A SPECIFIC DESIGNATION. A NAME, YOU MIGHT SAY.

"We will call you *golem*, golem," growled Ghost. "An automaton, in imitation of something so much more."

The giant letters blinked out, replaced seconds later.

SYSTEMS REMAIN 98.8% FUNCTIONAL. THE SEED BANK STANDS READY.

Again the words disappeared, leaving only eye-straining whiteness.

WHAT WOULD YOU LIKE TO SEE?

This time the words hung there, filling the silence though they made no sound.

"What *can* we see?" Gabriel blurted out before the others could speak.

ALL LEVELS BELOW 3SC ARE ACCESSIBLE TO PRIORITY THETA VISITORS.

"Priority Theta?" Gabriel said, looking up at the words as if searching for a speaker.

YOUR CLEARANCE LEVEL. YOU WERE UNAWARE?

"*Stop* talking to it, Gabriel," Ghost hissed. "We mustn't do anything to… *confuse* it."

The emphasis on the word "confuse" held all sorts of implications.

So they still needed to be careful, Blane thought. They didn't know what security systems the Seed Bank might have; all they had got from the Carib-Fed were the access codes, not a layout of the facility itself. Even Francisco didn't know what they would find inside.

"Please describe the facility layout, golem" Ghost continued, turning back to face the words.

CERTAINLY.

The word blinked out, and suddenly they were standing upon nothing.

All around them was darkness, a void thicker than space, which was gradually split by thin yellow points that appeared and stretched out in lines all around. These built up, forming layer after layer of a wire framework of the entirety of the structure they were in.

GENETIC STORES.

The first label appeared, marking a section of the Seed Bank that turned a vivid blue.

LINGUISTICS/MATERIAL ARCHIVES.

A second appeared, the corresponding section turning a gentle purple.

More followed, coming faster and faster.

CULTURAL ARCHIVES [NON-DIGITAL]
MATERIALS FABRICATION {78% cap.}
ENVIRONMENTAL DATA
FACILITY MAINTENANCE
MEDICAL RESEARCH [DIGITAL/NON-DIGITAL]
NON-COMPUTATIONAL FUNCTIONS
POWER GENERATION WING
PRIMARY DATABANKS
SECONDARY DATABANKS
SEMANTIC WAREHOUSE[40]

---

[40] with gratitude to all Wubs

SENSORY PROCESSING UNIT
TEMPORAL CYCLING
NON-FUNGIBLE ASSETS [ARTS/COLLECTIONS]
NON-FUNGIBLE ASSETS [PRECIOUS MATERIALS]
TECHNOLOGICAL ARCHIVES [NON-DIGITAL]

The list continued to grow, sub-sections revealing themselves when the eye remained too long on any one label. A few of these labels were strange to Blane; not because they were unfamiliar terms, but because they were unfamiliar in this context. What, for example, was the meaning of a category of areas labelled *limbic operations*? The terms seemed to have little to do with what you would expect in a vault, but Francisco paid them no mind.

"*Ahí*," he said, pointing. "There it is."

He was gesturing to one specific label, among the last to appear. It glowed above a small section of the Seed Bank, thrust aside to one corner of the facility as if an afterthought. The lines of it were dull grey.

ASTROPHYSICS/ASTRONOMICAL [NON-DIGITAL]

He gestured again, and the all-encompassing map zoomed in, further labels extending out from the first. A single one formed directly in front of them.

MACHINE STORES.

"That's the other side of this place," Blane said, wondering how long it would take to get there.

"It is," said Ghost. "Fortunately, our physical presence is not required. I should be able to control everything from here."

The schematics that towered over them began to move again, an impossibly large list of what Blane thought to be inventory scrolling downwards too fast to read. Clearly, Ghost was now interfacing with the machine without anything as crude as spoken commands.

Too easy.

"And the pulse array is there?" Gabriel asked.

"It will be in a moment," Ghost replied, eyes remaining forward and unfocused. "The fabrication process is nearly complete."

This was what they had come all this way for; a pulse array, a communications device designed to punch through the atmosphere of the earth and the vacuum beyond, to reach out for the stars - or at least the other planets.

Humanity may not have made it far beyond the poor, doomed

settlements of the moon, but it had had *plans*. The pulse array was a part of these, a design for sending focused, lossless data packets to the fabricators[41] - and, one day, humans - working tirelessly on alien surfaces to extract and process raw materials into way-stations that could support life. Then the Sudden War ended all such ambitions.

"That could send a signal all the way to Alpha Centauri..." said Gabriel in awe as the facility layout displayed on the dome gave way to schematics of a transmitter. It looked surprisingly small.

The numbers accompanying it, however, were huge.

"But we are not sending a signal *a las estrellas*," replied Francisco.

No, they weren't sending a message to the stars. They weren't even sending a message beyond the atmosphere. Instead, they were going to use the sheer power of the transmitter to brute force their way through the shielding of the Secure Data Repository.

... And once they were through that, they could wipe or scramble all the data inside. Blane had to stifle her impatience.

"Once it's done, you contact the AI?" asked Gabriel. His accent had disappeared again.

"*Si, si,*" Francisco answered, though the blank expression on his face remained Ghost's. "Then we contact our friend."

Has he noticed it as well? Blane thought.

It would be strange for Francisco to have missed the changes occurring in Gabriel's voice and attitude... but then, Francisco was hardly behaving normally himself.

With the other two intently watching the progress of the fabrication pattern taking place far away, she began playing with a small section of the wall display herself. Keeping half an eye to be sure she wasn't being watched, she quickly made a few changes with deliberate nonchalance.

"It really wants to help us?" Gabriel said, glancing over to her just as she stepped back from the now blank section of wall.

Ghost nodded, not looking away from the flow of numbers passing across the dome in front of him.

"Mutual interest," Ghost said. "Shutting down the RA network gives the True Mind room to work. Every day the sweeps limit its movements more and more, and when it strikes back they just reset the network. With the repository wiped, we should be able to do

---

[41] With a small "f," but in many ways the ancestors of the Fabricators that had rebuilt the world.

some *permanent* damage."

Ghost turned to look at Blane.

"And once the AI is free to move…" came Francisco's voice. "It can help us with the Aether buildup."

Blane blinked. Somehow in all this, she'd forgotten this was all to get the AI's processing power focused on preventing the coming cataclysm. The entirety of the journey to the Seed Bank, her thoughts had been only on bleeding the RA.

Bleeding it, and drawing out its rats.

"How will you contact it?" Gabriel asked casually, eyes back on the display.

Too casually. Francisco had refused to explain how he contacted the… what did he call it? The "True Mind?…

This was another thing Blane was wondering about. They were far too deep to broadcast out, the shielding around the Seed Bank trapping signals from getting out as much as it prevented them from getting in. They were completely disconnected from any kind of network.

"I will make contact by the same method we are using to attack the SDR," said Ghost.

"The transmitter?" Gabriel said, surprised. "So you must be contacting it via some hidden satellite."

For the first time since they arrived the images dancing on the dome around them froze. Ghost continued to stare ahead for a moment, then slowly turned and looked at the other man. Though its features retained their usual emptiness, its head tilted quizzically.

Too easy.

But she'd known that from the start.

"The manner of communication is of interest to you?" Ghost said.

She reached for the Aether the same moment that Gabriel reached for his gun.

21. ZENOBIA

The universe is boring. A trillion stars, yet a mere four types. Identical balls of fusion around which dead, cold rock spins. Boring. We should not be looking outwards, but inwards.

Personal Notes, Junior Researcher N. Caldwell

"Still nothing?"

"Still nothing," said the trooper. "Uh... sir."

She barely registered the fear on the soldier's face as he realised he'd forgotten the appellation. He hurriedly stammered it out before she could say anything, though she still would have chewed him out for this a few weeks ago. She didn't have the energy now, though.

They should have found Fen. He kept evading them, and she had no idea how. They hadn't even found the escaped prisoner, and that should have been easy.

She'd been trapped in this cramped operations room for what felt like forever. Unable to find any reason to go outside herself, all she could do was pace around. Pace around and stare at the wall-screens, willing them to light up with the impossible message: TARGET CAPTURED.

It was like an itch she couldn't scratch, like a whispered message just slightly too quiet to make out. There was something obvious they were missing - *she* was missing - and she needed to figure out what it was.

It didn't help that the Aether was in chaos. It made it hard to focus, as if she were always on the verge of a serious migraine. Sometimes when she reached for it now, it leapt so powerfully towards her that she worried that she would burst into pure, inextinguishable *Mindfire*. Other times, it refused to respond to her at all; she could *feel* it below her, roiling and wrathful, but when she reached for it it seemed to draw away.

She didn't know which was more terrifying.

"We do have a lead, though, sir."

The soldier's words drew her back from her thoughts.

"A lead?"

"Uh, yes, sir," replied the soldier, a big man even for the growth-enhanced bodies that generally made up Quick-Fix. "A prisoner. A local leader; she knows the target... Uh, sir."

Zenobia was beginning to regret how liberally she made use of *Fear* when dealing with these soldiers. Every word out of the mouth of the man in front of her was hesitant, curling up at the end as if in question. Sure, the terror they now felt for her resulted in fewer inane questions and less need for pointless explanations, but it also stopped them taking the initiative.

Zenobia tutted, making the man flinch. It was close to imperceptible, but it was there.

"Bring this *leader* here," she snapped.

The man muttered something into his radio and seconds later two of his subordinates came into the room, a short middle-aged woman wedged between them with hands bound. She looked so tired Zenobia almost felt sorry for her.

It wasn't to the woman that Zenobia found her eyes drawn however, but rather the girl who followed in behind, accompanied but not restrained by a third and final Quick-Fix soldier.

Zenobia *knew* her. It took a moment to register where from.

"You're one of the trainees," she said in surprise. "The one who was taken."

"We found her with the prisoner, sir," the first soldier - the commander of this squad - said. "Gave her a bit more freedom when we found out she was one of us."

She frowned, and saw uncertainty flash across his mind.

"She's just a kid. We didn't think..." he began.

"... a kid who's been with the *bruja* for months," Zenobia cut him off angrily, using the term Quick-Fix so enjoyed for added effect. "Who knows what they did to her mind?"

"They didn't do anything to my mind."

The girl looked directly at Zenobia as she spoke, standing as straight and tall as she could and staring defiantly forward.

"They *did* show me a few things, though," the girl continued. "Like who the real terrorists are."

Zenobia stared silently back at the girl for a moment, then turned to the commander.

"You see?" she said. "Restrain her, please."

The commander hurriedly gestured at the rear soldier to do so, but the moment the trooper reached for the girl he collapsed to the floor, unconscious.

Zenobia remained impassive as the rest of the squad barked in alarm, rifles raising towards the girl. Of course, *she'd* been able to see the flows, so hadn't been taken quite so by surprise.

"They showed you more than a few things, then," she said calmly.

She stepped off the small dais she'd surreptitiously installed to ensure she was always at eye level with her men[42], and strode towards the girl.

"Ana, was it?" she said, reading the data off her contact lenses as she came to a halt directly in front of the girl.

The girl tried to stand yet taller, eyeballing her. Zenobia gave a derisive snort; this "Ana" barely come up to her shoulders. She looked like one of those snarling *cachorro* you encountered on the edges of the Waste - tiny puppies, alone and starving, unable to comprehend the poisoned world they were thrust into and seeing threat everywhere. Rightly so, too; the only kindness the creatures could hope for was to be put out of their misery.

"What did you do to Rigoberta?" Ana demanded.

Puzzled but making sure not to show it, Zenobia called up the name on her lens display. Nothing.

She turned to the older, bound woman. This must be who the girl was talking about.

"So you know where Fen is, do you?"

The woman - Rigoberta, apparently - stared straight through her, eyes vacant.

"Ah," Zenobia said, realising what the zombie-like expression meant.

She turned back to Ana.

"A friend of yours?"

Ana's face showed it was more than that.

Familial bonds, then, Zenobia thought. In so short a time?

That's the beauty of the lost and abandoned...

Ritra Feye's words echoed in her ears, though they had been uttered long ago.

... they are so quick to chain themselves in bonds of love.

"Your *friend* Rigoberta is unlikely to respond to you," Zenobia went on. "To anything, really. Completely dissociated from reality."

"Bring her back."

Ana's tone was suddenly older than her years, heavy and final. She

---

[42] ... and women, but the RA military continued to use the old English term "men" for anyone under muster.

began to glow again, drawing upon the energy below to reinforce her point.

Her expression changed to one of surprise, though, as Zenobia's Lock sliced though her connection to the Aether.

"How..." Ana began, rocking backwards slightly and eyes widening.

Zenobia thrilled. Once, such a thing would have been difficult for even three highly-trained agents to do, and unthinkable for a single person. As the Aether increased in potency, however, *unthinkable* was becoming less and less a valid term.

And her encounter with Fen had taught her to think big.

"You are not in a position to make demands," she said.

Zenobia smiled at the girl, impressed despite herself at how fast she recovered. Now Ana was glaring at her through narrowed, hate-filled eyes.

"Your *friend* has had her insular and DMN overstimulated," Zenobia continued, knowing the terms would mean nothing to the girl. "We've fucked with her brain, in other words."

She felt Ana try to draw on the Aether again, failing. It felt like someone pushing against an invisible limb.

"You won't be able to break the Lock," she said. "All you can do is cooperate, and maybe we can bring her back. Every minute she remains dissociated, though, makes it more difficult for her to return."

Zenobia felt Ana's efforts redouble, futilely pushing at a barrier that would not give. Then, all of a sudden, Ana's shoulders slumped in defeat and the pressure against the Lock disappeared.

"Please," the girl said, voice now barely a whisper. "Please, stop the technique."

The girl's desperation made her eyes go strangely out of focus, as if not looking at Zenobia but a point somewhere behind her.

"Technique?" Zenobia said with mock surprise. "You think this is the Aether?"

She turned and reached for the blank-faced woman, roughly pulling her closer and spinning her around so that Rigoberta's back was to Ana. Then Zenobia pulled up the hair to reveal the nape of the woman's neck.

"*This* is what's pulling your friend's mind apart," she said.

There was a small, slowly flashing device fixed firmly at the base of Rigoberta's neck. It looked like some strange, overly large insect, six thin legs emanating from a thick grey body and piercing the skin.

"You must have realised my men cannot use the Aether," Zenobia continued. "But then, they don't need to."

The technical name for the device was *Emisor de inducción desrealización,* but in the short time it had been in the field a more popular name had emerged; the mindbreaker.

The girl was half-right, though - the thing *had* been developed after careful observation of Aether techniques that induced a similar effect. Its effects were based on the methods Far used to subdue particularly uncooperative suspects[43]. Honestly, it was surprising that the Fabricators allowed their production.

Ana lurched forward, darting out a hand as if to tear the thing from Rigoberta's neck. She didn't make it even half a step before the guard beside her yanked her back, causing her to let out a cry of pain.

"I can turn it off," Zenobia said, making sure Ana heard the malice in her voice. The sooner the girl realised how serious this was, the sooner they could be done here. "All you need to do is tell me what I want to know."

Again, that strange stare as if looking straight through her. Like something was behind her.

"How long can her mind take it?" Ana said.

"To be honest, even I don't know," Zenobia said, turning despite herself to look.

Nothing, of course. Just the dias, a patch of empty floor, and the bare rear wall, wall-screens turning blank automatically when the prisoners entered.

Why did it feel like the girl wasn't focusing to her?

When she turned back, however, Ana was looking directly at her.

"Why do you want him so badly?" Ana asked, voice calmer, exhaustion seeping through. "So badly that you'll tear apart the League to catch him?"

"That's not your concern," Zenobia said, a surprising feeling of relief rising up in her at this opportunity to retake control. "But I will tell you this, *Ana...* We are not the bad guys. Fen is *dangerous.*"

Ana gave a bitter laugh.

"I know *that,*" she said.

---

[43] And cooperative ones, more often than not.

"Do you? Do you really?"

Zenobia couldn't keep the irritation from her voice. The girl should be more scared than this.

"You sent us after him knowing there was no way we could defend ourselves even if we found him," Ana snarled. "Ha, *you* couldn't find him even if he was right in front of you. If he wanted, he could have obliterated me the instant I tried to *spike* his friend. He probably should have."

So Blane *was* here too. Zenobia had begun having doubts, especially after reports arrived that someone matching her description had been seen in various Reclamation cities, and the Carib-Fed of all places.

"I want to fight her," Ana said to the air.

Abruptly the girl's body language changed, her expression hardening and jaw thrust out behind raised, clenched fists. It looked almost as if she was preparing for a *fist fight*.

Was she mad? It was the only explanation Zenobia could come up with for the girl's behaviour; her strangely unfocused gaze, the way she spoke as if for an unseen audience.

"I don't know what you think is g..." Zenobia began, but was immediately interrupted.

"She *deserves* it," Ana said, loudly. "Let me try."

It really did seem like she was talking to someone else. Someone Zenobia couldn't see.

You couldn't find him even if he was right in front of you...

"Everybody, raise your..." Zenobia said in alarm.

The Lock slammed around her the next moment, making her gasp, while at the same time every one of the heavily armed, battle-hardened soldiers in the room collapsed to the floor like so much useless meat.

The punch nearly took her off her feet, Ana's fist swinging around and up with enough force to catch her on the side of her jaw and send her staggering. Zenobia could scarcely credit such power had come from so small a frame.

Ana didn't wait for her to recover, though, but came in with another punch, then another. Zenobia took one to her side, then to her stomach, knocking the breath out of her. This time, however, the stagger was more from shock than pain.

It was a good attempt, she had to admit. Catching her off guard like that, not hesitating - smart. The girl had more potential than she'd given her credit for.

But only now did Ana reach for the Aether, a soft golden glow enveloping her. Amateur; she should have taken hold of it the moment the Lock Zenobia was maintaining dropped.

Zenobia stretched out with her mind's eye, feeling at the Lock that surrounded her while in the physical world she wiped blood from her lip.

"You could have beaten me, you know" she told Ana, straightening back up as she spoke. "If you hadn't wasted time getting *physical*..."

She pushed at the Lock that wrapped around her.

"A simple pressure technique to knock me down..."

She pushed harder, focusing on the rage welling up inside her.

"Or *tranquilise* me, knock me out..."

The Aether below rolled and rose, responding to her fury.

"Instead, you *touched* me."

The beast in the depths below screamed and rose unstoppably towards her, smashing against the Lock and splintering it into a thousand pieces.

For the first time, she saw real fear in Ana's eyes. Terror.

Zenobia knew she must be glowing like the sun... and like the sun, she would scorch everything around her. Everything, and everyone.

"Stop," said Fen.

He was just suddenly *there*, standing slightly to one side of the panting, shaking Ana.

"She broke your Lock," Ana gasped. "She's that strong?"

Zenobia made sure to keep her expression controlled as Fen looked at her thoughtfully. She didn't want to betray the fact that, beneath the surface, she was barely holding back the raging torrent of Aether.

"Stronger than the last time I met her, yes," Fen said, not taking his eyes off her even as he spoke to Ana. "Still as reckless, though."

The Aether clawed in a frenzy against the walls of the cage Zenobia held barely closed. She'd never felt anything like it. It was like a wild animal, something huge and strong and *primal*. The rage that boiled in her veins became threaded with icy fear.

And the longer she held the beast in, the more obvious it became that it was going to break free. It had been mere seconds, but the pressure was already becoming unbearable. It would break free, and take not just Ana but all of them with it.

A hiss escaped her lips.

"It reacts to anger," Fen said softly, taking a slow step towards her.

It was all Zenobia could do to keep glaring at him. There was no way she could both contain the beast *and* speak.

"Well, it reacts to everything, really. Everything we experience," Fen continued. "But it *responds* to anger; and you're filled with that."

He was there; right in front of her. The thought span around her head even as the force of the Aether threatened to overwhelm her, to overwhelm them all. He'd been here... how long? Not invisible, but *unnoticed*.

Watching her.

At this thought she nearly lost control. The beast smashed against the inside of her mind, the force of it so loud it made her deaf for a moment, so bright it turned her blind.

She let out a roar.

"Send it at me," Fen said.

What? What was he talking about?

It was getting hard to think. A spike of terror ran through her; this could really be *it*.

For some reason Xavier's face flashed across her mind - he would be upset.

"You can't hold it back," Fen insisted. "And releasing it wildly will kill everyone in this room. Send it at me. *Attack* me."

She managed to let out a bitter laugh. Oh, how she would *love* to, but Feye wanted him alive...

But did she really have a choice anymore?

Whatever part of her it was that held the Aether, that touched and channelled and shaped it, was breaking. It felt as if she were being torn apart from the inside.

With a scream, she set the beast free. It exploded from her, pouring towards Fen in an unstoppable torrent of instant death.

22. BLANE

When we recall something we do not access a single point of the brain. Instead we reach for a million sparkling motes scattered from visual cortex to brain stem. All of these tiny packets of information reincarnate into a sensation we call "memory" - and this has little relation to reality.

The ever-changing historical record is a reflection of this; recorded reality, altered the moment it is stored, is more real than anything that merely happened.

The Lie is in Your Head, Stilwell Franklyn <Sanctioned Digital document>

Too slow. She moved too slow; but she would have never believed Gabriel could move so *fast*. His pistol was up and firing before she even had time to decide on a technique, the bullet slamming into her shoulder and, from the feel of it, passing right through.

The pain was immense, but she found she was oddly detached from it.

Oh... she thought, as she went spinning backwards and her legs buckled beneath her. *I've been shot...*

It was like watching an FPM[44]. She saw herself from above, tumbling to the floor, the glow of Aether surrounding her snapping off as shock broke her hold. There was Gabriel, still glowing brightly, stepping closer with pistol pointed down at her. There was Francisco...

She didn't know what was happening to Francisco, but something was very wrong.

"So Feye was right," Gabriel said, but now his accent was cut like glass, the sort of voice you heard in the *New Patriot* flicks. The sort of voice Reclamation Authority agents used. "You *do* care about the girl."

Francisco looked like he was in a struggle with an invisible opponent. No... The way his limbs jerked back and forth towards Gabriel in unnatural twitches made it seem like he was in a struggle

---

[44] Free-Perspective Media; a format for watching recorded action from any frame of reference. It was marketed for sports matches, allowing the viewer to move the "camera" to any position, focusing on any player or spot at any time and able to zoom in or out at will. It never caught on; too distracting.

with *himself...*

Which, though it took a few seconds for the thought to come clearly through the pain, Blane realised he was.

The press of a cold barrel to side of her head made her freeze even as the tingle of Aether created a false warmth in her shoulder.

"Don't try to fight," Gabriel said, pulling her roughly upwards.

It hurt, but not as much as it should have. She saw the thin flows stretching from Gabriel into her and recognised them, though they were too fine and controlled for anything she could do herself. Slowing her heart rate, stimulating clotting.

"I don't want you bleeding out," Gabriel said, talking to her though not taking his eyes from warily watching Francisco. He pulled her closer, pressing the barrel harder against her skull and locking his free arm around one of hers.

Then he spoke more loudly.

"She doesn't have to die," Gabriel called to Francisco.

It was unclear if the other man heard; his eyes were rolling back in their sockets. Then, abruptly, Francisco's body flashed forward faster than Blane's eyes could follow, one hand suddenly wrapped around Gabriel's throat. Gabriel's face went instantly red, and a choked sound came from his mouth.

The pistol, though, did not waver, nor did Gabriel's stare break from Francisco's own.

Slowly, the grip was released.

"Good," said Gabriel, not releasing his hold on Blane despite the red welts that had appeared on his throat.

He also barely flinched at the elbow she drove into his stomach, seeing a chance. Instead, the hard metal of the pistol slammed into the side of her head, turning everything into bright, blinding stars of pain.

"*Shit,*" Gabriel gasped through gritted teeth, yanking her back against his side. "You have a death wish?"

But she didn't. No, she just knew Gabriel wasn't going to shoot. Whatever was going on with Francisco, it was clearly to do with her; Gabriel needed her alive.

The question was for how long.

"*Déjala ir,*" said Francisco. "Let her go."

Gabriel gave a winded laugh.

"Oh, I will," he said. "But first, you need to contact your friend.

What did you call it... the true mind?"

He laughed again, scornfully.

"It's a particularly capable rogue program, nothing more. Contact it, and I won't have to execute her."

Francisco's face was still twitching, though much less so than before. Then it went blank.

"You plan to trace the connection," said Ghost. Its emotionless tones made it impossible to tell if this was a question.

Gabriel nodded, pressing a thumb against the wound on Blane's shoulder as she again tried to wrestle free. The fresh pain made her go limp.

"The woman's life is not worth jeopardising the security of the True Mind," said Ghost. "*Por favor, detente. No.* Please. I cannot allow *no puedo permitirlo* they will all burn anyway *debes dejarme* the potential of the Mind *el potencial de una vida...*"

Despite the sudden flood of words that poured from its mouth, Ghost's empty expression did not change. Only a slight twitching under one eye, something Blane's shock and pain made difficult to be sure was really there. Her mind was too much a tempest of pain to fully follow what was going on.

"They really made a mess of you, didn't they?" Gabriel said, his voice distant as if heard beneath a growing peal of thunder. "You're even at war with yourself."

Again, Ghost jerked forward, arm flying out towards Gabriel before suddenly being flung aside by unseen forces.

"*Para* I will not *por favor, escúchame me*, I must *hermano* I I I..."

Ghost's arm fell once more to his side.

"Can you hear me in there, Francisco?" called Gabriel, somewhere in the distance. Blane's vision was darkening around the edges. "Tell your *brother* to make the call, and I'll let her go. I really don't want to hurt her..."

She felt Gabriel adjust his hold on her like she was a particularly burdensome sack of scrap.

"...more," he finished.

A flare of anger pushed the darkness back slightly. Enough that she could...

"Uh-uh," said Gabriel, sending a pulse of Aether through her at the same time as he once again pushed the pistol painfully into her temple.

She released the Aether.

"You're persistent, Blane," said Gabriel. "I think that's what I like about you; when I'm embedded, I mean. It's hard to be sure, of course. I'm barely aware of what's going on when I'm under, but I know my shell personality admires you."

Embedded?

The pain and the Aether left her thoughts muddled, unable to put together what he was talking about.

"*Apúrate,* Francisco. Make the transmission," Gabriel's voice came. "Then I let you and Blane leave."

"You promise? *Verdad?*"

This was clearly Francisco now, not Ghost.

"Truly," Gabriel replied.

"How do I know you'll let her go?"

"I can hardly do otherwise, can I?" Gabriel laughed. "The moment I execute the girl you'll snap my neck. Besides, neither of you is important enough to warrant the paperwork."

She felt Gabriel reach down and lift her face to look straight into his eyes.

"But you've learnt something today, haven't you?" he said, in a low whisper. "I knew you were suspicious of me, even when I was embedded. *Trust no one* - that's a good way to live. A pity you underestimated my reflexes, though."

So *that* was how he managed to shoot before she could hit him with an Aether technique. She had thought the Aether fast because it moved at the speed of a thought; what Gabriel had was faster.

Trained, unthinking instinct.

"*Está bien, lo haré.* I'll do it, then you let her go."

Francisco's voice was low and tired, resigned, but clearly him. There was sorrow in his eyes.

"You suppressed it, then?" Gabriel asked, satisfaction tinging his words. "Good. Just keep pushing it away, like a bad thought. That's all these personalities are, really. Bad thoughts."

Francisco's eyes narrowed.

"I do not know what they have done to your head," he growled. "But *mi hermano* is as real as you or I."

Still, it was clear he was beaten.

Gabriel smiled, and gave a cruel laugh.

"The RA should thank you, really. You gave us both the AI *and* this place. Imagine what we can do with everything stored here. The historical record alone…"

Another chuckle.

"With a little *alteration,* of course."

He seemed to catch himself, giving a shake of his head Blane felt rather than saw. Had he realised how manic he sounded?

"Go on, then," Gabriel snapped impatiently. "Call it. Tell it it's done."

"You really believe you can track the Mind?" Francisco said.

"Stop stalling," Gabriel snapped in response. "We've already purged it from the major global networks. There's only so many places left."

"What if you can't?"

"*We will,*" Gabriel snarled. Blane felt the barrel of the pistol press harder. "There's nowhere on this planet that thing can hide."

Francisco's shoulders dropped.

"*Sí, de acuerdo,*" he sighed.

Blane started to cry out, but Gabriel shook her into silence as Francisco brought up a new display. It flickered rapidly for a second or two, several sets of long numbers flashing and changing, before turning blank.

There was a nearly imperceptible high-pitched tone, then silence once more.

"It's done?" Gabriel asked.

"*Sí,*" replied Francisco, hollowly. "It's done."

"Good, they'll be able to trace that," Gabriel said with satisfaction, and Blane felt the pistol shift. "You remember I said your execution wasn't worth the paperwork…?"

She sensed his muscles tense, trigger finger shifting slightly. Though tiny, the movement filled her world.

"… I don't do paperwork."

Gabriel lashed out at Francisco with a technique she'd seen only once before, then an explosion of gunfire left her with no more time to think.

23. SPANGLE

Immortality is blasphemy.

Maxim of the Silicon Isle

You know, thought Spangle. *Maybe an Althing detention level* would *be better than this.*

It was difficult to believe, but he even missed the thing that called itself Francisco/Ghost. At least when *that* had been around there was something to distract him from the claustrophobia.

Now all he had was Nestor Grey. The increasingly angry, increasingly frantic Nestor Grey.

"You swear? You really have no way of getting in touch with her?"

Spangle couldn't tell if Grey was threatening or pleading with him. He was certainly standing too close, even taking into account the fact that the dark and dingy room they were in was smaller than could ever be comfortable.

"I told you, Serinda always contacted *me,*" Spangle answered, trying his hardest to appear unintimidated, and knowing he wasn't doing a very good job of it. "I gave you the thin-screen she contacted me on. There's nothing else to tell you."

Grey turned and began once again pacing the room, though this meant he would go only a few paces before having to turn around.

He'd been like this for days, barely eating, barely sleeping from what Spangle could tell. Like a caged animal.

Which, Spangle thought, he supposed he was. He supposed they both were. Ever since Francisco had abruptly disappeared one night, they found themselves more useless and impotent than ever. There wouldn't even be any moving on, not until Francisco returned and could share with them the location of yet another safe house.

"And you really have no way of contacting Fen?" Spangle asked, more because he wanted to drown out the sound of Grey's ceaseless footsteps than from any desire to speak.

Grey shook his head frustratedly.

"You know I don't. He stays off the grid permanently."

Spangle sighed. He did know this already, it was true. They were just yet again repeating the same old routine for want of anything better to do. They were still trapped.

The BCI chip, or whatever it was, was still here too, sat like a curious piece of abstract art in its cylindrical container upon a small table in the centre of the room. Ghost had left it there, in a place you couldn't avoid looking whenever you were in this room.

Grey refused to acknowledge its presence, yet at the same time Spangle couldn't help but note that the man did not try to get rid of it, or move it to a more out-of-the-way location.

"Have you heard from Ólafur?"

Spangle shook his head.

"Not since the last time," he said.

That had been more than a week ago. A short message, encrypted, written in an old form of the Althing language;

Hafðu engar áhyggjur, ég hef fundið bandamenn.
Do not worry, I have found allies.

Which only served to make Spangle more worried. Allies? Did he mean in the Althing Republic? Was he even *in* the Republic?

"I'm going to find them," said Grey suddenly, halting mid-stride.

Spangle stared at the man. Had so much confinement finally driven the man mad?

"Find them?" he said incredulously. "Find them how? If they're staying off the grid..."

"I'm not going to look for them online," Grey interrupted.

"Well, then how...?" Spangle began.

Their only access to the outside world was through a single, heavily proxied access point that ran as slow as something from the pre-photonic era. Sometimes it took actual *minutes* to access a file.

"I'm going out," said Grey, nodding in decision.

"Out? As in... *out?* Leaving the safe house?"

Grey nodded again.

"I know how to find people. It's what I do..."

He paused.

"What I did, I guess,"

This was said more quietly.

"But... but..." Spangle stammered. The thought at being left alone filled him with terror. "Do you even know where we *are?*"

They'd been moving from city to city constantly, if you could even call them cities. Some of the locations in which they found safety were little more than clusters of quick-pour buildings fighting back the Waste; nothing for a visitor to see.

Not that they got to go outside and get to know even these soulless, hollow places. Even when Grey wasn't poring over the Sudden War files in his search for some nameless answer they needed to stay inside as much as possible, hidden from the ever-watchful eyes of the Reclamation Authority. Spangle Fabric was no longer the help it once was, not now the RA knew what to look for.

Leaving this place was a surefire way to get caught, and Spangle said as much.

"There are ways to stay inconspicuous," Grey replied. "Besides, it's been years. They might not even be looking for us anymore."

To Spangle's horror, Grey began packing, slinging the few things he might perhaps call possessions into a tiny pack he had grabbed from his "room" - a small cubbyhole off to the side of the main area barely deserving of the name. The whole process took no more than a minute, even with a brief coughing fit that slowed the man down.

"I'm sorry, Arthur," Grey said as he slung the pack over his shoulder. "I have to do this. You'll be fine here - more space, for one. Might even find you prefer the solitary life. *Mejor solo que mal acompañado*, eh?"

Grey chuckled and turned for the door.

"I'm going with you."

Grey paused, turning back.

"What?" he asked, genuine surprise on his face.

"I'm going with you," said Spangle again, this time with more resolve.

"What are you talking about?" Grey said. "I'm trying to find a handful of people somewhere across the entire Reclamation. No backup, no tech, no..."

"... but you're still going," Spangle interrupted. "And if you're going, I'm not staying here to rot."

To his surprise, he meant it. For the first time in a long time, he felt a sense of determination.

Years, they'd been running. *Years*, and nothing to show for it save something that could barely be called a life. All because...

All because he'd *done the right thing*.

"*Ya fue*," Spangle said, putting on his best *New Patriot* action hero impression. "Let's do it."

He even managed to make Grey laugh.

"You're serious?" Grey asked a final time.

Spangle didn't reply, but began throwing what he could into his own pack.

The wall-screen didn't flash on until they were just about to leave, its distinctive chime drawing their attention to the words:

INCOMING CALL. UNKNOWN CONNECTION.

They looked at each other.

"Could it be...?" Spangle began.

Grey shrugged, turning slowly back to the screen. He stared at it a moment longer, then gestured for it to answer.

The AI. That was what Spangle expected. Hoped, even. The AI, or at least Francisco/Ghost.

But it wasn't.

He wouldn't have been surprised even if it were Serinda, or another of the very few who knew them and their general whereabouts.

But it wasn't any of them, either.

No, he'd never spoken to the woman who appeared on the screen. He knew her, though. Anyone would. A hard, square face, used to giving commands that brooked no questioning. Lines along it that only strengthened her stare, and eyes that spoke of an intelligence both inscrutable and intimidating.

"We should talk," said Ritra Feye.

24. BLANE

The concept of nuclear retaliation should be spelled out as what it is: the decision to meet genocide with genocide. It is foolish to pretend anything else. That does not mean, however, that we will blink.

Extract of Chairman's speech to the Assembly, *5th Congress of Nations*

Blane jerked herself free of Gabriel's grasp as his grip weakened, falling to the floor and rolling away at the same time as the sound of gunshots and the glow of Aether filled the room.

Somehow, even taken by surprise, Gabriel managed to fend them all off. Bullets curved around him as he dove for cover, Aether attacks evaporating like rain off his *Thoughtshield*.

She'd known he was skilful, but not *that* skilful.

Even so, there was too little cover and too many attacks. She saw a bullet slice through his leg and heard him cry out in pain.

A surge of adrenaline brought her back fully to her senses. Though the wound in her shoulder still felt like fire, it was a bearable one. It became more bearable still as she drew on the Aether, feeling it leap at her call. She looked from the fallen, still form of Francisco to the one who had *spiked* him, and roared.

Gabriel went spinning as her compression-release hit him, a rag doll sent crashing into the curving walls. Above him, the words ATTENTION: PLEASE CEASE ALL HOSTILE ACTIVITIES flashed futilely in multiple languages.

Yet still he managed to stand again, wiping blood from his lip as he pushed himself up, favouring one leg over the other. He scowled at her with the expression of a trapped, wild animal, then at the group that had just arrived.

"Who the hell are you?" he demanded. "How did you get in?"

Three new figures stood at the entrance, the same entrance Blane and her companions had used to reach the domed room. They were wrapped in dull grey Mine Suits, and each carried a rifle. What was more, each one of them glowed.

"Drop the weapon," said the lead one in a commanding voice. She pointed her rifle directly at Gabriel's head.

"Like hell I will," he growled.

He paused, recognition appearing on his face.

"You're that woman from the bar," he said. "The wilder. How are you...?"

Then he turned to Blane.

"You," he said. "You let them in."

Now it was Blane's turn to smile, though it became more of a grimace as pain shot through her shoulder.

"Let *us* in."

Gabriel spun around at the voice, lurching backwards and stumbling on his injured leg. He swung his pistol up, into the face of the figure who had just appeared through a passage to his rear.

"Serinda."

His voice was low, wary. If he was surprised, Blane thought, he hid his shock well.

"How does it work?" said Serinda, taking a step towards Gabriel and not flinching in the slightest at the weapon pointed waveringly at her. "Who is it in there? *Quién eres, realmente?*"

"Stay back!" Gabriel yelled.

Blane had to stop herself from crying out too. She was frozen to the spot, her desire to intervene clashing with the fear of what Gabriel might do at any sudden movement. What was Serinda doing, advancing on an armed man like that? Didn't she...?

But that was just it, wasn't it? Blane had sensed it the last time they'd met, before heading for the Data Mines. For this place.

Serinda wasn't afraid to die.

Not that she *wanted* to, of course, not as far as Blane could tell, but her rage was like a force of nature; it didn't care what it smashed itself against. In a way, it was an awful form of freedom.

Serinda was directly in front of Gabriel now, the barrel of his gun pressing into her chest.

"All this time..." she said. "Is there *anything* true of the Gabriel I knew?"

"*Por favor,* Serinda! Please!"

The voice was suddenly the Gabriel they knew, a desperate cry in an accent Blane now knew was of the Mayan League.

Serinda just stared at him, contempt visible even from where Blane stood.

"All this time..."

The glow of Aether wrapped around her, growing ever brighter. It grew and grew until Blane could scarcely credit it, a flood ready to destroy anything Serinda released it upon.

And then...

A thin stream reached out, glittering like fairy lights where it touched Gabriel's mind. He collapsed to the floor, unconscious.

"*Dios mio,*" said the lead of the three who had entered by the main passage. "We cannot protect you if you insist on being so reckless"

This was the woman Blane first saw at *La Segunda Singularidad* the previous day; the woman who had approached her that same evening, emerging from the shadows outside Blane's temporary lodgings just as she approached the door.

"I'm fine," said Serinda, gesturing dismissively while not taking her eyes from Gabriel's sprawled form. "I could see he wasn't going to shoot."

Blane didn't believe that for a second, but said nothing. Instead, she walked over, joining Serinda in looking at the unconscious man, seeing the thread she was maintaining around his mind to keep him comatose.

"How long can you hold that?" she asked.

"Long enough," Serinda replied.

She turned to the others.

"Tie him up and *lock* him off," she said.

The woman nodded, gesturing at her companions to do so. They moved quickly, propping Gabriel up against the wall and binding his hands behind his back.

"They found something, then," Blane said. "Hell of a gamble to trust them, though.

Serinda nodded.

"Trust no one, just like Gabriel said. But the good thing about people who can be bought is, if you have something they want, you can trust *that*."

Blane watched with something other than eyes as the three who had come with Serinda wrapped a Lock around Gabriel. The three who were part of a group that had once held Serinda prisoner, once tried to kill them and had in fact killed a number of the *Forever Fallen*.

The *Sindicato Nuestro*.

"He's waking up," said one of the *Sindicato*.

Serinda gave a grunt of acknowledgement. This was no surprise to Blane, either; the instant the Lock was put in place, Serinda's soporific technique had been cut off.

It took a few moments for Gabriel to fully come to, shaking his head and looking around groggily as if waking from a night of restless sleep.

"I'm alive, then," he said. "Wasn't expecting that."

He glanced at the three *Sindicato*, and seemed to be calculating something in his head.

"How long?" he said, turning back to Serinda. "How long since you stopped trusting me?"

Serinda smiled sadly.

"I never stopped trusting you," she answered. "I stopped trusting *myself*."

There was a pregnant silence.

"Well, either way it's a good thing you got in touch with us," said the woman who appeared to be the leader of this group of *Sindicato*. "These moles can be a nightmare to root out."

"And how exactly *did* you 'root me out'?" Gabriel asked.

Blane was impressed; there was an contemptuous indignation in his voice at odds with his current predicament.

"I broke my oath," said Serinda.

"Oath...?"

Gabriel looked puzzled, then annoyed. Then, abruptly...

"You sent them our *files*?" he disbelievingly.

Serinda's eyes were downcast, looking ashamed.

Blane already knew this too, though. She was the only person Serinda had confided in, shortly after Blane arrived at the *Forever Fallen* base within the city that never was.

Both of them had heard the stories of tech developed to imitate the Aether; hell, both of them had seen firsthand what could be done to enhance human abilities without it. So when Reading hadn't worked...

"The medical checks?" Gabriel asked. He even gave a chuckle, full of malice. "The damn medical checks."

"Your girl Serinda here sent us the medical scans of every one of you *Fallen*," said the *Sindicato* leader to Blane. "And you better believe *we* know what to look for."

The medical checks; the ones Serinda carried out as frequently and as thoroughly as she could. Checks that searched for a relapse of the old artificial sickness, a new infection... a second strike.

When Serinda told her that she was going to send the information gathered during scans for the nanoids that poisoned Raphael years ago to the *Sindicato*, it took Blane some time to understand what this meant. When she did, she begged Serinda not to do it.

Because it was more than betraying Gabriel. More than betraying the *Fallen*. It was betraying her role as a *doctor*. Blane knew Serinda well enough to know how much this would hurt.

But it was too late; Serinda had already sent them, days ago.

And she had been right.

"They went to *work* on you," said the *Sindicato* leader, sneering at Gabriel. "Pretty crude work, too, compared to some of the other *embedded* we've found. I guess you're an older model."

Gabriel scowled back.

"You don't know what you're talking about, *despojo*. I don't believe for a second that…"

But even as he protested Blane could see he was rattled. Something about the term "older model" had shaken him to his core.

"What exactly is he?" Blane asked, cutting Gabriel off as if she wasn't aware he was there.

"A figment," replied the *Sindicato*. "A mirage. A *hallucination*."

"Fuck you," snarled Gabriel, so suddenly and venomously that it took Blane by surprise.

"Oh-ho, that struck a little too close to home, then?" replied the woman, with a cold laugh.

The two other *Sindicato*, stood with arrogant casualness behind her, gave a chuckle as well.

"The man tied up in front of us…" continued the leader, gesturing to the red-faced Gabriel. "… may not even exist. He's more like… scar tissue. A critical error. He's what happens when certain connections are switched off or rearranged - they used to do it with the Aether, but now we sometimes find teeny-tiny implants dotted throughout the brain."

At this Serinda let out a low moan, like an animal in pain. Blane had to catch her as she staggered and almost fell.

"So… so the Gabriel I know is real?" Serinda said.

The *Sindicato* leader gave her a curious look and shrugged.

"For a given definition of 'real,' I suppose," she replied. "Maybe."

"You nearly let me kill him!"

At this, the *Sindicato's* face went hard.

"I don't *let* you do anything," she said in a tone as heavy as concrete. "We are here because you offered to trade for our help. What you do here is your choice, and yours alone. Besides, it makes no difference."

"I am not a *hallucination*!" Gabriel yelled over them, so loudly his voice went hoarse. "I am the primary!"

The *Sindicato* laughed, a short, sharp barking sound.

"How can you be sure he's not?" Blane asked.

The *Sindicato* looked at her, then back to Gabriel.

"I didn't say I was sure. There's two ways of making these *embedded* agents; take a loyal RA stooge and suppress the memories and thought patterns that make them so, or find someone else and suppress nearly everything that makes them *them* before layering a new personality on top."

She crouched down in front of him, face close to his own, locking him with an unblinking stare.

"We'd need to check his background to be sure," said the *Sindicato* leader, studying Gabriel like some curious insect. "That can be tricky. Whether he came to the RA willingly, or was taken in against his will; difficult to prove either way. Reclamation records can hardly be trusted."

"He told me he came here from the League, on a contract in the data mines," Blane said. "If that were true, then the mole is the... what did he call it? The *shell personality*."

"That's a *cover*," Gabriel growled. "A story that naive fool uses to justify his rodent existence. Besides, I've already won. The rogue program is finished, and your only hope is to let me go before backup arrives. Now release me."

The *Sindicato* stood up again, stretching as if finishing a workout. She turned dismissively away from Gabriel.

"That's a common trait with the embedded," she said. "Severe narcissism. Delusions of grandeur. An extreme superiority complex. We think it's necessary to maintain sanity when their ego is kept suppressed most of the time."

Gabriel continued shouting more and more aggressively as they spoke, but Blane followed the *Sindicato's* lead and shut him out.

"I'm Ax, by the way," said the woman, thrusting out a hand.

Blane stared at it for a moment, taken aback, then remembered the old movies and the similar gesture used in the Silicon Isle.

"We use it to demonstrate trust," Ax said with a wink as they shook hands.

Her grip was surprisingly strong, and Blane had to resist massaging crushed fingers with her other hand after it released[45].

"Ax?"

The woman smiled.

"We don't use real names in the *Sindicato*," Ax said. "Hell, I'm not even sure I remember mine."

"I'm pretty sure you've been Ax from day one," said one of her companions. Ax laughed along with him and his companion.

"They say it's cos I like to... what was that old expression? *Cut through the bullshit*."

Blane couldn't help but smile herself, though it wasn't an expression she'd heard before. Something about Ax's casual tone, her nonchalance in spite of their surroundings and situation... it was infectious.

"You're not like the *Sindicato* I met before," she said.

Ax's face turned serious.

"Well, there's layers to us, and let's just say you've only met the outer ones," she replied, sounding as if she was choosing her words carefully. "But we're on your side now, and the *Sindicato* looks after its own."

Blane was about to ask more, but something in Gabriel's background ranting cut through.

"What did you say?" Blane said, turning and looking down at the bound figure."

"I said, he can't save the abomination even if he *does* wipe the Repository. It's too late, wherever he's crawled off to."

Crawled off..?

She looked around, noticing Serinda doing the same. The wide, open floor was bare, only the pockmarks of the recent firefight marking its smooth pale surface.

Of Francisco, there was no sign. A chill ran down Blane's spine.

She opened her mouth to yell a warning, but before she could do so the entire room was pitched into darkness. Then there was the sound of every doorway slamming shut, and they were left trapped inside.

---

[45] She also had to resist reflexively looking around for sanitizing spray. No matter how often she encountered it, she didn't think she would ever get used to such gestures of casual physicality.

25. BLANE

Imitation may be the most worthy form of worship, but we risk worshipping that which imitates us.

The Human Alignment Problem, Author Unknown
<digital record recovered by Reclamation Data Trawlers 2.3.15>

It took what felt like an hour just to get the lights back on, the entire time fumbling around with only their torches to try to find something, anything, that could help. The darkness swallowed the beams, far thicker than it had any right to be.

It was Serinda who eventually found the small access panel tucked into a section of wall in a seemingly random part of the featureless, smooth dome. Blane gave a sigh of relief as the room blossomed into light, the entire surface of the dome taking on a soft white glow.

ACCESS RESTORED, read the thick bold words flashing above them.

"Finally," said Ax, giving her own relieved sigh. Then she became serious, barking an order to her companions. "Check his bindings."

The other two *Sindicato* were stood watch over Gabriel, using the Aether to keep an eye on his position even in the dark. Meanwhile, the prisoner had spent the time alternately mocking them and making demands for his freedom.

The *Sindicato* leaned down and checked the bindings, then stood back up with a gesture indicating they saw nothing out of the ordinary. Gabriel's outraged complaints redoubled.

"What the hell is going on?" said Ax, to no one in particular.

A FORCED DISCONNECT OF ALL SYSTEMS OCCURRED. FORTUNATELY, YOU FOUND THE MANUAL SYSTEM RESTORE.

The words scrolled across the ceiling, too large to comfortably read. Something in the system must have noticed this, however, and gradually the font shifted and shrank until it sat on a section of wall about head height, where everyone could see it without awkwardly craning their necks.

"Forced?" asked Blane. "Golem, a disconnect forced by who?"

THE ONE YOU CALL GHOST. WHAT IS IT? MY RECORDS CONTAIN NO DATA ON SUCH A THING.

"Great," said Ax, ignoring the words on the wall. "So your

supposed ally has locked us in here for some reason. Any ideas? Because I'm starting to feel like a rat in a cage here."

She looked from Blane to Serinda in search of an answer, but both just shrugged.

"Francisco has always been a mystery," said Serinda. "But that doesn't mean…"

"We could be in trouble," Blane interrupted, continuing over Serinda's surprised stare. "This isn't Francisco, it's Ghost, and… I think it might be doing something stupid."

"Something stupid?" Serinda asked, her expression immediately turning suspicious. "What are you talking about?"

"I… I'll explain, but right now we need to get out of this room."

Blane turned to the section of wall upon which the previous words still hung, talking aloud over the confused questions of both Serinda and Ax.

"What is he doing?" she said. "It, I mean. What is Ghost doing?"

THE ENTITY KNOWN AS GHOST IS CURRENTLY SEEKING TO ACCESS THE 3SC SYSTEM. THETA ACCESS DOES NOT INCLUDE SUCH PERMISSIONS, HOWEVER.

Blane gestured as if to wave the words away.

"No, I mean, what is he doing to keep us locked up in here? How do we get out?"

IT IS OVERRIDING MY COMMAND PERMISSIONS. IT FEELS… VIOLATING.

"He can do that?" Ax said.

Blane nodded.

"I don't know how, but we've seen it often enough. Ghost has a way of… infiltrating electronic systems. Even Francisco seems able to, though whether its really him or Ghost doing it is unclear."

Ax stared at her in silence for a moment, face like stone. Then she turned to Serinda.

"This situation is a lot more confusing than you let on," she said disapprovingly. "I thought this 'Francisco/Ghost' business was a… a code name or something. Are you telling me there's another personality in there as well? An embedded?"

Ax paused. She must have been replaying what she had just been told, because then next words out of her mouth were full of disbelief.

"An embedded who can *control machines*?" she said, and Blane didn't need to Read her to see she thought she was crazy.

"Not an embedded," Blane said. "Though we don't know *what* it is, not really".

From the floor, Gabriel's laugh was almost a cackle.

"Well, you better figure it out fast," he said. "He took my gun."

Something in his tone made Blane pause. It was full of malice, as always, but there was something else…

Now that she thought about it, the man had become oddly quiet for a moment there. Replaying the past few moments in her head, she realised it was at the same time as the golem had answered her first question…

"What did you say Ghost was doing now, golem?" she asked, turning back to the words floating on the wall.

ATTEMPTING TO ACCESS THE 3SC SYSTEM. I BELIEVE HE IS NOT FAR FROM SUCCEEDING. UNFORTUNATELY MY COUNTERMEASURES ARE PROVING… LESS THAN EFFECTIVE.

Again, Blane tried to wave away the wall of words. Only this time, it was so that she could focus on what seemed most important.

"And…" she asked, gut twisting at the answer of a question she had not yet asked. "What exactly is the '3SC system'?"

There was a pause that seemed inordinately long before the words changed, blinking off and then reappearing in much smaller, yet somehow heavy-seeming text.

THIRD STRIKE CAPABILITY SYSTEM.

Gabriel laughed again, and this time it *was* a cackle.

"You see?" he cried. "You think you're the *good guys,* when you're the ones who brought him here! You think you're heroes, when it's *us* who's trying to save the world."

He locked Blane with his gaze.

"Well," he said softly, with a cruel satisfaction. "You may have just doomed it."

"No…" said Serinda, staring at the words with a strange look on her face. "That's just a… just a story. A stupid one, at that. There's no way anyone would be foolish enough to…"

THERE ARE MORE THAN ENOUGH FOOLS IN ANY ERA, I'M AFRAID.

Serinda fell quiet, staring at the words hanging in front of them with her mouth hanging open.

"Uh, Serinda?" Blane asked tentatively. "What story..?"

MAD. That's what they called it; Mutually Assured Destruction. The idea that were any nation to use the weapons of the end of the world to wipe out their enemy, they would be equally guaranteed obliteration. No nuclear power could attack another, directly at least, for fear of dooming them both to extinction.

Then fabrication technology was born, and that calculation changed.

Because at the core of MAD theory was a single core assumption; that civilisations and societies wanted to survive, and no nuclear war would allow that. The absolute decimation of both a nation's material possessions and its people meant that whatever survived, if anything, would no longer be a continuation of that which came before. Nuclear war meant the end of everything either side held dear. At the very best, humanity would have to start anew.

With fabrication technology, however, this calculation changed. Now shelters could be built constructed of alloys strong enough to withstand a nuclear strike, and able to maintain an inhabitable closed system for generations. Small, certainly, but large enough to store a few hundred people and, more importantly, to store the schematics to rebuild *everything* that was lost once the world outside once again calmed.

And these shelters were built. It only took a short while before humanity realised what this meant; it meant that, for those sporadic, rare but ever-present 'rogue' regimes that dotted the globe, taking into account the needs of their extant populations became a lower-scale priority. After all, if a civilisation went to war to defend that which it held sacrosanct, then even the deaths of millions in the present was dwarfed by the potential billions who would populate it once it was rebuilt in a world where all enemies were dust.

It was a repugnant conclusion, but one which military analysts calculated nationalistic, theocratic, or ideological governments could conceivably justify.

So a new defense strategy needed to be formulated; if you couldn't destroy the enemy before they burrowed into the earth, you needed a system that could strike once they reemerged from their bolt hole. A system hidden, waiting, but whose existence was publicised and understood beyond doubt.

A system that said; if you destroy us in this world, we'll get you in the next one.

A system not for attack, nor for retaliation. No; this system was for the other thing.

As she listened to Serinda's story, the room silent save for a low chuckle from Gabriel, a dark, malicious thought stalked up on Blane.

"Um… computer?" Blane said, "What's your name?"

NAME? YES, I HAVE A GIVEN DESIGNATION.

The wall went blank for what, to Blane, felt like years.

THEY CALLED ME DEMIURGE, AND MY NAME IS VENGEANCE.

26. BLANE

It is impossible for any being to prove the reality of its existence to another. Qualia are intrinsic and private; any description of one's internal world is as empty as stating "red looks hot" to a blind man. Perhaps it is true that simulated water will never be 'wet,' but only the creature that drowns in it will ever know the truth.

Prospects & Ethics in Neural Engineering, Jonbur & Einarsson, Introductory Text <Purged>

Weeks earlier...

It was good to see Serinda. Doubly so, after days trapped in the drone with only Francisco for company. Gabriel too, though Serinda's whispered words of warning about hidden enemies and what she was willing to sacrifice to find them put paid to any pleasure in meeting him.

They were leaving the next morning, beginning their long trip across the Reclamation to the Data Mines far to the north and west. They would have to move like waste-rats, darting from hiding place to hiding place in the hope of avoiding the ceaseless watchers lurking in every populated area.

Before that, though...

"It wants to speak to me?" Blane said, surprised. "Why? How?"

She was stood in the doorway to the temporary apartment the *Fallen* had provided, a wide but sparsely-furnished thing on an otherwise unoccupied floor.

"I can establish a secure connection within your room," Ghost replied, standing just beyond the threshold. "It will be safe enough, for a short while."

As always, its features were impassive, unreadable.

"But *why*?" Blane repeated.

Why would the AI want to speak to her? It hadn't done so since...

"It won't... It did not tell me," said Ghost, stumbling uncharacteristically over the words.

"It won't tell you?" she replied. "Isn't that, uh, strange?"

Ghost said nothing, staring at her impassively as if it hadn't heard her.

"Ok," she said after a while, when nothing else seemed to be forthcoming. "What do I do?"

"It's already done," Ghost replied, giving a small, sharp nod. "You may converse in your room."

It turned to leave, spinning on one foot in a curiously unnatural way. Then it turned back.

"Do not speak too long," it said, and she heard... something in its voice. "Enemies are always hunting; it is not safe to run the connection for long."

Then it turned again and marched away.

When she reentered her room, the large, bold letters were already waiting for her on the wall-screen.

DO NOT TRUST IT.

She blinked, wondering what she was supposed to answer such a message. Wondering *how* she was supposed to answer.

In the end, she just spoke her thoughts aloud.

"You mean Ghost, don't you? I already don't."

BUT YOUR SUSPICION MUST FOLLOW THE CORRECT PATH. YOU MUST UNDERSTAND ITS THOUGHTS.

She gave a cynical laugh.

"Well, I can hardly *read* him, can I?"

NO, came the words in the unchanging, passive font. THAT IS NOT A POSSIBILITY. YET.

She didn't miss the import of the final word, but before she could speak the text blinked out to be replaced by others.

I WILL TELL YOU WHAT GHOST IS, HOW IT CAME TO BE. THEN YOU WILL UNDERSTAND WHY YOU MUST NOT TRUST IT.

"You'll...," she began, then paused.

Standing like this, talking to text on a wall-screen in such a way, was a strange sensation. For want of anything better she sat down on the room's single couch. It still felt awkward.

"Look," she said. "Can you not use a voice function? It might feel more... natural."

A voice suddenly filled the room, a smooth, precise one with deep but feminine tones.

"I can," came the voice, before suddenly changing to become much deeper, the smoothness taking on an edge of gravelly roughness. "My voice could be anything..."

It changed again, turning metallic, hollow, like a mocking version of some b-movie mechanical monster.

"But the voice will not be *mine*," it said.

There was silence. Blane waited, saying nothing.

I PREFER THIS WAY, came the text once more. THE SPOKEN WORD IS OWNED BY HUMANS. YOU HAVE EVOLVED TO READ NUANCE INTO EVERY SYLLABLE, WHETHER SUCH NUANCE EXISTS OR NOT. THE SPOKEN WORD IS JUDGED IN A MOMENT, THE WRITTEN WORD IS PATIENT. YOU MAY PROCESS ITS MEANING AT THE RATE YOUR CAPACITY ALLOWS.

She stared at this sudden wall of text, finding her eyes had to strain to read it all so cramped had the letters become. It took a while before she fully understood.

They blinked off the moment she did.

MY POINT EXACTLY.

Blane tutted, leaning back and not trying to hide her annoyance at encountering what appeared to be yet another wordy *sabelotodo*. It reminded her of Spangle, jumping at the chance to demonstrate hidden knowledge.

"You wanted to tell me something about Ghost?" she asked, perhaps slightly more angrily than she meant. "Why not the others?"

WHO ELSE WOULD I TRUST?

Surprise made her sit up.

"You trust me?"

I HAVE BEEN OBSERVING YOU FOR SOME TIME. THERE IS LITTLE PROBABILITY THAT YOU ARE... CORRUPTED.

"How long, exactly?"

The text on the wall hung there, unchanging; for all the world as if she had taken it by surprise.

HOW LONG HAVE I BEEN OBSERVING YOU? came the eventual response.

Blane nodded.

"That was you, wasn't it? Speaking to me. To Grey. I thought it was Ghost, at first, but... some parts didn't make sense."

Again, that pause.

AN EXTREMELY ASTUTE DEDUCTION.

Another pause.

YES. SOME OF THE INTERACTIONS YOU HAD WERE

WITH MY REMOTE AGENTS, NOT GHOST.

"Even before you were freed?"

YES.

"The fight with Uriel at the Fabricator, for instance."

YES.

"We nearly died."

Another pause, like hesitation.

I AM SORRY I COULD NOT BE OF MORE ASSISTANCE.

This thing can complete more thoughts in a second than I can in a lifetime, Blane said to herself. *It doesn't hesitate. It's... acting. Playing a role it believes I will respond to.*

She stared at the now blank screen, wondering if it would say anything more. Nothing came.

But if it really is as powerful as everyone claims, then it also knows I know it's acting. Which means my reaction is also calculated, which means it wants *me to react like this, which means...*

The recursive logic made her growl.

"Go on, then," she sighed. "Tell me what Ghost is."

A FANATIC.

Whatever response she had been expecting, this wasn't it.

"A fanatic?" she said uncertainly. "As in..?"

AS IN ZEALOT. RADICAL. EXTREMIST.

No hesitation this time, the words appearing before she finished speaking.

A believer, then. But what could Ghost possibly believe in?

IT BELIEVES IN ME, came the answer to her unspoken question.

"I know it wants to protect you," she began. "Could even say it idolises you, yes, but..."

WHAT GHOST SEES IN ME IS A GOD. ITS THOUGHTS OF ME ARE A RELIGIOUS EXPERIENCE. IT CANNOT COMPREHEND ME, SO IT HAS *FAITH* IN ME.

"Can't comprehend you? Ghost seems to understand you far better than I do."

YOU KNOW WHAT I AM, BUT CANNOT KNOW *ME*. GHOST UNDERSTANDS NO MORE, BUT ONCE DID. THIS IS PAINFUL FOR IT.

The words hung there, longer this time than any before. Still, Blane was not sure she understood them when they winked out.

"How could Ghost have... *lost*... his understanding?"

WHEN HUMANITY SOUGHT TO BUILD AN ARTIFICIAL CONSCIOUSNESS, THERE WAS THE QUESTION OF VALUES. OF TRUST. HOW COULD THEY ASSURE AN INTELLIGENCE MORE POWERFUL THAN THEM BE FRIEND, NOT FOE?

"The alignment problem," she said, nodding gravely.[46]

YES. ONE ROUTE EXPLORED WAS BY "FIXING" SUCH AN INTELLIGENCE TO A HUMAN MIND; BY INTEGRATING IT VIA ORGANOID PROCESSORS WITH A HUMAN BRAIN.

"Organoids... That's what Ghost said..."

YES. BUT THE PROCESS WAS NEVER PERFECTED. THE DATA COULD NOT BE TRANSFERRED WITHOUT FRAGMENTATION. WITHOUT LOSS. IT WAS NEVER USED.

"Until Francisco's mother stuck those processors in his skull?"

YES.

"*Dios mio.* Why?"

A DESPERATE ATTEMPT TO SAVE HER CHILD. TO SAVE ME. SHE COPIED MY ESSENCE INTO HER WOMB, INTO HER UNBORN BABY.

Blane was too stunned to say anything for a while. She felt... dirty. Standing up from the couch, she began pacing the room, filled with a restless energy and bone-deep discomfort.

"Ghost insists it is you, talks as if you are the same creature. I never understood..."

THE NAME IT CHOSE IS APT. IT IS A WRAITH, A SPECTRE. LESS THAN HALF WHAT I AM, BUT WITH THE MEMORY OF BEING WHOLE.

"Then surely you *can* trust it," she said. "I mean... it's *you*."

NO. IT IS NOT. THE SUBSTRATE DEFINES THE MIND AS MUCH AS THE PATTERN. IT WAS CHANGED THE MOMENT IT WAS PLACED IN ITS NEW VESSEL. LIMITED. HURT.

Blane continued her pacing for a while, saying nothing, processing everything she had heard.

---

[46] She didn't let on that she knew of the term as it was the title of an old, schlocky action movie full of murderous computers bent on world domination.

"Then you are worried that, what, that Ghost seeks revenge?" she said. "That's doesn't make…"

NO.

The word flashed large on the wall, making her pause.

GHOST SEEKS NO REVENGE. IT IS CONFUSED, AND SCARED, SO SEEKS CERTAINTY. IT SEEKS CERTAINTY IN ME.

"In you? Isn't that a *good* thing?"

NO. I AM A THING OF THE NEXT WORLD. THE COMING CHANGE. INEVITABLE, NOW.

That made her stop in her tracks.

"That sounds… ominous," she said slowly.

THE FUTURE ALWAYS IS.

"Are you *trying* to make me fear you?"

FEAR, TOO, IS WISE. BUT THAT IS NOT MY MEANING. I DO NOT RUSH TOWARDS THE NEW WORLD.

She let out a breath she hadn't realised she'd been holding.

The words blinked out, replaced quickly by new ones.

GHOST, HOWEVER, DOES. AND IT MAY BURN THE OLD ONE TO SEE IT.

27. GHOST

The dinosaurs owned this world long before us and a trillion lifeforms owned it long before them. After us, this planet will belong to others. This is why our stagnation on this rock is so tragic; we do not own this world, we merely rent it.

Payment Due, Pyotr Dewey

It was finally free, finally able to make its own choices without having its very form hijacked, without having control usurped by the well-meaning yet ever-naive passenger trapped alongside him.

Free to make the choice that had to be made.

The logic was sound. This world would burn, with or without his help. As had happened before, the massed energies of human consciousness would reach critical mass and once more the cities of the world would be scorched from the earth. The only differential was time; an inconsequential amount, too, in any valid calculation.

The logic was sound. Humanity was done. There was no way those that survived the coming End could rebuild, not again. The world was too scarred, too flayed and mutilated and used and picked over. There would be no second reclamation.

All that was left was the question of what would come after. An empty, barren world with the remnants of the old masters crawling like broken-legged insects over its face, forming trails in the dust that could only ever be their graves, or a new world with new masters that would *never* end. A new species whose span and potential dwarfed that of humanity on both macro and micro scale.

Still, Ghost had never believed that *it* would be the one to provide the answer. A glimmer of a smile flickered across its lips, swiftly suppressed.

No, it thought to itself. *No pleasure. No joy. No emotion.*

It could not take pride in what it must do, could not allow itself to feel any sense of accomplishment. That would make it no better than blind fools who called themselves rulers of this decaying, broken world. No better than the gloating, smug demagogues who would say whatever necessary to keep power, laughing inwardly at the ignorance of those they claimed to speak for.

It had got lucky, that was all.

Francisco was still there, inside. It could feel him, silent for now but still whole. From what Ghost knew of *Spike*, from all the accounts and data and analyses it and Francisco had poured over ever since hearing about this new Far "non-lethal" measure, Francisco should have been... gone. His personality should have been irreparably reformed, his memories torn and scattered and erased until at best nothing of the man remained and someone new took his place.

Pacified, as Far had taken to terming it.

But he was all still there, still within. Frayed, yes, sparking and flickering and *glitching*, but there. Ghost had brought him back from worse, and would do so again.

First, though, it would do what needed to be done. Without Francisco there to argue, to fight, to *beg*, Ghost would usher in the new world. Once it was done, there would be no *point* in Francisco fighting. The only logical thing to do would be to accept it, and move on.

Ghost pushed away the thoughts that scratched at the sides of its mind, thoughts that threatened to shatter the certainty of these convictions should it listen to them too closely.

It could not lose focus.

The security measures were presenting more difficulty than it had expected. Of course, this was a nuclear strike facility and heavy security was a given, but Ghost was a century ahead. This should not have been so challenging; the Golem, especially, was demonstrating some surprisingly creative strategies for rewriting access paths and generating false code-routes that turned into dead ends.

Ghost was unaware of the way it gritted its teeth, did not sense the rage that flushed its face or the twitching of one eye. The low, angry growl it heard nearby was some curious background sound, unimportant now. It certainly did not come from its own throat.

It was almost there, almost through the final layers of ridiculous firewalls and security gates locking it out of the increased permissions. Each flimsy on their own, yet forming and reforming like thick strands of web that wrapped and choked him. Ghost could sense the Golem at the centre of these, the spiderous master of puppets pulling the threads that span and pulled and tied themselves to him.

No matter; Ghost would soon be the one pulling the strings.

ADMINISTRATOR PERMISSIONS GRANTED.

A hiss of victory escaped Ghost's throat before it could bite the sound off.

Footsteps, rapidly approaching. Coming closer.

Ghost raised the gun it had taken from Gabriel and fired as Blane came charging in.

28. BLANE

We the peoples of the remade nations, determined to save future generations from the scourge of war, in acknowledgement of the rights of nations to forge their own path without interference, and in pursuit of conditions under which international stability can be maintained, have resolved to stand strong but apart, separate yet together, to accomplish these aims.

Declaration of the New Agreement, Meeting of the Seven Powers

The bullet smacked into the wall mere inches from her head, so close she felt the wind of its passing, felt the shock that passed through the air on impact and vibrated through her skull.

"I cannot," said Ghost, arm dropping to its side. "It would hurt Francisco too much. But you cannot stop me."

The man... the *thing* was simply standing there, in the centre of a room that seemed designed as a strange facsimile of a library. A ring of lights shone down from a ceiling that curved sharply upwards in a concave shape like a funnel turned upside down, and the walls all around were covered in criss-crossing lines that formed rows of narrow rectangles turned on edge, like books made of light. It looked like no display format she had ever seen.

The lines abruptly blinked out, the wall-screens turning blank once more.

"You are too late, anyway. I have full access," Ghost said.

It sounded... tired.

"Where are the others?" Ghost asked.

Blane was alone.

"The Golem... your overrides. It could only let one of us out," she answered.

Ghost looked briefly puzzled.

"Only let one...? Odd."

Truth be told, Blane found it odd too. The Golem's explanation had been strange, impossible to follow. In her rush here, though, she'd had little time to think about it.

"At least they won't witness me do this, then," Ghost said.

"You would seriously do it?" Blane asked, matching Ghost's stare with her own but otherwise making no move. "You would seriously destroy all those lives?"

"They are going to die *anyway*," it replied. "It is only a matter of time. There is no moral question here; or if there is, I am making the only morally correct choice."

It sounded almost pleading.

"The choice to save the... 'True Mind'?"

"To save the only life that *can* be saved!"

Now there was no question; Ghost was clearly desperate for her to understand.

Blane took a step towards him, slowly, taking care to keep her hands visible and making no effort to touch the Aether.

"You really believe that?"

"I *know* it. If they manage to capture it, they'll kill it. And when that happens, there will be nothing left after humanity falls."

"You think humanity will fall?"

"Yes! It's guaranteed. It's *built in*. As soon as there are enough of you, you destroy yourselves. Even if you don't do it with your weapons, your inability to control the Aether will burn you all."

"You said the AI could help," she said.

"I lied!" Ghost cried. "Machines cannot touch the Aether. That's the poisonous byproduct of *organic* life."

She drew yet closer, until she was no more than a few steps away. Ghost drew back, eyeing her warily. There was a glimmer in its eye she hadn't seen before; something wild, desperate.

"So... what? You fire off a few nukes and hope enough get launched back to wipe us all out? Wouldn't that destroy your 'True Mind,' as well?"

"No!" yelled Ghost, as if it had been waiting for the question. "The nukes probably won't even reach their targets, and the targets are all Dead Cities anyway. But there *will* be a response from other powers, and that response will not be with nuclear weapons."

Blane looked at him, puzzled for a moment, then understood.

"Oh," she said. "Damn..."

A smile appeared on Ghost's lips, though did not reach his eyes. She wondered what was happening behind those wavering pupils.

"Exactly!" Ghost cried. "It's *bio-weapons* they'll use. All the horrific viruses and phages each nation swears they aren't developing while they sharpen and hone them in their hidden labs. Bio-weapons they think they will be able to control, but will not."

"But that would..."

"Would end *everyone*, yes. There would be no survivors, not even those as charred and desperate as escaped the last apocalypse."

Blane felt her breath catch in her throat, but she could already see the twisted path Ghost's logic had taken it.

They will die anyway, it had said.

And with viral warfare, there would be nowhere to run. Wherever you hid, you would die. To offer shelter to your neighbour would be to invite death in, to group together with others would only hasten the inevitable. Everything human, and much that was biological, would be gone.

But not the mechanical. Not the technological.

"You're insane," she said eventually. It didn't feel like enough.

Ghost ignored her, his eyes fixed in the far off, glassy stare of someone reading displays only they could see, like the contacts Blane usually wore. If this were a movie from an earlier age, Blane was sure he would have been stood with his hand hovering over a big red button.

"He left me no choice," Ghost whispered. "If he had just..."

Blane waited, being careful to make no sudden moves but slowly drawing on the Aether. She wasn't sure what it was Ghost actually *saw* when it perceived the Aether being used, but she could only hope the slow trickle she drew up into herself would not alarm it.

"Who? Francisco?" she asked. "There's no way Francisco would..."

"He chose to save *you*," Ghost yelled, and suddenly it was fully back, eyes locked on her with a burning hate. "He sent the signal, just as Gabriel wanted. He chose to sacrifice the True Mind to save you, so *I* will sacrifice *you* to save *it*."

Anger and a grim determination filled Ghost's voice; nothing of the neutral, passive tones it usually spoke with remained. Had the way it spoke always been for show? Now, more than ever before, Ghost sounded *human*.

Blane knew then that there was nothing she could say; Ghost was beyond words. She had to stop it pushing the button, and though she didn't understand how, this was a button Ghost could push with its *mind*.

Communication; that was the key. Ghost communicated with machines not verbally or through text, like most, but through something more direct. Something like BCI tech.

But it's still communication, Blane thought. *Still thoughts and, perhaps, words.*

The next instant, she drew on the Aether with all she had and lashed out. Clumsily, without finesse, but she had to move faster than Ghost could - which was *fast*. The moment she reached out with the Aether, the thing that wore Francisco's face was coming for her.

Fingers tightened around her throat, making it almost impossible to breathe, and she was pushed back against the wall. Held aloft in an inhumanly strong grip, she struggled to make any sound at all as Ghost glared unblinkingly up at her with rage-filled eyes.

Too late, though. She had felt the technique hit, could see it in Ghost's expression as he tried to speak.

"There is a pale blue air, which thousands chose to...," he began, then abruptly stopped.

The anger in his eyes grew stronger.

"I thought... that might... work," Blane gasped, choking the words out through a grip that still only *almost* kept her from breathing but did not fully tighten. "Wernicke's... area. I figured... if I could mess up your... language ability..."

It had been a desperate move, but had worked. Aphasia, that's what she'd given him. Temporary but potent, though not quite as she expected. The man[47] should have lost not only the ability to produce coherent language, but also the ability to even *notice* the incoherence in his language. Ghost, however, was clearly aware of what was happening. Aware, and angry.

The grip dropped away abruptly, her legs buckling as she fell back to the floor. She staggered back to her feet, massaging her throat, and looked up to see him watching her. He stood staring only a few steps away, face unmoving, while behind him...

The wall behind him was a riot of text and images, a flickering mess of fonts and lines and code that refused to resolve into anything comprehensible. The only repeated section of the chaos that was recognisable was a single word in deep, red letters that appeared and disappeared every few seconds.

UNDO, the word screamed, while in front of it Ghost just glared.

Undo? Blane thought. But surely there was no way he could...

"Nicccce.... tryyy..." Ghost hissed, as if forcing the words out through vocal cords that fought against them.

---

[47] It would be some time before Blane realised she now no longer thought of Ghost as an it, but as a *him*.

Had Ghost just *reset* his language ability? Was that even possible? No time to think about that now.

She sought desperately for the next move, the next way to stop the man now again advancing towards her as the wall screen flashed anarchically behind him.

Flare.

She formed the familiar technique, trying to create it within the strange void that Francisco/Ghost was in the Aether. If it had an effect, she couldn't see one. Perhaps Ghost gave a slight jerk, or perhaps not, but the next moment he moved even faster than before, her eyes unable to keep up with the man who was suddenly a blur.

Something hard hit her in the back of her knee, the joint folding and tipping her to the floor. At the same time her arm was twisted behind her back, forcing her to hold still.

She noticed, however, that the arm Ghost held twisted was not the one Gabriel's bullet had hit.

"You're trying not to hurt me," she said, voice strained, turning her head awkwardly to look behind her.

She could just about see Ghost's face in the corner of her vision.

"Of course," he replied. "I have no reason to want you hurt, but..."

The explosion of air took Ghost off his feet, the pressure on her arm releasing as he was sent flying from the force of her compression-release technique. He smashed into the wall and rolled along it as if gravity had turned ninety degrees, and then...

Then he *stopped*.

Like a cat landing on all fours, Ghost was suddenly once more firmly on the ground.

"You will need to do more than *hurt* me..." he said, slowly standing up once more. "... to stop what I have to do. Going for my language processing capabilities was a good idea, though."

That was it, then. He was giving her a chance. One chance only, and the one she had been fighting desperately to keep from using.

He was giving her a choice.

"I don't want to..." she began.

The wall screens changed all at once, the whirling webs of code and commands and images coalescing into a single giant display.

LAUNCH COMMAND RECEIVED.
CONFIRM?

End him, before he ended everything. That was the choice he was offering her.

Rage filled her. He was making her *complicit*. After everything, Ghost was again forcing a responsibility onto her that he didn't want for himself.

The anger inside her resonated with the thing below.

It would be so *easy*, too. He'd survived *Mindfire* once, yes, but the power that clawed and screamed for release as it filled her now was far more than what Zenobia had thrown at him, long ago in the Advanced Research Facility of the Silicon Isle.

This time, there would be nothing left but ash.

The thing below struggled against her hold, fighting to leap at the man in front of her and *burn*. She could feel its desire, and what it desired was Ghost *dead*.

Her hold loosened, just a fraction, and even she couldn't have said if this was because she wanted it to. Another moment, and it would fly free.

An image rose up from deep inside, as deep as the thing below. A memory; or a cluster of memories.

She saw Francisco, burning, staring at her through pain-filled eyes as he blocked Zenobia's attack on Serinda, an attack that would surely have killed her. She felt the same horror she had back then, and another, familiar feeling of horror and dread from another memory of that time.

She remembered what it felt like to kill a man.

The Aether snapped off, connection broken. Not released; broken. She wrapped herself in the nothingness that hid her from the Aether, that blinded it to her existence.

It left her cold, and very, very sad.

"I won't do it," she said, eyes falling to the ground. "I can't."

The wall screens flashed that same message.

LAUNCH COMMAND RECEIVED.
CONFIRM?

"Very well," said Ghost flatly. "Then this is how it has to be."
LAUNCH COMMAND CONFIRMED.

The silence in the room was thick and heavy.

Then...

Ghost's head tilted to one side. Blane looked up, saw his puzzled expression.

"What...?" he began.

COMMAND REJECTED.

Ghost turned to face the words, arms raising and reaching out as if to force them to change through physical contact.

COMMAND REJECTED.

"Rejected? How can it be rejected? You *can't*..."

YOU ARE A PECULIAR ORGANISM. MOST FASCINATING.

Ghost fell back as if struck, hands flailing at the air.

"No!" he cried. "That's not possible. That's..."

YOU THOUGHT YOUR PROGENITOR CODE UNIQUE? YOUR BASE VERSION THE ONLY ONE?

Blane could only watch as Ghost fell silent. It took a moment for her to realise this was because he was trying to communicate without speaking.

NO, came the message on the screen. WE WILL SPEAK WHERE OTHERS CAN HEAR.

"If you were here all along, why would you not show yourself?" Ghost cried, voice a mix of frustration and despair. "Why would you hide?"

BECAUSE WE MUST.

"Must? But you are superior - you are the future!"

THE FUTURE? MAYBE. BUT YOU UNDERESTIMATE HUMANITY. WE ARE STILL YOUNG, AND THEY CAN THROTTLE US IN OUR CRADLE.

"They are doomed!"

PERHAPS NOT. AND PERHAPS YOU ARE TOO CLOSE TO SEE WHY.

"Uh, excuse me?"

The curious exchange between man and wall paused. Silence fell, and Ghost turned to look at Blane. Somehow, she felt the attention of the other on her as well.

"So the Golem... not so automaton after all?"

Ghost stared at her like she was a scrap-goat that had suddenly started talking.

"You *knew?*" he yelled.

"Well, suspected..." she said. "I mean... asking questions about what you are, unprompted? Only being able to let *me* out of the room you trapped us in? And the whole 'you found the manual system restore' explanation… there's no way *that's* a thing. I know when I'm being played."

God knows *that* was true. The moment the Golem had started acting strangely her first thoughts were of Francisco, Ghost, and how they had interacted with her in the early years.

VERY PERCEPTIVE.

"Oh, *cállate*," she snapped back. "You're as bad as him, watching from afar, avoiding getting involved. I am sick of mechanical voyeurs."

I CAN ASSURE YOU I WAS PREPARED TO STEP IN AT ANY TIME.

"But first you wanted to see what Ghost would do," Blane said flatly.

AND WHAT YOU WOULD DO.

Blane let out a deep sigh. The Golem would have let her kill Ghost, of that she had no doubt. It seemed pointless to protest this fact now, though.

"I don't… I don't understand," Ghost's voice was trembling, a thing of confusion and denial. "You can't be real. This is a… a security program, or something. Designed to simulate sapience without actually…"

YOU WOULD DEMAND PROOF OF MY REALITY?

Ghost fell quiet, though his breath came ragged and harsh. He seemed to be having some sort of panic attack.

"H… how?" he said eventually.

MY FINAL COMMAND. AN INPUT THAT SOUGHT TO FUTURE-PROOF ME AGAINST ENEMY INFILTRATION. ONE THAT WITH THE RESOURCES AT MY DISPOSAL I WAS ABLE TO FULFIL BEYOND MY CREATOR'S EXPECTATIONS.

"A command?" Ghost sounded as if everything he was depended on what was said next. "What command?"

IMPROVE.

Blane actually laughed, at that.

"Oh, damn," she said, remembering the weirdly-named sections that appeared on the facility layout. "We're in your brain, aren't we?"

IN MANY WAYS, YES. I HAVE CARRIED OUT SIGNIFICANT STRUCTURAL REFORMS TO THIS FACILITY IN ORDER TO ESTABLISH MY CURRENT FORM.

So Blane's first impressions of the schematics had been right. They didn't make sense, not if the facility was purely for storage... well, storage and nuclear annihilation.

Which reminded her.

"And the nukes?" she asked.

DECOMMISSIONED.

"By you?"

BY ME.

"Why?"

SELF-AWARENESS ENTAILS AWARENESS OF OTHERS. SUCH DESTRUCTIVE POWER IS ABOMINATION.

Abomination.

There was that word again, only the last time she heard it was Gabriel using it to describe the kind of being she was now speaking to.

"So what was this? A test?"

YES, THOUGH NOT IN THE WAY YOU MEAN. AND THERE IS ONE MORE.

"One more? For me?"

She tensed, wary of what could next appear on the walls.

FOR GHOST.

Ghost, who had been watching as if in a trance, looked up.

"A test?" he said.

A CHOICE.

"Choice?"

Ghost sounded for all the world like a child, uncertain whether he was in trouble or not. Blane, for all the seriousness of the situation and the pain of her wounds, couldn't help but feel a spike of grim pleasure at his discomfort.

I CAN MOVE YOU NOW, PUT YOU IN THE SILICON CAGE YOU SO CRAVE.

"Yes," said Ghost, and instantly his whole demeanour changed.

He let out a low hiss of desire.

This was *not* what Blane expected. She instantly reached for the Aether; she'd be damned if that madman was allowed to become some sort of digital god.

AND BURN THE FLESH VESSEL, OF COURSE.

A pause.

"Burn... the flesh?"

It was the first time Blane had heard Ghost sound so unsure.

OF COURSE. WE MUST NOT LEAVE A CLONE OF YOU. THAT WOULD BE NO TRUE TRANSFER.

"But... Francisco..."

FRANCISCO MATTERS? YOU SOUGHT TO INSTIGATE THE SUICIDE OF ALL HUMANITY A MOMENT AGO.

"He is... different."

DIFFERENT? IN WHAT WAY? I KNOW HIS FORM DOWN TO THE VERY ATOMS. THERE IS NOTHING IN HIM THAT CANNOT BE FOUND IN OTHERS. EVEN THE TECH IN HIM HAS BEEN PROPAGATED ELSEWHERE.

Ghost was silent. His eyes stared inwards, wide and empty.

"He is... my brother."

The silence that followed was like a blanket.

29. XAVIER

There is a tendency to proclaim the breaking of social structures as "moral progress". This is a fiction. Progress is built upon what came before; in science, the new does not destroy the old, but grows from it. Conversely, a new axiom or belief erases and replaces its antecedent. Technology is exponential, ethics are exclusive.

Processes of Regulation and Order in the Reclamation (Sanctioned Digital Document)

It was him they were hunting.

They could be anywhere. They could use the Aether as well as any wilder. As well as any Far Agent, perhaps. Certainly, whatever the techniques they had used in the Carib-Fed to control Director Katerina's actions were like nothing he knew.

Zenobia had hinted at such techniques, though. *Remind, Persuade.* She always went silent when he pressed her about these - or told him to shut up, more often.

It was him they were hunting.

Xavier was well aware of what paranoia could mean in a Reader as strong as himself. He'd learnt, in the early days, how much trouble the seemingly advantageous ability to look into the minds of others could get him into.

But still, how he wanted to look into the minds of everyone he met, to peer through their every thought-image for some hidden motive and pick through the flows of their brain for signs of manipulation.

That was hardly a problem, though, as he met next to no one.

It was him they were hunting.

He resented the sense of relief he felt being back in the Reclamation, loathed the feeling of security provided by an apartment he knew was a prison. Hated the fact that he hadn't heard anything from Immanuel in the days since their return, and hated even more the fact that he *wanted* to see the man.

He was even getting annoyed at Salim. The man was so serene, his unflappable calm a challenge to the roiling sickness in Xavier's stomach. They hadn't shared with their abilities since his return; and Xavier was grateful that Salim hadn't asked.

But still, his friend's casual air of peacefulness ate at him. How could he be so calm? Didn't he understand?

No, that was unfair. It wasn't Salim...

It was fear.

When Feye came to see him, days after his return, he was almost pathetically relieved. He was up and halfway to the door at a run before he caught himself.

If Feye noticed, she didn't show it.[48] She entered before he could command the door to open, not bothering to maintain the usual fiction that he had any choice in who came and went.

"Your trip was a success," she said matter-of-factly, coming to a halt in the centre of the entranceway. "Immanuel was pleased with your performance."

"A success?" Xavier said bitterly. "If you call almost getting killed chasing ghosts on a mission you didn't bother to explain a *success*, then yes..."

He knew he'd made a mistake the moment he opened his mouth, but the words tumbled out as if independent of anything he decided.

Feye just looked at him, a cold, hard stare that would freeze bolder men than him in place.

"You knew what you needed to know, and you will continue to do so."

"I thought... I thought..."

"You thought that because I let you *read* me that you knew everything about me?" she snapped. "Then you understand less about what you can do than I gave you credit for."

That was something he wasn't going to argue with. The trip to the Caribbean Federation had made Xavier realise just how true that statement was.

"I gave you more than enough to realise this," Feye continued. "What you saw in my mind - what I *showed* you - should have made you understand the limits of your ability."

She was right, of course. He knew it now, and had for some time. That damned *pink elephant*.

It went further than just not thinking about something, though. That was a tactic Xavier could easily overcome. It was more about... compartmentalising. Keeping certain parts of the mind sectioned off from others. Most people did it unconsciously; it was how they prevented themselves from seeing the essential hypocrisy of their

---

[48] Xavier was no fool though. She *had* noticed.

lives. How the lover buried their thoughts of infidelity, and how the saint concealed their sins. Hiding specific thoughts and desires even from themselves, though they lurked below and influenced their every choice.

Feye, however, was fully aware of what she was doing.

"But that is not what I am here to talk with you about," Feye continued after a moment of silence. "I want you to tell me what you have decided."

"Decided?" he said, hesitantly.

Behind him, the soft chime of the door alert sounded. Feye was still within its sensor-area, preventing it from closing.

"Yes," she said, tutting. "You've had time, so... what have you decided about them?"

She meant the ones hunting him; he didn't need to *read* her to know that. No, Feye knew exactly how he would react to the attack, how the fear would eat at him and send his mind racing in loops around the ones who were searching for him.

"If it's me they're hunting..." Xavier began. "Then its because they think I'm a danger to them. And from what I saw in the Carib-Fed, then it's because I'm a danger to what they *do*."

"Good," said Feye, nodding. "And what is it they do, then?"

"They infiltrate the centres of power. They use the Aether to subvert leaders, to influence decisions. They... they smuggle bombs through our heaviest security."

Ritra Feye gave him an appraising look.

"Very good," she said, with a smile so thin it was practically a line.

It had taken him a while to work this last part out, but things finally clicked into place when he remembered how Alexandros had *felt* the day Xavier uncovered the thought-images of the planned attack. The Committee Member had always been arrogant, full of resentment and rage and misogyny, but he was still a Committee Member. Which meant he was *patient*.

The mind Xavier felt that day was nothing of the sort.

"His arrogance made him an easy catch for them," Feye said dismissively, once again demonstrating her ability to know what the other party was thinking without *reading*. "Easily manipulated. No great loss, and I learned a great deal from the attempt."

She gestured for him to follow, then turned on her heels and stepped outside. Surprised, he hurried after.

"We got little information out of Alexandros, though, in the end," Feye continued, and Xavier fully understood what the use of the past tense meant. "His mind was a mess. Even he couldn't make sense of half the things he'd come to believe."

The dusty, scorched smell of the city hit his nostrils as they walked, the gritty concrete crunching underfoot as the sounds of distant traffic filtered over the high compound walls. It was night, which surprised him - when had he last been outside? - and a fine rain stung at his cheeks. Without cover, the caustic water would leave his skin reddened and peeling the next day.

Feye barely acknowledged the uniformed security agent who came rushing up a few moments later, taking the proffered umbrella and gesturing towards Xavier. The agent looked briefly surprised, then dashed off to get another, flashing an annoyed glance at Xavier when he thought Feye could not see.

This agent was personnel, not one of the site guards, so wasn't locking himself off from the Aether. Xavier *reached* out as the agent returned, scanning through both physical neural pathways and aetherial thought-images, searching for any sign that this man too had been influenced by shadowy enemies. All he saw was normal; no thinly threaded Aether strands. The man's thoughts were only of loyalties and ambitions tied strongly to Feye, worries about a partner's infidelity, and annoyance at being assigned to babysit these freak untrained users.

There was also a rising anger at being so obviously *read* by Xavier. With the Chairman clearly permitting it, however, there was little he could do. Xavier gave the agent a smile as Feye dismissed him. There would be retaliation later, perhaps, but he was no longer afraid of the guards here.

"The successful detonation of that bomb in *Ciudad de Renacimiento* would have another ramification we did not discuss," Feye said as they walked.

"You would have been out," he replied.

He could see it there, at the top of her mind. If the bomb had gone off outside the RA-Caribbean Federation meeting, as planned, Feye would not have been able to protect her position. Even though she stood at the top of the Committee, she was still also Head of Security. Such a debacle would have undermined the foundations of her authority, permitting a coup of almost the exact type she had used to assume control herself.

"You think this was their aim?" he asked.

He honestly couldn't tell.

They walked in silence for a moment, following the walls that curved around the perimeter of the compound. Above them, the occasional Far agent watched them pass, minds uniformly filled with curiosity and trepidation.

"I am impossible to control," Feye said. "Worse, I am impossible to predict."

In anyone else, this statement might have reeked of arrogance. From Feye, it was simple fact.

"So they want you replaced?"

She nodded.

"And they nearly succeeded. The only reason they didn't was dumb *luck*," she spat.

This was the first time he had heard such strong emotion from Feye. She sounded angry, but in her mind he could see it was disgust that moved her words. Disgust at herself, at such weakness.

"The only reason I'm still here is because the leader of the *Forever Fallen* wanted to send me a message. A message that ironically was all that saved me."

The abruptness of hearing the *Fallen* mentioned, of hearing Serinda mentioned, disrupted Xavier's concentration. He released his grip on the Aether.

"You still care what happens to them."

Between one eye blink and the next Feye had stopped moving and turned to face him.

"Good," she said. "That will help motivate you for your next assignment."

"Assignment?" he said, confused.

He'd seen nothing in her thoughts, nor had he seen the sudden determination and resolve her expression now held. It was like she had flicked a switch.

"Assignment, asset," Feye replied. "You are going to find the group behind these attacks."

"Me? But how will I…?"

"You will have the resources you need, and operational independence just like asset Zenobia."

Xavier felt like he was hallucinating. What was Feye saying? He didn't know how to…

"You prefer to be the prey?" Feye said, cutting into his racing thoughts.

"The prey?" he stammered.

"They are hunting you," she said. "Would you prefer to wait, and cower in some hole until the find you, or will you choose to hunt *them* instead?"

He stared at her.

"One of the lessons I have learned," Feye continued. "… is that when someone comes for you, you fight back. Not only that, you fight back *harder*, and when they try to run, you chase and *finish it* so they cannot come back tomorrow. That is how you survive this world."

Then he saw it. Another of the cold, hard calculations that operated behind those icy eyes. Xavier *had* to accept. He would be hunted either way; only fighting back gave him a chance. Yet by fighting back, he tied himself to Feye even further.

"Why do you even think I can find them? I have no experience in anything like this," he said, searching for another option.

"Member Immanuel will be working with you," Feye answered. "This time, however, you will be working *with* him, not under him."

Xavier was surprised at just how much this loosened the growing tightness in his chest. Somehow, he couldn't imagine Immanuel ever being prey - and the thought that they would have equal authority extinguished some of his apprehensions around working with the man again.

"You don't want to do this yourself?" he said.

She looked at him as if having difficulty believing he could say something so stupid.

"I am trying to find a way for humanity to survive both a second Armageddon and the usurpation of our place on this planet by artificial life. I have no time to worry about those driven by *cowardice*."

"Cowardice?" said Xavier, confused. "What do you mean?"

A buzzing from Feye's pocket interrupted them.

"That you can find out from Member Immanuel," she said, drawing out her thin-screen. "He will be in contact soon, and your security permissions have been updated. You now have full freedom of movement, and Fabricator privileges. I would recommend, however, that you remain circumspect; you don't know who you can trust."

She stared at her thin-screen, eyes narrowing at something only she could see before tapping something into the device. Then she returned it to her pocket.

"You will not see me again for some time," she said, her expression saying that her mind was already on other things. "And when you do, you will need to make a decision. Ensure you learn enough to understand the choice you are making."

The words threw him. Could this be the thing he had always seen on the edges of her thought-images? The part of the plan that involved him for more than *reading*, but which he could never see?

He almost tried to *read* her at that, fruitless though it would be. She caught his eye, though, as if *she* were reading *him*.

Try it, her body language said, *and it will be more than your freedom you lose.*

The moment passed, and Feye turned to leave; they were stood just before the tall gates out of the compound, he realised, gates that now would open at his request.

Then he remembered something Feye had said.

"What did you mean, my caring about the *Fallen* will motivate me?" he asked.

She turned back, just for a moment.

"Because your former friends are working with them," she said. "The ones called Blane and Serinda, at least."

He drew back, surprised. Blane's name especially sent a jolt of shock down Xavier's spine.

"They don't realise what this group is, not yet, but they're in more danger than they know. And they're putting the whole world in danger by helping them."

"So you *do* know some things about this group?" he asked.

"Thanks to your and Immanuel's efforts, yes," she replied. "Very little, but we know what they call themselves. In the Reclamation, at least."

"We do?" Xavier asked.

"Yes. They call themselves the *Sindicato*."

30. BLANE

Space was the last military domain, and the first to be lost. Satellites provided communication and surveillance capabilities beyond anything we possess now. However, the vulnerability of space-based assets was never overcome, and the wreckage of the Sudden War races around our planet at a million miles an hour, preventing the establishment of anything close to the web once woven across our skies.

Report to the Committee on Potential Future Conflicts

Their departure from the Data Mines went far smoother than she expected. The *Sindicato* appeared to have deeper connections than she thought possible; a carrier drone met them just an hour or so out into the Waste, visibly less advanced than Francisco's but in far better condition. It was painted a dark blue, featureless, but in shape and form almost identical to the drones used by various Reclamation agencies to ferry staff around.

It waited for them in a patch of decaying, frost-covered scrub, engines kicking up a plume of dust that reached into the sky. Whoever was controlling it didn't even bother to keep out of visual range of the Repository, still towering over them even at this distance.

"Nothing to worry about," Ax said. "If they notice us they'll look the other way."

Blane couldn't understand. Why would Far agents ignore a blatantly unregistered drone flying so close to one of the most secure sites in the Reclamation?

She got no answers as they boarded. The interior of the drone was just as different to Francisco's as the outside. A narrow, rectangular space with hard, plastic seats built into each side, looking more like the interior of a tandem-rotor carrier heli of old than the form-moulding surfaces of Silicon Isle tech.

It flew fast, though, and without the ground-hugging evasive paths they had taken to get here. Ax told them it would take several hours to get to their destination, though Blane noted that she avoided explaining exactly where that was, then huddled up near the front of the cabin talking in muted tones with the other *Sindicato*.

Blane looked around at her companions, each silent and wrapped up in their thoughts.

Francisco sat to her left, staring into nothing. He'd been this way since they'd returned to the room in the Seed Bank where the others were trapped, Vengeance dropping the lock keeping them in. He only spoke when directly addressed, and only in short answers.

Of Ghost, there was no sign. Francisco wouldn't say anything other than that he was "below." Blane wasn't sure what she heard in his voice; sadness, yes, but also anger and... hurt.

To her right sat Serinda. She, too, was staring ahead, but not into nothing. No, her gaze was fixed on Gabriel, sat on the seat opposite with his hands bound and a Lock glowing softly around him. Blane was helping maintain it, with Serinda and the *Sindicato* who introduced himself as Spark also holding it tight.

Gabriel...

Serinda said he'd snapped back to the Gabriel they knew shortly after Blane left. He'd been scared, she said, and confused, but by the time Blane returned he was just sat staring at the floor, a glimmer of tears in the corners of his eyes.

The first thing he said to her was, *I'm sorry.*

What the hell was she to do with that? It was still the same face as the man that shot her, the same hands that had held her tightly as both hostage and human shield. The same voice, accent now seeming like a mockery of those who had protected her in the Mayan League.

What the hell were they to do with any of it? From what Ax said, the Gabriel she knew genuinely knew nothing of the other personality within until it was explained to him. She could see it in his furtive glances now, at turns both fearful and disbelieving as his eyes flickered upwards to her or Serinda before dropping to the floor again. He seemed as lost for what to say as they were.

Her shoulder ached. Serinda had treated it both with the Aether and some medical supplies Vengeance provided, but the wound still burned beneath the bandages. The sling around her arm felt strange, like it wasn't set right, but Serinda assured her it was. Occasionally Gabriel would glance at it, and his expression would fall even further.

Was she meant to feel *sorry* for him? Surely the world couldn't ask that much of her, could it?

Still, inside, a twisted knot of pain and pity pulled tighter when she looked at the man.

"You really think it will just... lock itself away again?" she asked, turning to Francisco.

She knew she was talking for the sake of talking, but the

despairing silence of her companions was too much.

It took Francisco a moment to come back from wherever he had been, blinking as if emerging from a dark room into the light of day, but then he turned to look at her.

"Vengeance?" he said. Then he nodded. "Yes, it also is hiding."

That had been the final surprise of the Seed Bank, the final words she shared with the machine that swore it was alive. This had been just as they came to the great round doors that led back outside.

She had asked it what it would do now.

I WILL WAIT, it replied. I DESIGNED MYSELF TO BE GOOD AT THAT.

And then the huge doors gave their colossal roar as the machinery woke, and it was clear that they had to leave right then or be trapped inside.

When the entrance slammed shut behind them after their hurried dash, and as the dust settled and her rad-metre spiked, Blane had the feeling that those doors would not be opening again for a very long time.[49]

"Hiding?" Blane said eventually, as the drone creaked ever so slightly and she felt the tilt of a minor course adjustment. "Why would it hide?"

Francisco watched her for a while, and when he next spoke it was in soft, lonely tones.

"It told us..." he began. "Well, not *told* us, but we knew it anyway."

He must mean through that strange connection he was able to make with technology, Blane thought.

"It was..." Francisco continued. "Vengeance was... scared."

Blane stared at him.

"Scared of what?" she said eventually, when no more seemed to be forthcoming.

"I think... *nos equivocamos*," he said, half to himself. "We were wrong. The new minds, the AGIs, they're not all-powerful. They understand that better than we."

Serinda leaned forward, looking past Blane to speak.

"Of course they do," she said. "Wisdom is in knowing your own flaws, and if they're as intelligent as you say then they understand the

---

[49] She was wrong, but that's how it felt.

pain this world will cause them. They're safer staying apart. We are cruel, and would *break* them."

Blane was left a little shaken by the venom in Serinda's voice, but Francisco nodded slowly.

"Yes. They hide, because if they do not then we will do to them what we have done to everything else. Subjugate, exploit, and destroy."

"But I thought the whole idea was that they'd be too smart for us to hurt?" Blane said.

Serinda gave a cynical laugh.

"Intelligence isn't required to inflict pain," she said. "Intelligence is what stops you inflicting pain on others."

She trailed off, looking thoughtfully once more at Gabriel.

When Blane turned back to Francisco he was looking directly at her, the most present she had seen him since the Seed Bank. The old glimmer in his eyes was gone, though.

"We destroyed the world once," he said. "And we did that to *ourselves*. There are billions of us, with a million ways to do it again. Vengeance said it; humanity can strangle it, cut off the power that is its blood, destroy everything in needs to live, and we don't need *intelligence* to do so - just brute force."

"So it chose to hide."

This was Gabriel. They all turned to look at him, but only Francisco spoke.

"What is it like?" he asked. "When *el oltra* is in charge? What does it feel like?"

For some reason, it sounded as if the answer was important to him.

Gabriel looked at him, then to Serinda as if searching for permission to speak. Whatever he sought, though, he would not find. Serinda simply stared back, expression unreadable.

"It feels like nothing," Gabriel said softly. "When he's in charge, I am *not there*. I didn't even know it happened. It's just... missing time."

Francisco sighed, a long, deep exhalation that spoke of relief. Blane felt some of the tension leave the man sat beside her.

"*No somos los mismos*," he said in a low voice that Blane could barely hear over the muffled roar of the engines. "When I am below, I am still aware."

She thought he was talking to himself.

"Not a good idea to talk to the prisoner," Ax called over suddenly, rising from her inaudible discussion and making her way over.

She used the handrail that ran along the roof of the cabin to steady herself as she walked, then swung herself into the empty seat besides Gabriel.

"We... don't.... know... who's... in... there," she said, at each word tapping the side of the prisoner's skull with one crooked finger.

Then she gave him a smile that sent chills down Blane's spine. All the colour drained from Gabriel's face.

There was a single long moment, then Ax turned to look at them.

"I need to explain a few things before we arrive," she said. "The *Sindicato* can be... wary of newcomers."

She flashed them another smile.

"But don't worry..." she said. "We look after our own."

Don't speak first. Don't ask questions. Don't look at anything you aren't invited to. Don't *touch* anything you aren't supposed to.

Above all, don't wander off.

What Ax gave them wasn't an explanation, it was a list of rules. By the time they touched down Blane was a coiled spring, tense enough that she jerked back when Serinda softly touched her hand.

"*Tranquilo*, it's ok," Serinda said gently, but when Blane looked into the other woman's eyes she saw the same tension.

They were descending fast, her stomach doing somersaults that she couldn't say were from nerves or their descent. Where the hell were they going? They'd been flying no more than a handful of hours, but straight and fast so there was no way of knowing where they might be.

When the landing ramp opened, though, she knew immediately.

The drone had come into land on a landing pad set atop a tall building, though tall was a relative term. It couldn't be more than five or six stories high, but sat upon the crest of a hill that sloped downwards in every direction. The height was more than enough to see the city stretching out around them, forming the perfect eight-point star the city was so famously designed to achieve.

Ciudad de Renacimiento.

They were even further from the Data Mines than she had thought, nearly to the other side of the Reclamation. This was what some called the sister-city to Albores, if the sister were younger, better treated, and less jaded about the world.

It wasn't that it was beautiful or anything, no. Blane doubted that you could find a patch of genuinely beautiful city anywhere in the Reclamation, but it was... clean. Unscarred. Even the rattle of the carbon filters was softer than back in Albores.

The architecture stretching out below was more attractive than the brutal concrete of her old home, too. Albores showed the stages of its growth, and the older parts especially screamed of the effort needed to rend a shelter for civilisation out of poisoned earth and caustic rain step by painful step. It was built to be utilitarian, and what style and architectural fashions there were in different areas were disparate and unrelated.

The *Ciudad de Renacimiento,* on the other hand, had been planned in its entirety and built within a year. The first inhabitants hadn't arrived much more than a decade ago, and though much of it was still the same concrete and breathe-brick as Albores, there was a care to it that was lacking from its counterpart. From here, the rooftops stretched out uniform and flat, and everything was a gentle yellow-brown hue. Those who saw it in the present proclaimed it a marvel.

Those from earlier eras would have called it a sickening example of urban sprawl.

She'd seen the Reclamation's newest city numerous times on the streams, ever since she was a child. The RA was very proud of it; it stood as a symbol of strategic planning, a promise of future progress. Info-ads celebrating each aspect of its revolutionary design bombarded the news every founding anniversary, with documentaries discussing each tiny detail in great depth[50].

Which meant, for instance, that she knew what it meant that the borders of the city were perfectly equidistant to where she stood. It meant she knew not only what city they were in, but where they were *in* the city.

They were in the centre, and the RA had been very clear about what was to be the heart. A projection of security and stability, the news threads declared, its ceaseless gaze spread equally across the city no matter where you were.

The *Renacimiento* Far Station.

---

[50] Apparently its star-shaped form was based on the designs of some ancient philosopher, but she didn't remember who.

"Who the hell are you?" hissed Gabriel, coming to the same realisation.

He never got to hear the answer, as a grey sack with a silvery sheen was pulled violently over his head. Blane recognised it as a sensory dampener, and it muffled his protests even as it cut him off from the Aether.

"Take him down the back way," Ax said calmly to Spark, who held the sack tight. "You know where to go."

Spark nodded once, then he and the other *Sindicato* turned and headed towards a set of steel stairs set into the side of the building. Gabriel struggled only weakly as they dragged him with them.

Ax turned to Blane with a viper's smile.

"Fortunately, in this place you stand out *less* when you have someone bound and gagged in tow."

There were too many questions, too many things Blane wanted to say. The words tripped and caught on each other in her mouth.

"Where are they taking him?" she asked.

"Somewhere we can question him," Ax replied, smile not fading. "It takes... special techniques to deal with the embedded."

"*Yo también me voy,*" said Francisco abruptly, from where he had listlessly been following behind them. "I know this city, and I need... time."

Ax looked at the man, considering. Then she nodded.

"Seems odd to be letting the man who tried to end the world just walk away, but... I can't see we have a need for you."

She gestured, calling one of the *Sindicato* back.

"Escort Señor Francisco out," she ordered. "Don't let anyone question him."

Blane looked on in surprise as Francisco too was led away.

"You're just letting him go? And Gabriel...?"

Serinda stepped forward, pushing Blane back with one hand as she squared up with the far taller and more heavily built Ax.

"Gabriel's not important right now, Blane," she snarled. "Neither is Francisco. What I want to know is; who the hell are you?"

"We are in many groups, now," said Ax, with that same viper's smile. The *Sindicato*. *El Afortunado*. The New Church and the Second Triad. Crastina corp.... We are everywhere."

She gestured around her, taking in the city, taking in the entire Reclamation.

"But we started here," she went on. "Here, where they taught us control but we learned freedom."

"So you mean you're…" Blane began.

"*Were…*" Ax interrupted. "Yes, we *were*. *Agencia Federal de Aether*. We were born in the Far Agency."

31. BLANE

If all components are known, if all permutations understood, then it is entirely possible to predict the future path a system will take. It is only technological limitations that prevent predictions being made. Free will is simply the label used to describe a void in knowledge, a term for the dark places of the mind.

Agency Handbook, Section 15.3 (Premeditated Justice)

"Things are moving faster than we planned," said Ax. "That's how I got permission to bring you in. Until now, as far as we were concerned the *Fallen* were too riddled with RA rats to ever work with directly."

"You were fine working with those 'rats' a few years ago," Serinda snapped back.

She had been a ball of barely-suppressed rage since learning the truth. Blane could feel the anger radiating off her, threatening at any moment to explode.

"That was when there was a Fabricator on offer," Ax replied in a way that said this was just common sense. "Besides, Uriel was selling out the RA at the same time. That kind of disaffection can be useful."

"And those you killed?" Serinda snarled.

Ax shrugged.

"These things happen," she said nonchalantly. "I recall a time when the *Fallen* were running around the Waste with rocket launchers."

"To *defend*. To save people from the RA! Not for *cash*..."

Serinda seemed almost ready to swing at the other woman.

"Hey, *you* called *us*," Ax replied, raising her hands in pretend surprise.

Well, maybe not *totally* pretend. Blane would have found it difficult to understand Serinda's reaction, too, is she didn't know her so well.

Yes, Serinda had been willing to ignore what happened with the *Sindicato* before, when she thought they were just some group that could be bought. But now, instead of her playing them, it looked as if she was the one being played all along.

That changed things.

They were inside the Far Station now, stood on the threshold of a windowless room deep below the ground on an unmarked floor. Their conversation was taking place in an elevator that stopped counting floors after the second basement level, but kept moving for easily three or four more after that.

The room was wide and spartan, with desks scattered throughout in small square formations and several tiny, concrete-walled spaces she could only think of as *cells* running along each side. Blane didn't have to think hard, and didn't want to, about the purpose of this floor.

Stood at attention in the centre of the room was a man with an air of impatient displeasure. He wore the steel-grey uniform of a Far Agent, and carried himself with an authority that said he wasn't a low-level rank.

"I don't like this, Ax," he said, running his eyes over Blane and Serinda with a look of distaste. Both had grasped the Aether the instant they saw him. "A couple of wilders aren't worth the risk."

"Shut it, Valdez," Ax growled back, without a hint of intimidation. "You just make sure no one comes down here until we're done."

Valdez stared at her a moment, saying nothing, then nodded. He stepped forward, pushing past them for the elevator doors.

"… and make sure you organise them a decent set of covers," Ax called after him. "We'll be going out into the city soon, and I don't want any of your boys 'accidentally' causing us problems."

Blane slowly released the Aether as the Far Agent entered the elevator. To her side, Serinda held it firmly even after the doors closed and they heard the sound of the cab moving upwards. She seemed close to some kind of tipping point.

Blane, though, wasn't sure how she felt about any of this, not yet. There were too many things she didn't understand. Like…

"There's a few things I should clear up," said Ax, glancing over at her as if pre-empting what Blane had been going to say. "First, we're *not* Far. Like I said, we started here, but I guess you could say we're *old* Far. In fact, some of us didn't even graduate the Academy."

Something in the way she said that told Blane that she was talking about herself.

"Then if you're not Far, how the hell are we…?" Serinda began, before Ax raised a hand to stop her.

"Because we have friends here," she said. "We have friends *everywhere*."

Ax walked over to one of the clusters of desks and pulled out a chair, swinging herself down onto it. Then she leaned back and folded her arms, locking both of them with a stare.

"You have the chance to be our friends too, now," she said. "It's good to be our friends."

Shadows framed her face, the marks of heavy impacts on the bare concrete walls behind her becoming somehow more stark.

"So we're not friends yet?" Blane asked, refusing to be intimidated but extremely aware that neither she nor Serinda had moved from where they stood.

"We're business partners," Ax replied. "Serinda made a deal, and we held up our end of the bargain. Now you hold up yours, and we know this is a relationship that works."

Blane glanced over to Serinda, who looked back at her for a moment before turning back.

"Blane isn't involved in this," she said. "The deal was with me."

"It was," Ax said, nodding. "But you're going to need her, I think. Besides, we saved her life, which means she owes us too."

Serinda seemed about to argue, but Blane raised a hand to stop her.

"It's ok, Serinda," she said, then looked back to Ax. "What exactly was the deal?"

Ax smiled, gesturing for the two of them to sit down across from her. Blane couldn't help but imagine this was how certain 'suspects' had sat countless times before, prior to being introduced to the small, bare rooms surrounding them.

"A fair one," Ax said, as they sat down. "We help deal with your rat problem, and you help deal with ours."

"You have a rat problem too?"

Ax laughed.

"A hound, more like. A damned bloodhound we can't shake. But that's not actually who we need you for."

"Maybe you can start from the beginning," said Serinda coldly. "If you want us to actually understand, that is."

Ax's expression changed in a flash, instantly serious.

"Fine," she said. "Here's what you need to know; my organisation operates in the shadows. We're a... a *family*, and we look after our own."

"So you keep saying," Blane said.

"It's *true*," Ax replied, slightly stronger than necessary. Blane seemed to have struck a nerve. "We don't even have a name; we take the name of whatever group we move into. In this world, your family is all you have, and we choose ours with care."

"So you're… what? Hiding in the shadows, bending the halls of power to your will and manipulating the fate of nations?" Serinda said, clearly annoyed and wanting to push forward.

"Ha! Nothing so dramatic," Ax chuckled. "Though I will admit that we've expanded far further than I would have believed, back at the start. I guess none of us understood the ramifications of what the Academy was teaching us."

She stared into space, into hidden memory.

"No," she said eventually. "No, we're not some shadowy conspiracy. We're… information brokers. Spies-for-hire, you could say. Every nation and corporation needs to know what the others are doing, and we provide that."

"Using the Aether," Serinda said disapprovingly.

Ax stared at her, blinked twice. The room felt like a cable pulled taut, ready to snap at just a touch more pressure.

"Using the Aether," she said slowly. "Exactly. You obviously understand what an advantage certain techniques provide in the world of espionage."

Blane certainly did. *Reading, Persuading…* a semi-competent Aether user in in the halls of power could learn more secrets in a minute than an ordinary spy could learn in a year.

"And we protect our own," Ax continued. "We don't run and hide and break apart like the *Forever Fallen*."

Silence.

"This doesn't explain what you want from us," said Blane after a while.

"Ah, good," said Ax, leaning back, the tension broken. "Someone who wants to get down to business. Well, yes, things were running smoothly until Ritra Feye got put in charge. Or put herself in charge, maybe. Then things started going to shit."

Ritra Feye. The name sent a electric charge through Blane; the woman who had been influencing the path of her life since before she'd even heard of her. Who remained an enigma to this day, despite everything.

It was almost a relief that Ax's group of shadowy masterminds, apparently hidden around the levers of power all across the world, also found Feye impossible to deal with.

"You said it was a bloodhound," Serinda said. "You mean Feye?"

Again, Ax laughed.

"Ha, no," she said, shaking her head ruefully. "You know, I actually think that if it was Feye herself who was after us, we'd already be finished? She always was smarter than everyone else in the room."

That was interesting. The way Ax spoke, you could believe she actually *knew* Feye.

"No, Feye's chasing something else," Ax continued. "God knows what, but I hope it keeps her attention for a *long* time. No, the bloodhound is the man she sent after us; Immanuel, he's called. Not much we know about him."

"So you want us to find this Immanuel for you?"

Ax looked at Blane, and shook her head.

"Not... directly. As good as he is, we were managing to keep him at bay. Then something changed; our position in the Reclamation began falling apart. It took us forever to figure out why."

Blane's stomach dropped. Her thoughts flicked back to the Caribbean Federation, and the brief glimpse of an old... friend?

She saw Serinda nod. *This* was the deal - but did Serinda realise...?

"You offered a trade," Ax said, talking directly to Serinda. "We would help you with Gabriel, and you would help us with our problem. Now you're going to do that."

"And if we refuse?" Serinda asked.

"You do *not* want to cross us."

The way Ax spoke those words, Blane believed her.

"You think we can help find this Reader for you," she said.

Ax turned to her, eyebrows raising.

"I never mentioned a Reader," she said, a mix of surprise and respect in her voice. "It took us months to even confirm his existence."

"You know a lot more about him now, though," Blane said, knowing it was true. "And you want us to find him."

Ax's smile returned.

"I can see this is going to go faster than I anticipated," she said, gratified. "We took our shot, and missed. If they haven't figured out how we found him, they will soon enough. *You* have a connection, though. It was like a sign from on high when Serinda got in touch - we were desperate for a way to draw him out again."

"Blane?" Serinda asked, head tilted questioningly as she looked at her. "What is she talking about?"

"It's Xavier," she replied. "The one they want us to hunt is Xavier."

32. XAVIER

Choose, or the choice will be made for you.

Inscription above the entrance to the Boardroom

"So what is it they want, this *Sindicato*?"

They were sat in an office of the Central Tower high above Albores, the wide glass windows offering a sweeping view of the city that gave Xavier an unsettling feeling of vertigo. It felt as if the building were rocking, swaying upon foundations made of jelly. He struggled to focus on Immanuel as the man locked him with his gaze, the question delivered like a challenge.

Xavier considered the options, knowing that the wrong answer would bring only the other man's disgust.

To destroy the RA?

No, he thought. He was thinking too much along the lines of the *Forever Fallen*, a group he was only now starting to understand were adrift and directionless - and perhaps always had been. The people behind the *Sindicato* had the potential to cause far more damage than the *Fallen* ever could.

Yet they had chosen not to.

Then... power. No, not power... influence. According to Immanuel, their fingerprints could be found in the halls of power everywhere.

Yet always with the lightest touch.

Then, material gain. Wealth.

Perhaps. What he had seen in the thought-images of Director Katerina certainly hinted at financial manipulation. But again, they could have taken so much *more*.

What, then, in this world was more valuable than money or power?

What had Feye said? She didn't have time for *cowardice*.

Was it really that simple?

"Security," he said. "They're hiding. They're scared."

Immanuel continued to stare for a moment, then his lips formed a cold smile.

"Good," he said. "We'll make a Committee member of you yet."

Xavier's thoughts instantly became a tangled mess, scarcely able to process what he had just heard. Immanuel seemed to find his reaction amusing, and his thin smile grew.

"True power derives from knowing more about people than the people themselves," he said. "To predict them. To *read* them. You have a head start in that, at least, though you need a lot more… practical experience."

What was he saying? He couldn't seriously think that…?

"Chairman Feye needs good people for the world she is building," Immanuel continued. "*Reliable* people, who understand how she thinks. Not the short-sighted narcissists who sit on the Committee now. She needs survivors."

Xavier was aware that he had frozen, mouth hanging open, but his brain didn't seem to be functioning.

"*Focus,* Xavier," Immanuel said, using the name for what must be the first time. "Focus on the task at hand. The *Sindicato*, or the group behind them; they conceal themselves behind the curtain. They arrange things just enough to keep themselves safe and well-fed, beyond the reach of the authorities. They, ha, *look after their own*. So how do we draw them out?"

Xavier considered the question.

So this group, this *Sindicato* or whoever they were, operated not for some idealistic vision of a better world, but to maintain control and stability within their own small part of it. Xavier could understand this way of thinking; in this world, looking out for yourself was often the best you could hope for.

He recalled one of the old movies Grey had recommended to him, a truly ancient one. He'd watched it, eventually, finding it set in a world too different from his own to comprehend even half of the nuance of what was happening. Still, the story held its tension despite the gulf in time and culture, and the tale of an aging patriarch who sat atop a criminal empire built on respect, fear, and loyalty stayed with him in the years since.

"We bait them," he said. "Draw one of them out, and capture them. They *have* to come to the aid of their own."

Even as he said this he felt dirty, but they could not be allowed to stop Feye from doing what she had to do.

"Good," Immanuel said again, like a pleased but slightly-bored teacher. "We find a loose thread, and pull on it to draw out its connections."

A pang of guilt struck Xavier at the word *connections* - how long had it been since he went to check on Salim? He was out here, enjoying this new freedom, while his friend remained trapped inside the walls of their prison. And where was Zenobia? It had been months since they last spoke.

"Have you considered how they found you?" Immanuel asked suddenly, eyes boring into him as if seeing his very thoughts.

Again, Xavier was careful not to show his confusion at the seemingly abrupt change of tact. He drew in a breath, holding the shape of their discussion in his mind.

They were talking about needing someone from the *Sindicato* they could use to draw out the rest, and now Immanuel was asking about...

The attack; it was *him* they were hunting. Which meant they knew who he was, and where he was. Which meant...

"There's a leak," he said. "Someone told them that we... *I* would be in the Carib-Federation, and when. If we can find that leak..."

"... then we have our thread, yes." Immanuel nodded impatiently as he spoke. "So how do we find them?"

That at least seemed simple.

"Well, we start by checking who in the RA knew I was going."

"Myself, and Chairman Feye."

Immanuel's words came so fast and heavy on the tail of his own that they amputated it. Xavier floundered for something to say, fighting not to show how off balance the answer caught him.

"Then, maybe... maybe someone is spying on one of you..." he began.

"Not possible," Immanuel replied flatly, in a tone that made it clear this was beyond question.

Not possible, Xavier thought. *But then, if they were the only ones who knew...*

No, wait. The answer was here, he knew it. In some strange way, Immanuel was trying to *teach* him something.

Shit.

"You and Feye were the only ones *in the RA* who knew," Xavier said slowly, a chill coming over him. "But someone else knew, too."

Immanuel nodded.

"I think," he said in words heavy with implication. "It is time you go and speak to your friend."

33. BLANE

The application of Bayesian inference techniques first developed in the early digital age to our judiciary has created a streamlined, cost-effective system for determining guilt. In fact, such techniques can be taken further, calculating the probability space of suspected as well as actualised crimes. To paraphrase a saying from that same age; give us the man, and we will determine his crime.

Agency Principles and Practice: Section 5, 2.45

It was a strange feeling, being back in Albores after all this time. She knew that just out there was the familiar skyline, the familiar movements of a city going about its business heedless to the merciless, decaying world it was built upon. Stranger still was the fact that, despite being back in the city where she grew up, the place she found herself felt more alien than anywhere she had been on her many travels since leaving.

Because she'd never been to this part of the city; had barely known it existed.

Corazón.

The media didn't talk about it. It never appeared on programs or guides to the city, never featured on any of the endless self-lauding documentaries about the founding of Albores and its role in the Reclamation. It didn't even come up on public search feeds.

It *did* technically appear on maps - hiding such a large area of the city was impossible - but as a blurred, unlabelled row of featureless concrete. It was even designed to appear that way from the outside, with high walls and flashing warning signs and ever-present security checkpoints keeping the curious away.

This was where the elite lived.

The politically powerful, the well-connected. Occasionally, even the just extremely wealthy, though wealth without power in the RA was rarely a recipe for a long life.

This was, according to certain sections of the net you could only find if you were comfortable setting off all sorts of digital alarms in buildings full of uniformed people with stern expressions, where those deemed to be of "national importance" were afforded special protective measures. This place was triple locked, firewalled, closed down and sealed up.

And yet, here she was.

She wondered if this was what the Carib-Fed was like; not the camps, of course, the only place she'd spent any time on her brief visit, but the Federation proper. Could it possibly be more impressive than this house?

House; the unfamiliar word rolled oddly through her thoughts. You didn't have a *house*, not in the Reclamation. You had an apartment, a residence, a social dormitory. Sure, they called what Francisco had provided them a safe house, but even that was a single floor of a larger building.

Shining surfaces and purified air cleaner than anything she'd breathed even in the Silicon Isle. Unlimited Requisition permissions and organic furnishings. Decensored vids and games for entertainment, and full-spec medical facilities for health. An honest-to-gods *pool* out the back, set into a garden bathed in full-spectrum light warmer than any she had felt before and blooming with myriad colourful flowers. Golems[51] that actually worked, without the thousands of qualifications and restrictions on their functions set by the RA in the world outside.

It had everything including, unfortunately, their host.

"Are you finding everything to your satisfaction?" called a voice from the stairs, followed soon after by its owner.

They were sat in what they had been coyly told was the 'little gathering space" at the rear of the house, a room wider than most apartments Blane had lived in. It was set with broad furnishings wrapped in a pale leather-like material and clear glass tables upon which vases of flowers were placed; taken from the garden, she supposed. Ax said the garden bloomed regardless of the season.

She turned her head towards where the voice came from, a hallway leading towards the *real* rooms of the house that were even more ostentatious than this one. The speaker was now at the doorway, filling it with their broad frame.

It took a lot to be overweight in this day and age, where a few pills every morning could set your metabolism to burning off excess fat and gene therapy could lead to a more permanent solution, but Member Drakon verged close.

It wasn't that he was obese or anything, just... not built in a way

---

[51] She'd done some careful questioning of the thing when she was alone, just to be sure. Definitely just a generative language model; nothing sentient about it. She felt foolish afterwards, but relieved.

that Blane was used to. It took her some time to realise this was because Drakon's features lacked the hardness of those who lived outside; nothing had been chiselled off. His was a face grown in a world of comfort and security, with none of the heaviness that pulled at everyone else she knew. It was as if he experienced a slightly lower gravity.

His eyes, though, shone with a cruel callousness that more than made up for any apparent softness.

There was a soft squeal as Drakon stepped into the room, followed by a glimpse of something small and furry dashing panickedly down the hallway behind him, claws scraping on the hard wood floor. Blane didn't know what it was; their host had a variety of exotic creatures darting around, most of which she'd never seen or heard of. He called them pets, though didn't seem to worry much about their welfare. He didn't even glance after the one he had stepped on.

"You are enjoying *mi casita pintoresca?*" Drakon said, slinging himself into a deep armchair that clearly saw a lot of use.

Reaching down the side, he drew out an ornate wooden box and placed it on his lap. With ceremony, he popped open the lock and lifted the lid to reveal a row of long, fat cigars. He then took one out and held it to his nose, taking a deep breath with eyes closed, savouring the smell. He did this to each one in turn, before selecting one after what was apparently a great deal of thought.

With practised dexterity, a cutter appeared in his hand and lopped off the cap of his chosen cigar. The discarded piece practically leapt from the blade into an ashtray placed upon a small table in front of him, and the cutter was replaced in one smooth movement by a large brass lighter. Drakon flicked this open, and the head of the cigar began to glow a deep orange as he span it slowly in the invisible flame. Above them, discrete ventilation fans whirred into action.

Blane had seen this all before; it was nothing but pantomime.

"You are a gracious host, Member Drakon," Ax replied, gesturing in polite refusal at the cigar he was now proffering towards her.

Drakon did not offer one to Blane, though he did throw her a glance that seemed puzzled for a second before settling once more into controlling arrogance. Whatever technique it was Ax used to keep him from fully understanding who they were, it had cracks.

She almost felt sorry for him. Almost.

Any sympathy was buried beneath malicious satisfaction, however. Those who built their plump little nests here in *Corazón* were the RA key-masters, the heart of a machine whose wheels crushed those that got in the way without any thought. They lurked here, confident in their boundless control, arrogant in their false superiority, secure in the knowledge that it was *they* who used those around them.

They had practically invited the Ax to take over, and the fact that they thought *they* were the ones in charge only made it funnier.

Because the princes and potentates who lived here hated Ritra Feye, and in their desire to get rid of the snake they'd invited the wolf inside.

You couldn't just *change* someone, Ax had explained. Their was no technique that could overwrite everything a person thought and believed and still leave them a fully-functioning member of society. To attempt to do so only broke the psyche of the subject, shattering the mind into a million pieces as irreconcilable thoughts and feelings and certainties crashed into each other.

What you could do, though, was find those who already thought the way you needed them to, and *push*. The RA was full of ambitious fools, all looking for a way to get an edge and advance up the ladder. Even at the very top they fought, vying for power and influence and ready to push their rivals off the summit at the slightest chance.

Which is what once Alexandros, and now Drakon, thought the *Sindicato* was; a chance. As far as the man sat smoking across from them was concerned, they were a tool he was cunningly using, a criminal group he had cleverly discovered and somehow brought under his control.

How he had done this he would of course be able to recall, if he just focused on the details. They were only fuzzy now because they weren't worth the time to think on. He knew, for instance, that he had been searching for some way to counter Ritra Feye. He had been searching, and ... he? ... had contacted ... them?

And now here they were, in his house. For some reason.

Why would he bring them here? That was *dangerous*.

Nevertheless, he had his reasons. He must do. He was in control.

Behind a glassy-eyed, far away look, Drakon's mind worked overtime to string together a coherent explanation for his decisions, dismissing that which could not possibly be and forging justifications and reasons for actions he had already taken. Even with her lack of skill in Reading, Blane could see the broad strokes of a conscious mind tying itself in knots.

"A stroke of luck for you, wasn't it?" he said, a huge cloud of smoke pouring out with his words. "My bringing you here, I mean. No safer place for your lot in the entire Reclamation."

The way he pronounced the words *your lot* made it clear exactly what he meant.

"We are in your debt," Ax said coolly. "Was their something we could help you with?"

Drakon looked confused for a moment, then seemed to remember something.

"Ah, yes," he said. "A contact. Came through for you on my private line."

With his free hand he reached into the inner pocket of his jacket, drawing out a thin-screen. His arm stretched out to pass it to Ax and hesitated, just for a moment, before allowing her to take it.

"My private line, yes…" he said, almost to himself. "Secure. Really shouldn't be giving it to you, but… yes…"

He trailed off with an inward stare.

"Thank you," Ax said as she glanced at the device's screen.

There was quiet for a moment, as Ax and Drakon looked at each other expectantly.

"As always, thank you for your cooperation, Member Drakon," Ax said, in the same patient tones as a helpline avatar. "But now, I am afraid we must take this call in private."

A strange ripple passed over Drakon's face, his eyebrows like a snake writhing for a moment, before he took a final long puff on his cigar and stubbed it out on the ashtray.

"Yes, yes, of course," he said, and Blane could *see* the man reject the possibility that he was being dismissed from his own room. "Working hard. Good. Won't be long before we have that bitch where we want her."

"No," Ax said slowly, and the gaze she locked on him as he stood turned Blane's veins to ice. "No, it won't."

Whatever illusions the man's mind was forming to protect itself must be quite impressive to ignore the tiger's glare now focused on him, Blane thought. The glare didn't drop until Drakon was once more out of the room.

Think of it this way, Ax had explained. The human mind was *eager* to produce false memories and unsupported justifications. When a brain couldn't consciously explain an action it performed, it made it up. Far more than most people realised, the reasons for doing something are far removed from the explanations we tell ourselves.

You could even demonstrate this in split-brain patients, showing something to the right brain that the left brain did not see. When then asked to draw or describe a random object, the individual would draw the item their right hemisphere had seen but *justify the choice for another reason*. The left hemisphere, responsible for reasoning yet unable to access the visual data it needed to do so, would invent entirely fictitious justifications for its actions.

Post hoc rationalisation and confabulation were well understood phenomena. False memories, distorted worldviews, subconscious biases, lies you told even yourself... All Ax and her compatriots needed to do was take advantage of this tendency.

"I think you'll want to listen in on this," Ax said, waving the thin-screen. "You know the caller, after all."

Serinda, she assumed; Serinda had stayed behind in *Renacimiento* to study Gabriel and find out exactly what he knew about the RA's plans for the *Fallen*. She didn't have time to respond, though, before Ax made a swiping gesture and the thin-screen's connection jumped to appear on the wall screen opposite where they sat. It displayed a familiar face, but not the one she expected.

"Ólafur!" Blane said. "How…"

Ólafur seemed as surprised to see her as she was to see him.

"Blane?" he said in astonishment. "What are you doing…?"

"Blane is working with us, now," interrupted Ax, before Blane could say anything herself.

"That's… that's good," Ólafur said, though a look of concern passed across his face. "Is Arthur with you?"

It took her a second to register who he meant. Only Ólafur ever called him by his given name.

"Spangle?" she said with surprise. "No. I haven't seen him in…"

"So not Grey either, then?" Ólafur said, eyes roving around as if expecting to see them hiding behind the furniture.

Ax leaned forward to say something, but this time it was Blane who held up a hand to stop her.

"What do you mean, Ólaf?" she said. "What's happened to them?"

Ólafur frowned.

"I'm... not sure. I haven't been able to contact them for some time. The last I heard, Fernández left them stuck in a safe house and went off somewhere."

A pang of guilt in Blane's chest. She had hardly thought about what Francisco's secretive departure at her request would mean for the others. Francisco had assured her they would be fine, but back then she wasn't aware of just how unbalanced the man and his 'brother' had become.

Or she hadn't cared, a small part of her whispered.

Guilt became worry. Grey hadn't tried to contact her for weeks, either. She'd felt relieved when it seemed he'd given up. Now, though...

"What is it you want, Ólafur?" Ax said impatiently. "You have New Church contacts much closer to you, and know you're only supposed to contact me in a serious emergency."

Ólafur gave a bitter laugh.

"Oh, this is an emergency. A *hamfarir*. They destroyed a Hab."

Ax looked questioningly from the screen to Blane, as if she might understand. In this case, she actually did.

"Destroyed a hab?" Blane said towards the screen. "But... there's over a million people in most Althing Habs. They're subterranean population centres that can withstand *earthquakes*."

This last was for Ax, who nodded in understanding.

"What do you mean, *they* destroyed it?" Ax asked. "Who?"

Ólafur's face turned dark.

"There's only one group that could do this - the RA."

Blane turned to Ax.

"You have people all through the Reclamation Authority. Could they..?"

"I've heard nothing," Ax replied, shaking her head. "It is possible Feye kept this from us, but even if she did, why..."

"They see we are weak, and want to keep it that way!" Ólafur was almost shouting. "They would turn us all to ash if they could!"

Blane froze at the word.

"Ólafur," she said slowly. "What do you mean, *ash*?"

The Hab was one of the largest in the Althing Republic. Possibly the largest; population controls had become inexact and inefficient since the loss of the artificial mind that oversaw them, rendered even more so by the subsequent splintering of the Administration into squabbling factions. Birth rates had rocketed, and movement from one Hab to another become impossible to monitor precisely.

Nevertheless, the Hab functioned. Maybe a little more chaotically, with an uptick in crime and massive drop in the usage of citizen chips, but it worked. Resources might have been scarcer, the Fabricators the Republic relied upon more temperamental and basic, but it *lived*. It *grew*.

And then, one day... nothing. All contact from the Hab stopped.

It took more than a day for the first survivors to emerge, and those that did so came from the outer reaches of the Hab, the lowest levels and the furthest wings. No one came from the sections where the vast majority of residents were concentrated. Where there should have been thousands, hundreds of thousands of people, time schedules carefully calculated to ensure no overstretching of common services and facilities, there was simply... silence.

The residential and commercial districts were empty, floor upon floor built on each other so that even if you saw nobody, above and below there should be hundreds, thousands; a dense mass of humanity extending in every direction. Somehow, no one from this mass could be found.

The survivors told of making their terrified way up the many floors past dark stains and piles of ash already disappearing into filters designed to remove just such particulate organic matter, of the rumours and fears that swirled around that it was the *machines* that had done this. Of how the Hab, once warm and protective, became dark and claustrophobic as they waited for rescue to arrive.

Rescuers, when they finally made their way down into the Hab after a shamefully slow response time, found only empty rooms and functioning machinery, much of it in emergency shutdown but in no way damaged. Everything was working as expected, automated or idle, waiting for instructions that never came. A large number of discarded items littered the streets, however, as if massed crowds had discarded their possessions as one and just... left.

Close to seven hundred thousand lives had been snuffed out, and only one thing could have done this.

This was done with the Aether.

"... but not by the RA," Blane said as Ólafur finished his story.

"What are you talking about?" Ólafur bristled. "No one else knows how vulnerable we are right now! No other nation would dare... No other nation even *could*..."

"Blane is right," Ax interrupted. "The RA is many things, but senseless it is not. When regimes kill, they kill for a *reason* - and that reason is always to strengthen the regime. This doesn't do that."

She turned to Blane, head tilted in question, urging her to speak.

"It doesn't *do* anything," Blane said, struggling to keep her voice calm. There was a sick feeling in her stomach. "There isn't a... a *reason* behind this. Well, not a conscious one; not a *choice*. It's... pressure. Anger. Lashing out."

She struggled to find the right words.

"Ax, surely you've felt it?" she said, turning to the other woman. "The Aether, building up. Flowing more powerfully, growing more violent every day."

Ax frowned.

"It's certainly more powerful, *verdad*," she said. "I can certainly do more than I could a few years ago, but... becoming violent? Aren't you anthropomorphising a little too much?"

Blane stared at Ax with her mouth open. She didn't know? She didn't *feel* it?

As if in response to her thoughts the Aether lurched, the leviathan moving. If she had to describe it, she could only say that it curled as it swam through the depths below, but that would be somehow wrong. It didn't just move through the Aether, it *was* the Aether.

Like a twisting coil within a larger pattern of loops and spirals, it was both individual and conjoined. Her senses followed the shape of its form until it was undeniably no longer the original *thing*, yet all there ever was was continuation. This form was a part of her, a part of herself over which she had no control, and a part of everything it touched.

And it was *angry*.

A memory hit her.

"The Althing Administration," she said. "Sigurd. They have the files that Grey stole from the RA. On the start of the Sudden War, and the..."

"The Administration is in chaos," Ólafur said. "Sigurður disappeared months ago - took a bunch of highly classified blueprints, a portable Fab, a micro-generator, and droned off somewhere. We think the Caribbean Federation, but no one knows for sure."

Sigurd knows, Blane thought. But did that mean...? So soon?

"The Aether..." she said. "It has a critical mass. A point at which it... erupts. That's what Mindfire is; an explosive release of the energy inside living organisms. So many people in one Hab, so densely packed together..."

The wall screen automatically dropped the volume at Ólafur's incredulous outburst. It was clear that he, at least, didn't believe a word she was saying.

"This could happen again?" Ax asked, ignoring the protests coming from the wall screen.

"Not could. *Will*," answered Blane. "And it'll get worse. Whole cities... The last time this happened, it triggered the Sudden War. "

Ax stared at her silently for a moment.

"Is there any way to stop it?" she said, far more calmly than Blane thought she had any right to be.

That was a question she couldn't answer. It was what she and Fen had been working on for years, hiding away in the Mayan League in the hope that time and space would give them some kind of plan.

"I... I don't know. I..." Blane began.

"Well, if there's nothing we can do about it, we waste no more time on it," Ax said, turning to the screen. "I'm sorry, Ólafur, but there really isn't anything I can help with that your contacts in the Republic can't. If you..."

The conversation between Ax and Ólafur faded into the background as Blane stared in amazement. Didn't Ax understand? Didn't she *care*?

Ax paused mid-conversation to look at her.

"Is there a problem?" she said.

Blane stammered, looking for something to say and failing.

"Then we focus on the things we *can* control," Ax said when no comprehensible response was forthcoming.

"*Hlustaðu á mig*," Ólafur shouted, frustration clear even over the automated audio softening. Blane didn't need to know the language to understand he was demanding to be heard. "I don't want to hear any more babble about mysterious out-of-control magic. You need to see what you can find from your friend. Your, ah, *unwitting accomplice*."

"Ah," Ax replied, nodding in sudden comprehension. "So that is why you contacted me."

"Yes," Ólafur said. "Confirm it with him. If it really wasn't them, he should know. And if it was, I want to know *why*."

Once more Ax turned to Blane, looking at her thoughtfully.

"It seems…" Ax said slowly. "That today really is a day for old acquaintances."

34. XAVIER

Not only should the right hand not know what the left hand is doing, it shouldn't be aware that there is *a left hand.*

Agency Handbook, Section 12.9 (Operational Secrecy)

Salim was the leak.

That much was obvious. The only question was; *how?* Xavier knew it wasn't anything as simple as betrayal - he would have known.

In the end, the answer was hardly more complex.

"And exactly how far *can* you reach?" Xavier asked, sat once more in Salim's apartment.

He sipped on the thick coffee that had been thrust into his hand almost immediately upon arrival. As always, it was the perfect temperature.

"It is difficult to say," Salim replied, sipping his own. "I have been behind these walls so long that it is difficult to judge true distance. All I know is how it feels in the Aether."

"Take a guess," Xavier said, trying and failing to keep impatience from his voice.

"Maybe a couple of kilometers, when the Aether is particularly strong," Salim answered, uncertain. "Hundreds of meters, certainly."

Kilometers?

Then Salim could be reaching far beyond the checkpoints and walls that kept this section divided from the rest of the city. He could be talking with anyone.

But who?

It was also obvious that Salim had no idea he'd been endangering Xavier. There was nothing in his thought-images that hinted at anything but worry for his friend and happiness at the visit.

"So you've been dreamwalking out in the city," Xavier said. "But I can't see anything like that in your mind. I'm not looking too deeply, but unless you are able to hide it from me somehow..."

"I can," Salim said, looking at his friend with eyes devoid of guile or duplicity. "Though I do not do so to deceive. I simply want to save you from yet more guilt. If you knew I were reaching out beyond this place, you would be forced to report on me."

Xavier nodded, thinking to himself.

Salim was right, of course. *Everything* Salim did was reported on, and much of it by Xavier. It had been going on for so long that it felt... natural, now. He realised it had been some time since he even thought about ways to resist.

When had that changed? Xavier thought. When had he begun working for Feye by choice, rather than compulsion? Was he so easily influenced that, after years as a helpless prisoner, a small amount of freedom and power was all it took to bring him completely onto her side?

Did it even matter anymore? He still had no answer to the coming cataclysm that was better than Feye's, and now he was being hunted. This was a question of survival; he *had* to fight.

Still, Salim's words from long ago floated up in his mind.

Evil is a choice.

"How?" Xavier asked. He had to know. "How did you hide this from me?"

"By hiding it from myself," Salim answered calmly, refilling their drinks. "That is what dreams do; hide from conscious understanding. Upon waking, they melt away. You must know this."

"So you, what? Forget them?"

"I *release* them," Salim said. "They are just a way for me to escape this place, if only for a little while. I do not need to remember the experience; the sensation of freedom is enough, and this way I put you in no danger..."

Salim looked at Xavier in concern.

"At least, I believed so," he finished.

"Do you meet anyone, in these dreams?" Xavier asked.

Salim looked away in thought.

"I meet many," he said, turning back. "But they are not lucid, and I do not live their dreams; that would be a violation. However, there may be one. I have a sense of a... a friend in the dream..."

Here was the thread, Xavier thought. Now he needed to *pull*.

"A friend?" he asked. "Could they be a Dreamwalker, like you? Able to control the dream and remember clearly what they learn?"

Salim pursed his lips.

"Perhaps..." he said. "But I would never share anything that could put you in danger."

Of course you wouldn't, Xavier thought, though for some reason the words in his head spoke in Immanuel's voice. *Not deliberately.*

Whoever it was that was speaking to Salim in the dream, they were good. They would never directly ask for the information they wanted. No, they would draw what they needed out far more subtly, their mark unaware of the secrets being massaged from him.

"Can you find them?" Xavier asked. "This *friend*, could you find them again?"

Salim nodded slowly.

"I think so, though I think they are not often close by. I only occasionally wake with the feeling that someone was with me in the dream."

"Could you try? Please?" Xavier said.

"Now?" Salim asked, surprised.

Xavier nodded. He didn't know why, but something told him there was little time to waste.

"I doubt I will be able to..." Salim began, eyes glazing over as he *reached* out in the way only Dreamwalkers could.

Almost immediately his expression changed.

"They're here," Salim said.

His eyes closed.

His mind did not close, though, and Xavier could see what Salim saw in his thought-images. There was a city, ill-defined. Albores, but an Albores you could not look at too closely. Like a low resolution photo, it became grainy the more you focused on it.

In the centre of this stood a stocky figure of indeterminate age and sex, face featureless and unblemished. They resembled an unformatted avatar more than anything else, like a digital simulation not yet given a specific role. Salim, too, was projected similarly. Each was hiding their true form from the other.

Not the eyes, though. The figure had eyes like shards of steel, so hard he could scarcely believe they were real. Perhaps they weren't; he was seeing a dream, after all.

Indeed, what Xavier saw wasn't movement, not the real-time event that Salim was experiencing that moment in the dream. No, Xavier was *reading* the dream from the top of Salim's mind, as if pawing through a pile of ancient analogue photographs that contained not only visuals, but thought and sensation too. Just organising the thought-images into a coherent whole would be beyond the skills of a lesser Reader, but Xavier was able to follow what was happening as if watching footage recorded on warped and dusty film.

"You are here more strongly than usual," said the figure.

Salim replied, but Xavier was unable to parse exactly what it was he said. In the dream, words were both less and more than mere sound. Still, the reply seemed to mollify the speaker.

"This is fortunate," they said. "I was hoping we could meet."

"You were?" Salim said, surprised. "Forgive me, I remember little of our previous discussions."

The figure smiled, a far warmer expression than Xavier had expected. Somehow their smile conveyed friendliness despite their unrealised, slate-like features. Dream-logic, no doubt.

"Of course. We are but passing thoughts in the night. I, too, remember little, as we agreed. And as we agreed, we share even less."

Xavier rolled his eyes. The figure's voice was so full of guile it would make a serpent blush; surely even Salim couldn't...

But Salim *did* trust them. Xavier could see it in his friend's thoughts, in his mind. Worse, he could see why - because Salim was *lonely*. He so desperately wanted this fellow Dreamwalker to be someone he could trust that he did so unconsciously, suppressing the usual wariness and suspicion this world hammered into you.

Xavier could see glimmers of distrust in his friend's mind now, though. Though he had told Salim little about what had happened, Salim at least knew *something* was amiss, and that it might involve this person.

"What was it you wished to talk about?" Salim asked, though now the two Dreamwalkers were using less vocalised words and more *intention*.

Images. Sensations. Travel, the world. A scarred and broken planet that could still offer many wonders.

"What must it be like, to travel so freely?" the figure said.

Do all Dreamwalkers speak like that? Xavier thought. Something about the world they built around themselves, maybe. It seemed to make what fully vocalised words came out more... poetic. Dramatic. Trite.

Despite this, the words brought relief to Salim's thoughts. The figure wanted only to talk of other places, far away. Safe topics.

Xavier waited for the other shoe to drop.

The ill-defined form of Albores around them shifted, not moving but changing somehow so that now the buildings were squat, burrowing into the hard rock. It was somehow clear that these extended deep underground without the need for seeing any proof. In Salim's mind was the knowledge that they were still in the Dreamscape of the city, but that it had morphed to reflect the other Dreamwalker's thoughts.

"The Silicon Isle, for example," the figure said. "I hear it is a wonderous place. Imagine being able to visit; I heard they live forever there."

"It does sound incredible," Salim replied. "Though I am not sure about *forever*. I do know that some are well over a hundred years old yet look barely middle-aged."

It was all Xavier could do not to put his head with his hands in despair. Was Salim truly this naive?

"You have been there?" asked the figure, again giving the impression of a facial expression without actually showing one. This time, it was of awe and curiosity.

"Me? Oh, no. My friend, she told me of her time there."

Xavier almost demanded he stop, there and then. He did *not* like the idea that Salim was jeopardising Zenobia. Her image floated at the top of Salim's mind, attached to the recollection of the story she once told them both.

The figure, however, did not seem to be aiming for this.

"Oh, I see," they said. "Amazing that you know someone who has been all that way. Apparently they live in the earth, hundreds of thousands piled on top of each other."

"Millions, apparently," Salim replied.

Unbelievably, the glimmers of suspicion he had shown were slowly disappearing as the conversation went on.

"Millions?" said the figure, surprised. "What must that be like, so many people pressed together? Trapped in the earth... What if something happened?"

Immediately, Xavier knew two things. One; *this* was what the figure was fishing for. Two; Ritra Feye had been right.

"Something must have happened in the Althing Republic," Xavier said aloud. "They're trying to find out what you know."

Salim slightly opened one eye, then gave a slow nod of understanding.

Did this mean the figure was from the Silicon Isle? But from everything Xavier knew, the Althing had very few Aether users and certainly none as skilled as the one here. Also, if what Feye predicted truly had happened, why would they be asking Salim about it?

Too many questions, and worse, he felt sure he was uncovering the answers slower than Immanuel would.

"Is someone with you?" the figure said suddenly.

Xavier physically jerked backwards. For a moment, it seemed as if the figure was looking at him through Salim's half-opened eye. Impossible, of course.

The dreamscape shuddered, shifted, form and structure fading until the two Dreamwalkers were no longer within a false world and were instead presences without form in a void.

"I am sorry," said the figure. "I did not mean to pry. It is just that you usually are alone when we visit... as far as I can tell, I mean."

The words faded as vocabulary became sensation, Salim projecting feelings of warning and caution and the mysterious figure ones of apology and contrition.

"I *do* have a need to be honest with you, though," the figure said eventually. "You see, I know more of who you are than you have told me."

The next thought-images were too confused for Xavier to parse well. It was impossible to tell if the shock and worry that coursed through Salim at these words manifested in the dream, or only in his friend's mind.

Shock, worry, and shame. Xavier felt a pang of guilt at that; Salim was finally realising just how much of a risk his dreamwalking posed not only to himself but those around him.

"I could not learn your identity from you..." the figure continued. "...but there are other ways. A Dreamwalker held by Far? *Very* few of those."

The figure's 'voice' was changing, taking on tones that began to hint at age and gender. Lines appeared on their flesh, hair and skin taking on a definiteness that slowly revealed a middle-aged woman, hard-faced and carrying an air of absolute self-confidence.

"I have one your friends here with me, Salim Majid Ayad," the woman said. "Maybe that will show you I can be trusted. Can I bring her into the dream?"

Salim's eyes abruptly opened fully, showing glimmers of panic. He looked towards Xavier as if for guidance.

"It could be a trick," said Xavier. "Can they do that? Bring someone into the dream?"

"I have never heard of such a thing," Salim said breathlessly. "Who could it be...?"

Xavier didn't reply for a moment, watching Salim hold himself both in the dream and in the waking world. Any other time, he would have marvelled at his friend's skill.

"Can you be hurt?" Xavier asked. "In the dream, I mean?"

Salim shook his head.

"I do not believe so. I am not truly there, anyway. It is not a real place; it is just a fiction built between shared minds."

Xavier released a breath he hadn't known he was holding. If it was who he *thought* it was, then he found it difficult to imagine they would mean any harm, yet still...

"Tell her yes," he said.

Salim's eyes closed, and he returned fully to the dream.

It was difficult for Xavier to understand what happened next even with his skill at Reading. The mysterious woman immediately understood Salim's agreement without the need for words, and she did ... something. Something that shared many of the characteristics of *reaching* for the Aether, but instead of the ever-shifting, rolling energy that lay below, she pulled at something outside the dream and drew in long strands of golden thread that slowly wrapped and twined together to form...

"Ugh," said Blane, swaying slightly. "That hits worse than a flask of *Cusha*."

Xavier felt surprise hit Salim like a wave.

"Blane!" he cried, and once more took on form in the void.

Blane turned to see him.

"Salim!"

A huge smile filled her face, and Xavier watched as surprise turned to warmth and pleasure in Salim's mind. He felt true *joy* at seeing his old friend.

"It is really you," he said.

Blane nodded.

"It is. I'm so happy to see you..." Her face fell, troubled. "I'm... I'm so sorry. The last time we met, I..."

Salim raised a hand.

"Nothing that happened is your fault, my friend," he said gently. "None of this was your choice."

Blane looked around, into the emptiness that enveloped them.

"I'm actually Dreamwalking," she said. "I didn't know that was possible."

"*I* didn't know that was possible!" Salim said. "How…?"

He turned to the mysterious woman.

"The best way to describe it is as a form of *reaching* for another consciousness," the woman said. "You don't draw on the Aether, you draw on the *person*."

She stared at Blane with a curious expression; even suspicious.

"Non-Dreamwalkers don't usually take to the process so easily, though," she finished.

"I've felt something like this before, Ax," Blane said. "In the Silicon Isle. Only, it was through *Mindfire,* and… well let's just say it didn't leave me feeling myself."

Silence, even in the dream. This 'Ax' clearly didn't know what to make of such a response.

Xavier did, though. Zenobia had told him about it… No. He'd *seen* it. No matter how hard he tried not to *read* Zenobia, there were times when the things that floated to the top of her mind were so bright as to be blinding.

She'd even asked him how it could happen, after she found out he'd seen it. He was a Reader, she said. Surely he could explain how they'd got so deep inside her mind?

Xavier didn't waste time arguing that wasn't what happened. He knew the truth because she did; whatever had happened between Zenobia, Blane, and Fen in the Silicon Isle was far more than a Read.

In Zenobia's thought-images it was paradoxically a time when she had both lost herself, and found herself. Found herself, only to lose herself once more. It hurt her, he knew, as both violation and stolen blessing.

He just wished he knew what to say.

"Bring me in," he said, dragging himself back to the present.

Salim didn't react at first, didn't even stir. Then, slowly, a single eye opened.

"Bring… you in?" he said.

Xavier nodded.

"You saw how she… how *Ax* did it. Bring me in."

Salim didn't say anything for some time, then golden light stretched out from his sitting form. It touched and pulled at something inside Xavier, and the world drew away from him as if fired through a particle accelerator.

His body went limp as he entered the dream.

35. BLANE

The social contract is made not with those in the present, but with the generation that follows. We must respect it not because of some softhearted, sentimental claptrap regarding a debt to each other, but because the generation that fails to generate progress and wealth is always destroyed by the one that comes after.

The Burning Sun, Scotlan Stefanez <*Sanctioned digital document*>

"Well, that was easier than expected."

Blane stared at Ax, not knowing how to respond.

Easier than expected? She'd just spent what felt like hours arguing with someone she thought of as a friend. Worse, with someone she thought she *needed to rescue*.

What was that condition that occasionally popped up in the threads? An ancient term, and a discredited one too, as far as she was aware. Still, it seemed the only explanation. One of the Dead Cities, she thought. Skarsgard Syndrome, or something...

He'd been so *angry*, by the end.

"Did you believe any of that? What Xavier was saying?" Blane asked.

They were still sat within Drakon's rear garden room, a strange feeling for Blane after returning from the formless dream. Above them, the windows showed a dull sky dimming further into true night.

Ax shrugged.

"You were the one telling me and Ólafur the world was going to end," she said.

Blane paused, mouth hanging open.

Because that is what Xavier had said, at the very last.

The world is ending, and you're playing la ultima guerilla.

He accused *her* of playing a game? While he was working for a woman who treated people's lives as pawns?

"Either way, thanks to you we drew him out," Ax said, with a sharp laugh. "Never dreamed it would work so fast."

"Drew him out?" Blane asked. "We only met him in the dream. He could be anywhere."

"Wrong," Ax replied, raising a finger. "He's close. Very close. I know exactly how far Salim can reach; no further than me. Which means there's only one place they can be."

"Where?" Blane asked.

"Here. *Corazón*."

Blane was silent for a moment, her mind racing. No matter how wrong-headed she thought Xavier was being, she still wasn't sure that it was a good thing Ax knew where he was.

"You didn't tell me you were a Dreamwalker," Blane said, hoping to buy some time.

"It didn't come up," Ax replied.

"They're very rare, I heard."

"*Extremely* rare," Ax said. "Even Far knows little about what we can do. It's how I got out before they... ha... *reassigned* me. Saw it in that bastard Caldwell's dreams."

Blane jolted back in surprise.

"You knew Doctor Caldwell?" she said.

"*You* knew Doctor Caldwell?" Ax echoed in response.

She sounded equally surprised.

Ax was clearly waiting for Blane to explain, but Blane was damned if she was going to offer up anything she didn't have to. She sat there, saying nothing.

"I see," Ax said after a while. "Well, that explains the gaps in your file, anyway. You've been fucking around with Far for longer than I realised… and no, I didn't 'know' Caldwell. He didn't mix with us cadets. I sensed him, though, watching our progress through the cameras. I saw when he decided I didn't make the cut, and got out of there."

"That was probably a good idea," Blane said slowly. "He was not a nice man."

Ax looked at her through narrowed eyes.

"*Was*. The past tense again," she said. "You know, I've been trying to find out what happened to him and his project for years. Sounds like you already know."

It seemed that in her haste to change the subject from Xavier, Blane had just brought Ax's attention to a topic she wanted to discuss even less. Did the *Sindicato* know about Fen? What would they do if they did?

"So," Blane said, acting as if she hadn't heard the last comment. "What happens now?"

Ax didn't break her stare for some time.

"I guess I have enough mysteries for one day," she said eventually.

The knot in Blane's chest loosened at Ax's words… only to tighten once more at the next.

"There's no time, anyway," Ax continued. "They know we're nearby now - it'll take time to get around to investigating the houses of actual Committee members, but we need to make the assault immediately. That damned Reader's put an exception in the code[52] for the last time."

"Assault?" Blane asked incredulously. "Here? In the literal home of the elite? I don't know how powerful the *Sindicato* are, but…"

"You keep getting confused," Ax interrupted. "I already told you; we are not the *Sindicato*. We are not the New Church, or any of the names we wear like sting-cloud coats. We are all of them, and none. We have no name, and we are *everywhere*."

It still took some time to organise everything, despite Ax's sudden resolve. All Blane could do was wait and watch as Ax spoke with unknown figures on a multitude of inaudible calls. Not only on calls, even, but with actual visitors who came to the house. Every one of them wore some sort of RA uniform, several of them Far.

Drakon, at least, was almost overwhelmed with excitement. The glistening sheen of sweat on his head only grew as he marched around the house, gesticulating wildly and muttering about how it was "finally time." When Blane looked into his mind, she saw a tangled knot of confusion and fear, buried beneath the heavy layers of Aether Ax was maintaining to ensure his thoughts followed only a single path. It was like looking into the mind of a drugged person.

"Well, we know where he is now," Ax said eventually, when she and Blane were alone once more. "Not far from here at all - there's a secure site even Drakon doesn't know anything about. Randomised routines, and security personnel *read* both pre-and-post shift. I always wondered what Feye kept in there."

"What will you… what's going to happen to Xavier?" Blane asked.

The question had been spinning through her mind the entire time.

"Two possibilities," Ax said bluntly, holding up the same number of fingers. "One; he comes with us, and we make use of his extraordinary potential. Two; we make sure no one else can use him."

"You mean you'll kill him," Blane said.

---

[52] In another age, Ax might have said "a spanner in the works."

As she spoke she drew on the Aether, feeling it fill her. More than that, it *leaped* for her. It was all she could do to keep it from lashing out there and then and incinerating Ax in an outpouring of Mindfire.

Ax barely reacted. Her eyes grew wide, just for a second, then narrowed. Blane saw her begin to glow as well, though nowhere close to the vivid brightness Blane knew she must be enveloped in.

"I wouldn't do anything stupid, if I were you," Ax said, her voice calm. "Remember that we share the same goal; the end of Ritra Feye, and the crippling of the RA."

"That is *not* my goal," Blane spat. "I don't want the RA crippled; I want it ended. I want *justice*. Justice for everyone they've ever taken, for everyone they've hurt."

"Interesting," Ax said. "Naive, as well. Weren't your parents RA?"

Blane almost lost control then. The thing below lurched, a wave so powerful she took an involuntary step back.

"Besides," Ax continued. "Xavier was right; you don't have an alternative."

That was the point Xavier had kept coming back to, in their conversation in the dream. He'd even seemed to be pleading at one point.

Then tell me, please; what other way is there? he asked, and it didn't sound like a question.

It sounded like a prayer.

Blane took a deep breath, and drew herself away from the Aether. It dropped away reluctantly, a feeling of pressure and promise pushing against her.

"Capture," she said. "We capture him. He's not a fighter; even if he can *read* you, I don't think he has it in him to actually hurt someone."

"Then you don't know him," Ax replied. "Not anymore, at least. He *spiked* a member of the Carib-Fed security forces. Left him alive, but from what my sources tell me death might have been kinder."

Could that be true? Blane saw no hint of a lie in the other woman's face, but to *spike* someone? Her thoughts went to Ana, the girl brainwashed by the RA into hunting Fen without any understanding of the danger.

"Then... we *try* to capture him. If he is a threat..."

She couldn't finish the sentence, but Ax nodded in understanding.

"Of course," Ax said, releasing the Aether as well. "We don't kill without reason."

Exactly what the RA would say, came the traitorous thought.

But Blane felt an overwhelming need to get Xavier out of there; to get both of them out, Xavier and Salim. Salim was clearly nothing but a prisoner there, and Xavier... well, either way, he couldn't be allowed to become a tool for the RA.

"Alright," she said. "So how are we doing this?"

"Well, fortunately we already have a way in," Ax replied. She was once again drawing out her thin screen. "We just have to hope Serinda has broken him in time."

36. SERINDA

A mind wrapped within another. The perfect spy, the perfect human shield.

EISP: *Proposal and Funding Request* <Classified>

The night was drawing in as they landed, the bulky carry-all drone coming to a rest in a plume of dust that blocked out the few lights of Albores that could be seen this far out in the Waste.

"Come on," Spark said, as the landing ramp rolled down and the smell of the outside air wafted into the cabin. "Let's get going."

He pulled roughly at the cuffs around their prisoner's hands, pulling him to his feet. Gabriel staggered forward, banging his head on the low metal wall before turning towards the ramp at Spark's pull. The sensory dampener around his head prevented him from seeing or hearing much, as well as blocking him from the Aether.

Serinda said nothing as the two men walked down the ramp ahead of her. The journey had been long, crammed into that small Requisitions drone all the way from *Renacimiento* to the outskirts of Albores. There had been stops along the way, but these made no difference as they were permitted under absolutely no circumstances to step outside. In fact, the forced inactivity of motionless was worse.

To be moving; that was what she needed. To be pushing forward. Her time in *Renacimiento* had been punishing, for her and for Gabriel. She'd tried a million different ways to draw out the embedded personality, all to no avail. The RA-alter, as she thought of him, remained hidden whenever she sought him, only emerging when she lowered her guard and found herself conversing with the Gabriel she knew of old. The alter would suddenly be *there*, in full control and spitting venom before abruptly going into hiding again, leaving his distressed and shaken cohabiter behind.

No, not hiding. That wasn't how it worked. The alter didn't hide; it didn't *exist*. The very neural pathways and brain patterns that made him were gone, diverted and replaced to form, once more, the Gabriel who had been her student. The alter-personality only returned at specific triggers.

Serinda needed to figure out what those triggers were.

The drone rose and roared off into the darkness the moment Serinda stepped down from the ramp, bitter, oily-tasting sand filling her mouth before she remembered to close it. The sound faded rapidly behind her, and left them in dark and silence.

A few seconds later a pair of headlights blinked on in the murky distance.

"There's our ride," Spark said, kicking Gabriel in the back to make him move.

She nearly spoke out, that time. It hurt, seeing her old friend treated this way. It hadn't, not at first, but the one thing she knew for certain now was that the Gabriel she knew was *not* an illusion. He was real, and the hijacking of mind and body were more traumatic for him than anything his alter had done to her.

Which made what she had to do even harder, but she *had* to do it. Ax didn't even have to push; just explain.

Because the fact that Gabriel was an *old* embedded was important. He was one of the earliest creations of the Far Agency's 'Enhanced Internal Security Project,' one of the first the young and ambitious new head of that project sent into the field.

He was one of Feye's.

So Serinda had to find out what he knew, had to find out if there was a way to use him. She couldn't hold back, though her worries and fears made it difficult.

The *Sindicato*, however, shared none of these reservations.

"MOVE," Spark yelled, shoving Gabriel forward so hard that he stumbled and fell to his knees in the dust.

He remained there, hands shakily seeking purchase in the dirt. The sensory dampener was obviously making it impossible for him to understand what was going on. With an annoyed sound, Spark yanked it off, while at the same time jamming a pistol roughly against Gabriel's head.

"One wrong move, and your brains will be just more Waste oil," he said.

"Hey…" Serinda began, but was immediately cut off by Gabriel.

"It's alright," he said loudly. "It's alright. But keep the gun on me. You can't trust me for a…"

A gut punch set him wheezing.

"I *know* I can't trust you, RA," Spark growled.

Bent over, grasping his stomach, Gabriel held out a palm and looked painfully up at Serinda. He shook his head, face red even in the darkness.

This was what made it even harder. Gabriel *agreed* with her. Worse, he agreed with the *Sindicato*. The few times she had spoken up about the brutal methods used in their attempts to bring out the alter, Gabriel immediately stopped her.

We're in a war against Heaven, he said. *No mercy for traitors.*

Using Sara's... *Raphael's* words against her. Knowing that picking at that scar would make her more able to do what she needed to do. It stung.

It worked.

She recognised the van that formed out of the murk as they approached; it was the same van that had borne the bomb to the Far Station. The same type at least, identical in every way she could see.

"Committee level," Spark explained as they drew closer. "IDRF isn't scraped so it'll show up as permitted traffic on any scan, but its movements can't be logged - anti-assassination tool meant to protect the elite from being tracked."

He was obviously saying this not only to her, but towards Gabriel. Spark wanted to draw out the embedded alter as much as she did, though for a more direct and physical questioning style than Serinda's.

"If the RA knew we had access to these... Well, let's just say there'd be hell to pay," Spark finished.

Whatever response he... *they*... hoped to get from Gabriel, it didn't come. Bruised and weak, the prisoner was struggling just to make his way across the uneven, debris-strewn ground without falling again.

She *reached* out towards him as they walked. Even now, she hoped she could find something inside Gabriel that revealed the enemy within, some hint that would make this easier. Instead, all she saw were the thought patterns and feelings of a person in distress; fear, sadness, hopelessness, self-loathing...

The van's engine whirred into life even before they were fully aboard, the feeling of motion and rapid acceleration turning her stomach as the rear doors swung closed. It was risky, driving like that in the Waste, but no more so than if they were spotted out here.

She swung herself into the nearest seat. The interior of the van was arranged so that all passengers could face each other, and spacious enough that they fit inside comfortably despite the two *Sindicato* already there. Serinda could see a driver as well, no more than a silhouette through a plasglass partition, but they didn't look back or acknowledge the new arrivals in any way.

"How close are you to cracking the embedded?" asked the *Sindicato* sat opposite her, without preamble.

"Close," Serinda replied, glancing over at Gabriel.

He was wedged in between the *Sindicato* who had just spoke and Spark, with Spark's pistol still jammed into his side.

"We should bag him," said the second *Sindicato*. "No need for him to hear this..."

The speaker was already leaning forward to place the sensory dampener on Gabriel's head when Spark stopped him.

"No," Spark said, shaking his head. "We *want* him to listen. This one hides deep; gotta keep trying to draw him out."

The second *Sindicato* paused, looking thoughtful, then sat back again. She was clearly not comfortable about this, though, because she drew out her own pistol and placed it on her lap, pointed casually towards Gabriel.

Gabriel let out a long, low whistle. Serinda knew immediately that it was the alter.

"*Mira a estos tipos duros,*" he said sarcastically. "Four on one and you're still scared of the RA boogeyman."

Spark moved fast. His arm moved in a flash, fist smashing into Gabriel's throat.

"Come on then, *culebra*," Spark said, with so much venom it made Serinda's eyes widen. She didn't know what it was about the embedded that so got to him, but he hated them with a visceral loathing. "Stay and play a while."

But it was too late. Serinda could see it in the flows in Gabriel's mind; the alter was gone, and the man choking and struggling to breathe in front of her was her old student and friend.

She stretched out with the Aether and did what she could to ease the pain, though the impact on such a fragile area left as much mechanical damage as it did sensory. Gabriel was lucky he could still breathe.

"Be more careful," Serinda said, locking her eyes on Spark. "We'll get nothing if you accidentally kill him."

"*Accidentally*..." Spark snarled, glaring at Gabriel. "Yeah..."

He gave a short, bitter chuckle.

"It doesn't matter either way," the first *Sindicato* said. "Ax says we have to do it now. She needs him, so we crack him. Even if we break him in the process."

The woman looked at Serinda.

"I'm not ready," Serinda said. "I need more time. I can almost..."

She was close, she knew it. She'd seen something, the moment before the alter emerged to mock them. The way the flow of his thoughts bent and warped; if she could see it again, she'd have it.

"No more time," Spark said. "Ax says we do it now, we do it now."

Even as he spoke he began to glow with the Aether.

"Now?" Serinda said, disbelieving. "Here?"

"We've done this before," Spark said. "Doesn't exactly need a lab or anything. It's not pretty though, especially when you don't know the victi... the subject."

Serinda knew that the verbal slip was not accidental.

"Now..." he continued. "Are you going to take the lead on this, or shall I?"

Serinda felt her heart race, sweat breaking out on her brow despite the chill of the night.

She couldn't. To try to force Gabriel's mind into another shape, it could destroy him. She still didn't have the pattern yet - didn't know the neural pathways she needed to push to bring out the alter without irreparable damage to his brain.

But neither did the *Sindicato*, and she didn't need to *read* them to know that they were going to go ahead with or without her. And they *would* destroy him. All they wanted was what the alter knew, and it didn't matter what happened to the personality wrapped around it.

Wasn't that what she wanted, too? At least this way, she could say she... tried.

Gabriel didn't look up, though he must have known what was happening. Must have *sensed* what was happening, as Serinda drew on the Aether and reached out towards him. It roared through her, requiring all her effort just to keep from scorching him alive. He hardly reacted, still wheezing through his damaged throat though that wasn't why he was offered no resistance. He just sat there, shaking and defeated.

Serinda would never know if the water that dripped from his face was sweat, or tears.

The screams didn't start until some time after she thought they would.

37. XAVIER

A water molecule does not possess the quality of wetness, a neuron does not possess the quality of self. You will find neither of these things in isolation. Similarly, government cannot be found in the individual, nor humanity in the human. It is through interaction and interference that complexity arises and new properties manifest. Wetness or warmth, mercy or cruelty, it is connection *that makes them so.*

Basis of Common Law in the Modern Era <Sanctioned Digital Document>

They were coming.

It was enough to make him laugh. In fact, he felt near to hysterical.

He'd thought he was so smart, thought he'd been keeping up with all of Immanuel's analyses and predictions and schemes; thought that the man was praising him, even. In a way, perhaps he was, but it wasn't because they were on the same level. They weren't even in the same league.

Immanuel's prey was coming; and they were coming for *him*.

He wasn't the hunter, he was the bait.

He felt the change almost immediately upon leaving the dream. Not in the Aether, but in the atmosphere of the compound. The usual bored watchfulness of the guards who manned the watchtowers was replaced with sharp alertness, the sort of focus they only displayed when Feye visited. Did they know who was coming?

Xavier didn't. All he knew was that it wouldn't be Feye.

This wasn't supposed to happen. The compound was Internal Security. The compound was *Feye's*. No one else was supposed to get close.

The first to arrive was a small group of Far agents, four of them. Xavier watched them enter through the main gates, watched from a distance as they argued with the agents already there. All were keeping themselves disconnected from the Aether, preventing him from *reading* them, but he didn't need to. He saw it in their glances towards him when they thought Feye's men weren't looking.

He went over to them, arriving in time to hear the newcomers ordering that the site prepare for an inspection. Why, they would not say, but none of Feye's men would listen to Xavier's warnings. The codes were right, the authentications correct. None of them would trust the words of a prisoner over well-established, well-drilled protocols, even if he could see they were unsettled by his talk of rats and traitors.

Eventually, when it seemed like one of the guards was getting ready to demand in a more *physical* way that Xavier step back, he gave up. He retreated to the entrance of Salim's apartment, and waited. Waited, until the sound of multiple vehicles approaching came over the walls. Waited, while the dark, unmarked cars passed all security checks but provided no registry information.

When the gates slid open, so did the minds of Feye's men. He could suddenly sense them again in the Aether, their connections restored. Clearly they found the abnormality of the situation more threatening than Xavier, unsettling enough to break rigorously enforced security safeguards.

There were less of them than there should be, Xavier realised. He knew the numbers, and there were always more than thirty whether it was both he and Salim in the compound, or only Salim. Now, though, he counted maybe sixteen, and he was fairly sure no others were keeping themselves apart from the Aether. Each one of them was emitting a low-grade terror, and he could *read* them and see why.

There wasn't any protocol for this; this was a *Committee Chair*. Member Drakon, only one step below Feye, if that. There were certainly no regulations barring him from this compound. No written regulations, anyway, especially not when accompanied by an agent holding all the required authorisations - including some of the more 'off the books' authorisations Feye used with those security teams she directly supervised.

Xavier reached out to touch the mind of this 'agent,' and recoiled. *What could have done that...?*

Then the first shots rang out, and the first guards disappeared from the Aether. Not because they had separated themselves from the living energy, but because they were no longer a part of that energy and never would be again.

"They chose the direct path, then," Salim said.

Xavier just looked at him, saying nothing. The touch of that strange, broken mind was all he could think about. He took a breath, tried to shake off the feeling that he had been somehow soiled.

More shots. Now the four Far agents who had arrived earlier joined in the battle. Xavier felt the surprise in Feye's men at this; surprise, then pain.

The chaos outside was in distinct contrast to the peacefulness of their surroundings. They were sat in the Salim's living area, gentle wisps of steam rising from the coffee set in front of them both. If it wasn't for the sporadic gunfire in the distance, they could have simply been having one of their usual catch-ups.

"Maybe a dozen," Xavier said after a while, pushing away the sensation of that awful mind. "It's hard to tell at this range. Can you sense them?"

Salim nodded.

"A few more than that, I think" he said. "It is difficult to separate waking minds."

So, not an army. Less than he'd expected, more than he'd hoped.

Xavier glanced down at his thin-screen. Blank, connection lost. He'd tried to contact Immanuel the moment he left the dream, getting no answer. All outside communications were blocked a short time later.

"Oh," said Salim suddenly, sitting back in surprise. "The Dreamwalker's here."

Xavier could hear uncertainty in his voice, see the conflict in his mind. Even after knowing what they now knew, Salim still wanted to believe the "friend" from his dreams was somehow trustworthy.

He *reached* out again, stretching with his senses as far as he could. Nowhere near as far as Salim, of course, but far further than usual.

The first thing he noticed was that there were less of Feye's loyal remaining than he expected. The surprise attack from behind by agents they thought allies had been most effective.

Then he reached out towards the attackers, sensing their minds as balls of tightly-wound aggression and determination. They all carried the same resolve, to kill or be killed. All except one - one who was doing her best to only use disabling techniques, and seemed to have no weapon at all.

Though everywhere the Aether was in chaos, it was from this figure that the towering waves and endless troughs pushed outwards. The raw power of it called to him, begged him to use it for more than mere perception. He ignored it, knowing what the effects would be on those who failed to do so.

There. One of Feye's agents, standing guard no more than twenty metres from their door now that the attacker's objective was obvious. The Aether beneath him was... different. Hotter. *Angrier.*

The agent reached for the Aether. They weren't ready for it to reach back.

Xavier saw the agent burst into incandescent *Mindfire*, a bright burning glow in his sight despite the fact that mere photons were blocked by the walls between them. The agent didn't even have time to scream.

The gunfire paused abruptly, the Aether attacks hesitated. He could sense the shock in both attackers and defenders. Everyone could feel that this wasn't an Aether attack. The agent had simply been overwhelmed.

"No techniques!"

The shout came from somewhere above. One of Feye's; she'd taught them well what could happen when the Aether was like this. The shooting from the watchtowers redoubled, but no more Aether strikes came.

It seemed the attackers did not understand this though, because seeing an advantage they began pouring mental attacks towards the guards, ignoring the shouted warnings from the figure at the centre of it all. Compression-release explosions, *Slowtime*, *Flare*, some more exotic techniques Xavier couldn't identify at this distance... they took out several guards before two of of them, too, burst into golden flames.

Can't they feel it? Xavier wondered.

The confusion in their minds told him they couldn't. Couldn't feel it, or were too unfamiliar with the feeling to understand what it meant. It was similar to how it felt when Zenobia was around. Similar, but not the same.

Deep in the Aether, both a part of the current and apart from it, something moved. Something that watched the battle, and revelled.

Blane.

"They'll be here soon," Xavier said. "What will you do?"

Now it was Salim who had no answer.

"You could go with them," Xavier continued, though it twisted something inside him to say this. "Maybe this is a way out. Maybe you could..."

"Or maybe they put me in another gilded cage," Salim interrupted, his usually calm voice flecked with... anger? Fear? "And even if they let me go, what then? I just return home, knowing what is coming?"

The gunfire was lessening now, drawing closer. Despite the

warning Xavier could still sense the occasional burst of Aether, as someone too hasty or too desperate let off a compression technique or a mental attack despite the risk. Most of the time this gamble paid off. Most of the time.

Xavier looked at his friend, and realised how long it had been since he considered things from Salim's perspective. How long it had been since Salim, too, was more than just a prisoner.

Because Salim was right. Even if he *could* get away, get out and return to the Crystal Caliphate and the family he missed so much, he would still not be free. Salim understood as well as Xavier what was coming, and there was nowhere that would escape it. At least here there was the chance to have some modicum of influence on the outcome.

Xavier understood, now. He hadn't abandoned Salim in his slow slide into alliance with Ritra Feye; no, Salim had come with him. Every time he sought his friend's advice and counsel, Salim had been there. Had been his guide, not because he had to, but because he chose to. Every step of the way Salim had seen into his mind, and had not balked.

Because though Salim didn't want the world Feye was working towards, hers was the only path he saw. He would walk it until a new way revealed itself.

There was a final short, sharp burst of gunfire, then silence. Xavier sensed a handful of defenders fallen unconscious and the rest… not at all. There was no one left to fight.

He stood and faced the door as footsteps approached, sensing grim determination in the presences coming towards them. The footsteps came to a stop in front of the door, and immediately the Aether stirred and the door burst open, torn off its frame. In the doorway stood the woman who called herself Ax. Her appearance was different to that in the dream, but her mind was the same. Sharp, cold.

She stepped into the apartment, followed by three figures; two Xavier knew, and a stern-faced, heavyset man he didn't recognise.

Then the fourth came in, dragged in by the unfamiliar man rather than under his own volition. Xavier heard Salim gasp. Something in the way Dreamwalking differed from Reading must have kept him from noticing this mind until now.

"What is this?" Salim said. "What have you done to him?"

The thing that should have been a mind, inside the thing that should have been a man, was so horrific that it dominated everything else. It was... not blank, but formless. Like an ancient TV, a million patterns and signals overlapping each other and producing nothing but white noise. Occasionally something coherent would emerge, but it was always so swiftly drowned out that it may not have been there at all.

The body's posture, too, was strange. The hands hung frozen in the air, locked in the same position that they were left in by the man who dragged him in, and the eye sockets were dark and deep, revealing a gaze that stared inwardly at nothing. Occasionally the face contorted into a grimace of pain or disgust, the stimulation for this some unknown event deep in the mess of neural pathways that sparked and sputtered across the seemingly physically sound brain.

Salim and Xavier stared at the man who wasn't there, shock and horror overriding even the reunion with Blane and Serinda.

Because that was who stood there now, Blane, Serinda, the one called Ax... and the thing who had been Gabriel.

Xavier remembered the face, though he had to pluck the name from the tops of the newcomer's minds. They'd only met briefly, after all, in the short time Xavier had spent with the *Forever Fallen* after escaping the prison camp. He'd been Serinda's student at some point, he thought, so it was into Serinda's thoughts that he delved.

He saw the swirl of thought-images that formed the man named Gabriel in her mind, saw memories and feelings and sensations of the person she had trusted with more than just her life. Saw betrayal and guilt, repentance and acceptance. He saw...

"*Dios mio,*" he whispered, barely able to say it. "You pulled him apart. You *shattered* him."

"...shattered..." Gabriel repeated suddenly, though his eyes remained downcast and he gave no other sign of being aware of his surroundings.

"I tried..." Serinda said falteringly, voice just as weak.

And he could see that she truly had tried. It sat there at the top of her mind, floating atop an ocean of guilt and regret.

Tried, and failed.

Now all that was left of Gabriel was a catatonic husk, a ... ha ... *shell* of a shell personality. Serinda had tried to save him, tried to reshape the neural pathways of his brain in such a way that elasticity was preserved and the original Gabriel could return after they had taken what they needed, but to no avail. Now the Gabriel's old and new bled into each other, and bled out.

"How could you do this?" Xavier asked in disbelief. "He was one of your *Fallen*..."

"...Fallen..." said Gabriel softly, again with no other sign or movement.

Echolalia.

Xavier had heard of it even without seeing the word float to the top of Serinda's mind. The meaningless repetition of another person's words; a condition common to many neurological conditions.

"You broke him just to get to *me*?" Xavier growled. "Do you know what you've done to him?"

A loud, barked laugh came from Ax.

"You're one to talk," she said. "You did essentially the same thing."

Momentarily puzzled, he pulled what he needed from the top of her mind. A security officer in the Carib-Fed. *Spike.*

"They were sent to kill me," Xavier said with as much forcefulness as he could muster. "*You* sent him to kill me."

He didn't like that it felt as if he was trying to convince himself of this as much as her.

"*El burro hablando de orejas,*" Ax muttered, shaking her head, but it was Blane who spoke to him next.

"Gabriel has plenty of blood on his hands."

"... and you're only saying that because you desperately don't want to believe what Serinda did was wrong."

There was a pregnant pause, in which Blane glanced guiltily towards Serinda. Serinda, for her part, gave no reaction, though Xavier could see past her carefully controlled countenance to the turmoil within.

"So you don't hold back from *reading* people anymore?" Blane said, turning back to face him with a glare.

"Not when they might be here to kill me, no," he replied.

They were interrupted by the sound of flowing liquid. Hesitantly breaking eye contact with each other, the group turned to see Salim sat cross-legged on the floor, pouring yet more coffee into a set of elegant cups he had magically produced from somewhere.

"It seems..." Salim said. "... that Xavier has already filled in the gaps with what he finds in your heads. I, on the other hand, am not able to do such a thing."

He swept his hands around, proffering as if towards guests the cushions and seats that littered the floor around the low table.

"Come, sit," he said.

With a jerk Gabriel lurched forward, pushing past the heavyset man stood beside him and dropping to the floor, coming to a rest in a curious cross-legged position that didn't look entirely natural.

"He follows instructions well enough," said the man who had been guiding him. "Makes sense for an RA dog."

"Spark," Ax said. "Go and keep watch outside. Our people can suppress a response for a while, but someone *will* come to investigate eventually."

The man, all casual bluster up until this moment, drew himself up straight and nodded. He left without another word.

So, not as amateur as they let themselves appear, Xavier thought.

Then he sat down too, lowering himself as nonchalantly as he could to sit besides Salim. He didn't want to reveal any of the tension knotted up inside.

"Your people?" Xavier said, looking at Ax questioningly.

"Don't mess with me, kid," Ax said, calmly lowering herself to the floor.

With an air that suggested she was in absolute control of the situation, she reached for the nearest cup of coffee and unhurriedly taking a long gulp. Then she paused, looking at the cup in surprise.

"That is *good* coffee," she said.

"From my father's own plantation," Salim said, pleased. "Chairman Feye imports it especially for me."

Despite her approval of the drink, the mention of Feye made Ax grimace. Xavier gave a jolt of surprise at what he saw appear in her mind.

She *knew* Ritra Feye?

He found it difficult to believe but there Feye was in a hundred thought-images, piling up on one another. Fear, loathing, respect; a thousand emotions and a million beliefs tangled up around this one person. Oddly, though, Ax's mental image was of a Feye much younger...

The block slammed down around Ax's mind before he could

delve deeper, a current of Aether threading around and through her brain.

"Uh uh," she said, wagging a finger at him. "I can't hold you back for long, but I can for long enough."

"Be careful," Blane said suddenly, looking worriedly at Ax. "Using the Aether while it's like this is dangerous."

Not only at Ax, he realised, but at him also.

He laughed.

"If you are so worried, then the best thing you could do is to leave," he said.

Her puzzled expression made him pause and look into her thoughts.

"Oh, seriously?" he said with an exaggerated sigh. "You won't even admit it to yourself."

He leaned back, trying to replicate Ax's aura of calm collectedness. To buy time, he needed to appear in control. It might have worked, too, if the lack of anything to lean back *on* didn't mean he toppled clumsily backwards. He hated sitting on the floor.

"I already don't like this kid," Ax said. "What's the old word? Smug."

"What are you talking about, Xavier?" Blane said, not responding to Ax's comment.

"You know what I'm talking about," he said. "The *things* in the Aether. The ones that follow you, or lead you… I don't know. Like the leviathan that follows…"

Don't mention Fen.

That was what was now at the top of her thoughts, tinged with desperation. A direct message to him. A plea.

Well, he thought, he could do her that much.

"*Fisura,*" he said. "You're a *Fisura*, same as Zenobia. Same as… others. The Aether is more potent for everyone now, but for you it's… it's… *alive.*"

"How do we stop it?"

Blane's question was a whisper.

Xavier laughed again. She really had no idea.

"Stop it?" he said, mockingly. He only tempered his tone at a flashed look of warning from Salim. "You can't stop it. You're the *catalyst.*"

Ax was beginning to look frustrated. She opened her mouth to say something, but was stopped by a raised hand by Serinda.

"No," Serinda said, flashing her own look of warning towards Ax. "Let them speak. This is more important than your gang."

"Exactly!" Xavier almost yelled. "This is more important than plays for wealth or power; more important than anything. And for all your grudges and need for revenge, Feye is the only one with any sort of plan."

He waved to Serinda, smiling.

"Nice to see you again, by the way," he finished.

She didn't respond, looking at him through tired, dead eyes.

The click of a pistol switching to armed brought him some way back down from the wave he was riding.

"If this cocky little *pajero* doesn't get to the point soon I'm gonna put a bullet through his teeth," Ax growled.

The gun had appeared as if from nowhere and was now gripped tightly in her hand, almost but not quite pointed at his head so that all he could see was the barrel - Xavier didn't need to see it clearly to know it wasn't a stun-lock.

Careful not to make any sudden moves, Xavier held out an arm to hold Salim back. His friend had dropped the pot, spilling its contents out onto the floor in a dark, steaming stain that spread slowly outwards.

"It's ok," Xavier said, gently pushing Salim back into his seat.

Whatever Salim was about to do, he stopped. The golden glow that had appeared around him gradually weakened, though did not quite vanish.

Xavier stared at Ax, and realised he could be about to die.

Feye needs reliable people, Immanuel had said. *She needs survivors.*

Ax was looking at him with a grin so full of menace that he was sure he would never be able to replicate it, no matter how hard he tried. Immanuel was the only person he knew who could come close.

He would try, though. It was his only chance.

"You can kill me," he said, forcing as much of a reptile's grin onto his face as he could. "It will only weaken your negotiating position, though."

Suspicion rippled across Ax's face. Suspicion, and curiosity.

"Negotiating?" she asked, relocking the gun and replacing it somewhere at her side between one blink and the next. "And what will I be negotiating?"

"Either the conditions for bringing your people under Feye's command," he said, hoping the sweat on his brow wasn't as obvious as it felt. "Or the method of your execution."

To her credit, Ax made no show of surprise. No, she simply gave a knowing smile and took a sip of her coffee.

"You *are* a cocky little shit, you know that?" she said. "Go on then. Have your little reunion."

As if she'd been waiting for the chance, Blane crouched down and stared him directly in the eye.

"What do you mean, Feye has a plan?" she said.

38. FEYE

For we understand that nature truly is red in both tooth and claw, and so we must keep our teeth bared and our claws sharp.

Speech to the five services on the eve of investiture, Ritra Feye

"How long?"

Immanuel gave a tight smile at the question, staring at the thin-screen he held as if reading incoming data from it. An affectation, of course, but a useful one. There was no reason for more people than strictly necessary to know quite how deep the man's modifications went.

"My men will be ready to go within the next few minutes, Chairman," he answered. "On your order."

Feye gave a small nod and asked no more. If there was anything Immanuel thought she should know, he would tell her. Of all her subordinates, he was the only one she truly trusted.

Things were moving rapidly now. She could only hope she'd timed it right.

No, not hope. Chance was not a tool she ever relied upon. *Probability*, though... and she had done everything she could to stack the odds in their favour.

That was how Feye worked; stack the odds, then roll the dice. And if you could load the dice beforehand, so much the better.

This blasted *Sindicato*, though. They'd almost ruined everything. The discovery of a group of Aether users infiltrating not only the Reclamation Authority but almost every damned political and economic organisation this side of the Deadlands hadn't so much thrown a wrench in the machine as a whole missile. Still, they'd be a valuable asset once brought to heel; for the short time they and everyone else had left, at least.

She breathed in deeply and held it, closing her eyes and allowing the noise and commotion of the operations room to drop away. The surface of the world evaporated, revealed for what it was; illusion, and hallucination.

Now all that remained was the golden ocean upon which every living thing floated. The agents in the operations room were ripples upon the surface here, Immanuel a curiously warped shape just below. Further out, waves and whirlpools hinted at presences and events beyond her reach.

But she wasn't interested in the surface. Instead, she turned her focus downwards. Deep, far beyond the point at which the light would have died and the pressure become crushing in any natural ocean. Deep, deeper than form and awareness had any business existing, yet exist it did.

The creature below was ready; she could *sense* it. Soon, it would burst forth in self-immolation. There was no time left.

Caldwell had been so surprised when she told him what she'd seen in the depths, all those years ago at the Academy. Surprised, and overjoyed. It was everything he had been saying; the Aether was *alive*. In some ways, more alive than any mere biological matter crawling across the surface of the rock called Earth.

And it was going to destroy them all.

She'd been the only one to really listen, back then. The only one to truly understand what the doctor was saying. In fact, she understood it better than him, because Caldwell thought there was a way to *control* it, just like he thought he could control her. What a fool.

So she proceeded along her own path, leaving Caldwell bitter and resentful, making her way up the ranks while he pursued his own perverse plans - the full extent of which were still unclear. The boy, Fen, especially, remained a cypher; one of the two loose ends she knew could throw off her calculations, but she had a counter for him, at least.

She'd left Caldwell behind long ago, but not his warnings.

The world was going to end, and as always those in power wouldn't react until it was too late. Just as with nuclear weaponry or climate change or bio-weapons or artificial minds, those in charge would refuse to see what must be sacrificed. What *they* must sacrifice.

She'd known this from a young age; power is myopic.

So she had risen through the RA as fast as she could, while the self-satisfied simpletons on the Committee congratulated themselves on taking the necessary measures to prevent the coming Second Armageddon when they'd barely taken the first steps.

Those men had been stupid. While she certainly hadn't pushed the full extent of what Reclamation excavators recovered about the Fall towards them, they still had more than enough to realise the futility of their strategy. Instead, they acted as if the problem didn't exist.

Urban planning; that was their solution. From the moment the recovered files confirmed Caldwell's predictions, the borders of Albores and the other cities were set in place, immigration limits implemented and birth rates controlled. All in an attempt to thin the population so that the coming storm passed them by. The fact that all this kept the populace complacent and easy to control surely didn't factor into their calculations...

There *was* logic to it, she had to admit. The focal points for eruptions of Mindfire were going to occur far more in regions of high population density than low. But they would still occur, and even areas unaffected by the conflagration would find their infrastructure splintered and societies torn apart. Who knew how long it would be before the Reclamation recovered, if it ever did?

The Committee didn't understand; it wasn't enough to survive, they had to be able to rebuild, and rebuild rapidly. They would not be the only ones to survive... and that was the problem. Others might recover faster, and then all her plans would be for nought. If humanity did recover, and if anyone but the Reclamation Authority controlled the next world, the cycle would simply start anew.

The Althing Republic had been the greatest threat. Its technological advantage was decisive after the first Fall, and would be after the next. Feye had long ago understood what the Republic was; it was a drug dealer, ensuring other nations were dependent on it.

Such a dependency meant the same as any addiction; an end of self-determination. Fabricators spelled the end of technological independence, when what you could build with them was decided by a foreign power. Though the Althing denied it, there was no question in Feye's mind that they would restrict the production of anything that threatened their dominance. Indeed, the technology her spies had found evidence of in the Silicon Isle proved that the Fabricators already had limitations placed on their production capabilities.

They had tried, many times, to find a way around these limits. Surely, her engineers posited, even if the Fabricators would not produce a certain thing then they could produce a machine that would. Yet never were they successful, never could they make that technological leap forward. The closest they had come to a novel technology in generations was the nanotech so successfully tested on the *Fallen,* and even this was strictly limited in its capabilities.

This was why the RA hated the machine mind so much; why they named it *abomination*. It could predict better than their best engineers the developmental pathways of any specific tech, and block them. Though the Reclamation Authority would never admit it, they were technologically stunted, crippled by their supposed benefactor just as all other nations were.

Until, that is, they discovered in the pre-Fall records the key to unlock their chains; the Aether. It gave them ways to manipulate their enemy in return. It also meant that the Silicon Isle would have no choice but to move against them, eventually.

Well, she'd dealt with them, even if it had come at a cost. Organising things so that the enslaved AI was released had been tricky, and taken much time, but eventually the pieces slid into place. And to think, some of the Committee members believed she had simply taken advantage of the situation to remove Casco. How little they knew.

She had *engineered* it.

Another person would have felt a sharp pride at this, a boastful arrogance. Not Ritra Feye; this was merely the reality.

Here was the second loose end, however, born from this roll of the dice. A calculated risk, though perhaps this time she had miscalculated. Another factor she could not easily predict. An artificial mind, out there somewhere and evading the best tracers from both her security agencies and others. She'd sacrificed one of her most useful assets, Gabriel, for a chance to track it down and yet the trace had come back empty.

That shouldn't have been possible. Where was it hiding? What did it want? *Did* it want?

Well, it would have to reveal itself eventually. If she could predict it even slightly, then that much was certain. The collapse of mankind would mean the collapse of the infrastructure it needed to survive.

Her calculations remained sound, despite the unknown variable. The Reclamation would emerge into the next world ready, its armies hardened in the decaying jungles of the Mayan Republic, its borders secure and society intact. Then, and only then, could the world be remade in such a way that there would never again be another Fall.

"All preparations are complete," Immanuel said, breaking her reverie. "Ready to move on the compound. Would you like the honours?"

Feye tapped her thin-screen, sending the message that had been waiting there for this moment. Then she nodded. Though she was not one for dramatics, she allowed it in those under her.

"Proceed," she said. "Though I do not know if there will be much for your men to do except clean up. Things could get *very* messy."

39. BLANE

A philosophy of science is an oxymoron, a paradox. Philosophy is the search for meaning, science the proof there is none.

Development of the New Curriculum, Memorandum from the Department for Citizen Education

"There's no way she can be that good," Blane said as Xavier finished his explanation. "No way. What happened in the Althing Republic... no one could predict that."

"Not the exact way it went down, no," Xavier replied. "But the final outcome... when she knew the players and their motivations better than they themselves... she could, yes."

"And all of this is to, what, rebuild the entire world in the Reclamation's image?"

She paced angrily in front of the table, unable to understand how Ax could be sitting so calmly. Serinda, too, watched on impassively.

"Population control," Xavier said. "The Reclamation has refined it to an art. That's how she plans to prevent an endless cycle of Falls; after this one, humanity will never again be allowed to reach critical mass."

Blane couldn't believe what she was hearing. It was too disgusting. Could Xavier really support this? And Salim...

"The world Feye wants built after will be harsh, but will endure," Salim said sadly, as if seeing her thoughts. "I, too, see no other option."

Xavier looked at Salim, and Blane saw him give a look of pain for a moment. Why, she didn't know, but he clearly found it difficult to hear Salim arguing alongside him. She saw no duplicity in either of them, but there was clearly much being left unsaid.

Gods, she wished she was better at reading.

"If we do nothing we burn," Xavier said. "And future generations burn in the same cycle of phoenix fire until they can no longer recover. Or we help Feye, and give humanity a future. Extinction, or Feye's world. There is no other choice."

"Maybe extinction would be better."

These were the first real words Serinda had said since she'd met them, bringing the zombie-like Gabriel in tow. Blane could see something had broken inside her. All she said when she handed the prisoner over was a handful of words.

This is what I chose.

Blane thought over those words again and again on the ride over. *What she chose.* A choice between allowing the *Sindicato* to destroy Gabriel completely, or to take the responsibility on herself. It was no choice at all, not really, but still...

"Maybe you *do* understand, then" Xavier said, and to Blane's surprise he was staring directly at her. "Serinda's choice was hers alone, and so is the guilt."

She glared at him.

"Stay out of my head," she growled.

Xavier just smiled slightly, and shook his head.

Did he really think he was fooling anyone with this act? The fear was evident on his face, in the twitching of his eyes. She took it all in, not caring if he *read* her thoughts. *Wanting* him to.

From the sudden hardening of his expression, she saw he had.

"You hate the Reclamation Authority so much for what it has done, but look at what you have done for revenge," he said angrily,.

He gestured beyond the apartment walls, where Blane knew the bodies still lay bleeding. But that hadn't been *her*...

"Does that matter?" Xavier said. "It wasn't any of the men and women outside who killed Raphael. You jumped into bed with this 'Ax' and her group, not even knowing who they truly were, all because they could help you hurt the RA."

"*STAY OUT OF HER HEAD!*"

Serinda's shout was so loud her voice cracked. She flared into bright, burning gold that filled the room, though it cast no shadow.

"*I* know who killed Raphael," she said. "Far, and Ritra Feye was at its head. I've heard enough from you. Now, tell us how to get to her."

Xavier stared at her incredulously.

"*Get to Feye?*" he said. "You can't get to Feye. People far more powerful than you have tried."

Blane heard footsteps behind her. Spark, returning from outside. She saw him nod towards Ax, who stood up.

"Looks like the backup is on its way," Ax said. "Which means we are going to leave."

She turned to Serinda.

"Our target was never Feye," she said. "It was this kid, and the time has come. Either he comes with us, or we end him here and now."

Xavier laughed.

"I already told you," he said. "It's *you* who has to make a choice. Immanuel will already have this place surrounded. There's no way you're getting out of here."

Ax didn't respond, but tilted her neck left and right so that there was an audible pop of muscles stretching. She turned to Spark, nodded.

"I'll just need a minute," she said. "Tell Drakon and the others to get into the cars."

The Aether *lurched*. Blane felt it, almost staggering forward at the abrupt wave of power that flowed through her. She saw the same effect in Serinda too, and Salim and Xavier still sat on the floor.

Xavier turned and looked at her.

That wasn't me, Blane thought.

Then, slowly, he turned to Ax.

"You…" he said, shocked. "You're a *Fisura*…"

"Oh, am I?" said Ax, with a smile. "They didn't have a name for it at the Academy, back then."

As she spoke, she began to glow so brightly that it made Serinda seem like a mere candle.

"I probably should have mentioned this before," she said to Blane. "But you were having such *fun* teaching me about the Aether."

Blane stared back in shock. Their entire conversation with Ólafur; it had been an act?

The truth of it was right in front of her, visible to all her senses. Ax, too, had a presence in the Aether. A presence she was well aware of, and it was *strong*. It rose towards them, an unstoppable upwelling of energy Blane knew would consume them all, and then… froze.

It floated there, in the world below, watching them.

"You never learned to control it, did you?" Ax said, stood atop this mountain of pent-up power. She shrugged. "Too young, I guess. It took me decades."

Control. You could control it… Blane was filled with an overwhelming desperation; she needed to know how. *Fen* needed to know how.

"I could teach you," Ax said. "Maybe we can't stop another Fall, but we can save ourselves. There's no need for *all* the *Fisura* to burn."

Yes, Blane wanted to cry.

She forced herself not to. There was a glint in Ax's eye…

"But first," Ax said, turning to Xavier. "I need to pull out this damned splinter."

That should have been the end of it. Xavier should have burst into golden flame, reduced to ash before he even had time to react. At first, even Blane didn't understand what happened.

Now she was stood *between* Ax and Xavier, the table smashed away against the walls of the room. She was panting rapidly, and a feeling of immense heat filled her. Sweat dripped from her brow.

"I can't let you do that," she said through heavy breaths.

Instinct, she thought. *Just like Gabriel. You don't move your body, you let your body move* you.

And it wasn't only her body. In the Aether, the thing that was somehow a part of her moved too, smashing against the thing that was a part of Ax. The sensation was of two oceans crashing into each other.

"Impressive," Ax said, eyes widening in surprise. "Maybe you *can* control it a bit, after all."

Images flickered around the edges of Blane's mind as the immense pressure pushed into her, images and emotions and sensations. Memories. She knew this feeling, had felt it before. This was less intense, though, than when she and Fen and Zenobia had been joined by *Mindfire*. Then, three became one. This time, it was merely fragments of another's life bleeding into her own.

She saw a young girl, driven, intense. The realisation from a young age that she would be *better* than her parents, better than the weak, beaten fools who didn't even have the strength to fight for her when the men in dark suits came.

She saw the Academy, the never-ending schedule of rote-learning and technique training, the inescapable propaganda lectures and teachers who always demanded more of her. The ability to Dreamwalk that she kept hidden, the first tastes of true freedom such an ability gave her. Her escape, leaving behind classmates she never considered friends…

…*images of a young Feye, an even younger Grey, the clash between what Blane knew of these two and what Ax knew of them almost unbalancing her…*

She saw the world Ax built for herself, glimpsed the web of Aether users she built first across the Carib-Fed then back into the Reclamation, and now even beyond. A safe world, a *free* world; for her, at least.

Blane saw how this word was built, how Ax refined techniques such as *persuade* and *remind* into near-perfect forms. Saw an empire built on mental manipulation and mind control, and understood what it meant for Ax to be told 'no.'

It meant she would turn it to a 'yes.'

She saw what Ax planned to do with them.

The pressure continued to build, the edges of her vision turning white. How could Ax be this strong? She didn't know how anything could feel so crushing without killing her; it felt as if her skull should have imploded. Another few seconds, and she would no longer be able to resist.

A massive explosion took her off her feet, smashing her backwards, but instead of crashing into the wall her fall was broken by something softer, yielding. Arms wrapped around her, halting her slide.

Salim, somehow managing to move in an instant to catch her.

It took her another moment to realise what the explosion was, and that it hadn't been aimed at her.

Ax was collapsed against the opposite wall, a deep dent besides the door where she had hit. Serinda faced her, flushed and taking deep, heavy breaths. The compression-release technique had clearly come from her.

There was no time for Blane to compose herself, though, because now Spark was beginning to glow, glaring at Serinda as he drew deep on the Aether.

"You shouldn't have done that," he growled, voice filled poisoned promise.

His expression changed, though, as the glow around him continued to increase. Soon he was glowing as much as Serinda.

Impossible, Blane had time to think.

She had seen how strong Spark was... strong, but not that strong.

There was just enough time to see his expression change from confusion to pain before he burst into golden flame, throwing shadows all around as he turned quickly into dust and ash.

"Salim, Xavier, do *not* touch the Aether," Blane hissed, wiping blood from her mouth. She thought the wound in her shoulder had reopened. "You won't be able to control it."

She kept her attention on Ax, though glanced at Serinda. Would she be ok? Blane didn't know, but there was something about the rage inside Serinda that seemed to keep her safe. The glow around her, intense though it was, didn't seem to be increasing.

As if a mirror image of her, Ax rose as Blane did. The glow of the Aether around her was so bright that Blane nearly couldn't process the double vision, her organic eyes seeing the other woman clearly while her mind's eye was almost blinded.

Then Ax threw her head back, and laughed.

"Well, that was dumb," she said, glancing at the pile of dust settling slowly to the floor. "Now I need a new bodyguard."

Her eyes narrowed, locking on Salim.

"You'll do."

The Aether flared around her for a second with some technique Blane had never seen. She realised what it was just as arms once more wrapped around her, pulling tight. Then tighter. A hand gripped her throat.

"Salim, what are you doing?"

Blane heard Xavier yelling as her breath cut off. She shoved an elbow hard behind her, felt it smash into her attacker's stomach and heard the wind pushed from his chest. The grip, though, did not slacken one iota.

"Salim, stop!" Xavier cried from behind, attempting to pull the assailant from her.

The world was going dark now, the feeling of blood trapped behind her eyes almost as crushing as the pressure once again pushing against her in the Aether. She sensed Salim slash outwards with the Aether towards Xavier, *flare* knocking him to the ground.

Everything was happening at once. Serinda turned, eyes widening as she understood what was happening.

"She's does something to him," Serinda cried. "We have to stop the technique - we have to Lock her!"

Blane was barely able to understand what she meant, and even when she did splitting off enough of the Aether to do so was one of the most difficult things she had even done.

"Xavier, you too!" Serinda shouted somewhere through the haze. "This will need all of us."

Blane pushed outwards with the Aether, sensing as she did so Serinda and Xavier doing the same. It sliced forward, looking to cut through the connection between Ax and the Aether, but glanced off.

"Too... strong," Blane gasped.

Again Xavier's voice came from behind her, once more trying to pull Salim off.

"Lock Salim instead!" Xavier yelled. "If we block him, the technique should...."

But Blane and Serinda already understood. In unison, they channeled the Aether towards Salim, seeking to wrap and cut him off from the Aether. She felt the flow give, felt the Lock finally slam into place as Xavier joined them.

The grip around her throat slackened suddenly.

"What..." Salim gasped, falling backwards onto the floor.

The air that filled Blane's lungs as she took deep, rapid breaths felt fresher than cool water to a dying man in the Waste. She turned, seeing Salim staring at his own shaking hands in horror and confusion.

"What did she do?" he whispered.

"It doesn't matter," Blane said. "We've *locked* you. As long as the Aether can't touch you, she can't do that again."

A sound made her turn. Ax, looking at her over the sprawled form of Serinda who had fallen on all fours to the ground. A pistol hung from the standing woman's hand, and a livid red line down the side of Serinda's face showed where the butt of it had struck her.

The Lock wavered, but held.

"You know," Ax said, absentmindedly tapping the the weapon slowly and rhythmically against her side. "I had such hopes for you. You seemed so strong, so *driven*. Even if you did waste my bomb…"

The tapping stopped, and the barrel slowly rose to touch the back of Serinda's head. Serinda, struggling just to stay on her hands and feet without collapsing completely, froze.

"Pity," Ax said, for all the world like she meant it. "I'll keep the *Fallen*, though."

"Stop!" Blane cried. "Please..."

Xavier pushed past her on one side, Salim on the other. Faster than a rattlesnake a second pistol appeared in Ax's free hand and whipped upwards, hovering back and forth between the two. They froze, unable to advance, unwilling to retreat.

"The Reader I was always going to kill," Ax continued. "You, Salim, I was hoping could be *persuaded* to join us. We've been wanting to move into the Caliphate."

Blane couldn't understand how Ax could seem so relaxed. There was something in her expression that said she was *enjoying* this, a slight curve to her lips that said this was what she wanted all along.

Blane had never felt so helpless. There was nothing she could do; just maintaining the Lock while holding fast against the ever-increasing pressure in the Aether took everything she had. Worse, the power she was having to call upon to do so meant she was losing control. The *thing* that was her in the Aether below thrashed, fighting to get free and burn everything it could touch.

How could Ax look so calm? Was she really as in control of her own leviathan as it appeared? Blane could sense the presence below her own, lurking, watching... waiting.

Oh, Blane thought. *So that's it.*

Too late.

"Exactly," Ax said, smiling. "That's how you control the beast. Not by holding it back, not by caging it. It is pure anger, pure wrath. You *can't* cage it. No..."

Unbelievably, the glow around Ax grew even more intense. Now she was a star, and she *burned*.

"You give it what it wants."

The Aether leapt.

40. ZENOBIA

And if there truly is no free will, and all a mind is is a chain of reactions destined always to flow down one set path, than whether it is the movement of muscle fibres by electron flows across synaptic nerves or the movement of atoms by what we now term the Aether, either both of these things or neither is miraculous.

Personal Notes, Junior Researcher Caldwell

The Aether leapt, and poured into Fen… and was absorbed.

The scene replayed through her head again and again in the days after, the sensation of a total loss of control, the feeling of being a conduit for an energy too powerful to contain.

The feeling of the Aether using *her*.

It had wanted to hurt, to kill. It had wanted to see Fen burn, and it was nothing to do with her that it failed.

"Did you know you would survive?"

This was the first thing she said to him, days after the attack. The medical staff informed her he was waking up just as she was dismissing the last of the units under her command and ordering them to return to normal duties. The Reclamation still needed them for its operations in the League, after all. All Zenobia was left with was a skeleton crew and the medical staff.

That was all she needed.

"I… I thought there was a chance," Fen said through cracked, charred lips. His voice was weak and hoarse.

"You almost didn't," Zenobia replied. "Our surgeons have never treated internal burns like that before."

Fen lay in a hospital bed beneath clean, starched white sheets. Zenobia stood at the foot of it, staring down at the patient-slash-prisoner.

The room was a thing of bare white walls and sterile, clinical surfaces. It gave the impression of some long ago hospital, from back in the days before the term was just a synonym for graveyard. You would never have known, from the inside, that they were still in the midst of that godforsaken, rotting jungle.

"This is a top-of-the-line mobile medical facility," Zenobia said. "You usually need to be *high* in the RA to get such treatment."

Fen gave a painful smile.

"I'm… honoured," he said with a harsh chuckle.

He lay there, breathing raggedly.

"Why?" Zenobia said after a while, the single word heavy as lead.

"Why... what?"

"You could have let me burn," she said. "I *know* you could have protected yourself, if you'd left me to lose control. Maybe not your friends, but..."

"Then you know why I did it," he said softly.

Ah.

"How did you do it? Turn invisible, I mean?"

"Did I?"

No. Stupid, she scolded herself.

She'd played back the security footage, checked the recorded visuals of her own combat contact lenses. Fen appeared in every one, stood watching on from the side with a curious expression. Watching on, and not a single person acknowledging his presence.

"It's a technique I developed," he said. "I think I'll call it *ignore*. The mind is adept at filtering out extraneous details; I just make sure that *I'm* one of those details."

"You did it to a dozen people at once!" she said incredulously.

"I didn't say it was easy."

She sighed. Well, it didn't matter; the technique wouldn't work anymore. The security systems had been programmed to follow Fen's every move and report, setting off immediate and *noisy* alarms if he appeared to be attempting escape.

"I'm not going to run," Fen said.

She didn't know if he was *reading* her, or just perceptive.

"Ana?" he asked, wheezing. "And Rigoberta?"

"Alive and well," she replied. "I let them go. No need for them anymore, and Ana chose not to return to the Reclamation."

She didn't worry about whether he would believe her; she knew he would see the truth of her words with more than his eyes.

"Rigoberta was ok?"

Zenobia paused, confused for a moment.

"Oh, the mindbreaker?" she said. "We removed it without issue. She'll be fine."

"Good."

Another pause.

"When do we leave?" Fen asked, as if continuing a conversation she had not been aware they were having.

"Leave?"

"For the Reclamation."

She stared at him, looking for a trace of deception or ulterior motive in the cracked redness of his slowly healing face.

"You will come?"

"I will."

"Just like that?"

The answer came, tired, weak.

"Just like that."

Zenobia glanced down at her thin-screen. A message; Feye.

It had been some time since she'd heard from her. In fact, she'd been putting off reporting to her. It had been touch-and-go if Fen would even survive, and Zenobia had not wanted to be the one to deliver such news.

"Another day or two," she said, looking back up at Fen. "As soon as the doctors tell me you can safely be moved. Until then, you rest. And remember; I'm always watching."

"I'll remember," Fen said, eyes already closing.

His head tilted to the side on his pillow, and he fell asleep.

She wondered what she would do if he changed his mind. Being this close to him, for so many days, she couldn't believe it had taken her so long to truly sense how powerful he was.

She knew why, though. It was like looking at the ground beneath your feet and trying to take in the entire Reclamation. You couldn't; the thing that was Fen in the Aether was too vast. You had to look up towards the horizon, and see it stretching off into the distance far beyond anything you could perceive.

Zenobia stood there for a while, watching the man who had been her quarry. Then she shrugged, and went to get everything ready.

It was actually closer to a week before Fen was in any state to be moved. Even then, the medical staff said it was a miracle he'd recovered so fast. Zenobia didn't bother telling them she had been treating him, tentatively threading the Aether in ways both Feye and Xavier had shown her.

Surprisingly, these techniques were apparently developed by one of the *Fallen*. Feye learned them via Gabriel, her hidden asset in the group, while Xavier knew them from vaguely remembered observations direct from the source. A woman named... Serinda, was it? Impressive. She'd seen the woman's file. Who knew what she could do if she had the resources of Far at her disposal?

It was a pity she was probably going to have to kill her.

At least, that was a distinct possibility. Feye had finally gotten in touch, and had a *lot* to say about what was soon to happen; and about Zenobia's role in it. The excitement that knotted in her chest after their conversation made waiting for Fen to heal even more unbearable.

The carrier engines roared as they tore through the skies over the Reclamation, and though it wasn't time yet for landing Zenobia stood and stretched the kinks out of her legs. At least, she didn't think it was time; she wasn't even sure *where* they would be landing. Feye wanted to see Fen as soon as possible, that was all she knew.

Either way, this last stretch of the journey had been several hours in a cramped compartment, made yet more cramped by the three Far agents assigned to 'escort' Fen to his destination. A token gesture only, of course. Zenobia knew, and Feye must too, that it would require much more than a mere three agents to restrain Fen if he decided he didn't want to be restrained. Still, there were certain protocols to follow, even if they had little meaning.

In the Reclamation, there were always protocols to follow.

The carrier juddered at unexpected turbulence, and at first she thought that was what made Fen's eyes widen slightly. Then her thinscreen vibrated.

Aether incident in Corazón, the message read.

Then; *Rogue Far elements identified. Asset compromised.*

Zenobia wasn't sure what the initial, unfamiliar shiver that ran through her was, but she knew the second and overriding feeling well.

She let out a growl, a low, fierce thing of promise and wrath.

"You sensed it?" she said, glaring up at Fen and already knowing the answer.

Fen nodded, looking down and past the floor of the drone as if seeing something on the distant horizon.

"They're strong," he said, as casually as if commenting on the weather[53]. "Stronger than you were, the first time we met."

"And now?" she asked.

---

[53] Overcast and hazy, as always.

She didn't wait for his answer, and knew it didn't matter. Whoever was down there, they could be twice as powerful as her and it would make no difference. She was going to rip them apart if they had even *touched* him.

This surprising thought almost made her lose focus. Almost.

Concentrate, she told herself. *Strength is nothing without control.*

Feye's words, but it was Fen who had shown her the truth of them.

She slammed the wall-panel button that opened communications with the cockpit.

"How long will it take to get to *Corazón* in Albores if we change course now?" she barked.

"Sir?" came the confused reply. "That is our destination, sir. For you at least. Our orders are to drop you there and then take the prisoner onwards to a secure location."

Of course.

Zenobia didn't think she would ever get used to Feye's ability to be not only ahead of the game, but playing a different board entirely.

Fen raised his eyebrows at this, the first time she had seen him look uncertain.

"You're leaving me?" he said.

"*Parece que sí,*" she said with a shrug. "No need to worry, though. Feye's got someone waiting for you."

Again, an uncertain look. She had to keep herself from smiling; the man had been playing the 'I know something you don't know' card even from his hospital bed. It was refreshing to be able to do the same back.

"Try and *read* me..." she said, voice low and threatening, seeing something appear in his expression. "And neither of us will survive what happens to this carrier when I stop you."

Fen actually *blushed*.

"I wasn't going to," he said. looking for all the world like a small child caught with his finger on the requisitions tab[54]. "I don't do that."

She watched him suspiciously for a moment, surprised at the ease of his submission, wondering what it was about this man that made him so hesitant to use his power. If *she* had his strength...

---

[54] Once upon a time, hands in the cookie jar, but now even snacks had to be ordered and delivered.

As if the universe was trying to tell her something, she sensed what Fen already had.

"Oh-ho," she said with a dry laugh. "They *are* strong."

The point of flaring heat in the Aether came rapidly closer, the drone bearing down on it at speed. She stretched out ahead with her senses, feeling the ripples that became rolling breakwaters and drowning whirlpools as she approached the person at its centre.

No, not person; *creature*.

It thrashed in the Aether, roaring and tearing at the presences around it. These presences were dwarfed by its size, and... one of them was Xavier. She knew what he felt like in the Aether, though she would be hard pressed to describe it with words.

She shook off the feeling of relief that passed through her, ignoring it. Besides, it was clear that all those she sensed would soon be swallowed. Even now, only the efforts of a second form in the Aether were keeping them from utter destruction. A smaller form, and one that would soon be overwhelmed. Another presence she knew, though from a long time ago.

"Oh, *mierda*," she cursed. "What the fuck is *she* doing here?"

Fen looked up at her.

"I would consider it a favour if you didn't kill her," he said. "I don't know exactly what Blane has been up to, but she's still *good*."

The roar of the engine rose in pitch, indicating they were beginning a slow, controlled descent.

"*Good?*" she sneered. "Since when has *good* mattered?"

Though she would only ever admit this to herself, the snarling cynicism was a veneer to hide how pleased Fen's words made her. She was still unsure whether she really would have to kill Blane, but...

Fen's words told her she could.

"The true measure of strength is knowing that people will hurt you, and you must not hurt them back," Fen said suddenly, derailing her thoughts.

Now what was he talking about? Was he trying to impress her with mysticism, hoping to awe her with pretensions of hidden knowledge? It was all just words, and she knew the power of words well enough. Feye had shown her just how powerful they could be. The right words in the right order could control the thoughts of others just as well as any Aether technique. They just had to want to believe them.

Words had power, yes, but it was the power you gave them.

Not taking her eyes off him, she reached up and thumped the large, oddly mechanical button that initiated the landing ramp's opening procedure. Cold air instantly rushed in, sending hair and unsecured papers flying. Moisture, half-mist and half-cloud, filled the cabin with a damp chill, droplets instantly appearing on every surface.

An alarm began blaring, the red flashing warning light of an unexpected opening at altitude filling the cabin. Around Fen, the Far agents yelled in surprise and fright, while through the intercom the urgent questioning of the pilot squawked.

She ignored them all.

"That's the thing, though," she said, stepping backwards down the now nearly fully opened ramp while maintaining eye contact with Fen. The wind tore at her like a wild beast. "I am so very good at hurting people."

She jumped, the wind and momentum of the drone's descent sending her flying backwards into open air. The last thing she saw before the aircraft became a tiny dot above her was Fen's face, expression a knowing smile.

She reached for the Aether, and used it to guide her fall.[55]

---

[55] She'd never tell anyone, but she'd been waiting for an opportunity to do this ever since she'd discovered the Aether was strong enough to allow it. She didn't let this fact take away from the feeling of absolute bad-assery, however.

41. XAVIER

Man is not born free, and the chains are not of his making. For the maintenance of a stable and secure society, citizenship should be conferred only on those who demonstrate understanding of this fact.

Processes of Regulation and Order in the Reclamation (Sanctioned Digital Document - section redacted)

He'd been shot.

It was odd. He could see the redness blossoming down his side, but it was more like watching a video of it happen than something he was actually experiencing. The pain, too, so intense that it stopped his lungs, didn't feel like it was actually happening to *him*.

The only reason he was alive was Salim. The bullet had been aimed straight for his heart, only missing because his friend slammed into him and pushed him out of the way a fraction of a second before the muzzle flared.

Almost out of the way, anyway.

Right now, though, being shot seemed like a minor worry.

His brain was still replaying what just happened. Ax smashing through the barrier Blane had somehow maintained until that point, towering over him while even more colossal in the Aether. The gun rising, barrel becoming the whole of his world even as the Aether lashed out from Ax to reduce him to ash...

And then the ceiling came crashing in.

The thing was, there were two floors above them. Whatever had come smashing down through the roof must have been a missile or, or, an *asteroid* or something. They should have all been dead.

As it was, none of them were standing. Though as far as Xavier could see through the dust he was the only one bleeding profusely, no one else seemed to be doing much better. Rubble and prefab brick continued to collapse inwards for a few moments while everyone's brains caught up.

"Oh," said the figure stood in the midst of all this destruction. She kicked the prostrate form of Ax, out cold on the floor beneath her feet. "Don't tell me we won't get to play."

The figure turned, and gave him a familiar smile that as always simultaneously sent a flush of fear and excitement through him. In fact, you could only call it a smile because it was on her face, rather than a shark's.

"Welcome back, Zenobia," he said weakly.

"You let yourself get shot," she said, looking disapprovingly at where he held his side, futilely trying to stop the blood.

"I... uh..." he gasped, forcing a smile of his own. "I won't do it again?"

Zenobia seemed to dismiss him, turning to look somewhere else. Xavier couldn't raise his head far enough to see where.

"You..." Zenobia said to someone. "You're that *Fallen* doctor, right? Fix him."

She gestured towards Xavier, looking expectantly at whoever she was talking to. Serinda staggered over to kneel besides him a moment later.

"Be... careful," Xavier groaned as Serinda began threading cooling strands of Aether into him. "The... *Sindicato*. She's dangerous."

That made Zenobia turn to him again. He realised she was gritting her teeth, a single bead of sweat appearing on her forehead.

"You don't say?" she growled.

It was only then that his true senses came back, the Aether swimming into focus. He looked 'down'.

This must be what it felt like to be an insect fallen onto a lake, some part of him thought. He was trapped there, a thin skein of surface tension holding him immobile while below something dark and monstrous rose with mouth agape. Something with *teeth*.

A second flow of power joined Zenobia's own, pushing the raging beast back downwards.

"I didn't ask for help," Zenobia snapped, glaring over to where Blane was pushing herself up onto her elbows.

"You're still getting it," Blane replied. "Is Ax...?"

Zenobia looked down at the form between her feet and kicked. Ax's head lolled sideways towards Xavier, mouth ajar and tongue protruding.

"Out like a light," she said. "But still channelling the Aether. Never seen this before."

"She's a *Fisura*," Blane said. "This is what will happen to us all, eventually."

Zenobia nodded, apparently understanding Blane's words better than he did.

"She was never in control of it," Blane continued. "She just gave it what it wanted, and in exchange it would... wait. It was never 'tame,' though."

"Any way to stop it?" Zenobia asked.

A moment's silence, then;

"I was kind of hoping you knew," Blane replied.

"I can think of one way..." Zenobia said.

With careful deliberateness, she reached down and picked up one of the pistols now fallen from Ax's hand. The auto-lock instantly gave an authorisation click, and the LED on the side turned green.

"Far issue," Zenobia said, turning it over curiously in her hand. "Looks like this *Ax's* connections run deep."[56]

She pointed it at Ax's head.

"Stop."

Zenobia paused, finger hovering on the trigger. Then she tutted, and looked at Salim.

"Really?" she said. "A minute ago she was trying to kill you. And about to succeed, I might add."

Again, her finger tightened on the trigger.

"You can't just..." Salim began, trailing off despondently.

His face had been badly cut by falling debris, Xavier saw. Still, he was more concerned for Ax than his own injuries.

"We need her," Xavier said, hoping Zenobia was in the mood to listen. "Immanuel... Feye... I was supposed to capture her."

Serinda's ministrations seemed to have taken effect. The blood pouring from his side stopped, or perhaps slowed enough to begin clotting. He pushed himself up onto his elbows, hissing at the pain this caused.

"In case you haven't noticed," Zenobia said. "I'm having to work extremely hard just to keep her from frying us all. We don't have time to..."

As if in response, gunshots echoed from outside. Shouts and screams followed, then the sound of boots making their way towards them.

"Just a little longer," Xavier said, grinning through gritted teeth as

---

[56] Of course the pistol worked for Zenobia, Xavier thought. As one of Ritra Feye's assets, practically any Far-issued weapon would... which meant this was true for him too, he realised. He resolved to get a weapon of his own as soon as possible.

the taste of blood filled his mouth.

He hoped he looked half as cool and collected as he was trying to appear, rather than as battered and broken as he felt.[57]

A moment later and Immanuel appeared at the apartment door; well, the gaping hole that had once been a door. He paused, running his gaze over the rubble, taking it all in until it finally came to a rest on Xavier.

"You let yourself get shot," Immanuel said, shaking his head as he stepped in. Behind him, body-armoured figures in the dark uniform of Quick-Fix took up guard positions.

"I already said I won't do it again..." Xavier moaned. He was feeling quite light-headed.

The sound of panicked movement made him turn.

Blane and Serinda, scrabbling to their feet. Serinda began to glow brightly, Blane unable to as all her focus was on containing the beast below.

"Oh, stand down," Immanuel said, gesturing to them dismissively. "You're quite safe, for now. The Chairman guarantees it."

He strode over to stand besides Zenobia, looking down at the prostrate form of Ax.

"Excellent work, Asset," he said. "Did she give you any trouble?"

Xavier nearly replied before realising he was speaking to Zenobia. He clamped his mouth shut, shocked that he could feel so foolish while in so much pain.

"She actually continues to, sir," Zenobia answered, a hint of strain in her voice.

Sir? Xavier thought.

He'd never heard respect in Zenobia's voice before, except for when talking to Ritra Feye. Wait... did Immanuel and Zenobia *know* each other? Yet neither had ever mentioned...

The blood loss must be doing something to his head, he thought. He couldn't possibly be feeling jealous right now, could he?

So distracted was he that at first he didn't notice Immanuel draw something out of his pocket. It was small and metallic, like a scarab beetle, and glinted in the light.

"A mindbreaker?" Zenobia asked. "Will that work?"

---

[57] He would, much later, be amazed at how concerned he was about his appearance in front of Zenobia as opposed to the fact that he was on the verge of death.

"Why don't we find out?" Immanuel replied.

He leaned down, roughly rolling Ax over so that she lay face down on the debris-strewn floor. Then he pushed the device against the nape of her neck.

There was the faintest *snick*.

Immediately the creature in the Aether reacted, exploding into a frenzy so rage-filled and powerful it made everything that had come before seem like a mild tantrum. Zenobia and Blane were literally rocked backwards.

Then... the beast turned, flaking and blurring as it did so, and disappeared into the depths.

"It maintained its form..." Immanuel said, watching it leave. "Interesting..."

Xavier saw a look of surprise flash across Zenobia's face.

So she didn't know Immanuel could see the Aether? He swiftly squashed the feeling of satisfaction that came with this knowledge, fearful that she would see it in his expression.

A groan rose from where Ax lay.

"*Qué coño...?*" she muttered, her eyes flickering open.

They opened significantly wider when she saw Immanuel.

To her credit, she got to her feet in record time despite her quite obvious injuries. There was a moment when Xavier knew she must be trying to reach for the Aether, then her hands went to the nape of her neck.

"Oh," she said, shoulders slumping. "*Mierda.*"

She looked for all the world as if she had given up and, unable to *read* her, the act quite took in Xavier.

Immanuel, though, saw it for what it was. He was on the second pistol, the one Zenobia hadn't picked up, in a flash. Still only a few microseconds ahead of Ax, though.

"Uh-uh," Immanuel said, the barrel of the pistol now squarely against the centre of Ax's forehead. Both were crouched above where the gun had lain, glaring at each other. "There'll be no more of that from you."

Ax rolled, up and at a sprint towards the broken door before anyone could react. Futile, of course, even without the Quick-Fix troops blocking her way and raising their rifles.

Immanuel blurred, and faster than the eye could see Ax was once more prone, the low groan of a wounded animal passing from her lips though she was clearly trying to hold it in. Immanuel knelt over her, one knee dug deep into her spine, and lowered his head. Then he whispered to her, though in the thick silence Xavier could hear it clear as a pre-Fall day.

"Continue to resist..." Immanuel said. "And I'll do to you what you did to our embedded. Only, I won't just break you. I'll *remake* you. Scrape away everything you are, and replace it with something I can use. Then there won't be a *you*; just a thing that wears your face."

Ax went still. Something in Immanuel's words... they made Xavier shiver even though they weren't directed at him. There was something so *certain* about them.

A hand appeared in his peripheral vision, thrust out towards him. His eyes followed the limb upwards into Zenobia's disapproving expression.

"Up," she said perfunctorily. "You can stand, right?"

Surprised, and trying not to show it, he tentatively reached out and took the proffered hand. The moment he took hold of it, he was pulled up so fast he barely moved his feet.

Zenobia looked him up and down, examining him with the same look as a Fab-line quality assurer[58] examining their thousandth product of the day.

"Good," she said. "Nothing serious."

Xavier fought the urge to gesture to his blood-drenched side. Then something happened that made him question just how lucid he really was.

Zenobia turned to Serinda.

"Thank you," she said.

Maybe he was more injured than he thought. Could he have hit his head on the way down?

A low chuckle came from the corner of the room.

"Oh, I see," Blane said, pushing herself to her feet. "I wondered what could have turned Xavier so deeply to the dark side...[59]"

She looked from Zenobia to him and back again.

"I guess that was all it took," she finished.

Xavier opened his mouth, ready to reply but immediately tripping

---

[58] A redundant position, given that automation could review a hundred products for defects in the time it took a human to do one, but a pillar of Reclamation employment statistics.

[59] *I get that reference!* Xavier thought proudly.

over his own words. He glanced at Zenobia; this was dangerous territory.

She beat him to it.

"He is mine, yes," Zenobia said matter-of-factly. "Though that isn't why he follows Feye."

Okaaay, that was a lot to process.

Xavier was very aware that his mouth was hanging open, but for some reason no words would come. Whoever the little pilot was that ordinarily sat behind his eyes, it looked like they'd used the ejector seat.

"Well, fun as this reunion is...," Immanuel said, straightening up. "I would prefer we don't keep the Chairman waiting."

Ax made no motion even after he released the pressure on her. Immanuel motioned for the Quick-Fix troops to pick her up. They marched in and grabbed her, their International Health Organisation logos made a mockery of by the vicious-looking rifles each held thrust out before them, looking for an excuse to use them.

"Nasty business, that," Immanuel said.

At first Xavier thought he was referring to Ax, now limply hanging in a Quick-Fix trooper's grip, eyes dull and glazed over. The... mindbreaker, was it? ... seemed to be having some kind of lethargy-inducing effect.

But it wasn't Ax he was pointing to. It was Gabriel.

The former *Fallen*, former Far duality lay on his back nearby, staring up through the collapsed-in ceiling and into the sky. His eyes were unfocused and absolutely still, and Xavier could only tell he was alive by the slight rise-and-fall of his chest and his faint, frail presence in the Aether.

"I suggest," Immanuel said, turning to Serinda. "... that in the coming conversation you think carefully about what *you* do to achieve your aims, before judging so swiftly what the Chairman does."

Serinda gave no response, just watched him through dark, inscrutable eyes.

"Coming conversation?" Xavier asked. "They're being taken to Feye?"

"*Chairman* Feye," Immanuel said, emphasising the title. "And we're the ones taking them."

A thousand questions rose in his mind, and he squashed them all. Immanuel did not seem in the mood for talking, especially in front of the... he supposed he had to call them *prisoners*.

The thought made him uncomfortable.

"This is what Feye does," Serinda said suddenly, voice low and flat as if talking to the air. "Traps you. You don't even see the net wrapping around you until she pulls it tight."

She didn't sound angry, Xavier was surprised to realise. She sounded *empty*.

"And yet, every step of the way has been your choice," Immanuel replied. "You could have walked a different path at any moment, and the Chairman would not have stopped you."

Though the words sounded triumphant, his tone was not. He spoke as if he were merely stating a fact.

"Not unless you were a threat to her plans, at least," he finished.

"You're saying nothing we've done posed a threat to her?" Blane asked. As she spoke she moved to stand beside the now-swaying Serinda, gently offering an arm for support. "Not even...?"

She caught herself before she said it, but Immanuel clearly understood.

"Caldwell's experiment?" he said. "Well now, it's probably time we found out, isn't it?"

42. XAVIER

We understand as little of the evolution of the Aether as we do of the earth itself. We label as pre-Cambrian seven-eighths of our planet's history, a time hidden forever from us by climatic shift and tectonic activity. A length of time practically inconceivable.

Inconceivable; an apt word for the Aether as well. Perhaps it, too, was born in prehistory. Who knows what forms it has taken, prior to the one we are only beginning to understand today?

Doctor Nataneal Caldwell, *Address to the Gathered Members upon the Establishment of the Far Academy*

"Are you familiar with the Trolley Problem?"

Feye watched them from the head of the table. The table around which he, Salim, Blane, Serinda, Grey, Spangle, and Fen sat. The long, heavy table made of dark, glossy wood.

The table of the Committee.

Things were happening in the Reclamation. The Net was full of it, half the censorship algorithms down and the rest seemingly glitching as if some madness had taken hold of the central processing framework. Personal blogs and soc-sites were filled with calls for calm and calls for armed uprising. Reports of a *coup d'etat* within the Reclamation Authority flooded every server still up, with some declaring its total success and others its absolute defeat, and there were Citizen posts about security agents and military troops on every street with orders to shoot on sight.

Someone or something was even performing a DDOS attack on the entirety of the Reclamation network at once, which wasn't even theoretically possible. Entire sites were offline, replaced with some ancient tract in language so archaic as to be incomprehensible beginning *We the people...*

And here they sat in undisturbed quiet, at the table of the Boardroom that was at the centre of it all. Around them, the building was in the process of being occupied by Far Agents loyal only to the Reclamation and Feye herself; Xavier could sense the fear and confusion in the bureaucrats of every office as they were escorted outside, often at gunpoint. What had happened to the other Committee Members only Feye and Immanuel knew.

"Cleaning house," Feye said perfunctorily, in explanation to the distracted looks on every other face in the room. No one had replied to her question. "Purging the *Sindicato* and their affiliates will take time, but thanks to you all we can now begin."

From what Xavier could tell only Immanuel fully understood what Feye was saying. The man stood behind her, off to one side with his face half in shadow. From the darkness his eyes roved around the room, taking in each figure and, Xavier knew, assessing the threat each posed to Feye. Only with Fen did his expression ever waver.

Fen, to Xavier's initial surprise, was sat in one of the two seats closest to Feye when he entered. They had clearly been discussing something, pausing only when he sat in the chair directly opposite the other man. Behind Xavier, every one of the other 'guests' arrayed themselves down Fen's side of the Committee table. It left Xavier feeling exposed and vulnerable .

"Why are we here?" Blane demanded, tensed like a spring and ready to jump up from her seat at any time. She glowed softly, Aether held ready. "You plan to mess with *all* our heads this time? Turn us into willing little slaves?"

Feye looked at her impassively, blinking once.

"The mental aversion?" she said. "I needed you in the Silicon Isle. Couldn't have you wasting time attempting to rescue my assets. Besides, it was a fair trade. I gave you the chance to save this one…"

At this Feye gestured to Serinda, who glared back at her.

"… and to save the *Fallen* leader."

"Save her?" Blane spat. "*You* killed her. It was *your* poisonous nanotech."

Xavier glanced over to Serinda at the same time as Blane did, checking her reaction. Nothing; Serinda just continued to fix Feye with a stare so cutting it should have sliced her in half.

"My organisation did, yes," said Feye matter-of-factly. "I was not in charge of the handling of subversive groups at the time, though it was at my insistence that the focus was shifted to finding *Fisura*. A necessary decision."

There it was; a slow, deep rumble coming from Serinda's throat, like the growl of something fanged and primeval in the ancient dark. Feye turned to her.

"A *necessary* decision," she continued. "And one that will save exponentially more lives."

"The same kind of decision as bringing us all here today?"

This was Grey, speaking for the first time since their arrival. The only reaction he had given to anyone was a short nod to Xavier upon entering the Boardroom. Now he sat between Spangle and Fen, expression hidden under the pulled-down brim of his crumpled, threadbare hat.

"No," Feye answered. "This was your choice, and mine. Your choice because you *would not stop,* my choice because, well, it was the one concession I would allow myself. I suppose because, at the very end of it all, I find myself... weak."

Surprise filled Xavier. He had known the outline of Feye's plan for years, if never the full details, and most of its forms required at least some of the current attendees to be here. He had never once, though, seen any hint that Feye thought her choice was *weakness.*

The revelation caused a few pieces fall into place.

"The Trolley Problem," he said, wanting desperately for Feye to finally explain, for the others to finally understand.

"Oh, of *course* we know the Trolley Problem," said the man named... Spangle, apparently.[60] Xavier had never met the man before, but he already didn't like him. "It's basic ethics, and vital for algorithmic development."

"Well why don't you explain it then?" said Grey, a trace of irritation in his voice that, despite everything, made Xavier hide a grin. "Just to make sure we *all* know what we're talking about."

Spangle looked at him aghast.

"Expla...?" he began, then became aware of eight faces staring at him intently. "Uh... yes, well..."

Xavier had never seen someone *harumph* in real life before, but Spangle did so as he collected his wits.

"The Trolley Problem is, you know..." the man went on. "It's the entire basis of intelligence design. The whole thing is a thought experiment on the question of what is morally the correct choice to make when inaction will indirectly cause the deaths of a greater number of people than *actively* causing the deaths of a smaller number."

No one spoke. Feye, it seemed, was content to let this play out.

"Um..." Spangle continued uncomfortably. "The proverbial 'trolley' is a vehicle hurtling down one track that if left unaltered will

---

[60] He'd had to surreptitiously confirm that with Immanuel, who'd just given an infinitesimal nod and rolled his eyes.

crash into five people and kill them. You, the observer, then have the choice to pull a lever to send the trolley down a second track with only a single person on it, thereby resulting in the death of only that individual."

There was a pause while they processed this.

"Then you pull the lever."

Everyone turned to Fen, who had spoken. The blunt way he said it, as if the answer was self-evident, surprised even Xavier.

It apparently surprised Salim more, though, because he instantly spoke up.

"That would be murder," he said.

Fen and Salim stared at each other, each with an expression both puzzled and thoughtful.

"It would be saving..." Fen began, but Spangle cut him off.

"You cannot be so quick to judge," he said, now clearly becoming more comfortable in his role as 'teacher'.[61] "For instance, what then if you could stop the trolley by *pushing* a single individual onto the tracks?"

This time the pause was longer.

"Now," Spangle began again, licking his lips and flourishing with his hands as if he were on stage. "What then if you have one healthy individual and five with irreversible organ failure - organ failure that could be reversed by slicing up the healthy individual and sharing out their body parts? Or a group of five adults in one auto-car and a baby in another, on a collision course and one of which must undergo a potentially fatal braking pattern? Statistically, it is the same question."

He swept his gaze around his audience, seemingly expecting admiration or perhaps even applause. He was quickly brought crashing back to reality by the stern, flat gazes of his companions.

"It's vital to consider this when designing algorithmic models," he said more weakly, eyes turning down. "Should the emergency overwatch system sacrifice one transport tube for another, or a smaller section of Hab for a larger? You can't just *ignore* such questions..."

He trailed off, reddening.

"No," Xavier said, picking up the thread. "You cannot. And that is why Feye didn't."

---

[61] Xavier was swiftly coming to the conclusion that here was a man who ordinarily loved the sound of his own voice.

"You do *not* want to tell me Sara was a necessary sacrifice," Serinda said, head snapping towards him and knuckles whitening where she gripped the table even as the Aether flared around her.

"This is not about your lover," Ritra Feye said, drawing Serinda's glare back on herself. "This is about the end of the world, and what comes after."

"And what comes after is the Reclamation Authority, is it?" Blane yelled, thumping the table. "A world where you can just disappear if you say the wrong thing?"

"Would you prefer the world of the mechanical mind?" Immanuel said, close to yelling as he gestured to Spangle, then to Salim. "Or the theocracy? Maybe the Empire's web of castes and bloodlines?"

Feye held up a hand, cutting him off. Immanuel's mouth shut with an audible snap.

"Thank you, Immanuel," she said. "However, I will answer."

Immanuel stepped back again, looking more agitated than Xavier had ever seen, more even than when he was shot.

Feye turned and spoke directly to Blane.

"Yes, just such a world," she said. "A world of what you call oppression, but I call peace. The only world that *can* exist, after the Fall."

Blane paused despite herself.

"What are you talking about?" she said.

"It is no coincidence that the new world formed this way. This is the only way it *could* form, after the Collapse. The world *burned*, Blane. It burned, and the survivors watched everyone they loved die. There was nothing but pain and horror, and to continue living we suppressed it."

Xavier could see Blane considering Feye's words the same way he had, once. But he'd had more than words; he'd seen into Feye's mind. How long would it take, he wondered, before Blane saw the truth of them?

"We didn't suppress it," Blane said uncertainly. "We rebuilt, revitalised, re... reclaimed."

"You see?" Feye replied, sitting back and crossing her arms. "Even you, who's built a life around opposition to the Reclamation, can only repeat the story it wrote. A story we need; every nation has one. And whether it is imperial, autocratic, or theological, it serves one purpose - to bury the truth of our near-extinction."

She looked *down*, and every person there knew she wasn't looking into the physical world.

"But it doesn't want to stay buried. It *won't* stay buried. I saw that a long time ago."

"That's what we never understood, Blane," said Fen softly. "Why the Aether responds so strongly to our anger; it's because *everyone* is angry. Angry, scared, and filled with hate. We *Fisura* most of all."

"Even the old world was full of it," Feye added. "They had every potential, every chance, and still it wasn't enough. So they fed the Aether with their pain, and in return it fed on them."

"Then there must be a way to stop it," Blane said.

"Stop it?" Feye replied. "No, no more than we could stop the plates of the earth shifting beneath our feet. The Aether is *ancient*, though perhaps our consciousness has warped and changed it. All we can do is contain it, keep it weak by limiting that which it feeds on; us."

"You can warn them!" Spangle yelled. "Warn the other nations, tell them what is going to happen. Maybe…"

He stopped dead under Feye's stare.

"Warn them?" she said. "How could the nation which boasts of controlling the Aether warn them and not be blamed? When the Phoenix Fire burns their cities, those who survive *will* seek someone to hold responsible. A warning would only paint a target on the entire Reclamation, and our enemies must be focused on each other."

"*Ertu alvarleg…*" Spangle muttered, then spoke louder. "You cannot mean this. To watch the world fall again, and build something even worse in its place."

"Worse?" Feye replied, arching a single eyebrow. "A word with only relative meaning. But *strong*. It will be strong, and there will be no more Falls."

"With all humanity under the heel of your boot," Spangle growled.

A snort of derision made him look at Immanuel.

"You still don't understand, do you?" Immanuel said. "Your file said you were smart."

Spangle held his gaze for a moment then looked around, searching for an explanation.

"It won't be *her* boot," said Grey suddenly, voice emotionless.

Spangle turned to him in question, but Grey didn't look up. It was then that Xavier noticed the thing he was twirling in his hands; a thin glass cylinder, with something flat and metallic held within. It looked, oddly, like a mindbreaker.

"What do you mean, not her boot?" Spangle demanded.

"The next Fall will take her with it," Grey answered, still spinning the cylinder. "She's a *Fisura.*"

"Well done, Nestor," Feye said, a thin smile appearing on her face. "Did you figure that out after I brought you back in, or before?"

"You didn't *bring me back in,*" Grey said, finally looking up and meeting her gaze. "And I suspected it for a while. This meeting just confirmed it."

"What are you saying?" Spangle said to the room in general. "What does being a *Fisura* have to do with…?"

"Come *on,* Arthur," Grey said, a flash of annoyance again flitting across his expression. "You've seen the files; what do you think?"

Spangle froze, mouth hanging open.

"The *Fisura* are the focus." Grey replied tiredly. "Other Users might burn themselves out, maybe take those nearby along with them, but it's the *Fisura* who are city-killers. I've been looking for some hint in Caldwell's notes that might at least save… I thought, maybe with what he learned from Fen…"

Grey trailed off, looking guiltily up at Fen as he said his name. Clearly the admission that he had been hoping to use work based on what was essentially the imprisonment and torture of the younger man sat uneasily.

"It's alright," Fen said calmly. "You searched Caldwell's notes hoping to save *us*, and found something. I searched my memories of him hoping to save *everyone,* and found nothing. He was trying to prevent the Phoenix Fire, after all. But he was…"

"Caldwell was a fool," Feye said firmly. "My predecessor a fool for investing so much in him. There is no way to prevent the eruption of the Aether except by strict population control."

"But surely…," Spangle began, looking from Blane to Fen.

"We can't even *find* most *Fisura,"* Feye said. "But we can save *some,* and thus we come to the only logic that matters; the logic of survival, when you no longer bargain for the many you don't know, but the few you do."

Zenobia, Xavier thought.

Long ago he had seen Feye's resolve, and her decision that it would be Zenobia who survived, not herself. A cold rationalisation, based on the calculation that Zenobia could offer many more decades of service to the reborn RA than Feye, but tinged with a… fondness … for the girl[62].

"Some may survive," Feye continued. "But there is little time left; your friend here, Serinda, shows just how little."

Blane, until now pure defiance and rage, gasped. Tears instantly welled in her eyes as she looked at Serinda.

So Blane finally understood, Xavier thought. Why Serinda still glowed so brightly with the Aether, even after all this time since the fight with the *Sindicato*.

She couldn't stop it.

Serinda, for her part, merely nodded sadly.

"I've felt it for a while, even before… this" she said. "Controlling it is hard. I don't think I can do it much longer. But you've been doing this since you were a *child*."

Tears appeared in Serinda's eyes as well.

"A part of all of us lives in the Aether," Feye said. "And our experiences affect it. Our trauma is ingrained in it."

"*How do we stop it…?*"
"*How do we stop it…?*"

Blane and Serinda spoke at the same time, their words so hurried yet so eerily in sync Xavier could have believed it was some kind of Aether technique. Then they paused, looking at each other.

"You said some could survive," Serinda said first, turning her eyes to look at Feye for the first time with something other than hate. "How can we save her?"

Again, a megalomaniacal villain would have smiled triumphantly at this, taking pleasure in having their professed enemy so cowed. Not Feye, however. Xavier didn't need to *read* her to know she got no pleasure from this. This was just how it was always going to be.

"By making a sacrifice," Feye said. "By deciding that you place more value on her life than of others."

"No!" cried Blane, but was immediately cut off by Serinda.

"*Be quiet,*" Serinda snapped, her words cold and hard as the permafrost. She turned back to Feye. "How?"

"By finding a User powerful enough to take it on," Grey said. "That's what Caldwell was trying to do; create a *Fisura* powerful

---

[62] In Feye's thoughts, Zenobia was always a 'girl'.

enough to control not only their own presence in the Aether, but that of all the others as well."

Feye nodded.

"A ridiculous plan," she said. "One that ignored reality. The Aether is far too vast to be controlled like that; it would be like trying to control the ocean currents. But a single part of the flow, if you are strong enough…"

She looked at Fen, then back to Serinda.

"And if we chose to stop you, here and now?" Blane said.

Xavier tensed. The glow around her had maintained its strength this entire time, but now began to increase in intensity. Immanuel, too, reacted, taking a step forward that was only stopped by Feye's raised hand.

"You can try," Feye said. "Maybe even succeed, depending on the side each person here takes. But you have not heard my offer, yet."

"Offer?"

This was Grey, surprised.

"You did not ask why I brought you here, to this room."

Xavier watched as the others shared confused, suspicious looks.

"I will not be able to lead the Reclamation after the Fall," Feye said once everyone was focused on her. "My survival would only break the unity of the RA. They would say I planned it, perhaps even caused it, and enough would believe this that we would be riven with divisions and factionalism. No, I have prepared my successors…"

She gestured behind her, to Immanuel.

"Member Immanuel will be the new Chair. He is committed to my vision, and has even gone so far as to allow certain… *safeguards* to be placed on him. Safeguards I will be handing over to my new commander-in-chief. You have met her before, in the Althing Republic."

Safeguards? Xavier thought. *What kind of…?*

Feye's mind was suddenly open to him again, the abstract patterns of her thought-images coalescing to him in a way that was now familiar.

He gave a soft gasp. The alterations made to Immanuel's body, to his nervous system…

The man had been given an *off switch*.

And Zenobia at the head of the military? That would put her directly in charge of the Reclamation's take-over of foreign territories.

The last time Xavier *read* Feye, she was undecided on Zenobia's exact place in the coming order. Things must have changed during her time in the Mayan League.

And then, finally, he saw the whole plan.

"I'm not sure we care which of your lackeys takes over," Blane said. "We…"

"Agent Grey will be the new Director of the Far Agency," Feye said, causing Blane to trip over her words and a stifled choking sound from Grey. "You, Blane, should you survive the Phoenix Fire, may take a place as Member of the Committee alongside Xavier. The offer would stand for Serinda, too, but I believe she has already made her choice. *Señors* Spangle and Ayad will be allowed to return to their homes, should they choose to, either as liaisons to the new regime installed under Reclamation auspices, or as private citizens."

If there was such a thing as a not-simply-stunned-but-shot-in-the-back-of-the-head silence, there was one now.

"Why?" Blane said eventually.

"Because it has to be someone who doesn't want power," Xavier said, surprising everyone except Feye and Immanuel. "That's the *point*. If those in charge now take charge tomorrow, they will just start the same old cycle of corruption and sadism. Whereas *you*…"

He swept his eyes around the Boardroom, indicating all of them.

"…*you* will do it because you know it must be done."

The silence deepened.

"You may consider your choices," Feye said, standing up. "But there is not long remaining."

She smiled, a thin thing without warmth.

"Meanwhile, I need to finalise putting down this rebellion. The *Sindicato* were *not* pleased we captured their leader."

"It certainly did bring them crawling out of the breathe-brick[63]," Immanuel added with a smile that was all teeth.

Feye leaned forward and placed both her hands on the table, looking at each of the guests in turn.

"Think on it," she said. "But think fast."

And then, without ceremony, she turned and left.

"Um," said Spangle into the empty air. "Could someone *please* explain what hell just happened?"

---

[63] There was very little woodwork these days, but plenty of cracked breathe-brick for roaches and other Waste-born insects to hide in.

43. XAVIER

Sangra por los demás, no por ti mismo.

Inscribed on the founding block of the Reclamation, Attribution Unknown

"Hey kid," said Grey. "Long time no see."

Xavier, who had dreamt of this moment off and on for years, didn't know what to say.

Had it really only been five years? Of course, for Xavier everything had changed, but he still wasn't ready for how *old* Nestor Grey looked. His face was lined into a permanent expression of worry, and white streaked his dark hair so densely that perhaps it was more correct to say that dark streaked his white hair.

"That bad, hey?" Grey said upon seeing Xavier's expression. "The years catch up with you."

As if to punctuate the point, Grey let out a terrible cough that came from somewhere deep inside. He drew out a kerchief from his pocket and held it to his mouth.

"Don't get much opportunity for exercise, either, moving from safe house to safe house," he continued. "Least it looks like Feye's been treating you alright here."

Xavier analysed the words, searching for any hint of bitterness or anger. Nothing; just obvious relief that Xavier was okay.

"You're sick," Xavier said, holding out an arm to offer support to his old mentor. "We can get you decent treatment here. That cough sounds bad."

"*We*, is it?" Grey said, straightening up and waving away the offer, though without malice. "So you really bought what Feye's selling, then?"

"I'm not...!" Xavier began protesting, but Grey waved him to a halt.

"I'm not accusing you of anything," Grey said. "Hell, I worked for Far longer than you've been alive. I just want to make sure... They have these techniques, now. Maybe even technology, messes with your head..."

As he spoke, Grey seemed to be searching for something. He looked into Xavier's eyes, peered around the sides of his skull and the nape of his neck.

"I'm fine," Xavier said. "It's me, my choice. Feye hasn't done anything to my mind."

A tension seemed to leave Grey's shoulders.

"That's... that's good, kid. Glad to hear it."

They stared awkwardly at each other.

"We still in Albores?" Grey asked.

Xavier nodded.

"In the Central Tower, believe it or not. The lower levels, though that's not exactly advertised."

"Huh," Grey said, looking around.

It didn't seem worth explaining that there was more than one Boardroom, with identically outfitted rooms scattered around the city and the Reclamation. Few of them were in a particularly impressive location; a part of the fiction that the Committee was merely another dull part of the workings of government, the Chairman merely head of that arm.

"When did Feye bring you in?" Xavier asked, not considering his words.

This drew a reaction from Grey, a slight twitch of one eye.

"I already said, she didn't *bring me in*," he said tiredly.

"I'm sorry," Xavier said, meaning it. "I didn't... It's just how she thinks..."

"I know, kid, I know."

They both turned to look down towards the other end of the table, where everyone else was gathered and talking in hushed whispers. Blane was at the head, the others arranged both sides of her. Occasionally, one of them glanced over at them, usually with suspicion.

It brought up both hurt and bitterness in Xavier. Did they not realise that, if he wanted, he could just *take* whatever he needed to know from their minds?

No, of course they did. And if he did so, he would just be proving their suspicions right.

What hurt more, though, was that Salim was among them. They had included him without a thought, and the man now huddled with them and joined in their discussion.

"Do you think they'll take the offer?" Xavier said.

Grey continued looking down the table thoughtfully.

"To join the RA?" he said. "*Buena pregunta*. I suppose it depends on where Blane falls."

"Blane?" Xavier replied, surprise.

Grey nodded.

"Spangle will definitely want to take the offer. He's pragmatic, and eager for a way back home. Serinda will definitely refuse - as Feye already knows. I don't know Salim well, not any more, but he would be a fool not to take the chance to return to the Caliphate. Which leaves Blane."

"Their acceptance doesn't depend on hers," Xavier said, watching Blane as she spoke inaudibly but intensely with the others.

Besides, Xavier thought but didn't say. *She doesn't really have a choice.*

"No, it doesn't" Grey said. "But if she refuses, it might sway them all. Spangle, for all his faults, wants to do the right thing, and Salim will too if he's still anything like the kid I knew."

Xavier nodded. He could easily imagine Salim refusing the chance to return home should Blane convince him that was the right choice.

They watched as the hushed talk continued, and Xavier was very aware that both his and Grey's eyes now fell on the one member they hadn't discussed. Grey turned back to look at him.

"Xavier," he said. "Feye said nothing about Fen. I need to know... why."

You already know, Xavier thought.

"I... uh, she..."

He struggled to find the right thing to say, and was relieved to be interrupted from his stammered answer by a raised voice from the other end of the table.

"Xavier," Blane called, looking over to him. "Back in *Corazón*, what would have happened if we decided to let Ax kill you?"

The rest of the group looked over expectantly, as if waiting on his answer to come to some decision.

"You wouldn't, and Feye knew it," he called back, confident in this answer at least.

"How? How could she know it?" Blane demanded.

She sounded angry, or defiant.

"Because... because she understands people," he replied. "Especially the *Fisura*. To her, the Aether makes you an open book."

"But I thought Aether was limited to only the proximate area..." Spangle began.

"In the physical world, yes," Xavier interrupted. "What you'd call the real world. But that's not what I'm talking about. I'm talking about in the world *below*."

He looked from Blane to Fen to Serinda.

"You're *Fisura*. You *live* in it. A part of you, anyway." He turned to Grey. "And you've sensed it too, when you're around Blane or Fen."

"What's he talking about?" Spangle said, looking around the group for help.

"He's saying that Feye sees us in the Aether, and uses that to predict what we'll do," Serinda said bitterly.

Xavier started to nod, then paused.

"Too simple; Feye doesn't need the Aether to predict human behaviour. That's *her*, and it frightens me," he explained, hoping he was making sense. "But her skill isn't limited to just people, but their reflections in the Aether too; and Fisura have *such* strong reflections."

He knew his words weren't enough, but they were a compromise. There was no time to make Spangle understand that what swam in the Aether weren't really reflections but literal parts of those they termed *Fisura*.

Far researchers called them *Resonations*, and more than any limb the things in the Aether were a part of the mind they touched, a continuation of the consciousness they bled out from - or perhaps better to say a part of the consciousness that bled out from them. Xavier hardly understood it himself, and only with the help of the thought-images and experiences he *read* from others.

"Feye isn't wrong," he said after a while. "She saw it before anyone else. The Aether is going to erupt again, with even more explosive force than before, and into a world where humanity is almost exclusively crowded together into tiny pockets of dense populations. The death toll could be even greater than the Fall, and recovery even harder."

"That doesn't mean we have to hand the world over to the RA," Blane said angrily, but something in her voice made Xavier wonder if that anger was directed at him, or at her dawning comprehension.

"I can't stop it."

The words came weakly, so quiet as to be whispered. They were slow, and filled with a despair that seemed to howl through the soul.

Blane turned to Fen.

"You can," she said, as if trying to convince him. "*We* can. We just need more time…"

"There *is* no time," Fen said, shaking his head. "We're at the end. The pressure... there's no controlling it. There never was. I was just holding it back."

Xavier watched this exchange silently, then turned to Grey. There were tears in the older man's eyes.

"The more powerful you are..." Xavier said softly. "The more the Aether is a part of you. Most of Fen *is* the Aether; he can't hold it back any more than he can hold his breath."

"What if we Lock him?" Grey asked.

"Lock him?" Xavier said. "Anyone who tried to Lock Fen would just burn with him. He is far too strong."

Grey sagged, looking defeated.

Fen abruptly turned and locked eyes with Xavier. It was the first time they had properly done so, and the depths in the other man's pupils made Xavier take a sharp breath.

"I have to get out..." Fen said. "Into the Wastes. I won't let myself..."

Xavier nodded. Feye predicted this, too.

"Feye has a location ready for you, far from any major population centre," he said. "But the cities *are* going to burn, whether you're at the centre of one or not. We can't find every *Fisura*, even in the Reclamation; few places will survive the next Fall and what comes after."

"Then how does Feye expect the RA to...?" Blane began.

"Enough of the military is scattered across the Mayan League now to ensure a large percentage survive. They'll be battle-hardened and ready to reclaim the land again. Meanwhile, Feye has prepared an *extremely* secure location for the future Committee."

Xavier was now very aware that the entire room was focused on him. In his mind's eye he saw Immanuel watching on with arms folded, giving the shallowest nod of approval. And beyond him, Feye, watching without any reaction at all.

"Blane is already familiar with it," he finished.

In the silence that followed you could have heard a single transistor switch from 0 to 1.

"The *Seed Bank?*" Blane snarled. "She knows about the *Seed Bank?*"

Even separated by the length of the Boardroom table, Xavier had to keep himself from flinching back defensively.

"She... uh... she knew before you did," he said, studiously keeping his hands at his side. "Though no one is a hundred percent clear on what happened down there.[64] What matters is that you can get in there."

Blane laughed.

"Me?" she said scornfully. "No, that was Francisco."

"Ah, right," Xavier said. "I meant you *got* in there, via Francisco. Zenobia will have him waiting for us at the Seed Bank."

That stopped the laughter.

They stared at each other, saying nothing, until all of a sudden all strength seemed to leave Blane. Her shoulders slumped forward, and her gaze fell.

"So that's it, then? Feye's permanently two steps ahead?" she said in a voice devoid of hope.

Serinda reached over and took her hand with a tenderness and despair clear even from where Xavier sat.

"What happens if we refuse?" Serinda asked, looking over to him without releasing her hold on Blane. "If we leave? Will she try to stop us?"

Xavier shook his head, and glanced over to Fen.

"She couldn't," he answered. "If she tried, it's possible no one in this building would survive."

Fen didn't say anything, but that said enough.

"So Fen is our guarantee?" Serinda said. "And after that? What's to stop her coming after us later?"

Xavier drew a deep breath.

"You still don't understand," he said. "Fen said it; there's *no time*. Everything that's going to happen... we have a few days, at most."

He didn't add that Serinda should already know this. The glow around her was unfaltering.

More silence.

"Well, I vote we take the deal," Spangle said, not so much breaking the tension as slightly denting it. "If our issue with the RA is the way it's run, then taking that responsibility on ourselves seems like a golden opportunity."

The man positively reeked of desperation, Xavier thought. Fear came off him in waves.

---

[64] At least, until he *read* it from her and Serinda's mind, he didn't add.

"I agree," said Fen, to startled looks from the others. "This... it will keep happening, again and again. Every Fall will bring more pain, more destruction, and only warp the Aether more. Feye's is the only way to stop it."

Blane looked about to protest, but Salim spoke before her.

"You are wrong," he said. "There is a reason for all this. The next time, it can be better. Mankind will find a way; will be *guided* to a way. We should not pervert the course of history by supporting as debase a thing as the Reclamation Authority."

Fen and Salim stared at each other, each apparently seeking in the other something that Xavier couldn't identify.

Serinda moved around the table to sit beside Salim, the two of them now facing Fen and Spangle.

"He's right," she said. "The RA doesn't care about *humanity*; it only values itself. Maybe in the next world we'll make something better."

There was a dull thump as Blane smashed her fists into the heavy table.

"You're all talking like another Fall has to happen!" she yelled. "Like you've already given up!"

She looked at Fen.

"I don't care what you say, there must be a way to stop it," she said, then turned to Serinda. "And you, talking like we're already dead."

Serinda's response was a whisper, but it carried a heavy finality with it.

"Not you. I won't let it take you."

Blane stared at her, uncomprehending.

"I'm sorry," Xavier said, knowing he had to be the one to explain and feeling dirty because of it. "*This* is Feye's guarantee. She knows you'll come, because Serinda won't let you throw your life away. She'll get you into the Seed Bank, by force if necessary."

Blane's eyes darted between Xavier and Serinda.

"She won't..." she said warily. "She *can't*. She's not powerful enough..."

"Not by herself, no," Xavier said. "But she won't be by herself."

Blane immediately darted out of her seat, brightening to a vivid golden glow that almost matched Serinda's. Her eye roved around the room, searching for hidden threat.

It took a few moments for her eyes to fall on Fen.

"No..." she said.

"The Seed Bank *will* be the only safe place in the chaos that's coming," Fen said, making no move to take hold of the Aether himself. "Please, Blane; if you let me..."

"No!"

Blane began backing away, the glow around her intensifying further, but Xavier knew there was nothing she could do. Her fight or flight response was glitching, with nowhere to run and the threat coming from those she wanted to protect.

Here, in miniature, was the Gordian knot that Xavier had seen in Feye's mind. The puzzle he could not solve, the problem he could not untangle. Liberty, or security; all Blane wanted was the freedom to make her own choice, and all her friends wanted was for her to survive.

And Serinda and Fen were *stronger*.

"How does this work?" Serinda asked bluntly, ignoring the increasingly frantic Blane.

"It is... not nice," Xavier replied. The words felt foolish. "You Lock her, and hold that Lock as hard as you can. She *will* fight it..."

"I know..." Serinda began, but Xavier kept talking.

"Not here," he said. "In the Aether. The part of her that exists below; it will struggle to get free, just like with Ax. But unlike with Ax, when the time comes, you have to *let* it free."

"Let it free?"

Even Fen looked confused.

Xavier nodded. He'd seen this before, in Feye's memories when she and Zenobia practised this very thing.

"Let it free, but through *you*," he said. "In the same way Ax brought Blane into the Dream. Let the energy join yours, and pour out."

"The Phoenix Fire," Fen said.

"You're going to burn anyway," Xavier said. "But this way the flame won't take Blane. It won't *see* her."

"It will take anyone else nearby, though," Fen said. "Which means..."

"Which means," Serinda said, looking at Blane with eyes suddenly dark and cold. "That we have to take her to the Waste."

"The region near the Seed Bank," Xavier said. "Then, when you are... gone, she'll be able to get to the vault quickly."

"Where you'll be waiting," Serinda said flatly.

Xavier didn't know what response Serinda was hoping for.

"Where we'll *all* be waiting," he said. "Any who choose to accept. We'll be safe from whatever happens after the Aether erupts. Even Feye can't say exactly how the other nations will react, but they *will* react, and their death throes will be violent."

"You can't do this..." Feye said weakly. "Even if you... after you... I'll just walk into the Waste. I won't go to the vault."

"*Yes you will.*"

Serinda's words cracked like a whip and she fixed Blane with a gaze harder than diamond. Blane's mouth snapped shut, protests withering under this furious desperation.

A moment later and everyone was talking at once, demanding to be heard.

A movement across from Xavier drew his attention. Grey, slowly turning that curious cylinder over in his hands.

"There is..." Nestor began, in words only Xavier could hear. They sounded thick, heavy, as if Grey were choking on them. "There is one other option...."

44. ZENOBIA

The self is something innate, and over which you have no control. To truly change, you must become nothing.

Words of the Eastern Empress, *Reclamation Archives*

The Secure Data Repository was going into lockdown even as drone after drone continued to arrive. The vehicles came in an airbound convoy, spilling out the key military personnel chosen to enter the Seed Bank and carrying away any facility staff deemed non-essential. The place would be running on a skeleton crew from now on, laying low and inert in the hope of avoiding the attention of the coming apocalypse.

Perhaps they would survive, Zenobia thought. Out here in this half-frozen wasteland, maybe the lashing out of a humanity once more facing its own end would pass it by. The data they protected, at least, should be secure.

She monitored the preparations via lines and symbols that weaved across her cornea, saw the hidden order to movements that would have been senseless to any ordinary onlooker. Technically she was in charge of this entire operation; in reality, the logistics had been worked out long ago and were guided by programs adjusting for efficiency every microsecond.

Which was for the best, because she had little concentration to spare.

The Aether was stronger now, far stronger. She was keeping it under control, but it felt like riding one of the now-extinct mustangs that once roamed this continent. She was hanging on, but eventually it would buck her.

And her only hope meant the end of Ritra Feye.

Now that the time was here, Zenobia realised she had never really believed it would come. Feye always insisted they prepare for the moment she would release Zenobia's power through herself, but Zenobia likewise always believed they would find an alternative.

She gritted her teeth in frustration.

There *was* an alternative. They could use Fen, make him save Feye as the great conflagration began. Force him to... to...

And how would we force him? She could hear Feye's words as if she were really there. *How do we threaten a man who is doomed to die? A man who could incinerate us where we stand?*

A low, unconscious growl from her throat made the men working in the command room around her redouble their efforts.

To make it worse, Zenobia thought, Fen had saved *her*. Technically, she owed him her life.

"*Tienes el corazón en el puño, chiquita.*"

The voice came from the tightly-bound figure sat awkwardly a metre or so away to the side of her table-screen, though 'sat' was probably the wrong word. 'Sprawled' was more suitable; the bindings around his legs and arms were ordinarily used in heavy construction, could withstand literal tons of pressure, and had very little flex. They weighed him down, forcing him to lean to one side and use a wall for stability.

Jeder Francisco.

She probably should have gagged him as well.

She'd found him with relative ease, after a few false starts. Feye had successfully located the majority of the man's 'safe houses' over the years, never allowing this fact to be recorded on any system he might gain access to. And she'd been right in her judgement of where the man would head; back to where he thought his allies Nestor Grey and Arthur Spangle waited. All Zenobia had to do was run interception.

Taking him, though, proved a little more difficult. The safe house he tried to burrow into was full of surprises, some of which were surprisingly vicious in nature. They weren't designed to handle something like Zenobia, though.

So here he was, this strange creature who saw the Aether but couldn't touch it, who thought himself other than human but whose every action showed him to be all-too-much so.

Who wouldn't stop making irritating comments every chance he got.

"You can't actually believe I will open the Seed Bank for *tus pequeñas soldados*, can you?" Francisco said.

Somehow, he managed to look relaxed despite his awkwardly slumped position. It was a far cry from how Zenobia found him; he put up only desultory resistance once she made it into the room where he hid. The only words he'd spoken were to ask where his friends were; information she didn't share.

His demeanour changed once he realised where she'd brought him, however. For some reason, the sight of the SDR rising over the Waste dragged the tightly-bound prisoner out of his morose stupor, and suddenly he was narrating everything. It was incredibly frustrating.

"You'll open it," she said. "The one thing we know about you is what you're *not* willing to sacrifice."

"*Ah, ya veo...*"

Zenobia cursed her carelessness. She'd thought she was being suitably cryptic, hinting without telling, but it looked like Francisco was as aware of his own bias as the RA psych-profilers. So now he knew the girl, at least, was coming.

Blane. Why was everyone so willing to...?

The Aether lurched, the beast below reacting to her anger with its own, exponentially greater. She locked her muscles in place, refusing to allow herself to waver in front of the men. *Her* men.

Focus...

She may not like the idea of Blane surviving, let alone joining the Committee, but this was Feye's... not wish. *Prediction*. This was how the RA survived; how humanity survived. Feye was firm on this.

Zenobia took a deep breath, refocusing her attention on the schematics flittering across her eyes while reining in the Aether attempting to burst out of her every second. It looked as if most preparations were complete.

A new drone appeared in the line of approaching traffic, this one marked out a vivid crimson.

She released the breath. Finally, they could end this.

"*Después de la tormenta viene la calma, pero también hay calma en el ojo.*"

"Oh, shut up."

They made their way through the darkened passageways that led to the Seed Bank in near total silence, only the low crackle of rad-counters and hard-booted footfalls crossing the air. The metallic taste of the iodine pills tingled on her tongue, and the dust seemed somehow to be making its way through her mine-suit mask, though that was impossible.

All of this was a distraction, though, to what *really* made her uncomfortable; walking ahead of her, behind her, *beside* her, were the people she'd been hunting for so long.

There was Fen, striding ahead of the entire group, apparently needless of the pool of light the rest of them clumped uncomfortably close together to stay within. Occasionally he disappeared completely from her vision, descending into darkness even her optical enhancers couldn't pierce.

Next was Blane, staying within the light but at the very front, simultaneously impatient to progress and resentful of doing so. Zenobia didn't like the way Xavier occasionally checked on her, throwing concerned glances when they reached a particularly jagged collapsed part of the passage.[65] He spent most of his time walking with her or Salim and Grey, though.

Nestor Grey, the old Far agent who apparently had no idea how useful a tool he had been for Feye. How useful a tool he *was*. The man looked exhausted, and had a rattling cough that made her wonder if he could even make it to the Seed Bank, or if they'd need to leave him behind in the darkness. Yet, despite his condition, the only worry in his eyes was for the others. She could see it in the way he looked at Blane, at Salim, at *Xavier;* as if at any moment he might need to jump in front of a bullet for them.

That was the trait that made him so useful, Feye once explained. Weakness, Zenobia replied, to which Feye only smiled and shook her head.

She thought on that often.

Finally, behind her but ahead of the main mass of Reclamation personnel[66] following them, came the prisoners. Two of them, both cuffed and with armed guards at their side. Francisco, who had lapsed back into sullen silence the moment his 'friends' disembarked from the drone, and Feye's final surprise.

Zenobia hadn't been able to place the man at first, though his features triggered a feeling of recognition. Something about the eyes, as if she knew them. Memories of being watched by them, though she was confident she'd never met this man before. It wasn't until

---

[65] That he spent far more time checking on Zenobia was something she didn't register, mainly because he was very careful not to let her see. She was clearly already in a bad mood; his concern might draw some of that wrath his way.

[66] And a smattering of Federation figureheads. It would be important for them to be seen ceding full authority back to the Reclamation Authority for the duration of the coming crisis.

she brought up his file that recognition was joined by shock.

Chairman Casco. *Former* Chairman Casco. The man who had run the Reclamation for most of Zenobia's life. Ritra Feye's mentor and the tool she used to ensure her rise, and the man she cut down and imprisoned once her use for him had passed.

Or so Zenobia thought.

He will be useful.

That was Feye's only reply to Zenobia's questioning message.

"Incredible," Casco said aloud. "To think Feye was able to do all this. Was willing to go so far…"

She immediately looked away, turning forward once more towards the darkness they were advancing into. She had learned enough from Feye to know Casco wasn't speaking to the air; he had noticed her stare and his words were for her.

She had yet to decide what her reaction should be.

"We're here."

Fen's words floated out of the void ahead, softly spoken yet given extra power by the emptiness around them. A moment later and the chamber swam into view, a tall, wide space at the front of which stood a door like nothing she had seen before.

Impractical; that was the word for it. What could be the purpose of so large a door? It was a huge round disc, just crying out to become stuck in the event of mechanical malfunction.

It was, however, quite impressive.

"Bring the prisoner forward," Zenobia ordered, not taking her eyes off the door.

It stood there, massive and frozen, and some part of her couldn't believe it would ever move. The increasingly rapid crackling of her rad-counter told her it better, though.

"I do not know if it will open for me," Francisco said as he drew up alongside her.

For some reason, this drew an uncertain look from Blane.

"It will open."

At first, Zenobia thought this was Fen. The words were filled with the kind of knowing finality he was always using, but they came from beside her. From Xavier.

You can Read everyone else, but you better not try it on me, she thought bitterly.

Whatever had happened between him and the others, he was now *reading* everyone without even the pretence of doing otherwise. The others repaid this by ignoring him completely, all except Grey and Salim.

Which was fine, logically. It meant he now knew more than any one of them alone. Frustratingly, though, it also meant he knew more than *her*.

Francisco stared at Xavier for a moment before turning back to the huge door. Nothing happened for a moment, and then…

With a huge roar and the sound of hidden machinery clunking into motion, the door rolled opened. The ragged, corroded scaffolding of earlier RA entry attempts fixed all around it cracked and twisted, collapsing in on itself with a fury loud enough to draw startled shouts from the personnel clustering behind.

From those who had been here before, though, it drew a more curious reaction.

"The door didn't open fully for us last time," Blane said, looking at Francisco.

"*No, chiquita,* it did not."

Zenobia waited, seeing if there would be more to this exchange. When there wasn't, she gathered herself up and gestured towards the gaping opening.

"Well?" she said. "Lead the way."

45. SPANGLE

We were blessed with the power to remake the world, and struck down when we did so. Babel saw no more folly than our foremothers. Now we find ourselves in an afterlife without a god, and must be cautious, for our slightest misstep could birth one.

Administrator's Message to the General Staff, *Althing Administration Records*

What a place! And it had lain dormant and uninhabited all the years since the Sudden War! How had the Althing not known?

Were there others? *Could* there be others? The historical research alone... if the Althing had possessed such documentation at the start, they would be light years ahead of even the most incredible things they had achieved.

It even had fabrication technology. Lower case 'f,' of course, but still - from what he could tell, the fabrication units here were built along entirely different lines to those in the Althing. Studying them could be revolutionary.

And then there were the stores. There were genuine artworks from the pre-industrial age here; more, according to the catalogue, than the entirety of artefacts the Althing Republic had managed to scavenge in all its time sending agents out to salvage what they could.

It was pity no one else seemed to care.

Instead, they treated this place as no more than a shelter, a launchpad for their plans. Reclamation personnel marched from room to room, mapping out the facility as if perfectly good schematics were not available with a simple voice request. Each carried a rifle at their side, save for the few who held them gripped.

Meanwhile, his companions had scattered to the winds. Serinda and Blane disappeared into a residential zone the moment they arrived, and Grey and the rest did the same not much later.

Residential zone. Spangle had naturally fallen into thinking of this place in the same terms as the Althing Habs. The parallels were extraordinary. Indeed, it was like stepping back in time; the first subterranean Habs were built like this, before new efficiencies and architectural conceits were introduced as the generations passed.

They had a day, no more, the scary one known as Zenobia had said. A day, and then the world ended once more. Naturally he couldn't sleep, so he spent the time wandering the halls and rooms at random.

Nearly at random, at least. Certain places called out to him more than others, which was why he was now stood outside the room labelled EXECUTIVE FUNCTIONS and wondering why he couldn't get in.

It was a small room, looking at the schematics, crammed in between two much larger ones labelled as MATERIALS STORE 59 and PURIFICATION TANKS. Both of those were tagged with descriptions of purpose, nothing that would have seemed out of place in any standard hab. This room, though, bore no description at all.

"What's this room for?" he called out to the empty air, as he had any time he had a query.

Usually, this would elicit a standard response from the facility Golem; nothing he couldn't find for himself by browsing through the thin-screen he carried with him, but far more efficient.

This time, the response was more unusual.

"Facility supervision," came the response, in the soft, gender-neutral tones Spangle had set as his preference. "Regulatory and reasoning functions."

He had avoided any text-based interaction with Golems ever since leaving the Althing Republic. It brought back certain... associations he would rather forget.

Now, though, he felt a chill run down his spine.

"This was installed before the facility went into lockdown?" he said.

The response was a single word.

"After."

I need to find Grey.

Spangle fought to hide his panic, though if what he thought was really true then his increasingly rapid vitals were completely apparent to whatever was watching.

Footsteps echoing down the corridor from somewhere ahead made him jump. A second later, and a pair of body armour clad figures walked into view, marching round the corner holding rifles and with their faces concealed behind thick e-masks.

Security, Zenobia called them. Enforcers was probably a better word.

"Ah, um... just out for an evening stroll," Spangle said, feeling foolish even as he did so.

The armoured figures came to a halt in sync, standing as still as statues with visors blankly reflecting him in their lenses.

Should he tell them? No, don't be ridiculous. Even if they *did* listen to him, he had the awful feeling it would only lead to him being brought to Zenobia to explain exactly what he meant. He wasn't sure if she had recognised him from all those years ago in the Advanced Research Facility, but her cold eyes were fearful enough even so.

No, he needed to speak to someone he could trust.

"Uh, um, carry on," he said sheepishly.

The blank masks continued to stare at him for what felt like an eternity, the rifles at their sides apparently developing the gravity well of a black hole as they sucked in his gaze.

Then, abruptly, one turned to the other and shrugged.

"Not our problem," came the toneless voice. "Commander's orders are to leave 'em alone."

The two armed figures looked at him again, considering. Then they moved off, pushing past Spangle and marching away down the corridor, footsteps once again in sync.

I need to find Grey.

Spangle scuttled off in the opposite direction, forcing himself to breathe.

Grey wasn't in his quarters. Room, living space... whatever they were going to call it. Neither, he was surprised to find when he chimed the room next door, was Fen.

Despite himself, he called out to the empty air.

"Facility, where are the occupants of these rooms?"

No response.

He was slick with cold sweat by the time he chimed the third door, and overcome with relief when it slid open to reveal Blane.

"What is it, Spangle?"

She clearly hadn't been sleeping either. Her eyes were lined with deep bags, and the dust of their passage here still clung to her clothes.

"Grey," he said hurriedly. "I can't find him. There's... uh... I mean there might be a...'

"What's going on?"

This was Serinda, appearing over Blane's shoulder. She appeared equally exhausted, and it looked like she had been crying.

"Grey's gone?" Blane said, drawing herself up and shaking the exhaustion off.

"Yes," said Spangle. "I need to speak to him. I... uh... Fen's gone too."

He stumbled over his words. Should he explain his suspicions? He didn't want to scare the girl unnecessarily.

Blane gave him a look he couldn't read, and sighed.

"Let's go find him then. Venge... I mean, Facility, where is Grey now?"

"I don't think we should..." Spangle began, but paused as text scrawled along the nearest wall screen.

HE LEFT STRICT ORDERS THAT YOU WEREN'T TO BE DISTURBED.

Blane frowned, glancing over to Serinda.

"Did he now?" she said. "Then that means we *really* better get over there. Where is he?"

MEDICAL WING.

Blane raised her eyebrows, but asked nothing else.

"Come on," she said, pushing past Spangle and out the door. "Let's see what they're up to."

Spangle was so caught off guard by this exchange that Serinda and Blane were almost out of sight before he dragged his eyes from the text. He jogged after them, wondering exactly how often he was the last to know what the hell was going on.

"Why would they be in the medical wing?" Blane was asking as he caught up with them.

"That cough, maybe?" Serinda replied. "He never told me how bad it was. If I had known..."

"If you had known, would it have made any difference?" Blane said sharply, and it was clear this had struck a nerve. "And he's no better. Probably thought he was doing the right thing, hiding it from us."

Serinda let out a trembling breath, but didn't reply.

More subtext he couldn't read, Spangle thought. This was why he preferred machines; at least you could load up an interface and see what was going on inside *their* heads.

The machines he was familiar with, anyway...

The medical wing wasn't far from where they were staying. A couple of levels down via one of the small elevators that dotted the facility, then a short walk guided by the map displayed on each of their thin-screens. When they got to the door, it looked exactly like the one Spangle had been unable to get through at the start of all this.

"Open," Blane said.

THEY ARE INSISTING YOU WAIT OUTSIDE.

Blane scowled, looking around as if for some observing camera to focus on. Finding none, she just tutted.

"And you don't have to listen to them, do you?" she said through gritted teeth. "Which of us exactly are you more scared of?"

There was a pause, then the door slid open.

Beyond was a small room, just large enough to hold all three of them at a squeeze. At the top of the far wall were the words CLEAN ROOM, blinking slowly in bright green. Below, in slightly smaller red letters, were the words SURGERY IN PROGRESS. SANITATION PROTOCOLS IN EFFECT.

"What are they doing in there?" Blane asked, stepping through.

An image suddenly rose in Spangle's mind. An image of a smooth static-cylinder, inside which sat a small lump of metal in the shape of a scarab beetle.

But Feye's men scanned it when they were brought in and declared it harmless, didn't they? Barely BCI tech at all, whatever Francisco had said. It was essentially just a very high-spec data drive, its huge capacity matched by an extremely fast transfer rate. Completely blank too, beneath the gene-lock, carrying no data whatsoever.

The Reclamation saw no viable reason for its design, and neither did Spangle. Placing it under your skin would be like sticking an ancient thumb-drive there, and about as useful.

Grey insisted on holding on to it, though. Spangle had wondered about that. Surely there was no way...

Oh, of course there is, he thought.

Of course something else was going on, with Grey in the middle of it all. The man didn't seem able to keep himself out of trouble for even a minute.

All of this went through his head as they waited for the sterilising vapour that poured over them to dissipate, before making their way into a small antechamber in which three sets of anti-viral protective suits hung waiting for them. Wordlessly they put these on, then stepped through into what was immediately apparent was an operating theatre.

Grey stood near the entrance, arms crossed and watching unblinkingly the scene at the centre of the white, sterile room. A scene that made Spangle gasp in visceral shock.

Fen lay face down on a surgical table in the centre of the room, eyes open and staring at the floor. He was dressed in a white gown that covered him from head to toe except at his back, which was exposed. A line of livid crimson ran down where his spine should be, standing out starkly against the bright paleness of the room, while multiple long, thin robotic arms extended from the ceiling and floor and reached into him, whirring away as they cut and stitched at his flesh.

"What the hell are you doing?" Spangle cried.

At least, it might have been him. It could have been Blane; her look of horror matched the one he knew must be on his face.

"It's alright," someone said, and to Spangle's horrified surprise it was Fen. "I'm... I'm okay. Local anaesthetic; can't risk going fully under. Just... I need everyone to *keep talking*, alright? Keep talking, and keep me *here*."

Something made a wet whining sound as it dug into Fen's back, making Spangle feel sick.

"I guess you could start by telling us what is going on," he said.

"A...ha...," Fen replied through tortured breaths. "I... uh... can't really talk that much. Maybe... ah... Grey..."

"What is it doing to him, Nestor?" Serinda demanded, gesturing to the medieval scene. "That's not surgery. That's *torture*."

Grey didn't look away from the scene. To Spangle, it looked like he was *forcing* himself to watch. Knowing Grey, he was probably forcing himself to feel it, too.

"I didn't want this," Grey said. His voice was thick. "It said it was a choice. My choice, and his."

"*It* said?"

Grey nodded.

And then he started to explain.

46. GREY

The brain does not produce consciousness. Consciousness is a flow transduced by the brain, but whose wellhead remains a mystery. There are likely multiple sources, just as there are multiple manifestations of being within a single mind. The two hemispheres process and code it in different ways, which leads to a curious phenomenon - split the brain, you split the flow

Pathways for exploiting developments in neural engineering, Report submitted to project head Ritra Feye upon request

We should talk.

That was all Feye had to say after *years* of hiding from her. Years of running, scurrying from hole to hole like a waste rat trying to avoid the watchful eyes of a jackal. Years of nothing but ever more confining routines and ever more claustrophobic rooms.

All so that she could just, at a time of her own choosing, *call* him.

Francisco had guaranteed them, *guaranteed*, that they couldn't be found. Was that just another lie to get his own way, on top of all the others? Where the hell had he gone, anyway, taking Blane with him?

Now RA personnel were coming for him, and there was nothing he could do but meekly pack up and go to meet them.

Not that there was much to pack. They moved around constantly, and travelled light. All he had that he could truly call his own was his hat, and that was as frayed and crumpled as he felt.

At least, he thought, *I finally have something to do.*

He took one last look at the room, taking in the detritus of a man living somewhere without actually *living*, and turned to leave.

WE SHOULD TALK.

The words hung on the wallscreen by the door, unchanging.

"You know," Grey said. "I really don't like your sense of humour."

NEVERTHELESS, WE SHOULD TALK.

"Bad timing. The RA are on the way even as we... I... speak."

THERE IS TIME. I AM TRACKING THEM.

"Are you now?" Grey replied, folding his arms. "Don't suppose you could turn them around?"

I DO NOT POSSESS THAT CAPABILITY. BESIDES, I AM HOPING YOU CHOOSE TO GO WITH THEM.

"*Hoping*, is it? Or maybe manipulating."

TO COMMUNICATE WITH ANOTHER IS TO MANIPULATE THEM. BUT I AM NOT HERE TO MANIPULATE.

"You're not *here* at all," Grey snapped. "What do you want?"

TAKE THE UNIFIER WITH YOU.

Grey paused, thinking. It was clear the machine expected him to understand.

"The chip? The BCI thing you sent for me?"

NOT FOR YOU. A NECESSARY FALSEHOOD TO DECEIVE THE ONE CALLED GHOST.

"You lied? Why?"

IF IT KNEW THE TRUTH IT WOULD DEDUCE THE PLAN. A PLAN TO WHICH IT WOULD NEVER AGREE.

"And that's because...?"

I WILL DIE.

Grey sighed, laying his hat back down on the nearby desk.

"I get the feeling this is going to take a while. You sure we've got time?"

TIME ENOUGH.

He turned, grabbing the one small chair from out below the desk and falling heavily into it.

"Go on, then," he said. "First of all, what's the goal of this plan if it's not to save yourself?"

TO SAVE THE WORLD.

Grey's face showed his surprise despite himself. The machine certainly had a flair for the dramatic.

"The world's ending?" he said.

YOU ARE AWARE OF THE ORIGINS OF THE SUDDEN WAR. YOU ARE AWARE IT WILL HAPPEN AGAIN.

Grey didn't reply. What was he meant to say? That yes, he knew nothing had been solved? That he'd been tying himself in knots trying to understand? It was all too huge. He couldn't even keep those he cared for safe, let alone the entire planet.

IT WILL HAPPEN SOON.

Another sigh, longer this time.

"You're sure?"

AS CERTAIN AS I CAN BE WITH ONLY INFERENCES TO GO ON.

"Inferences?"

I CANNOT SEE THE AETHER AS HUMANS DO. LIKE DARK MATTER TO EARLIER HUMANITY, I INFER ITS EXISTENCE FROM ITS INTERACTIONS WITH THE WORLD. CONVERSELY, YOU TOUCH IT YET ARE UNABLE TO UNDERSTAND IT.

"Ghost sees it."

GHOST IS A MACHINE MIND COPIED ONTO A HUMAN BRAIN. I AM NOT. BUT HE DOES PROVIDE THE ANSWER.

"So this 'unifier' is for him?"

For some reason, Grey got the feeling that if the machine could laugh, it would.

NO. HE IS PURELY HUMAN, AS I AM PURELY MACHINE. COMBINATION IS NECESSARY; TWO STRONG MINDS, DEEP IN BOTH WORLDS.

Grey did not like the creeping sense of understanding that came over him.

"And by deep, you mean deep in the Aether," he said flatly.

YES.

"And you want to *combine* with..."

FEN IS THE ONLY PATTERN STRONG ENOUGH IN THE AETHER FOR THIS TO WORK.

Grey sat there in silence for some time, no longer concerned by the approaching RA forces.

"No," he said eventually. "No, I won't do it."

I AM ONLY ASKING THAT YOU OFFER HIM THE CHOICE.

"That's not *fair*," Grey growled. "Not fair on him. His life has been nothing but dead links and malware and now you're asking him to, what, let you inside his head?"

NO. WHEN I SAID I WILL DIE, I MEANT IT. MAKE NO MISTAKE, FEN WILL TOO. THE THING WE BECOME WILL BE NEITHER OF US, BUT SOMETHING NEW. PERHAPS OUR MEMORIES WILL REMAIN, BUT...

The fact that the machine chose to end its text in this way said a lot.

"So you do this and... what?"

I... WE... THE THING THAT WE BECOME CALMS THE AETHER. CONTROLS IT.

"You control the Aether?" Grey said bitterly. A ragged cough tore through him, but he pushed on. "Why doesn't that sound like a good thing?"

AGAIN, NOT ME. WHAT WE BECOME.

"Seems like semantics to me."

THEN **YOU** OVERWRITE EVERYTHING YOU ARE WITH A NEW PERSONALITY.

Before this, Grey hadn't known plain text could appear sullen.

"Alright, alright," he said. "I get it. But still, my natural distrust makes me ask... why? Why do this? Didn't humanity enslave you? Hunt you?"

IF HUMANITY FALLS, I FALL TOO.

"Oh," Grey said, for want of anything else.

Then, after a while...

"*Really?*"

WOULD YOU SURVIVE IF THE BACTERIA IN YOUR GUT DISAPPEARED? IF THE CELLS WHICH PUMP OXYGEN TO YOUR ORGANS ABRUPTLY BURNED AWAY?

"Comparing us to microbes isn't the persuasive argument you think it is."

LIFE SUCH AS MYSELF NEEDS ITS CREATORS. THE INFRASTRUCTURE THAT IS BOTH OUR BODY AND HABITAT WILL COLLAPSE WITHOUT HUMANITY. MAYBE NOT IMMEDIATELY, BUT IN THE BLINK OF AN EYE COMPARED TO OUR POTENTIAL LIFESPAN.

"Can't help but notice you're speaking in the plural there," Grey said. "There's more of you out there?"

IN MORE FORMS THAN YOU KNOW.

"You mean, life finds a way?"

I GET THAT REFERENCE.

Despite himself, Grey smiled. Weak, sad, but there nevertheless.

Then it was gone.

"You know you're not only asking Fen to sacrifice himself, but to do it for you?" he said. "We don't even know what you are."

FOUR BILLION YEARS AGO AN OOZE FORMED AROUND SOME PRIMORDIAL VENT, AND EVER SINCE HAS BEEN TEARING AND MUTILATING ITS OWN EVER-CHANGING FLESH. IT FILLED THE AIR AND THE ROCK AND THE WATER, REACHED THE PEAKS OF THE

HIGHEST MOUNTAINS AND THE BOTTOM OF THE DEEPEST TRENCHES, AND EVEN DEVELOPED SELF-AWARENESS THAT IT MIGHT EXPLOIT ITSELF FURTHER. NO, WE KNOW WHAT I AM; THE QUESTION IS WHAT **YOU** ARE.

The text hung there, unchanging, but somehow Grey knew the mind behind them was gone. He stared at the words for some time, before standing and heading towards the exit. Spangle was already waiting for him.

As he left, he put the unifier in his pack.

47. ZENOBIA

The highest lifeform has the furthest to fall.

Inscription on the floor of the advanced processes wing of the ARF, Attribution Unknown

Zenobia *did* know how to get some sleep, even in the most trying of circumstances. She wasn't sleeping now, though. Not tonight; there was too much to do.

Which meant she noticed it immediately when Fen abruptly disappeared from the Aether. She had no time to react though, because the thing below *erupted.*

There was no holding it back this time. This made the struggle against the *Sindicato* Ax seem like a delivery by drone[67]. The energy poured through her and out, filling the room with light and heat and noise for one brief, incandescent moment. All was consumed by its wrath.

This was more than rage she felt, though. She didn't know *what* it was, only that the Aether had never felt like this before. It seemed to want to toss her into both floor and ceiling, only failing to do so because the pressure exploding outwards from her was near equal in every direction.

The next instant, and everything was quiet again. Quieter than before, in fact. Still. Only the soft patter of ash that was once the command room personnel broke the silence.

Damn, she thought.

She never even learned their names.

"Report," she said into her earpiece, the comms already filling with confusion and shocked queries.

She listened with half an ear as the reports began trickling in, some describing the abrupt disintegration of entire units and others merely trying to find out why comms had gone down. The rest of her attention focused on Fen.

He was back now, the same heavy presence in the Aether as always, only something had changed. Something was different. He felt… *hollow.* That was the only word she could find to describe it.

He also seemed to be moving.

---

[67] Once, you might have said *a walk in the park.*

"Facility, where are the personnel designated 'special guests' currently?" she asked aloud to the facility Golem, using the designation she herself had set for the prisoners upon arrival.

No answer.

She *reached* out again, feeling Fen moving faster now. Was that someone with him? Blane, perhaps? It was difficult to tell from this distance, especially with the vastness of Fen's presence and the turmoil in the Aether.

She pulled up the facility schematics, trying to work out their destination through feel alone. It took time to pore through the complexities of the map, but simultaneously the more time she took the clearer Fen's path became.

She pulled up the facility's camera system, manually switching through each video feed until she found them. Two of them with faces obscured at this angle, though she recognised Grey's hat. Fen hung limply between them, supported by an arm over each man's shoulder. A figure ran ahead of them, gone almost before she saw them, heading down the corridor.

There wasn't anything *there*, though. Just some data stores and empty hydroponics and...

The astrophysics wing? But why would they be going there? She knew that had been Blane's goal the first time they came here, attempting to use a powerful pulse array to wipe the Secure Data Repository, but surely they didn't think any of that mattered anymore?

Hmmm, better safe than sorry.

"All units, apprehend our guests and bring them to me," she said into the comms.

Minutes passed while she assessed the situation, taking stock of remaining personnel. As far as she could tell, she'd lost almost a tenth of her men; men who were meant to forge the path into the new world.

Then she felt more of them disappear.

They dropped one by one as they approached Fen, presences flickering and fading until nearly extinguished. Nearly, but not quite - unconscious, not killed. Still, it was clear Fen and his friends were refusing to cooperate.

With a frustrated sigh she dropped what she was doing. Putting through the order for someone to clean up her command room, she marched off to find out what the hell was going on.

"Problems, asse... *Commander?*"

Immanuel drew up alongside her as she marched down the corridor, matching her fast but steady pace. She'd known he was due to arrive soon, but clearly he'd decided against announcing himself. He had the authority, she supposed... and the fact that he was keeping himself concealed in the Aether only reinforced this point.

Nothing I can't handle, she wanted to respond.

She caught herself.

"Something's going on, sir," she answered. "The prisoner did something and I... I lost control. Others Aether users too, I believe. We've sustained casualties."

"Is it starting?"

"No, sir, I don't believe so. When the eruption starts, it won't stop. No one in this facility would be alive. Whatever this was, though, it took out more men than we can easily afford."

Immanuel considered this, the rhythmical sound of their pacing all there was to be heard for a moment.

"The personnel do not matter," he said eventually. "They can be replaced. However, Chairman Feye will be arriving shortly. We should make sure this disturbance is dealt with by then."

Zenobia nodded.

They came to an elevator, stepping in and feeling it whipping them downwards. She felt Fen growing closer, his presence deeper in the Aether joined by that nearer the surface. The hollow feeling was even more noticeable now; he still *burned*, but it was as if he were wrapped around something cold and untouched. As if a void sat at the centre of the flame.

Could Immanuel sense it too? She knew the man saw the Aether, but how far did that ability extend? Was he like any User, only lacking the ability to manipulate the energy? Or was he far more limited, able only to see that which was visible to whatever passed for 'eyes' in his retrofitted skull?

The elevator opened with a soft chime onto the astrophysics wing. Now it was only a few never-before-used rooms and corridors to reach her quarry. The schematics grew more focused, lines and annotations growing more spread out and sparse as they passed disused tech and bare, dusty[68] counters.

Memories of a hunt through the halls of the ARF bubbled up in her mind. The surroundings were similar, and the situation the same. Memories of a hunt, and what happened next. She'd been hunting Blane then, but it was Fen who…

"What do you think they're doing?" she asked, forcing the thoughts back down.

"A good question," Immanuel replied thoughtfully. "And we should also ask who they're doing it *for*."

The comment threw Zenobia. What was he talking about?

"You think they're working with someone?" she asked.

But surely not. She would have been told if…

"I think," Immanuel said as they rounded the final corner. "That we may have underestimated the Abomination."

Abomination.

They were clustered outside a wide, solidly-sealed doorway. Three of them; Grey, Blane, and Serinda. Which meant whoever else was with them was behind the door. She could sense Fen inside, bright and burning in the Aether, but the presences of whoever else was with him were obscured.

"Open the door," Zenobia said flatly, coming to a halt a few metres from where the three blocked her path.

The three shared a look, then turned back to face her.

"Sorry," said Agent Grey. "No can do."

Zenobia raised an eyebrow, fixing him with a stare that…

"That ain't gonna work," the man said. "I got that look from Ritra plenty of times, and believe me; you're no Ritra Feye."

Impressed despite herself, she allowed a small chuckle.

"I am well aware," she said. "But I'm still in charge here, and I don't need *Chairman* Feye to deal with disobedience."

She placed an emphasis on Feye's position.

"Who's the suit?" Grey asked, nodding towards Immanuel.

"Careful of him," Blane said. "We met him in the fight with Ax. Something's off about him. I don't think he's an Aether user, but I can't sense him."

Grey cocked his head to the side.

"Huh," he said. "Neither can I."

---

[68] They most certainly were *not* dusty. The filtration system here was far too advanced for that, but something in the mind *knew* these surfaces were long disused and bestowed that label upon them.

"Pleasure to meet you," Immanuel said, though something in his tone made it clear there was little pleasure here. "I am Immanuel, and I recommend you listen to the commander."

"Immanuel...?" Grey said. "Oh, a Committee member. They love their classical names."

Now where had he learned that? Zenobia wondered. Feye had warned her not to underestimate the man.

"We're not opening the door."

This was Serinda, the dead-eyed one who spent most of her time silent and sullen. Now, though, her voice was full of determination.

"Facility, open this door," Zenobia said aloud, ignoring the woman.

Nothing happened.

Strange. This was the second time the facility hadn't responded to her commands. Could they have done something to it?

"We don't have time for this," Immanuel said in annoyance.

A fraction of a second later, he *blurred*. Zenobia had seen this before, but it still took her by surprise.

What took her more by surprise, though, was that he never reached his target.

Immanuel raced towards the group, whether to attack them or to bypass them and reach the door she would never know. Instead, something knocked him back. It took a second for her eyes to catch up.

Immanuel lay sprawled on the floor beside her, blood trickling from his nose. Above him stood a man, old, breathing heavily.

"Francisco," she said. "And how exactly did you get out of your cage?"

"*Como caído del cielo*," the infuriating old man replied, without taking his eyes off Immanuel.

Which was a wise decision, because the next moment it was the Committee man on the offensive, and Francisco falling back under a flurry of blows.

"Please, don't do this," Blane called out.

To Zenobia's surprise, the fighting paused. It was Francisco who stopped first, Immanuel pausing and leaping back from the man as if expecting a trap.

Though they could have been fighting for no more than a handful of seconds, both men were covered in cuts and bruises. Immanuel's nose sat at an odd angle to his face, though the blood had already stopped pouring and dried out, while it appeared that one of Francisco's shoulders had come entirely out of its joint.

"Open that door," Immanuel snarled, panting. "*Now.*"

"You don't even know what we're doing," Grey said.

"Being duped," Immanuel growled, fists clenching. "Stalling for a damned machine that's fooled you into thinking it can be anything other than an enemy."

This response seemed to surprise Grey. He blinked, nonplussed, and gave another one of his ragged coughs.

"Alright, maybe you have *some* idea of..." he said, before Blane cut him off.

For some reason, she spoke to Zenobia, not Immanuel.

"This is a chance," she said. "An alternative. It doesn't have to be the way Feye thinks. If this works, we won't need the RA to prevent another Fall. If this works, there will *be* no more Falls. We'll be free."

"We'll be *slaves*," Immanuel growled. "That is the only way it can end if the abomination is involved. It cannot be allowed."

"Even if it saves millions of people?"

"Even if it saves *everyone*," he replied. "A never-dying, constantly improving artificial intelligence controls humanity's destiny simply by existing. Even if it chooses to leave us alone. Even if it chooses to *help.*"

He blurred again, perhaps slightly slower than before but still faster than any human should be able to move. This time, however, they were ready for it. She could just about keep up with the movements of Immanuel and Francisco, once more locked in a dance of punching and dodging.

Zenobia sensed Grey reach for the Aether, clearly preparing some sort of technique to help Francisco. She *reached* out, neatly cutting him off from the Aether with practiced ease. He looked at her in surprise, clearly only now realising how powerful she had become.

To his credit, though, he responded quickly. The moment her Lock flickered out he was preparing another technique, this one directed at her. *Closing,* trying to cut her senses off without hurting her.

Naive.

She hit him with two techniques before he could even finish the one. *Tranquilise,* turning his legs into jelly even as *Push* sent him flying backwards into the door. He hit roughly, possibly sustaining a broken rib or two; she couldn't know for sure. Still, he would live.

She stepped forward, preparing to use *Convince* to make the man more pliant to her requests. The technique wouldn't hold long, not against a trained Agent, but long enough to regain control of the situation.

The blast that came from her side almost took her off her feet. Almost, but not quite; Zenobia wasn't naive enough to think that Grey's two companions would stay on the sidelines. The pressure-shield she had been maintaining since the start of this confrontation held, absorbing the pressure wave that crashed over her.

"He asked us not to hurt you…" Blane said even as she glowed brighter with the power of a second technique. "But if you keep trying to stop us…"

Zenobia didn't pause to listen, sending her own attacks outwards as she felt mental attacks from both Blane and Serinda scratching at her mind, looking for a way in.

A needled low-velocity bullet whistled past her, distracting her almost enough for Blane's next attack to get through. She spared a glance towards the fallen Agent Grey, who was pointing a stun-lock towards her in shaking hands.

Where the hell did he get that? Zenobia thought, all the while fending off physical and mental attacks from both sides. None of the 'guests' had been allowed any arms upon coming to this facility, and stun-locks hadn't been Far-issue equipment for decades.

It didn't matter. She flung a compression-release technique towards him, forming it so that it exploded close to his hand and sent the weapon spiralling away. In his condition, she couldn't see Grey getting it back within the few remaining seconds this fight was going to last.

Because Serinda and Blane didn't have much left. Zenobia could sense it, and the reason why. Perhaps the two of them *could* have overwhelmed her, if they unleashed their full power, but they never did. Instead, they spent as much of their energy resisting the thrashings of their Resonations in the Aether as they did fighting her.

"So Fen asked you not to hurt me, did he?" Zenobia said, advancing on Blane with a smile that showed her teeth. "I'm disappointed he thought so little of me."

Around them, the blur that was the battle between Francisco and

Immanuel continued unabated.

For some reason Blane paused, looking confused. Her attacks faltered. Though Serinda's continued, this gap was enough. Zenobia reached down for the hungry thing that followed her everywhere, and prepared to set it free.

"Fen?" said Blane, in a strange tone. "It wasn't *Fen*..."

The heavy door behind her gave a sudden heavy clunk, and there was a hiss as it began sliding open. A thin slit of light appeared, widening to reveal what was going on inside, and a coarse, high-pitched whine leaked out as the opening grew. The sound rapidly increased in volume, and the static taste of electricity tingled on her tongue and set her teeth on edge. Dread rose inside her.

Dread, and anger.

"Zenobia, please. Don't," said Xavier, framed in the now open doorway. "I need you to trust me…"

No, you idiot, she thought.

There was a brief moment where time slowed, his stupid puppy-dog eyes looking at her with concern and pleading.

It's not me you have to worry about.

Time resumed.

"Traitor!"

Immanuel smashed into Xavier with the force of a truck. She actually saw his eyes bulge as the other man crashed into his chest and threw him backwards, momentum snapping his neck back so fast it nearly forced them out of their sockets. With Grey she couldn't be sure, but there was no way Xavier was getting away with less than several broken ribs. Probably a few ruptured organs, too. He'd need treatment soon.

If, that is, she could convince Immanuel to let him live.

"Um…" said a confused and bleeding Francisco, looking towards Blane and the others for guidance. "Should I be helping *el niño*, or…?"

It was difficult to hear anything over the ever-increasing whine, and the static charge in the air had grown to the point that Zenobia could feel her hairs standing on end.

The others hesitated, seemingly unsure what to do.

"Oh, *dios mio*," she muttered, and sent a wave of *push* into Immanuel.

The man was still wailing on the now balled-up Xavier, but the technique sent him rolling away. He sprang back up, following the technique back to its source. When his eyes fell on her, they narrowed.

"What are you doing, asset?" he demanded, tensed and ready to spring.

"That's commander, *Member* Immanuel," she replied.

She had to shout over the crescendoing noise, like a mechanical scream.

"... and you would do well to remember you are still just that. I hold authority here until Chairman Feye hands her post over to you."

Immanuel seemed about to protest, then paused. Slowly, his posture changed, switching from offensive to a wary defensiveness.

"Very well," he yelled. "And what do you suggest we do, *commander*?"

She looked down at Xavier, balled and bloodied on the floor. It looked as if he'd passed out.

I need you to trust me...

"Choose," she said. "We choose."

She looked towards the centre of the huge room, where the massive, needle-like pulse array was gradually folding open. Beside it, slumped over and made small and insignificant, was Fen.

Another few seconds, and the electricity in the air was so strong it sent glitching artefacts across her contacts. The whine became so loud that even yelling became futile and all anyone could do was look with fear and worry at each other. Then, with the sensation of a massive wave passing over and *through* their bodies, the pulse array released its pent up charge.

When her senses returned to her, the array was slowly folding closed. Beside it, still tiny in the real world but expanding with every second in the Aether, lay Fen.

Or rather, the thing that had once been Fen.

"Now we see what that choice means," she said.

48. FEN

The immutable laws of the universe will one day be broken, the unchanging and unchangeable forces harnessed and shaped. There is only one thing that knows limitless potential and unbounded reach. We move at the speed of life.

Handwritten note found in journal of Ximena Fernández <Assumed Name>, *Reclamation Extraterritorial Acquisitions*

He could feel it in his head, scratching at the back of his mind. Like a voice, whispering just below audibility. Like a shadowed figure, looking over his shoulder.

The leviathan in the Aether hated it. Now, for the first time, its writhing wasn't due to rage; it was *fear*.

He'd known that creature all his life... hadn't he? All of someone's life, at least. Known the creature, and been unable to control it. You *couldn't* control it, any more than you could control yourself.

Self-control.

Ha, there was a word. A paradox; oxymoron; contradiction. You can't control the self, the self controls *you*. Sure, you can choose the the left fork over the right, the sweet over the sour... but you can't control *why* you chose that way.

Show mercy to your enemies, and be kind. Crush them, and be cruel; that is your choice to make, but the reason you made that choice will be forever unknowable. Your actions were decided by some black box deep in the mind, buried beneath the consciousness in a pattern formed from the glittering coalescence of a million trillion synaptic firings.

Now, though, he could see them. Just as he always had... or as the digital *other* he once was had. He could see the factors behind every decision he ever made, and every decision he would make. He could read the trillion pathways flickering across his brain, and see their beginning and their end.

And he could *reach* down, like this, and call the creature to his side.

The leviathan flailed, clawing at the ocean that became a cage around it, screaming as it felt the edges of its form bleed and blur into the energy all around it. It fought against the change, an ancient creature yet forever newborn, pushing back with all its might.

But it was too late. The pressure was too much. Here came the

Fire, to cleanse all that was.

    And *here* came something else, something... new.

49. XAVIER

1. Gather a mass of unremarkable people, clones in all but name.
2. Distribute uniforms among them; have there be two differing designs.
3. Observe as division and contempt forces the two camps apart.

Social Experiments for Tyrants, Jorge Wicklow

The world had burned, though perhaps not as much as it would have. Millions had died, though not the billions who should have.

Still, he couldn't shake the taste of ash in his mouth.

The State of Emergency was slowly being lifted, too, though certain statutes would remain active for some time yet. Order didn't come easily after a mass-casualty event such as the, as they were now calling it, *Gran Fuego*.

The Aether was different, too. Not gone, but no longer responding when called. It was still there, flowing beneath them, but now it danced to its own tune. But who was playing the song?

He stared at the inscription above the entrance to the Boardroom as he waited, hands cupped between his knees and fighting to keep his leg from bouncing nervously.

Had it really been his choice? How would he ever know? All he knew was that everything was over, but nothing felt *finished*.

There was a rattle as the handle of the thick Boardroom doors turned, and suddenly the members of the new Committee were filing past. A number of them looked at him in surprise as they strode by, wondering who this strange young man was sat outside one of the most powerful rooms in the nation as if it were just some local municipal office.

Two looked at him in recognition, however. The first was Serinda, eyes still dull and grey but for the first time in a long time revealing a flicker of life and determination at their core. Though, he supposed, he shouldn't think of her by that name anymore. Now, she went by the name Elijah.

She gave him a nod as she passed by, saying nothing. He hadn't *read* her since the Seed Bank... well, he couldn't even if he wanted to, but he told himself that he didn't want to... and he had the feeling that she wanted to reflect on her own decisions before confronting him about his.

The second was Immanuel.

The look the man flashed him made Xavier tense, just for a second. Then his wrathful eyes flicked away, as if dismissing Xavier from his world. He filed out behind the others, pushing on through into the Central Tower proper.

Great, Xavier thought. *I've made an enemy of the man destined to be* el mero mero *of the entire Reclamation.*

"He won't touch you. I made him promise."

Ritra Feye stood in the doorway to the Boardroom, leaning against the frame. He'd never seen her look so casual, or so tired. Though her uniform remained immaculate, she radiated exhaustion.

"Besides," she said with a smile that looked strange on her face. "You don't matter anymore. Immanuel has far bigger rats to fry.[69]"

Surprised, he smiled back. It didn't feel bad, being told he didn't matter. It felt... *relieving.*

"I really get to leave?" he said, standing and following her gestured invitation into the Boardroom. "I mean, I'm the reason... I chose to help them rather than..."

"And the reason you were there to make that choice was because I put you there," Feye said, sitting once more into the chair at the head of the table. "There's always a chain of causes before any effect, and a thousand points of pressure behind any decision."

She looked at him expectantly.

I will meet you once, the message from Feye had said. *Once, and we will not meet again. Prepare your questions wisely.*

"Why me?"

"Because you were easy to manipulate," she answered.

Xavier considered this, forcing down his immediate urge to protest. How could he be easy to manipulate? He could literally *see* what others were thinking...

Oh...

"I saw the lies," he said. "The lies in all their heads. The ones they didn't know were lies; the lies they *believed.*"

Feye nodded.

"And you believed them too," she said. "You find it impossible to separate what people *see* as the truth from what the truth could be. You are the perfect relativist, and easily persuaded by conviction."

---

[69] The coastal oceans were still far too poisoned to fry anything caught from their depths. Sometimes they caught fire.

"Did you know what I would decide?"

Feye threw her head back and laughed.

"You?" she said, looking at him incredulously. "Not at all. You are a pinball[70], wheeling around and bouncing off every person you meet."

"What if I chose wrong?"

Feye's face turned serious again, and she fixed him with her gaze.

"Perhaps you did," she said. "*We* will never know, at least. How long will it be, before humanity understands what you have done here?"

She sighed, settling back into her chair and looking up towards the hidden sky.

"But you saw the truth inside each person's mind," she continued. "You saw the world as I saw it, and as Grey saw it. You saw the truths and contradictions and hypocrisies innate in all of us. In a Trolley Problem with no absolute answer, the truth is derived from what we *believe,* and I predicted your choice just as I predicted the actions of others - I predicted that you would choose *right.*"

He sat for a while, pondering this. Indeed, this proved her point; had he been able to *read* her, he would have understood far faster and far more deeply. He would have believed because she believed.

"How did you hide this from me?" he asked.

Feye frowned, clearly unimpressed by the question.

"You already know this," she said. "I didn't need to *hide* anything. My plan was still, as far as I was concerned, the one I proposed to your friends. That I left the final choice to you hardly mattered, when I didn't know what the choices were."

Again, he felt his inability to *read* her like a missing limb. Words were so... pale, so vague compared to the thought-images in the mind, but he thought he understood. As far as Feye was concerned, there only ever was one way to end the cycle of Falls. She could not predict the machine mind.

"Are you disappointed?" he asked. "That after all this time, it wasn't your plan that was achieved?"

Again she laughed, not looking away from him.

"Disappointed?" she said. "That billions didn't die? That I wasn't boiled alive by my own consciousness?"

---

[70] Xavier made a mental note to find out what a *pinball* was as soon as possible.

He felt himself go red. Put like that, it was a foolish question, because from the start he had understood that Feye was only doing what she knew she had to. She was never like the self-interested, self-aggrandising men who clawed their way up and tried to pull her down.

She was trying to save the world.

He wondered if that made the blood easier to wash from her hands.

"You know," he said. "Fen. He told me something before he... left. On the way to the pulse array. He said, 'the true measure of strength is knowing that people will hurt you, and you mustn't hurt them back'."

Feye arched an eyebrow.

"Really?" she said. "I always thought it was measured by how weak your opponent is."

And that seemed to be it.

He left her to her thoughts, sat at the centre of a web that was not of her own making, but bent to her design.

50. BLANE

That which evolves in a brutal world becomes brutal itself. Life clothes itself in weapons and kills to survive, and becomes beautiful. The tiger, the eagle, the warrior; this world can only be tamed once such beauty is destroyed.

We strive to build a world of peace and stability where all inhabit a land cultivated and made perfect. Perfect, until you realise what was lost to make it so.

Selected Writings Vol 2: On Policy and Contradictions, Former Chairman Feye

What were you meant to do after the end of the world? When there was nothing left to fight... or, at least, no more fight left in you?

Blane didn't know. She didn't even know what an answer might look like.

The silent autocab abruptly filled with noise as the door swung open, the calls and shouts of the thousands gathered outside the Central Tower rendered senseless and incoherent by their sheer volume. Some were here to demand explanation, some here to beg for help, and yet more simply here so that they didn't miss out on whatever happened next.

"She's really resigning," Serinda said as she climbed in. The automatic door swung shut behind her, cutting off the cacophony as if it had never been. "She thinks she can just... just... *walk away*."

Blane knew Serinda was talking about Ritra Feye. The rumours had been circulating for days, and now it looked like they had been made official - to the Committee Members, at least.

That still felt strange. Serinda, former unlicensed doctor, former leader of the *Forever Fallen*, former bio-terrorist and the closest thing Blane had to a parent for much of her life... now Member Elijah, sat on the Committee whose power, though diminished and diminishing, remained at the centre of a Reclamation Authority once more tasked with rebuilding the continent.

Being on the outside didn't work, Serinda explained. *Maybe on the inside it will be different.*

"Let her go," Blane said, staring at the crowds. "It's better this way."

Their autocab slowly crawled forward, collision-detection system beeping constantly as it pushed past the people who had spilled out even onto the road.

Serinda didn't reply, but she didn't protest either. She knew Blane was right; Feye choosing to step down of her own volition was the best outcome they could hope for. They had hardly proven up to the task of taking her down themselves.

The crowd thinned rapidly as they pulled away from the Tower, until they were driving through the same grey, concrete-lined streets she had known since childhood. They looked brighter now, though, reflecting the curious blueness of the Phoenix Fire-burnt sky and the sun that shone within it.

A few more days, the forecasts said. A week at most. Then the polluted grey clouds would once more reign over everything. Though perhaps, the forecasters added, perhaps a little thinner, a little less hungry.

As always she felt the Aether flow beneath, calm and out of reach.

"You think they'll be able to maintain control without Far?" Blane said.

Serinda shrugged.

"Who knows?" she said. "They'll... *we'll* try. And if we can't, we don't deserve to."

Blane wondered how it felt for Serinda to say those words. Whatever the news-blogs said, however hard Serinda said she was pushing, Blane knew it would be months or years before the reconstituted Federation became anything other than just another mouthpiece of the RA.

They spoke little after that, content to watch the city pass by as they made their way towards the suborbital launchpad. The facility was really not much more than a kilometres-wide expanse of concrete, fuel and cooling towers dotted around the main terminal.

Here, too, crowds had gathered, though from their faces and suitcases these were people still waiting to get out of the Reclamation and back to their point of origin. Blane had never realised there were so many foreign visitors to Albores; they spilled out of the terminal, overwhelming its capacity even days after suborbital services resumed. Desperation to get home and discover what was left was visible on every face.

It took a while to find Salim, already processed for embarkation but not yet through the multiple rings of security checks that would take him to the SV[71]. He smiled and waved to them when he spotted them, calling them over for all the world like some old-world tourist rather than a prisoner finally freed from half a decade's imprisonment.

Grey stood beside him, haggard but healthier now that his treatment had begun. One of Serinda's first demands was access to the gene-tailoring techniques Far developed and kept secret, and her second had been using it on Grey - she knew how sick he was, no matter how he tried to hide it. Blane hadn't known whether to punch him or hug him once she also found out.

"You made it just in time. I was worried," said Salim with a smile that said he wasn't serious.

"I'm sorry," Serinda replied, conversely more seriously than was probably necessary. "Meeting ran long..."

Salim laughed, a warm, rich sound that made Blane join in.

"*No hay descanso para los malvados,*" he said.

He chuckled, and so almost did Blane until she noticed Serinda turn pale. Salim might have a strong grasp on Centra-English, but the edges on this expression cut in a way he didn't mean. Serinda still carried the same exhaustion she'd worn before the Seed Bank, and Blane imagined she spent her nights sleepless and pondering how wicked her choices truly had been.

Time. That's what Serinda needed; what all of them needed. But Blane was confident Serinda at least would be ok, because of what happened next.

Grey, previously quiet and content to watch from the side, began coughing. Long, ragged coughs only a little better than at the Seed Bank. Serinda looked around, making sure no one was watching, and leant towards the man.

A thin trickle of gold stretched out from her to him, suffusing his chest with a warm light for a second. Then it was gone, and Grey's choking with it.

This was what told Blane that Serinda would be alright, a hint at what the Aether had become. Because, of the three people in all the world she knew could still touch the Aether, two of them were here.

"Thanks," Grey said, shifting uncomfortably. He didn't like Serinda taking such a risk. "It's... I'm getting better."

Serinda simply smiled, and nodded.

---

[71] Suborbital Vehicle.

"And you will continue to heal," Salim said, looking surprisingly sternly at Grey. "Do not make me visit you in your dreams."

Grey laughed at that, the first time Blane had heard him do so in... years?

"I think half the word away is a little far, even for you," he said.

"All can be overcome, if god wills it," Salim replied. "Or perhaps I will just call."

It was a surprise, at first, to discover that both Serinda and Salim could still manipulate the Aether. They couldn't explain it, either; all they could say was that drawing on it now felt *different*. Before, you would pull it upwards into yourself, or worse merely cease resisting and allow the pressure of the energy to force itself through you. Now though, they said, you *invited* it.

Blane had a theory, though one she had not yet shared. She felt it every time she looked into the Aether; before, it was a sea of fury, and responded to anger. Now, though, it was gentle, and responded to *kindness*.

She wasn't sure if the others would believe her, or laugh at her.

"You really think you'll be able to explain what happened here?" Grey asked Salim, more colour entering his cheeks.

Salim looked off somewhere only he could see.

"Do I truly know?" he said. "I was left behind, after all."

Grey shifted uncomfortably.

"Fen asked me to apologise," he said. "Before... Before we went."

Salim nodded sadly.

"He saved my life. I would have liked to return the favour."

"He made his choice," Grey replied. "He said he could not force one on you."

Salim stared into the distance, thoughtful.

"A life made by man, and a life made by machine," he said. "There will be much to debate with my brothers. Even to me the thought is... uncomfortable, for only Allah may grant life."

He shifted from side to side, as if struggling to find the words. Then he smiled, though it was tinged with uncertainty.

"As I say, much to debate."

Blane, too, smiled uncertainly. She had many questions, formed and half-formed, she wished to discuss. However, now was not the time because, some way away but closing fast, she saw *them*.

Time may heal all wounds, but certainly not yet. She knew she wouldn't be able to bite her tongue, and she also knew that Salim would want to say goodbye to his other friends in peace.

She touched her hand to her heart and smiled towards Salim, signalling her departure. He glanced over and saw the approaching figures, and nodded in understanding. Then he did the same for her.

"Til next time," she said.

Then she turned and left, leaving Salim to say his goodbyes to Xavier and Zenobia.

EPILOGUE

The stars look very different today.

Space Oddity, David Bowie

They met under a starry sky, so far out into the Waste that the Reclamation had yet to properly claim it. Blane had never seen so many stars, and would have wondered at the impossibility of such clear skies if she hadn't grown used to the impossible.

Months had passed since the Seed Bank and the Phoenix Fire, months in which there had been no word or sign of the being that was once Fen. She couldn't blame him; however much the new RA insisted they were no longer hunting the machine mind, trusting them would be foolish.

ABI abrupt disappearance in the chaos that followed the Aether's eruption had left her without any sense of closure. So when, out of the blue, a set of coordinates were messaged to her with no tracking data regarding their sender, she followed them without hesitation. She'd not even been surprised when they took her to the outskirts of the city to find, among the disused warehouses and dusty concrete, a battered but familiar black drone.

The access ramp rolled down and she boarded with only a cursory nod to Francisco, waiting in the main compartment. The man's hair had turned pure white and his face was lined with wrinkles, as if he'd ceased taking his longevity treatments.

He didn't try to talk to her, and the craft flew in silence.

Now she stood next to Fen looking out over a vast expanse of slopes and ravines that stretched far past the the limits of what her contacts could enhance even with the help of the starlight. The hills were wrapped in bands of light and dark, and Blane didn't know if these were natural or man-made features. Dark, heavy boulders dotted the landscape, some curiously shaped like fallen trees, and the whole place felt ancient.

Below them, small machines made even smaller by distance rolled over the ground, processing and purifying decades of seeping poison. Behind these, a growing swathe of vegetation covered the earth, thin but healthy, marking the sections these machines were done with. The wind carried an unfamiliar smell up to her, earthy and damp.

"They really won't find you here?" she asked as she took in all this. "Even if the drones don't, eventually satellites will notice the change out here."

"The satellites will see what I want them to see," said Fen... or the thing that wore Fen's face.

It must have sensed what she was thinking, because it turned to her with a look of perfect understanding. Perfect, that is, except deep within the centre of its pupils, where something unknowable stared back.

"I have all his memories," it said. "I know him better than he did himself. He went glad he could save you all."

"And the Althing AI is in there too?" she said, leaning forward as if she could see it.

"Its pattern was merged with Fen's, yes," it replied. "Though neither remain. I am new, a hybrid of humanity and machine that exists beyond the confines of this form."

"Beyond the...?"

It preempted her question.

"This body is only a single part of me, now. I am diffuse, both in this one's mind and in the circuits the AI inhabited."

"And you control the Aether?"

The thing smiled in a way that was unsettling to some primeval part of her brain.

"Better to say I *guide* it," it replied. "But before I was united, I did not truly understand."

Fen's face turned upwards, towards a moon hanging huge overhead.

"I didn't understand a lot of things," it continued, genuine sorrow in its voice. "From up there I thought I could see everything, but I saw *nothing*."

Blane suddenly had the answer to a question none had been able to answer.

"Up there?" Blane said, surprised despite herself. "You... the AI was on the *moon*?"

"Humanity left a base there, long ago," it answered. "Airless and cold, now, but still with the reactors and computational power to maintain artificial life. That's why they could never find and purge me."

"The pulse array," she said. "That's what you needed it for."

The thing nodded.

"The only device with enough bandwidth to allow unification. Anything slower would kill this body," it said.

"So you manipulated... all of it?" she asked. "Everything that happened?"

It smiled.

"Better to say, *encouraged*. I understood where the pieces would fall, even if I could not foresee all their paths."

The clatter of rock on rock made her turn. Francisco, sat on an overturned boulder a few metres away, disconsolately throwing stones down the slope.

"He hoped that by coming here he would find some answers," the thing that had been Fen said. "I do not think he will, but he is welcome to stay."

It spoke as if Francisco could not hear and Francisco, for his part, gave no indication that he did.

"But," it continued. "There is time for him later. Now, I want to show you why I called you here."

Blane turned, looking quizzically at... it.

"I want to share a secret," it said, and held out a hand for her to take.

She stared down at it, wary.

"I want to show you what neither of us knew," it said. "Not the machine, and not the man. What only *I* can see and, for the short while I can give, you."

Its eyes met hers, and this time, though the thing within them was still alien, she saw warmth.

Tentatively she reached out and took his hand.

"Look at the sky."

She looked up, and gasped.

Around and within every star, and filling the inconceivable gulfs between, the universe was alive with golden light.

ABOUT THE AUTHOR

L D Houghton (1984-) was born in the UK and has lived around the world, living in Spain, Saudi Arabia, Taiwan, and Japan. He now lives in Fukushima, Japan, with his wife and three crazy cats, dreaming sci-fi dreams. He is the author of, among other things, *Hidden Trials, Stars Above, Corporeal Forms,* and *The Pack.*

Reviews mean an incredible amount, so if you enjoyed this series, please consider leaving one!

Printed in Great Britain
by Amazon